A Darker Night

Also by P.J. Brooke

Blood Wedding

A DARKER NIGHT

P. J. Brooke

CONSTABLE • LONDON

SOHO
CONSTABLE

Constable & Robinson Ltd
3 The Lanchesters
162 Fulham Palace Road
London W6 9ER
www.constablerobinson.com

First published in the UK by Constable,
an imprint of Constable & Robinson, 2010

First US edition published by SohoConstable,
an imprint of Soho Press, 2010

Soho Press, Inc.
853 Broadway
New York
NY 10003
www.sohopress.com

A copy of the British Library Cataloguing in Publication
Data is available from the British Library

UK ISBN: 978-1-84901-045-0
US ISBN:978-1-56947-624-6
US Library of Congress number: 2010007711

Printed and bound in the EU

1 3 5 7 9 10 8 6 4 2

Mixed Sources
Product group from well-managed
forests and other controlled sources
www.fsc.org Cert no. SA-COC-1565
© 1996 Forest Stewardship Council
FSC

En una noche oscura,
con ansias en amores inflamada
(¡oh dichosa ventura!),
salí sin ser notada,
estando ya mi casa sosegada.

On a dark night,
my heart was filled with love and longing
(Oh, happy chance!),
Unnoticed, I slipped out,
leaving my very self behind.

St John of the Cross, 1542–1591
'En una Noche Oscura', *Canciones del alma*, 1577

For my aunt, Margaret, who gave a small girl a love of books and poetry, and a whole world of happiness in very difficult circumstances.

Jane

Acknowledgements

We would like to thank Margaret Brooke, Chin Li, Shona Douglas and Jón Fairbairn for their comments on early drafts. We would also like to thank Gabi Pape, Carlos and Patty Janin, David Martinage, Virtudes Ruiz de la Rosa and María Eugenia Pérez Merino for their advice and support.

Many thanks to Krystyna Green, Imogen Olsen, Andrew Hayward and the team at Constable & Robinson, and to Jacqueline Anne Taylor of the Language Clinic, Granada, both for her research support, and for her final checks of the manuscript, which have added local colour and weeded out mistakes. Any remaining errors are, of course, our responsibility.

We are grateful to members of the Polícia Nacional de Granada for their advice and information on the operations of the Spanish police, and to Paco Martínez, a future judge, for his advice on Spanish judicial procedures. Our fictional police bear very little resemblance to the real forces, which would never have employed Max Romero in the first place.

Authors' Note

This novel is entirely a work of fiction. The names, characters and incidents portrayed in it are the work of the authors' imagination. Any resemblance to actual persons, living or dead, and events is entirely coincidental. Although we do draw on historical accounts for some events and figures, our account is fictional. Some localities actually exist, but our presentation of them is also fictional.

Chapter 1

The prison gate closed behind him. Nobody was waiting outside. No friend, no enemy. So, with his guitar in one hand and a cheap plastic holdall in the other, Paco Maya walked alone to the bus stop. There was a bus to the city centre in ten minutes. He lifted his face to the sun, and breathed deeply. They would come for him eventually. But he was free now. He was going home.

Paco got off the bus at the cathedral and walked towards the stop for Sacromonte. But there was María, still working the tourists outside the Royal Chapel. She hadn't changed. The same old gypsy scam. María glanced at him, then glanced again.

'*Coño*, Paco!' she exclaimed. 'You're out!'

She came over, and hugged him tight. Paco kissed her on both cheeks, drinking in her smell of patchouli, garlic and olive oil.

'*Sí*. I'm out at last.'

'I'll buy you a coffee, *carrajillo*,' she said, winking.

'*Por favor*, but just the one . . . for old times' sake.'

'We'll go to the Café Colón.'

They walked along the busy main road to the Café Vía Colón. The black-aproned waiter eyed them suspiciously, hesitated, and then came to take their order.

'This hasn't changed,' said Paco, admiring the gilt angels and mirrors. 'But I don't remember ever seeing so many tourists.'

1

'*Sí*, we've got an international airport now. So there's even more daft buggers around. Suckers for the old patter. Good for my business.'

Paco sipped his *carrajillo* coffee slowly, savouring with every sip the shot of local cognac. '*Gracias*, María. I've been waiting years for this. Have you seen Angelita?'

'She's fine, Paco. She looks more like her mother every day.'

Paco rubbed the back of his hand across his mouth. 'You know the old cow wants me to sell my bit of land?'

'Lucía's mother?'

'*Sí.*'

'Well, you'd get a good price these days.'

Paco frowned. 'But I can't do it. I just can't. So I told the old bitch to go to hell, and I haven't seen my daughter since.'

'Another one, Paco?'

'No. I'm off the booze. And I'm clean, María. I didn't mean to kill her, you know.'

María glanced at his scarred wrists. 'I know, Paco. So what are you going to do now?'

'Go home. Make a bit of money. See my angel.'

'You'll get the bookings soon enough. I heard your song on the radio. It's good. Really good.'

Paco shrugged. 'I just want my daughter back.' And his voice broke.

'*Hombre*, take it easy.'

Paco wiped his eyes with María's gaudy handkerchief. 'Abbot Jorge heard my confession in prison, and he knows my heart.'

'Perhaps Abbot Jorge can help you again.'

'I hope so, María. Look, I'll get this.'

'No. This one's on me, Paco. Just got ten euros off a real daft *guiri*. An Englishman, I think. Read his palm, and told him he was coming into money.' And she flashed a gold tooth.

Paco stood up and kissed María goodbye. He shouldered his bag, picked up the guitar and walked back to the bus stop. The Sacromonte bus arrived shortly after eleven. He could have walked on a couple of stops, and picked it up when it returned from its loop around the Alhambra and Barranco de los Abogados, but he wanted to see the green woods and the palaces again.

The buildings on Cuesta de Gomérez, the steep narrow road to the Alhambra, had improved. But the old guitar shops were still there. And Narciso might need a hand in his workshop.

The bus trundled through the old Puerta de los Granados, the Pomegranate Gate, into the lush Alhambra woods, fresh with the bright leaves of spring. It stopped a couple of times, then turned towards to the old gypsy village of Barranco de los Abogados. *Ay Dios Santo*! It had changed. The *gitanos* were selling up and moving. But not Paco. He would never sell. Not now. He'd see his days out in that house, just like his old man and his grandfather before him.

In the distance Paco could see the peaks of the Sierra Nevada, where the snow still lingered on the high tops. The bus turned and came back down to Plaza Nueva, then squeezed past the tourists on Paseo de los Tristes. The little river Darro still gurgled in its channel between the road and the cliffs below the Alhambra, but two of the old mansions on the left had become hotels. At the end of Paseo de los Tristes, the bus turned left up Cuesta del Chapiz, then right at the square of Peso de la Harina with its statue of Chorrohumo, the Gypsy King, and then into the valley of Sacromonte. Paco looked back across to the Alhambra, and then down the valley with the steep wooded cliffs below the palaces and the dry cactus-covered hills on the other side.

The bus passed his favourite bar, El Pibe. He would go there with his guitar. Get a few gigs and start earning again.

Would Angelita dance like Lucía did? He'd get her the best teachers . . .

The bus passed the old city wall and then the ancient cave houses of Barranco de los Negros, where the freed slaves

3

lived after the Christians threw the Moors out. The road snaked along the side of the Darro valley. Orchards and market gardens filled the valley basin. The bus finally stopped at the hamlet of Puente Maríano, sitting modestly below the great abbey of Sacromonte, the Abadía.

Perhaps he would ask Abbot Jorge to let him walk as a *penitente* in the Paso de los Gitanos, the Easter Procession of the Gypsies.

Paco got out of the bus and went into the tiny bar, which doubled as a shop.

Doña Constancia was still alive, brown and shrivelled as a raisin now, but still running the place. She peered at him.

'*Madre mía*,' she exclaimed. 'Is that you, Paco?'

'*Sí*. I'm back for good now, Constancia.'

'María Santísima del Sacromonte must have held you in her bosom. I always lit a candle for you.'

'I'm sure you did, Constancia. You're a good woman. I need some eggs, sugar, coffee, bread, cheese, sausages, and a bit of your nice ham if you have any in today. And olive oil.'

'*Sí*, Paco, my son. *Una cervecita* while you wait?'

'No, thanks. I'm on the wagon.'

'My, you have changed.'

Laden with food, Paco set off to walk to the end of the Sacromonte valley. He noticed a few bus stops, but no sign of any buses. The road turned into a track that led to the ruined monastery of Jesús del Valle. His feet crunched on the baked earth and the dry olive leaves still littering the track. He hoped he wouldn't see his neighbours. He didn't want to talk any more. He just wanted to be home. He was lucky: very few people were about. He stopped and paused when he came to the last house before his own.

Would his dog still be alive? Surely Conchi would have said if he'd died . . .

As Paco stood there looking at the old farm building, a small black dog ran up to him, barking.

'Negrito!'

The dog jumped up at him. Conchi opened the bleached wooden door of her house.

'*Por el amor de Dios.* It's Paco. *Ay. Mi Paquito.* Come on in. Don't just stand there like a *payo. Cerveza? Café?*'

'Coffee would be fine, Conchi.'

Negrito followed him inside, snapping at his heels.

'Look,' said Conchi. 'He remembers.'

Paco ruffled Negrito's ears, and the dog yelped with pleasure.

'I won't stay long. I need to get back to my place.'

'Nonsense, man. You look as if you haven't had a good meal in years.'

'That does smell good.'

'There, I knew you'd want something. I've got a good stew on the stove. Coffee first, and then we'll eat. Manuel's in town. Some business deal.'

'How is he, Conchi?'

'*Hombre*, we're all getting older, and you know he's not a well man. It's liver problems now. But how are you? I heard you had a heart attack.'

'*Sí.* Have to take it easy.'

'That's right, *amigo.* You don't want to go as young as your father.' She smiled at him affectionately. 'You've still got your mother's good looks, but *Dios mío*, you need to put on some weight.'

'I'm sure I will now I'm out. And you are looking good, Conchi.'

'I'm still dancing, you know. It keeps me slim.' Conchi straightened her shoulders, and clapped her hands in a flamenco rhythm.

'So how are the kids?'

'All grown up and gone.'

'María José?'

'Married a lad in Alfacár, and two babies already.'

'Marcos?'

'Gone to Barcelona. Hardly see the little bugger these days. And Nacho's got a flat in Granada – wants to be a chef.'

5

'So it's all change?'

'You've been away a long time.'

'*Sí*. But I'm here to stay now. Angelita's grandmother wants me to sell. She came round to the prison twice to get me to sign a bit of paper. But I won't sell.'

'You should think about it. We're selling up and moving into town ourselves. We're too old to manage all this land ourselves.'

'*Ay*! You've been a good neighbour, Conchi. I'll be really sorry to see you go.'

'*Gracias*, Paco. You've helped us as well. Don't worry. We'll still be around.'

'That's good. So how's my Angelita?'

'I heard she's fine. But we're not speaking to the grandmother these days, so I don't really know. *Hombre*, just don't expect miracles. Take it real slow with Angelita. She's been taught to hate you.'

Paco bit his lip, and then wiped his eye with a worn cuff.

'And be careful. The uncles won't be pleased when they find you're out. As far as they're concerned, hanging's too good for you.'

'Gregorio and Mauricio. Those bastards. I'll watch my back.'

'My, here am I talking, letting you starve. Come on through to the kitchen – it's easier to eat there.'

Paco followed her into the kitchen. The food did smell good, and he had forgotten how hungry he was . . .

'Is that a bus stop I saw at the end of the road?' he asked, wiping his mouth with a paper serviette.

'*Sí, sí*. That's new. The only problem is you have to phone if you want the bus to come out beyond the Abadía.'

'It won't do me much good then. I don't have a phone.' Paco pushed his chair back. '*Ay. Gracias* for the meal, Conchi. I haven't eaten so well for years.'

'Come back when Manuel is here. He'd like to hear your stories. We're away for a few days. Off to see my sister in Jaén.'

'I'll be round.'

Paco looked at Negrito, and fondled his ears. 'You coming with me, boy?'

Negrito thumped his tail on the floor.

Conchi got up, and fetched a broom, a mop and bucket. 'Your place'll be full of dust and cobwebs. Let me give you a hand.'

'I can manage!'

'Paquito, don't be so proud. You need a hand. I'll get your document box. You'd better take your deeds back with you.'

She fetched an old wooden box, and dusted it thoroughly. They set off together, Negrito excitedly running ahead, then darting back and jumping on Paco. They walked along the dusty track, between olives and the hills covered with prickly pear cactus, and then turned up a steep rutted path to Paco's home, an old cave house hacked out of the side of the hill. Paco rubbed his hand across his mouth then gazed back down the bare hillside to his old plot. Neat rows of beans and young potatoes stretched all the way down to the river on the other side of the track.

'Manuel's looked after my land really well.'

'Oh, he enjoys it. And you've got a well, so water wasn't a problem.'

'The thought of my land kept me going all those years inside, you know.'

'*Sí*, good flat land with water is worth its weight in gold. The radio said that there was only five months' water left in the reservoir, and the council needs to sink more boreholes. And my Manuel says those fools in the council are still handing out permits for new buildings all over the place, and golf courses too, when there isn't enough water for us anyway. Someone's making big money somewhere. But it's not the likes of us.'

'That's life for you.'

They turned the final corner. The first thing Paco saw was '*Asesino*' – smeared in red across the outside wall of his home. Murderer.

'The bastards. That's the last thing I need. If I get my hands on –'

'*Ay, Dios mío.* I'm sorry, Paco. It wasn't there last week. It'll be those devils Gregorio and Mauricio.' Conchi put her arm round his shoulders. 'Don't let it get to you, *hombre*. You're worth a thousand times more than they are.'

Paco released the padlock on the cave door, and then flung the single window wide to let in air and light. His few sticks of furniture were still there, and the picture of the Virgin of Sacromonte hadn't been touched, except by spiders.

'Nothing missing, I hope, Paco.'

'There's not much to go missing.'

Paco went to his chest of drawers, and put the wooden box in the second drawer.

Conchi looked around, sizing up the work that needed to be done. '*Ay*, Paco. This is no place to live on your own. You should find a wife and move into town.'

'I'll think about it,' he said. But he knew he wouldn't move. Not unless Angelita asked him to, and wanted to live with him.

'Come on, let's get this place sorted,' said Conchi. 'Have you got any cal? We'd better get rid of that scrawl right now.'

'I'll check my cupboard. Yes. There's a dry packet here.'

Conchi set to work straight away, while Paco mixed up the whitewash. She swept the floor, washed the single window, shook the sheets and blankets vigorously then laid them out in the sun. Paco plastered whitewash over the scrawled '*Asesino*'. Negrito ran around, barking furiously, rolling in the dust, and sticking his nose into the cobwebs.

'There's still gas in the bottle. Can I make you a coffee?'

'Thanks, but I must go now, Paco. I need to collect Manuel downtown, and then we're off to Ana's.'

'Thanks for all your help. I don't know what I would have done without you.'

8

'What are neighbours for? Just take it easy. We'll see you when we get back.'

She looked at the freshly whitewashed wall. 'You can still make it out. If I were you, I'd give it at least one more coat.'

'I'll do that later. See you when you get back. *Hasta la vista. Ciao.*'

Now, he was alone at last in his own house. He could relax. He was home. Angelita's mother, Lucía, would never stay here. But for Paco it had always been a bit of Paradise. And here, with just the sound of the doves in the rock face, sometimes his demons would leave him.

Dusk was falling. He took a chair outside, fetched his guitar, and started to sing quietly. His own song. The one that had won the prize in prison. For the first time in years he felt at ease. Now there was something to hope for. Something to do, something to work towards.

From his chair he could see the track which led towards Granada. He heard the sound of a car in the distance. The engine noise grew louder, and then stopped. Paco carefully placed his guitar against the chair, stood up, and walked to the edge of the dirt track. Two men were walking up the steep slope. His first instinct was to go inside for a knife. But no. It was a knife that caused the trouble last time. He stood still, silently waiting. The men approached slowly.

Chapter 2

Sub-Inspector Max Romero of the Policía Nacional de Granada opened the shutters to let in the morning sun, walked out on to his terrace and gazed over the old clay-tiled roofs of the Albayzín, across to the Nazrid Palaces of the Alhambra. Behind the palaces, only a little snow lingered on the Sierra Nevada, and the lower hills were already parched. He breathed in deeply, inhaling the sweet smell of jasmine. In the evening, the neighbourhood would throb with the rhythms of flamenco, but the only sounds now were the birds, and the guitar student next door anxiously practising for her next assessment.

Max went to the end of his terrace, and looked down the narrow street. The post lady was pulling her trolley of mail up the cobbled street as usual. She stopped at the door of his block of flats and pushed a bundle through the letterbox. Max walked down the three flights of stairs, and eagerly glanced through the mail. There was a letter for him, a thick envelope, with a printed address.

He returned to his flat with the letter. 'We hereby notify you that you have three months in which to vacate the premises at Calle María de la Miel Nº 27, 3B, Albayzín, Granada . . .'

No new lease. *Mierda*! Max looked around his small flat. It had its problems, but the view of the Alhambra was wonderful. He really didn't want to leave it.

As he was filling his water bottle from the cold tap, the doorbell rang. It was his new neighbour, Belinda.

'It's a good day for a walk, Max.'

'It is. Looks like we're going to be lucky with the weather.'

'Thanks so much for inviting me. I've hardly been out of the city since I arrived.'

'A pleasure, Belinda. You'll like the gang, and they'll all want to practise their English on you.'

' Max, you're looking a bit down. Anything wrong?'

'Bloody landlord's given me notice He's kicking me out in three months.'

'Oh dear. Your little flat's so nice. Can't you do anything about it?'

'No. It's standard stuff. I bet the old bastard wants to do the block up as tourist flats.'

As they walked down the little cobbled road of Calle María de la Miel, Max pointed to the decaying building. 'See that house? It's fifteenth-century, Moorish. And it's falling down because the council won't force the owner to repair it.'

'But the Albayzín's a World Heritage Site, isn't it?'

'It doesn't seem to make much difference. The landlord's waiting for the house to get so bad that he can legally throw the tenants out, knock it down and build flats on the site.'

'Is anyone doing anything about it?'

'Our Neighbourhood Association is doing its best, but it's an uphill struggle.'

'I'd like to join the Association.'

'Good idea. They'd be pleased to see you.'

Max and Belinda walked down Cuesta de San Gregorio and into the square by the church of San Gregorio Bético. A hippy baker was sitting on the broad steps, above the old washing-trough, selling her organic bread from a large esparto basket. They turned sharply left down the hill towards Plaza Nueva. On the wall beside the old town hall, someone had painted in huge letters: '*Semana Santa + Alcalde = Robo*'.

Holy Week plus the Mayor means Theft.

Underneath was a row of posters: 'Stop the Concrete. International Meeting. Old Trades Union Centre. Thursday.'

11

'You'll really like Carlos. He's an architect. Spends most of his free time campaigning to save the Albayzín.'

The walking group were waiting by the large fountain. A tall good-looking guy with cropped grey hair smiled at them.

'Hi, Max. And you must be Belinda.'

His English was very good indeed. He kissed Belinda on both cheeks. 'Max tells me you're writing a novel.'

'Trying to. I never realized how much work it was going to be.'

'Let me know if there's anything I can do to help. Max says I'm a mine of useless information about Granada.'

Max grinned. Belinda gave Carlos her best and sunniest smile. 'I'll take you up on that.'

'Okay, Belinda. Meet the gang. Giovanna and Maite are language teachers, and Miguel's doing postgrad work in Geography.'

Together they walked to the end of Paseo de los Tristes, crossed the old bridge over the tiny river Darro, and began to walk up Cuesta de los Chinos, the old route from the Albayzín to the Moorish fortress of the Alhambra. The stream flowing down from the Alhambra to the Darro had carved a deep valley, still cool and shady. The trees were in early leaf, and wild hyacinths were just emerging where a spring created a patch of damper ground. The group paused at the waterfall, where water gushed out of the ancient *acequia* from the Alhambra wall to join the stream, and then stopped at the plaque with a poem by Federico García Lorca.

With a bit of help from Maite, Belinda read the poem aloud. 'Wonderful, isn't it? The idea of water as a magical mirror which allows you to gaze into history.'

'Yes. Just imagine what Lorca might have written if he hadn't been shot.'

'That was in 1936, just at the start of the Civil War, wasn't it, Maite?'

'Yes. I've got a few books in English on the Spanish Civil War you can borrow if you like.'

'Thanks, I will.'

The group continued upwards, then passed under a double arch into the lush woodland which surrounded the old fortress. They walked past the Alhambra ticket offices and car park, then picked their way through a grove of mulberry and orange trees and emerged on to a minor road, which climbed upwards to the country park. They paused at the ruin of a Moorish palace, Dar-al-Arusa, the Palace of the Bride, and shimmied through a hole in the security fence, scrambled to the top, and looked out at the panorama of Granada ringed by mountains. They were already high above the Albayzín. Directly in front of them, piercing the city walls, was the church of San Miguel Alto. And to the right of the church, a network of old paths ran through the hills to Sacromonte and its abbey, la Abadía de Sacromonte.

The route now went upwards through a pine forest. As a jay flashed blue and chestnut, the path curved to their right. Suddenly, they could see the highest peaks of the Sierra Nevada, sprinkled with snow. And before them stretched rows and rows of olive trees, shining silver and gold in the sunshine.

'And here,' said Carlos, playing tourist guide for Belinda, 'we have a monument. "To the greater glory of God, Francisco Franco Bahamonde."'

'Amazing. After thirty years of democracy, there are still monuments commemorating that evil dictator.'

'Yes. There are probably more left in Granada than anywhere else in Spain.'

For the next hour, they walked through pinewoods, along the lip of the ridge which ran parallel to the Sacromonte valley. Way below them, a man was exercising a horse in a field, and a tiny black dog barked excitedly. Their path finally met a rutted farm track, and they turned left through a broken gate.

Carlos, who was enjoying showing Belinda the sights, pointed to a ruin in the valley. 'That's the old Jesuit monastery of Jesús del Valle.'

'This countryside is amazing, isn't it? And it's so close to Granada.'

'That's the problem. The only thing saving this valley from turning into a concrete jungle is the lack of good road access to Granada. When I was a kid, the Vega, that's the plain on the other side of Granada, was full of orchards and market gardens, and now it's shopping centres, houses and industrial estates.'

The track coiled downwards, carving itself into the stony clay of the hills, where wild lavender, thyme and rockroses flourished. On the valley floor they walked through olive groves, crossed a stream by a small bridge, and halted where two huge plane trees guarded the entrance to the monastery. Carlos checked his watch.

'Okay, *gente*. It's one o' clock. Lunch is booked for 3 p.m. I think we've time for a little look round.'

They squeezed past a broken barrier blocking the entrance to the monastery. A young man was already in the courtyard with his back towards them, poking at a pile of smashed marble and plaster. He turned round.

'Francisco!' exclaimed Carlos. 'What are you doing here?'

'I've been hearing stuff. Right now, I'm coming here every week to check up on things. Look at that. Some bugger's stripped all the marble from the chapel. It'll be the new owner, and he'll pretend it was vandals.'

'Any idea who's bought it?'

'I've been trying to find out all week, but they're being very secretive. It doesn't look good. Have you heard any more about the roads projects?'

'My friends in Planning think there's something big coming up.'

'Any chance of a leak before the conference?'

'I'll see what I can do. Oh, sorry. Max, Belinda. This is my friend Francisco Gómez. He's Chair of Granada Verde.'

Belinda looked the young man up and down. He was tall and wiry, brown as a berry with dark curly hair down to his shoulders. He kissed her on both cheeks. 'I'm very pleased

14

to meet you, Belinda. And I hope you'll join Granada Verde.'

'I'd be happy to help out . . . if my Spanish is up to it.'

Maite laughed. 'We always need help. How's the conference going, Francisco?'

'It's fine. Numbers are looking good. And how are things going with the procession?'

'Lidia can't make it now, so Margarita's going to do the final leg. She'll be okay so long as her father doesn't find out.'

'That's great. We won't be telling him.'

'Francisco, any chance you could show Max and Belinda around the monastery?' asked Carlos.

'Another day, *hombre*. I have to go now, meeting someone. *Vale*. See you guys on Thursday.'

Francisco picked up his staff, and walked away briskly.

'Okay, Belinda,' said Carlos. 'I'll show you round. But be careful, it's not safe. The kitchens were over there. This monastery belonged to the Jesuits until they were expelled from Spain in 1767. Its most colourful tenant was a Capitán Calderón who made a fortune in Constantinople and was buried in a black marble tomb in what's left of the chapel over there.'

Inside the ruined chapel, a mural of Bob Marley smoking a very large joint had replaced the usual holy fresco, and goats were stabled in what remained of the monks' kitchen.

'What a shame,' Belinda said. 'Can't someone find a good use for these buildings?'

'There are always plans, but they usually involve hotels, golf courses and luxury villas, and that means concrete all over these valleys.'

'Oh dear. But it's so close to the Alhambra. I'd have thought the whole area would be protected.'

'On paper, yes. But money rules here. Right, it's twenty past one. We'd better get a move on.'

The Club de Salud y Cultura set off along the valley bottom. The path recrossed the stream, now larger, and well over boot-level. Max tested a log which had been placed across the stream, and then he and Carlos helped Belinda and Maite across.

'There's a waterfall up there if you want a quick look,' said Carlos.

The waterfall was tiny, and half hidden by undergrowth, but white and orange butterflies danced in a shaft of light, and wild violets clustered round the margin of the pool. Belinda gazed at the little waterfall, and glanced at Carlos. Moving to Granada had been a good idea.

The group emerged from the woods at a big farmhouse with a large sign, 'Private Property. Beware of the Dogs'.

'Change of ownership here as well,' said Carlos.

They walked along the *acequia*, the little irrigation canal, past a ruined watermill and then turned right on to a broader path. Somewhere in the hills above them, a dog cried in pain. As they approached a small dirt track, the dog's cries became louder.

'Hey . . . that dog's in trouble. I'm going up to have a look.' And Belinda set off up the track.

'Belinda, you'll miss lunch. I'm sure the dog is all right.'

Belinda looked back at Carlos. 'I won't be long.' And then she continued upwards.

'You guys go on, and we'll catch up with you later,' said Max.

Belinda hurried up the track, not looking back. Max paused for breath and checked he had his inhaler. As he reached the top, Belinda dashed back towards him.

'Max! Come here. There's a dead body in that cave.'

Max looked at his watch. It was exactly 2 p.m.

16

Chapter 3

A man lay on the floor of the cave house. Francisco Gómez looked blankly at Max. 'I think he's dead.'

'Here, move aside.'

Max knelt down, opened the man's mouth to check the airway for obstruction, then felt for his pulse.

'Belinda, have you got a mirror?'

'Oh my God. I think so.'

She fished in her little bag. Max put the mirror close to the man's mouth. There was no mist. No pulse. The dog limped into the cave, and sat beside the dead man, crying. Belinda fondled the dog's ears, and the cry became a whimper.

'Okay. He's dead. I'll have to treat this as a crime scene. Will you both please leave the cave, and don't touch anything. Either inside or out.'

Francisco looked startled.

'I'm a cop,' Max said, closing the cave door as they all went outside. 'Have you called for an ambulance or the police?'

'I tried, but I can't get a signal in these hills.'

Max took his mobile out of his pocket. 'I'll call them.'

Francisco looked at him, puzzled.

'My mobile has a booster. I should get a signal. Yes. I can.'

Sargento Pedro Vidal, the duty officer at the Policía Nacional, answered.

'Pedro, it's Max. I have a dead man here in a cave. It's the first path uphill on the left at the very end of the Sacromonte road, about a kilometre after the end of the tarmac. Can you get a team out as soon as possible? No, I can't give you the coordinates. I'm fine, *gracias*. Just out for a walk. No, it's not a drunken hippy. He looks like a *gitano* . . . I'm sure they drink as much as the hippies. *Sí*, I should still catch the Real Madrid game.'

Max turned to Belinda. 'Can I borrow your notebook and biro?'

'Sure.'

'So, Francisco, what's the story?'

Belinda butted in. 'Max, let me get Francisco some water. He doesn't look too good.' She took some water from her rucksack, and Francisco drank thirstily.

'That's better,' he said. 'Thanks.'

'You okay now?'

Francisco nodded. 'I heard this dog crying, so I came up to look. He was sitting outside the cave door, howling, and I just . . . I pushed the door open . . . and there was this man, lying on the floor.'

'So you're here just by chance?'

'*Sí*.'

'Do you know this man?'

Francisco licked his lips and paused. 'No.'

Max raised an eyebrow.

'No, I don't know him. I've never met him before in my life.'

'Okay. I hope you didn't touch anything.'

'No,' said Francisco. 'I thought he had just blacked out or something.'

'Then why is his shirt torn?'

'Well, I . . . that was me,' said Francisco. 'I tried CPR. But I think he was dead when I got here. I did my best, but . . .'

Francisco's voice trailed off. Belinda handed over the water again. He sipped slowly this time.

'Okay, I'm going back in, but you two must stay out here until the police team arrive. Belinda, have you got a couple of clean hankies?'

18

'No, sorry. But I do have some silk walking gloves.'

Max squeezed the gloves on, pushed open the door and went back inside. The man was lying on his back, eyes closed. Max looked closely at his face. He must have been very handsome once, but his features were pinched, and his ponytail was streaked with grey. There were no obvious signs of rigor mortis. Beside the man was a chair, lying on its side. And some distance away was a guitar, face down on the concrete floor. Max went carefully through the dead man's pockets. He found just a dirty handkerchief, two used bus tickets and some small change.

The cave house was clean, but pretty basic. There was a single bed and a chest of drawers in one corner, a cheap rosary and a couple of framed photographs on top of the chest. The other corner served as a kitchen. There was a bottled gas stove, a few cheap glasses by the sink, and someone had carved an alcove into the rock to hold food and kitchen things. There was nothing else but the dead man, a guitar, and a framed picture of la Virgen de Sacromonte hanging from a nail in the wall.

Max went over to the battered chest of drawers. The top drawer was empty. In the second was a solitary shirt on top of a wooden box. There was nothing inside the box. In the last drawer there was underwear, and, underneath the pants, an imitation leather wallet. Max lifted the wallet from the chest of drawers and then opened it carefully. It contained about forty euros, an old letter, carefully folded and addressed to Paco Maya, and an identity card, the DNI.

He looked at the DNI photo and then at the dead man. They matched. The house had recently been cleaned. There were no obvious signs of drink, drugs or violence. Max went back outside. The wall of the cave was freshly whitewashed. But beneath the paint, he could just make out some letters . . . 'Asesino'.

Max checked the ground outside the cave. A few yards from the door there was a pile of ash. He carefully scooped it up and put it in an evidence bag. It was too much ash to be

19

a cigarette. It must be from a cigar. As he put the bag in his pocket, a car parked at the bottom of the path. Two uniformed police got out and started to walk uphill.

'*Joder*!' Max muttered. 'It's bloody Navarro.'

They hadn't exchanged a civil word since Navarro's suspension.

Before he reached the top of the path, Inspector Navarro had to pause for breath. His smooth jowly face was covered in sweat and his fat belly wobbled with the effort of the ascent. The younger guy, slim and very dark, had hardly noticed the climb.

'What's up, Romero?'

'Inspector Navarro, sir. This gentleman is Señor Francisco Gómez. He says he heard a dog crying, came up to investigate, and found a body inside the cave. He tried to revive the casualty, but without success.'

'So how come you and this lady are here, Romero?'

'My friend Belinda and I were passing below with other members of our walking group. She too heard a dog crying, came to help it, and found Señor Gómez and the dead man. I've checked for vital signs but there's no pulse and no breath. There are no signs of violence, as far as I can tell.'

Navarro grunted, and turned to Francisco Gómez. 'Why did you come up here? This valley must be full of yelping dogs.'

'I can't bear to hear a dog crying.'

'Hmm,' said Navarro. 'So why didn't you phone us when you found the body?'

'I couldn't get a signal in these hills. But then Belinda and Max turned up and Max phoned police headquarters.'

'So you two know one another?' Navarro asked Max.

'Not really. Francisco's a friend of some of the folk in my walking group.'

'So where's the rest of this group, then?'

'They went on ahead, and were going to wait for us in Casa Juanillo.'

20

'Okay. We'll want statements from all three of you, and the names of everyone in the walking group.'

Max and the two other cops entered the cave. Navarro bent down, and carefully examined the body.

'He is definitely dead. A *gitano*. Probably an overdose.'

'I've been through his pockets. His wallet with his DNI card was in the bottom drawer of that chest over there,' said Max. 'His name is Francisco Javier Maya Fuentes. It looks like he was known as Paco.'

'I hope you haven't damaged any evidence.'

'Of course I haven't,' said Max indignantly. 'And I had gloves on.'

'This isn't going to look good on my report, Romero. Did you tell the others not to touch anything?'

'Of course I did. But Señor Gómez may have touched a few things earlier. He attempted first aid when he found the body.'

Navarro glanced round the room. 'Nothing valuable here, is there? What a dump. Even if you've got no money, you've no need to live in a bloody cave!'

Max made no reply.

Navarro looked round again. 'Nothing much,' he said. 'I'll take a quick look outside. Okay, Belén,' he said, turning to the younger cop. 'Cordon this place off and take down their statements. And you three, empty all your pockets and bags.'

'Right,' said Belén. 'Names? DNI?'

'Sub-Inspector Max Romero. Policía Nacional, Granada.'

'Oh. Sorry, *señor*,' said Belén hurriedly. 'I didn't know.'

'That's okay,' said Max. 'New to the force?'

'Just a couple of days.'

Belén glanced at Max's stuff. Cash. Inhaler. Keys. Chocolate. Water. Sunhat.

'That's fine. *Gracias.*'

Belén then moved on to Francisco, took his statement, and went through the pile of items he had put on the ground. 'Lots of seeds you have here.'

21

'Yes,' replied Francisco. 'These are tree seeds, and those are wild flowers. I like to scatter them when I go for a walk. Anywhere that's bare or bulldozed. And I always have a bit of string with me to tie wild herbs together if I find any.'

'And this is your purse?' asked Belén, pointing to a small, red leather purse with an embroidered flower decoration.

'*Sí,*' replied Francisco. 'I keep my change in it, and a few euro notes. My niece gave it to me.'

'Do you mind opening it?'

Francisco opened it, and took out a ten-euro note, some coins, and a small photo.

'Very pretty,' commented Belén. 'A dancer. Your niece?'

'*Sí,*' replied Francisco.

As Sub-Inspector Belén finished taking Belinda's statement, the ambulance arrived, followed by Forensics, and then the duty judge, the *juez de investigación*. They all walked together up the hill. The judge, a young man in his mid-thirties and almost completely bald, introduced himself: 'Juez Emilio Martínez.'

'Inspector Ernesto Navarro. I'm the officer in charge. This is Sub-Inspector Belén. And this is Sub-Inspector Max Romero who just happened to be passing by below with his English friend here, Señora Belinda. They heard a dog yelping and came to investigate, and found this young man, Francisco Gómez, inside the cave with a dead body. Señor Francisco claims he too heard a dog crying, came to investigate and found the dead man.'

'I see. And who informed the police?'

'Sub-Inspector Romero did. Señor Gómez claims he tried, but couldn't get a signal.'

'Right. What have you got?'

'Looks like another bloody gypsy. Probably an overdose. No big deal.'

'That's for me to decide,' said the judge. 'I'll go and have a look.'

22

Ten minutes later the judge emerged from the cave house and examined the outside wall of the cave closely. '*Asesino*. I don't like that. Looks recent.'

He turned briskly to Navarro. 'There are a number of things I'm unhappy about. Treat this as a crime scene . . . I want a full set of photographs, fingerprints and footprints, plus everything I consider to be relevant documented and taken away for further examination.'

The technicians went about their business with quiet efficiency. Francisco sat outside the cave comforting the dog, while Belinda watched everyone and everything with fascinated interest.

The supervisor of the Forensics team emerged from the cave.

'What's the story?' asked the judge.

'It's too early to be sure, but the death's recent. Probably between half an hour and two hours before we took the body temperature. We may get something better from the autopsy . . . but I can't guarantee that.'

'Anything else?'

'There are signs of lividity – slight discoloration on buttocks and arms – so that suggests something between thirty minutes and two hours as well.'

'All right,' said the judge. 'I'll sign the order for the removal of the body. You can take it away as soon as you like now.'

He turned to Inspector Navarro. 'That's it for now. I'll be opening a case file.'

Inspector Navarro motioned to Sub-Inspector Belén. 'Okay, Belén. You take the DNI and check out the next of kin. Get someone on a doorstep tonight or tomorrow. Doubt if anyone's going to lose sleep over this guy though. Romero, anything else from you?'

Max flushed with annoyance. 'Just this one thing. I found what I think might be cigar ash over there. I've bagged it.'

'Bit slow giving this over, weren't you?' Navarro grunted.

Max did not reply.

'What about the dog?' asked Francisco. 'The dog's injured; he's been kicked.'

'So what's new? *Gitanos* kick their dogs all the time,' commented Navarro.

'Not in my experience,' said Francisco.

The dog looked up at the judge.

'*Bueno*. Let's get the dog to a vet for an examination. We might learn something.'

'What the –!' exclaimed Navarro. 'Who the hell is going to pay for it?'

'I would have thought your department, officer,' said the judge pleasantly.

They all set off down the path. Navarro went straight into his car with Belén, and drove off at speed.

'Not very polite, that Inspector Navarro,' said the judge.

'*Sí*,' said Max.

'Do any of you need a lift back to Granada?'

'That's kind of you, *señor*.'

'*Un momento*.' The judge looked around carefully at the patch of ground where the police vehicles had been parked. 'What do you make of this, Max?'

'There have definitely been other vehicles along here. It's all a bit confused, but those could be 4×4 tracks . . . a motorbike, and those are bicycles.'

'This should have been cordoned off as well. I need more pictures. I'll get Forensics back out.'

'It looks like rain. We could lose all the evidence if it does. Let's take some photos.'

Max borrowed Belinda's camera and took pictures.

'It's only one of those cheap disposable ones, Max. Will the pictures be good enough?'

'It'll have to do,' he said. 'Anyway, the lab guys can work miracles.'

Max got in the vehicle beside the judge, while Belinda, Francisco and the dog squeezed into the back seat.

'Are you new to Granada?' Max asked the judge. 'I don't think we've met before.'

'Just started here. My first case, you know. In fact, I've just started practising. My first case after years of useless learning by heart to become a judge.' He laughed. 'I got so nervous and frustrated with the process . . . well . . . my hair fell out. But I'm determined to treat all of the dead equally. So I'll make sure this case is handled thoroughly.'

Max smiled.

'I'll take the young man and the dog to the vet. Where can I drop you off?'

'The entrance to the Albayzín will be fine for Belinda and me. We can walk from there.'

The car stopped at the little Plaza del Horno.

'Belinda, sorry you missed lunch. I can make us a sandwich in my flat if you like.'

'Thanks, Max, but I'm shattered. Another day.'

'Are you still on for the Paso de los Gitanos on Wednesday?'

'Of course. That Navarro is a nasty piece of work. He doesn't like you, does he?'

'I complained once about how he treated a suspect, and he was suspended. He hates my guts. And the feeling is mutual.'

Chapter 4

The bells of Santa Ana rang out, long and loud. A minute later, the bells of Santa María de la Alhambra replied from the Alhambra hill. But no matter what the day, the bells always got Max to his desk before Inspector Jefe Davila arrived.

'You still on duty, Pedro?'

'On for the whole damn weekend. I won't even get to see the match tonight. But Málaga's going to get shafted. And Barça won't be able to catch up with Real. No chance.'

'We'll see,' said Max. 'Barça always comes through at the end.'

'Not this time, *hombre*. Have you managed to sort out that gypsy death?'

'Not yet.'

'It'll be drink or drugs. Mark my words.'

'Maybe.'

Max went to his office. Paperwork took up the whole morning. Just before lunch, his phone rang. It was Chief Inspector Davila's secretary, Clara Flores.

'*Hola*, Max.'

'Clara. How you doing?'

'Fine, Max. *Bien gracias*. But Señora Davila is being a pain. She can't go to her hairdresser's without phoning the boss twice. I'm sure he spends more time talking to her than the rest of the force put together.'

Max laughed.

'The boss wants to see you after lunch. He's taking long lunches these days. And he's spruced himself up no end. Expensive shoes and shirts, new watch. I suspect something's up. There's a woman.'

'You can't be serious, Clara. No woman would look twice at him.'

'Some can be desperate, you know.'

'Unlike you.'

'Well, Max, if you have it, there's no need to flaunt it.'

Max laughed. *'Vale, guapetona.* I'll be over at five.'

After lunch, more paperwork. At ten past five, he was in Clara's office, still waiting patiently for the great man.

Clara looked up from the pile of forms that she was checking.

'Sorry, Max, I don't know what has kept him,' she said. 'I tell you, he never used to come back this late. Looks fishy.'

Max smiled.

'I tell you, something's up. I can smell good cognac on his breath. And you know what a skinflint he is.'

There was the sound of running water from the washroom.

She cocked her head to one side. 'That's him back. He always drinks a glass of water now, and cleans his teeth. And then he phones the lady wife. You don't do that unless you're having an affair.'

'How do you know about that?' asked Max accusingly.

'It's what all the psychologists say,' she said, pointing to a pile of glossy magazines beside her desk. 'You should read these. You'd learn a lot about real life.'

The phone rang. Clara picked it up. 'Okay. You can go in now.'

Chief Inspector Davila was sitting behind his desk, absorbed in a file as if he'd been there for the last hour. After a minute or two, he looked up.

'Ah, Romero. Sit down. I have a note here from Inspector Navarro. This gypsy death. I'm not happy about the fact that you waded in before the duty officer arrived.'

27

'I'm sorry, sir, I just thought –'

'Well, next time don't think. Follow the rules. You should know the procedure by now. The body wasn't exactly going to vanish into thin air. And another thing. Navarro complained about you being slow in handing over some evidence.'

'Not true, sir,' said Max. 'Just an oversight on my part.'

'Romero, do I have to remind you that you've got your Promotion Board coming up next month? Stop messing about.'

'I'm sorry, sir.'

'Sorry's not good enough. I want to see a complete change of attitude. You're a poor team player. Our first rule is to support and cooperate fully with our fellow officers, no matter the circumstances. Is that understood?'

'*Sí, señor.*'

'And I have here a note from Judge . . . uhm . . .' Davila glanced at his files. 'Martínez. New chap, clearly no experience. He says that some details require further investigation. Something about a chair, a guitar, and the position of the body. He says he's opening a case file. Got a bee in his bonnet about foul play. Dickhead.'

Max said nothing.

'Bloody nuisance.' Davila sniffed, unfolded an immaculate cotton handkerchief, and wiped his nose. 'I hope this chap's not one of these new liberal types. Our judges have always represented the true Spain.'

'What would you like me to do, sir?'

'Do? As it's a new judge, I'll take full charge of this case. But you, my friend, will do all the legwork. And that gives you a chance to get your act together. You'll report first to Navarro. And if anything odd crops up, bring it to me at once. Remember your promotion is on the line. Understood?'

'*Sí.*'

'*Sí*, what?'

'*Sí*, Inspector Jefe. Fully understood.'

28

'Oh. One more thing. The judge has something here about a dog . . . taking it to the vet?'

'*Sí, señor*. There was a dog at the scene of the incident when we arrived, and it had been injured. The judge requested that the dog be taken to a vet, and he wants a full copy of the vet's report on the nature of its injuries.'

'He what? What sort of *idiota* is this judge? And who, pray, is paying the vet's bill?'

'The judge thought our department would, sir.'

'He did, did he? We'll see about that. I have a feeling about this new judge. I don't think he's going to last too long here in Granada. This is a conservative town, Romero. Never forget that. Pay for a vet indeed.'

'Is that all, sir?'

'Yes. Just watch your step.'

'You look a bit down,' said Clara, as Max passed her desk

'No. Didn't go well. Promotion's on the line.'

'Maybe he didn't get it up. Wait till next time.'

Max grunted and returned to his office. He phoned Forensics, and asked for the Chief Forensics Officer, Dr Guillermo Arroyo. He was a grumpy old bastard, but he and Max got on.

'Whatever you want, it's not done yet! Do you have any idea how busy we are?'

'I do, Guillermo. I just wondered how you were getting on with the Maya autopsy?'

The voice softened. 'Oh, is that you, Max? Just got in, and the phone's never stopped. Everyone thinks we can do miracles here. Maya, did you say? Che told me a quickie would be fine.'

'Oh, did he now? Bloody Navarro. Have you done it?'

'No, no time.'

'Could you find some time? We've got a new judge on the case, and he's keen as mustard. And I've got some concerns as well. Can you make it a full autopsy?'

'You should see our workload. Okay, Max, we might have it done by Wednesday. No promises, mind you.'

29

'*Gracias*, Guillermo.'

'Remember, you owe me one.'

'I'll remember.'

Max looked at his watch. There was still sufficient light to return to the gypsy's cave. And it was probably a good time to find some of the neighbours in. Whether they were willing to talk or not was another matter.

Max parked his car at the end of the Sacromonte road, and climbed up to the cave. The police padlock on the cave door was still intact. If that really was cigar ash he'd found, then there should be a cigar stub somewhere. He searched, but there was no sign anywhere of a stub. He poked around in a pile of debris at the side of the vegetable plot. Then he noticed it: caught between two dry leaves, a cigarette stub, filter-tipped. So maybe the dead man did smoke. Cigarettes. There was probably nothing suspicious about the ash after all. Max put the cigarette stub in an evidence bag, and walked back down to the main track.

The nearest house was a large *cortijo*, the one with the Dangerous Dogs sign. He looked around for a stick, just in case.

Stick in hand, Max set off for the *cortijo*. From the sound of it, there were big dogs somewhere close. As his hand reached for the gate, two mastiffs crashed against the fence. Max jumped back, and the dogs paused, snarling. Then a harsh voice called out.

'Diablo . . . Tigre. Down, you big bastards.'

The dogs turned reluctantly. A burly man wearing a security guard's jacket over dirty jeans was coming down the drive.

'*Huevón*. Can't you read?'

'Yes, I saw the sign. But I'm here on police business,' said Max, showing his ID.

'What do you want?'

'It's about a neighbour of yours, Francisco Javier Maya. You probably know him as Paco. Lives in the cave over there.'

'Neighbour? Never met him. Didn't even know anyone lived up there. I'm just the security guard.'

'This gentleman is a *gitano*, aged about forty. He plays the guitar . . .'

'Of course I've seen loads of *gitanos* around. It would be hard to miss them. And most of them have guitars, don't they? What's up?'

'We found Paco Maya dead, inside the cave.'

'Oh. Murdered?'

'Too soon to say, but I have to check up on a few things. Do you mind if I ask you some questions?'

'Go ahead.'

Max took out his notepad and biro. 'Do you have your DNI card?'

'Got it here somewhere. *Sí*, here it is.'

Max looked at the photo on the card, and then at the man in front of him.

'Fernando Pozo. You live out in Almanjáyar, I see. That's quite a way from here.'

'I work wherever I'm sent. This place is a bugger to get to. But the boss picks me up in the town centre, and drops me off here.'

'Your boss is?'

'Víctor Bustos. Owns Seguridad Victoriano. You might have seen our van around – "Your Security Is Our Concern".'

'Do you know who owns this place?'

'*Ni idea*. Never ask questions. The boss says that's wise.'

'Did you hear or see anything unusual yesterday?'

'Nah. Usual walkers on the path. But there was this tall guy with long hair on his own, looked like a hippy. I spotted him gawking through the fence. Told him to clear off, and he went. Then ten minutes later, there he was coming down the hill towards the *cortijo*. He'd circled round the back, crafty bugger. But the dogs got rid of him, no problem.'

That sounded like Francisco. 'What time did you see this guy?'

'He pitched up at half past one. Finally got rid of him at quarter to two.'

'How come you're so sure of the times?' asked Max.

'I'd got the footie on the radio. The match had just begun when I had to go and chase the hippy away the second time. The dogs were barking, you see. I wasn't pleased, I can tell you. I missed Seville's goal.'

'Anybody else come by?'

'*Sí*. Just after the dogs chased Nosy Parker, a bunch of walkers came by on the path. They had a couple of *guiris* tagging on.'

'How do you know they were *guiris*?'

'Well, she was wearing shorts, and had really pale legs, and he had this stupid hat.'

'Hmm, I see. Thanks. That's all for now. I think I should have a talk with your boss.'

'Doubt he knows anything. And Víctor keeps everything close to his chest anyway.'

Max returned to his car and drove to the dead man's nearest neighbour on the other side. He walked down a rough track to an old house covered with ivy and rang the doorbell. It didn't work. He knocked on the door, but there was no reply. A light was on at the back, so he walked around the side of the house. A woman with oiled grey hair scraped back in gypsy style was in the kitchen. Max tapped gently on the windowpane. The woman jumped, startled.

'Policía Nacional.'

She motioned to the back door, then opened it a crack.

'It's nothing to be worried about. I just have a few questions about a neighbour of yours, Paco Maya,' said Max and he handed over his ID. She examined it carefully, suspiciously.

'Paco!' she exclaimed. 'I hope nothing's wrong.'

'May I come in?' asked Max.

'I suppose it's all right. My husband will be home soon. We're just back from visiting my sister. We're best off in the kitchen. I was making a cup of coffee.'

32

Max followed her into the kitchen. The walls were covered with sparkling ceramic plates, and there were shining copper jugs on the window sill. He sat down on the flowered sofa.

'Paco,' said the woman. 'I hope nothing's wrong. He's never had much luck, that *gitano*. Just got out of prison a couple of days ago.'

'Out of prison?'

'*Sí*. In for a long while. Killed his wife, Lucía.'

'It's not the Paco who has a little daughter . . .' Max searched his memory. 'Angelita, wasn't it?'

'That's right. So you know him then?'

'No, but Abbot Jorge at the Abadía knew him well.'

'Knew . . .? *Ay Dios mío*. The Blessed Virgin of Sacromonte. Poor Paco. What happened?'

'We found him dead inside his cave.'

'*Dios santo*.' She closed her eyes and crossed herself. '*Sí*, he had a bad heart. You can't live the way he did and keep your health. Would you like a cigarette?' She took out a packet of filter cigarettes from her apron pocket and offered one to Max.

'Thanks. But I don't smoke.'

'May the Blessed Virgin protect him . . .'

'Here, let me help you. I'll make the coffee.'

Max stood up, and helped her to the little armchair. The water in the saucepan was boiling away.

'*Gracias*. Poor Paco. My husband has liver problems. You can go so quickly, can't you?'

'Sugar?' Max asked.

'*Dos, por favor.*'

Max made two coffees, both with two sugars. He would have liked milk in his, but didn't see any. He sat down and took out his notepad.

'Can I ask a few questions?'

'Poor Paco. Who would have believed it? Just out. The good Lord giveth, and the good Lord taketh away. You can call me Concepción,' she said taking a deep drag of her cigarette.

33

'Thanks, Concepción. It's just a few routine questions.'

'All right.'

'I know about Angelita. And there's an *abuela*, isn't there?'

'*Sí*. Carmen Espinosa. Angelita lives with her. There's his sister, Catalina. But Paco and Catalina aren't close, what with Lucía's death and all.'

'Do you know where any of these folk live?'

'No, not since the *abuela* moved away. And Catalina, I haven't seen her in years.'

'Any other family?'

'Not that I know. His *papá* died young, not much older than Paco, then his *mamá* died after he got sent down. Broken heart, I reckon. Did you know, Paco won the prison flamenco song contest?'

'No, I didn't know that.'

Concepción started to sing. Her voice was surprisingly good – low and powerful.

> 'Do what you can, Mother,
> To get me out of here.
> Do all you can, Mother, so I can die in peace,
> On the clean earth we own.'

'That was Paco's song. He wrote it after his mother died. That was the one that won the competition. Every time I hear it, I weep.'

Tears rolled down Concepción's cheeks. She took out a large handkerchief and wiped her eyes, then had another pull at her cigarette.

'Yes. I can understand that. You said he had health problems.'

'Bad heart, like I said. He'd been warned he might not have long to live.'

'I see. Did Paco own that cave?'

'*Sí*. And the land around it. Plus the plot on the other side of the track which goes all the way down to the river. The land's been in his family for years. And you know, he even had proper title deeds. I kept them here for him while he was in jail.'

'Do you still have the deeds with you?'

'No, I gave them back to him when he stopped off here on his way home.'

'Do you have any idea where he might have kept them?'

'He stored them in an old wooden box. I saw him put it away when he got home.'

'Where would that be?'

'In his chest of drawers. He didn't have many other safe places. Poor Paco. No bloody luck.'

'So he visited you, then?'

'*Sí.* I made him some food the day he got out of prison.'

'What day was that?'

'Wednesday. Me and my old man were going to stay with my sister in Jaén for a couple of days, and we've just got back today.'

'Can you remember what you talked about?'

'We had a bit of a laugh, talked about the old times, but mainly about his little girl. I tried to persuade him to move so he could see her more often. We're moving, you see. Had a good offer. At our age we can't cope with all this land.'

'I can understand that,' said Max. 'But Paco wouldn't move?'

'No, never. The grandmother wanted him to sell so that he could help the child, but he wouldn't.'

'Anything else you remember?'

'Not really. I gave him a hand to clean his house.'

'The cave?'

'*Sí.* I'd kept my eye on it while he was in prison.'

'Ah. We noticed it had been cleaned recently.'

'I like to see a home clean. We may be poor, but we can always be clean. All these lies about *gitanos* being dirty. I hate those lies.' And she looked with pride around her tidy kitchen.

'Did you notice anything unusual about the cave?'

35

'*Sí*. The wall had *Asesino* written on it in red paint. Paco gave it a good coat of whitewash, and he was going to give it another coat later.'

'*Asesino*,' said Max. 'What do you make of that?'

'Lucía's brothers. A real couple of bad ones. I never let my boys near them. The brothers probably heard Paco was getting out.'

'Do you know their names and where they live?'

'They're nasty bastards. You won't let them know I gave you their names, will you? I don't want trouble.'

'I know that,' Max said. 'We'll keep your name out of it.'

'All right. They did threaten poor Paco. The Blessed Virgin will protect me. Their names are Mauricio and Gregorio. They live somewhere in Almanjáyar. But I don't know where. The grandmother might know. She dotes on those boys, still thinks the sun shines out of their backsides. She'll do anything for them.'

'Have you seen the grandmother recently?'

'No. Not since she moved from around here. We quarrelled over those damn boys of hers, so we don't speak any more. That's all I'm going to tell you.'

'That's okay,' said Max. 'Thanks very much for your help. Can you think of anyone else who might have wanted to harm Paco?'

'No. Nobody. Apart from the brothers and the grandmother. The old bitch hated him.'

'Okay. Did Paco have his guitar with him when you saw him?'

'*Sí*. He never went anywhere without it. He said that his dog and his guitar were his best friends. Looked after it better than a baby.'

'We found a little dog outside the door of his cave.'

'That would be his dog, Negrito. We looked after him while Paco was in prison. Negrito still remembered Paco after all these years.'

'The dog was injured when we found him.'

'Injured? He was fine when I left.'

36

'Could Paco have kicked him?'

'Paco? Never. Even if he were blind drunk, he'd never hurt that dog. Poor Negrito. We're moving to a small flat. Can't really have a dog there. Where is he now?'

'We took him to a vet.'

'Vets are useless. And cost a fortune. A few fresh herbs would have helped. But who'll look after poor Negrito now?'

'Someone's offered to take him in.'

'That's good. The dog's old now. I'd like to see him die happy.'

'*Gracias*,' said Max, standing up. 'Just one last question – did Paco smoke cigars?'

'Cigars? You must be joking. Do you think we're made of money?'

'Cigarettes?'

'Not now. The man used to smoke like a bloody chimney, but he got clean in jail. Didn't do him any good though, did it?'

'I notice you smoke filters,' said Max.

'*Sí*,' she replied, stubbing out her cigarette in a ceramic ashtray. 'The doctor says I should give up, but well . . . what is there in life if you can't have a smoke or a little drink now and then?'

'Not much,' Max agreed. 'Did you smoke when you were cleaning out the cave?'

'*Sí*, I always have one after I've worked hard. A sort of reward.'

A car drew up outside.

'That'll be Manuel, my husband.' She went to the front door. 'Manuel,' she called out. 'Paco's dead. A cop's here, asking questions.'

'It's okay,' said Max, joining her at the doorway. 'I'm just going. Did you see Paco when he came out of prison?'

'No. Only Concepción did. Poor Paco. No luck, *este gitano*.'

'Can you think of anyone who might want to harm him? Concepción told me about the *Asesino* sign.'

'The Espinosa family hated him. But we all knew he didn't mean to hurt Lucía. It was tragic what happened. Bloody tragic.'

'Thanks for your help. If you remember anything else, call me on this number.'

Max drove back towards Granada along the Sacromonte road. There was quite a distance between Concepción's small *cortijo* and the nearest group of houses. More *gitanos*. They all knew Paco or knew of him. They'd heard he was out of prison, but hadn't seen him.

Max finally arrived at the hamlet of Puente Maríano, underneath the Abadía. He could do with a beer. As he parked the car in the tiny square, the sky suddenly turned dark. A swarm of bees was passing overhead. Max hurried into the bar. There was a tiny, shrivelled woman behind the counter, perched on a high chair.

'*Una cerveza, por favor.*'

She slid off the chair and served Max with a bottle of San Miguel. No glass.

Two grizzled old chaps, bottles in hand, were hunched in the corner. They glanced up at him, and then looked away as soon as they saw his uniform.

'I thought it was going to rain,' said Max to nobody in particular. 'But it was a swarm of bees.'

'We could do with rain,' said one of the grizzled chaps. 'My goats could do with a bite of green.'

'Sure could,' added the other. 'I've never known the rains to be this late.'

Max turned to the woman behind the counter. 'I'm making a few inquiries about a Paco Maya; lives at the end of the Sacromonte road. Do you know him?'

She shot a quick glance at the two men. 'Maybe.'

'Have you seen him?'

'Might have.'

'He was found dead in his cave yesterday.'

'*Paco!*' exclaimed the woman. 'But I saw him on . . .' She stopped and then added, 'He seemed fine then. *Normal.*'

38

'That would be Wednesday, the day he was let out of prison,' said Max.

The three old folk stared at each other. Then one of the men spoke. 'So we understand.'

'Did any of you see him?' asked Max.

Another pause.

'No. Just me,' said the woman. 'He came in here to buy some things. Straight out of prison like. A few eggs, bread, oil.'

'Any cigarettes, or a cigar even?'

'No. No cigars. Are you kidding? But no cigarettes this time. Said he'd quit smoking for good. He was off the booze too. Who would have thought it?'

'Did you get the impression that he was worried about anything?'

'No. Just happy to be out. He desperately wanted to see his daughter.'

'Angelita?'

'That's right. Left here with a smile on his face.'

'No car?'

'Car? Never had one. He had to walk from here to his place. Quite a distance.'

'Have you seen his wife's brothers around?'

She shot another glance at the two old men. 'Lucía's brothers? No, I've never seen them.'

The two men both shook their heads. Max paid for the beer, and left. He had an uncomfortable feeling about this case. But no idea why.

Chapter 5

Max looked at his watch. It was late, but he should let Jorge know about Paco's death. He drove up the steep, dusty road to the Abadía, rang the bell, and waited until one of the priests answered. The Abbot was in the workshop, helping with the preparations for the procession on Holy Wednesday, Los Gitanos.

The workshop was a scene of organized chaos, with Abbot Jorge apparently in the thick of it. Max smiled. The Abbot's shirt was bloused over his ample stomach, his sleeves rolled up to the elbows, but Jorge was doing his man of the people show, which meant just standing around making suggestions, while a team of *gitanos* were doing the actual work.

Three women were easing elaborate cloth garments on to a statue of the Virgin of Sacromonte. One man was polishing candlesticks, two others polishing the Virgin's copper throne. Next to Jorge were two men whom Max did not know. One was a priest. Jorge turned and saw Max standing in the doorway.

'Max,' he exclaimed. 'Come on in, you heathen, and give us a hand. This is where all the hard work is done for the Insigne, Pontifical, Real, Colegial, Magistral y Sacramental Cofradía del Santísimo Cristo del Consuelo y María Santísima del Sacromonte.'

Max smiled again. 'Known to us ordinary folk as the Cofradía de los Gitanos – the Brotherhood of the Gypsies.'

In spite of all his radical pretensions, Jorge loved all the extravaganza of the Catholic Church.

'Max, you really should join a *cofradía*. It'd make a true Spaniard of you.'

'Jorge, you know I find it all a bit . . . well . . . over the top. Not my scene really. Look at this cloak . . . velvet and silver thread.'

'Yes. It's gorgeous, isn't it? Let me introduce you to our great benefactor, the man who paid for this fabulous cloak. Max, this is Don Andrés Mendoza.'

A tall, thin man with his black hair swept back, dressed in a smart grey suit, stepped up and shook Max warmly by the hand.

'Sub-Inspector Max Romero of the Policía Nacional,' said Max.

The other man, a priest who looked like an El Greco portrait, smiled.

'And this gentleman,' said Jorge, 'is Monsignor Mateo Bien, the Archbishop's adviser . . . and my chess partner. He's a great networker.'

'Very much so,' said Andrés Mendoza. 'I came into a fairly substantial sum of money, and wanted to make a donation to a *cofradía*. I asked Monsignor Bien, and he suggested the Cofradía de los Gitanos. And Abbot Jorge here felt the Virgin needed a new cloak.'

One of the *gitanos* stopped his work and turned to Max. 'Yes, this is our way of honouring God. When we carry our Most Holy Mary of Sacromonte through the streets of Granada, we want her to look her best. It's an honour for us all.'

'Quite right,' added Jorge. 'Even when people were hungry around here they always insisted the Virgin looked her best.'

'Looked her best!' exclaimed Max. 'Just look at her crown.'

'Fabulous, isn't it?' said Jorge. 'Cost a fortune.'

'Okay, okay,' said Max. 'I should know better than to discuss religion in Catholic Granada.'

Jorge laughed. 'It's just that we believe in external professions of our faith. We're not miserable sods like you Protestants in Scotland.'

Monsignor Bien and Andrés Mendoza both smiled.

'Abbot Jorge,' said Andrés Mendoza, 'it's been a pleasure working with you. I too am delighted with the cloak, and pleased that in my humble way I can honour the Virgin. And it's an honour to be associated with such a famous *cofradía* as Los Gitanos. But we really have to be going now.'

Jorge beamed, and embraced the two men.

'Thank you, Don Andrés,' he said. 'We'll be in touch soon, I'm sure.'

'Of course. The Abadía has a place deep in my heart, and it will be an honour to help restore it to its former glory.'

'And thank you, Mateo . . . I really appreciate this.'

Mateo Bien handed Max his business card. It was small and elegant, with the Opus Dei symbol, a cross embracing the world. Max rummaged in his pocket and found one of his own. It was slightly crumpled.

The two men shook Max's hand, nodded to the gypsies, and left.

'Well, Max. What can I do for you?'

'Sad news, Jorge. Paco Maya's dead. He was found in his cave yesterday.'

'*Ay* . . . Poor Paco. But he wasn't due out until next week.'

'He was released a few days early.'

'*Ay* . . . such bad luck. He was so looking forward to seeing his daughter. I will offer a funeral mass.'

'Paco?' said one of the gypsies. 'Killed his wife, didn't he?'

'That's right,' said Max. 'But he was still a good man.'

'And he helped us when we needed help,' said Jorge.

'Some *gitanos* have bad luck . . . all their bloody lives,' commented another of the gypsies.

'They do that,' said Jorge.

'I have to go now, Jorge. It's getting late.'

'Come back soon. I have something I'd like to discuss with you privately.'

Chapter 6

On Palm Sunday morning, Max's car nosed its way along Calle Isabel la Real, negotiated the tight corner on to Cuesta de la Lona, and passed the Moorish gate of Puerta de Monaita, overlooking Granada. The clay-tiled roofs of the old houses on either side of Calle Elvira crowded the foreground. The green and white domes of Renaissance churches, San Jerónimo, San Juan de Dios, San Justo y Pastor, and the cathedral dominated the middle distance and then the unending sprawl of tower block suburbs faded into the hills of the Sierra Elvira.

Max's cousin Juan had spent the night in the little flat above his offices in Calle San Juan de Dios. He'd been at another business dinner. Now he was waiting at the kerb, with flowers, a cake for Isabel and a couple of things for the kids.

'I got you some flowers for *abuela* Paula, Max.'

'*Genial*. Good idea.'

'Thanks for the lift. My car will be back from the garage tomorrow. How's the new car then?'

'Great. And thanks for getting such a good discount.'

'No problem. So how's things?'

'A disaster. Sodding landlord's just given me notice to quit.'

'*Qué*! Your lovely little flat?'

'*Sí*.'

'And your Promotion Board for Inspector?'

'It's at the end of this month, and I've still got loads of preparation to do.'

'*Ay*! That's bad timing.'

They took the motorway to Motril and the coast. The suburbs of Granada went on and on. There were still derelict farmhouses waiting for the bulldozer, next to the smart new residential blocks, and some old folk were trying to grow vegetables in the spare scraps of land between car showrooms and industrial estates.

'Oh Christ,' said Max. 'This is becoming so ugly.'

'Yes. But that's progress for you. Helps my business.'

'Hmm. And how is business?'

'Slow. But it'll pick up if I get into the Brotherhood of the Bell, la Cofradía de la Campana.'

'I didn't think that was your thing.'

'Get real, Max. The networking opportunities are great for me. There are a couple of big builders in it. Guys with connections.'

'Hmm.'

'And it turns out our *abuelo* was one of the founding members, but don't mention that to Paula. It'll just upset her.'

'I won't. No point in distressing her.'

'Good man. You know, there are some nice new houses on the way to Cenes, and, strictly speaking, they're not on the market yet. But I know the developer so I could probably get a discount for you to buy off-plan, and then you could make a killing in a couple of years.'

'Juan, I'm not moving out of the Albayzín. End of story.'

Half an hour later, Max turned the car off the motorway and headed into the mountains towards the town of Diva. They passed through Diva and out along the Jola road to a large farmhouse overlooking the river. *Abuela* Paula and Isabel were waiting to greet them, the younger woman gently supporting the older, who grasped her walking stick determinedly.

'Oh, Max, Juan.' Paula hugged them both tightly.

'*Abuelita, abuelita*. It's so good to see you.'

'*Ay*, Max. Lilacs. How lovely. You remembered how much I love them. And Juan, you found my favourite cake.'

Juan grinned at Max, who slipped his arm around his grandmother's waist. As they walked towards the house, Leonardo and Encarnita belted back along the lane on their bikes.

'*Papá, papá*.'

'Leo, Nita. Mind Daddy's arm.'

'I'm fine, love, I'm fine.'

'Did you get my book, Daddy?'

'My Seville football?'

'I sure did. Would I forget?' said Juan.

Isabel rounded up her brood and despatched them into the house to wash their hands, and then disappeared back into the kitchen.

'Lunch should be ready in half an hour,' she called. 'Do you want to get changed, Juan?'

'No, just a little glass of wine, and I'll be ready to face those kids. Ah, Max, here's Anita. Just on time.'

Anita Guevarra's small car crunched up the driveway.

Max opened the car door, and pecked Anita on the cheek. Paula embraced her warmly.

'How are you, my dear?'

'I'm well, Paula. I'm sorry, I didn't have time to change. I had to go out and interview a witness this morning.'

'Don't worry, my dear; you look lovely in your Guardia Civil uniform. Doesn't she, Max?'

'Very.'

'Green does suit you, my dear.'

The big garden table had been pulled out of winter storage, back into its old position where the sweet chestnut tree was already casting a delicate shade with its fans of soft new leaves. When all were seated round it, Isabel brought out a large platter of seafood cooked with tomatoes, garlic, saffron and olive oil, rice cooked in fish stock, a golden, wobbling bowl of home-made mayonnaise and a jug of spicy

45

sauce of roasted red peppers, pounded with garlic and capers to a rich purée.

'But this is not paella,' said Juan.

'No. It is my new recipe,' said Isabel.

Conversation buzzed backward and forward across the table: worries about the impact of the proposed water-bottling plant on Diva's water supply, Leo's football team, and plans for young Encarnita's First Holy Communion. When she thought no one would notice, Anita's bright smile faded a little as she looked at Max.

'So have you heard from the Mayor yet?' Max asked Paula.

'*Sí*, he's agreed in principle we can open up the mass grave. But there's a legal process to go through.' Paula turned to Anita. 'Did you know, my dear, there are still families who don't want the grave opened?'

'Really? But you have so many friends in the village. I'd have thought . . .'

'The Quiros brothers are worried about potential costs – tightwads. And the Campos family don't want another newspaper article denouncing their *abuelo* for supervising some of the executions.'

'After so long?'

'After so long.'

'The Lorca family don't want his grave opened, either,' said Juan. 'Quite right. No point in opening up old wounds. We've got to look forwards, not backwards.'

'*Bien*,' said Paula. 'But we need to give those who were murdered in the Civil War a decent burial.'

'I know how you feel, grandma, but we shouldn't burden the younger generation with problems which aren't theirs. And that's what Cardinal . . . what's his name, said.'

Paula looked tired and upset. 'Juan,' she said, 'I just want Antonio properly buried before I die. I can't leave him lying in a pit in a ravine. He was my brother.'

Juan fell silent.

'*Ay por Dios*,' said Isabel. 'Why can't we just forget the Civil War? Sometimes I think this village has a ghost at every table.'

'Because there *are* ghosts at every table, Isabel. And wishing won't make them go away. The dead need justice,' said Paula.

Juan concentrated on his dark chocolate and almond cake.

'The cake's a bit dry, *abuela*. Shall I get some cream?'

'No, Juan, it's as it should be. Where did you buy it? Pâtisserie la Giralda? I hope not.'

'No, *abuela*. I did not.'

Anita looked at Paula with a half-formed question on her lips.

'My dear, the present owner's grandfather was an informer for Franco. I would never buy anything from that shop.'

Leo looked at his great grandmother, and gently punted the new football under the table at his uncle.

'*Tio* Max, can we have a kickabout? Please. Mum, I've eaten everything.'

Isabel looked relieved. 'Of course you can, dear.'

'All right, kid. Let's try out this new ball then. Juan, you coming?'

'Sure. I've still got my old skills. I can still beat you to a pulp.'

The three went off to a worn patch of flat grass at the end of the garden.

'Thanks, kid,' said Juan. 'Right. Let's have penalties. *Tio* Max'll be goalie.'

Max saved the first penalty from Leo. Juan carefully placed the ball, stepped back four paces, grinned at Max, stepped up to the ball, and slid it into the left corner.

'Gooooal!' he yelled, and punched the air.

'Who won?' asked Isabel when she finally got them back for coffee.

'Leo did. The boy's got real talent. Takes after his *papá*.'

As Max sipped his *digestivo*, he turned to Paula. 'Sorry, *abuela*, I have to get back early.'

'Oh, so soon?'

'Really sorry, but I'm working on a case.'

'I'll walk you to your car, Max,' said Anita.

Max kissed Anita goodbye, in a brotherly sort of way. She hugged him, but Max didn't hug back.

'Shall I see you soon, Max?'

'I'm really busy at the moment. I'll call you as soon as I can.'

'Max, we need to talk. How about a meal together?'

'That's a good idea. I'll check my diary and give you a ring.'

'That's what you always say these days.'

Paula called from the table: 'Drive carefully, *cariño*. I'll phone you tonight.'

A few fat drops of rain splashed on the windscreen as he drove through the Granada suburbs. Ten minutes later a traffic cop halted the car.

'*Joder!*' said Max aloud. 'Bloody Holy Week.'

The procession, el Paso de la Cofradía of Jesús de la Sentencia y María Santísima de las Maravillas, was approaching.

Five men, robed in black velvet and carrying banners on heavy silver poles, appeared round the corner, followed by a group of black-clad musicians playing a sombre march on drums, clarinet and trumpets. Robed, masked penitents marched behind them. Then came the tragic tableau of Jesus, sentenced to death, chained to a pillar, and whipped by Roman soldiers. The statues were life-size, the blood very bloody. And in the distance he could see the great, swaying bulk of a baroque image of the Virgin of Sorrows, cloaked in red and cloth-of-gold, enthroned on her *palio*, and carried shoulder-high by a sweating team of *costaleros* to bless the streets of Granada.

Max did a U-turn and escaped through the back streets. By the time he reached his flat, the phone was ringing.

'Maximiliano.'

'*Hola, abuela.*'

'Maximiliano, you are being unkind to Anita.'

'But –'

'You hardly spoke to her, and when she looked at you she seemed so sad. What's wrong, Max? You can tell your *abuela.*'

'*Abuela* . . . things are a bit difficult right now.'

'Have you met someone else?'

'No, *abuela.* No.'

'So what's the problem, then?'

'It's just . . .'

'Max, she's a lovely girl and I don't want you making her unhappy.'

'I don't want to make her unhappy either.'

'That's good . . . But?'

'*Abuela*, the spark's just gone out of the relationship.'

'So you don't love her any more?'

'Well . . .'

'Maximiliano, you should do the right thing and tell her in plain words.'

'But *abuela*, I don't want to hurt her.'

'If you don't want to hurt her, you should be honest and make a clean break of it.'

'But *abuela* – oh, that's my milk boiling over. Have to run.'

'Maximiliano, if you were here I'd read your forehead, and I'd know if you were fibbing.'

There was a gentle click as Paula put the phone down.

But Max knew she wouldn't let the matter drop. Great things, families.

Chapter 7

The rain finally came on Monday. Max lay in his bed, listening to the heavy drops splashing on to his terrace. He padded to the living-room window. The jasmine in its terracotta pot was dripping water. And beyond the rooftops, the Alhambra was shrouded in cloud, apart from a shaft of light touching the Torre de la Vela.

Dolores next door was practising her *saeta*, the flamenco psalm to the Virgin. If the rain stopped, and her Virgin, la Virgen de la Esperanza, left her home church, Dolores would stand on a balcony downtown tonight, and sing, alone and unaccompanied. The procession would stop, the crowd would fall still and silent, then Dolores would have her moment. But right now, things weren't looking good. Neither for Dolores nor for la Virgen de la Esperanza. Rain would spoil the big day for both of them.

Max took a quick shower, dressed, and munched a bowl of muesli. After breakfast, he took out his notebook and updated his 'to do' list on the Paco Maya case:

1. Talk to the boss of Seguridad Victoriano. Find out who owns Cortijo de los Angeles.
2. Talk to the sister, Catalina Maya, then to *abuela* Espinosa. Locate Lucía's brothers, Gregorio and Mauricio Espinosa.
3. Get prison report on Paco Maya's health.
4. Check if lab results back yet.

5. Get vet's report.
6. Get tyre photos blown up in lab.

Umbrella in hand, Max walked down the steep, wet streets of the Albayzín. A stream had already taken over the pathway in Cuesta de San Gregorio. Along Calle Elvira, he dodged the puddles where mud was flowing from the building sites. In Plaza de la Trinidad, where heretics had been burned, the trees still hadn't recovered from a savage pruning. The sight of the mutilated branches reaching to the sky made Max feel very uncomfortable. Just as Easter did.

He clocked in and walked up the stairs to his office, his boots leaving muddy prints on the freshly mopped tiles. On the second floor, Comisario Principal Bonila and Comisario Felipe Chávez were talking in the corridor. Chávez looked up as Max walked towards them.

'Max, we were just talking about you.'

Max paused. 'Good things, I hope.'

'Well, nothing bad. If you're free at the moment, could you come into my room for a second?'

'Certainly, sir.' Max followed Chávez into his office.

'Sit down, Max, and make yourself comfortable. We need a bit of help. You've probably seen the posters in town for this Anti-Globalization conference.'

'Sí. They seem to be everywhere.'

'They've got permission for a march and demonstration. We are worried there might be violence, and we don't want a repeat of Genoa.'

'But the Genoa demonstration was huge,' said Max. 'And there seems to have been a lot of police provocation there.'

'I agree,' said Chávez. 'The Italian police really messed up. So we want you to go through the websites to see if there's anything which would help our planning.'

'I'd enjoy that, sir.'

'Good, and we'd like you and Sub-Inspector Belén to attend the conference. See if you can spot the violence brigade, and get names and photos.'

51

'I may be recognized,' said Max.

'We've thought of that. But your fluent English will be invaluable. And Roberto Belén won't be known. So even if you get chucked out, he'll be able to stay.'

'But I'm on a case at the moment.'

'We know. We're going to ask Davila to release you.'

'I'd rather not, sir, if you don't mind.'

'Is there a problem, Max?'

'We're still awaiting the autopsy, sir.'

Chávez glanced at him, sharply. 'So you think there's more to it than Davila reported?'

'Yes, sir. Plus, we have a sharp new judge on the case who's keen as mustard.'

'I see. So the new judge might cause us grief if we don't do it by the book?'

'Something like that.'

'Let's compromise, shall we? You spend a little more time on the case now, but the priority is to check those websites and attend the conference. Then you can go back on the case.'

'That seems fair, sir. But what will I tell Inspector Jefe Davila?'

'I'll sort that out. Any serious problems, just let me know.'

'Thank you.'

'We'll be having a meeting tomorrow lunchtime, 2 p.m. prompt.'

'I'll have the report.'

Max saluted and left. He went into the secretaries' office. There was a fax on one of the machines, from the prison. Paco Maya had had a chronic heart condition. Any strain might have provoked a heart attack. Max photocopied the report, put the original into an envelope, went downstairs, and slid it under the door of Navarro's office.

He returned to his office, switched on his PC and checked his emails. There was a message from Navarro.

'Next of kin is a minor. Daughter, Angelita. Lives with grandmother, Carmen Espinosa, at Calle Libertad, N° 7,

Haza Grande. Grandmother informed Sunday. Only other known relative is a sister, Catalina Maya. Address unknown. Interview grandmother, track down and interview sister.'

Max picked up the phone and dialled the vet.

'*El pobrecito*. Poor little thing,' the vet said. 'Looks like some bastard had kicked him hard. Fortunately the guy wasn't wearing heavy boots, so there are no broken bones. But the dog is badly bruised. The injury is definitely recent.'

'Can you tell what sort of shoes?' asked Max.

'Sorry. We can tell the difference between a kick and, say, being hit with a stick, but we can't go much beyond that.'

'*Muchas gracias*.'

Max then checked the address of Seguridad Victoriano. It was quite close as well. So he could go and see the grandmother, stop off at Seguridad Victoriano, then on to Almanjáyar to track down Lucía's brothers. Max walked to the car park and got into his car. It had stopped raining. It didn't take him long to drive to the grandmother's house in Haza Grande.

On Calle Libertad, three boys were cruising around on bikes and another boy was showing off on a mini motorbike. Max watched them for a while. Flamenco blared from an industrial-strength sound system, perched on a window sill, and a dejected-looking donkey stood tethered to a lamppost. Max knocked on the door of number 7. A stout, unhealthy-looking woman wearing an apron and carpet slippers answered.

'*Qué*? The cop's been here already.'

'I know,' said Max. 'My sincere condolences for Paco Maya's death.'

'Only what he deserved,' she retorted.

'Do you mind if I come in and ask a few more questions?'

'I was just going out. You can ask them here.'

'*Vale*,' said Max. 'I take it you and Paco Maya did not get on.'

'After what he did to my beautiful daughter, what do you expect?'

'And Angelita?'

53

'She knows what the bastard did to her *mamá*.'

A pretty young girl, eight or nine years old, appeared round the street corner, munching something from a paper bag. She saw Max, looked at the boys on the bikes and started to run towards them.

'Angelita, inside this minute or I'll leather you. Tomasito, Nico, Rafa – go home! Now!'

The girl looked at her grandmother balefully, but went inside. The boys stared at Max for a moment, then cycled off.

'So that's Angelita?'

'*Sí.*'

Max continued: 'Paco had a sister, I believe – Catalina.'

'*Correcto.*'

'Do you know where I can find her?'

'*Ni idea.* Haven't seen her for years, ever since she walked out on my Mauricio. Left him broken-hearted. The nasty bitch.'

'Could you tell me where I can contact Gregorio or Mauricio?'

'No.'

'All right. I'm told you went to see Paco in jail to get him to sell his land.'

'Who told you that? That nosy cow, Concepción?'

'But it's true, isn't it?'

'*Sí.*'

'But Paco refused to sell?'

'*Sí.* I told him it was for Angelita, but he wouldn't listen. I told my boys, and they said he was a stupid, selfish bastard.'

'So your sons knew you wanted Paco to sell?'

Carmen Espinosa stared suspiciously at Max. 'So what?'

'Where can I find your sons?'

She paused. '*Ni idea.*' And with that she slammed the door shut in Max's face.

The offices of Seguridad Victoriano were located down a side street tucked between dingy grey blocks just off the city centre. Max knocked on the office door and entered. A

54

woman in a tight red dress was sitting behind a desk, painting her nails an even brighter red than her dress. She looked up and smiled coquettishly.

'*Un poli*. Well . . . what can I do for you?'

'I'm looking for the boss,' Max said.

'What a shame. And there I was thinking that you might be looking for me. I could do with a body search.'

'I'd have to arrest you first.'

'I'd look forward to that.'

'Maybe some other time,' said Max. 'When I catch you doing something illegal.'

'I'll look forward to that as well. I'll have to think of something deliciously illegal.'

She scraped her chair backwards, and shoved open the door of the inner office. 'Víctor. There's a *poli* here. He wants to see you.'

Víctor was a small grey man in a crumpled suit. He looked at Max. 'Don't tell me the cops need protecting now.'

Max laughed. 'No. Not yet. But the way things are going we will do soon. No, I'm here to ask about a property you are protecting, El Cortijo de los Angeles, at the end of Sacromonte.'

'*Sí*. That's one of ours.'

'Do you know who the owner is?'

'It's a company. Gredas SA.'

'And the owner?'

'*Ni idea*. The fewer questions you ask in this job, the longer you live.'

'But they pay you in advance?'

'Of course. Our company policy. Never take on a job until the cheque's cleared or we get cash up front.'

'How were you paid for this job?'

Víctor paused and looked at the woman in red.

'Cash,' she said.

'*En efectivo*,' he echoed.

'And you have a receipt?'

'Sure. We pay our taxes, you know.'

'You don't happen to have the receipt here, do you?'

Víctor looked at the woman again. '*Sí*. We do.'

'Could I see it?' asked Max.

Víctor paused, 'Don't see why not.'

The woman opened her desk drawer and took out a big black ledger.

Max looked at the receipt. 'Received from . . . an illegible scribble . . . the sum of 5,200 euros . . . but there's no legible name. And that's all you know?'

'That's all we need to know,' said Víctor.

'Quite a lot of cash to hand over. How did he pay it?'

The woman smiled at Max. 'Ten five hundreds and two one hundred notes.'

Víctor scowled.

'*Gracias*,' said Max. 'You've been most helpful.'

'We're always pleased to help the police,' said Víctor, returning to his office at the back.

'My name's Gloria. Remember that arrest. I'm still thinking about something really wicked to do.'

'I'll remember,' said Max. 'If you recall anything else to do with this case, phone me. Here's my card.'

Max returned to his car, drove towards the blocks of grey flats of Almanjáyar, then looked for somewhere safe to park. He called out to a bunch of young men lounging on the kerb. 'Is there a Policía Local here?'

They looked at him as if he were from another planet.

'*Ningún idea*,' one of them finally replied and then spat on the pavement. 'Don't think we have one of them here,' he added, turning to his mates.

'Never heard of one,' they echoed.

Max sighed and started his car.

'You could ask the *poli* in Granada,' one of them called out.

A little further on, there was a church with its gates open. Max parked the car inside the gates, and went to look for the priest. The priest was in the sacristy, folding his vestments. Max coughed and the priest turned. He was young and fresh-faced.

56

'Father Gerardo Arredondo,' he said, and shook Max's outstretched hand.

'Sub-Inspector Max Romero from the Policía Nacional,' replied Max. 'Sorry to disturb you. But I'm looking for two gypsy brothers, Mauricio and Gregorio Espinosa. I believe they live around here. Do you know where I can find them?'

'Ah. Don't know them, but I know their mother. And I know Catalina, Mauricio's *ex-novia*. She was a regular at our women's refuge before she left him.'

'So Mauricio has a record of violence?'

'I'm afraid so. His brother as well.'

'You don't know where I might find Catalina?'

'No. She's just moved and I don't have her new address yet. She moves around so Mauricio can't go and pay her a visit. But she comes back here to help with the refuge. I have a mobile number for her.'

The priest fished in his pocket for his own mobile, checked the contacts list and wrote the number down.

'*Gracias*,' said Max, carefully folding the piece of paper. 'Can you think of anyone who would know where the Espinosa brothers live?'

'Well, there's the mother, of course.'

'Tried her. She wouldn't tell me.'

'*Sí, típico*. I would have expected that.'

'Can you think of anyone else?'

'Not anyone who would tell you.'

'That's unfortunate.'

'But there's a good chance they might be in the Bar Gitano. If they aren't in town, sometimes they go to Nerja.'

'Where can I find this bar?'

'At the end of the street.'

'*Muchas gracias, padre.*'

It was a surprisingly long walk to the end of the street. It began to rain, and Max lengthened his stride. The Bar Gitano was a rough, unwelcoming place.

'*Un carajillo?*' asked the barman.

'Just *un café con leche*.'

The barman stared at Max's blue uniform, and grunted. The bar was full, noisy when he entered, but now uncomfortably silent. The barman banged the coffee down in front of him, poured the hot milk until it ran over the top of the cup, and shuffled away. Max cleared his throat.

'I'm looking for two brothers, Mauricio and Gregorio Espinosa,' he said. 'Anyone know where I might find them?'

'Don't live around here,' said a skinny guy, stroking an ugly dog's ears.

'Never heard of them,' said a fat man in a dirty shirt.

Max stood up, and stared around. Two pony-tailed guys, who looked as if they might be brothers, were sitting in a corner sipping their *carajillos*. Max walked towards them.

'Excuse me, *señores*. Do either of you know Gregorio or Mauricio Espinosa?' he asked pleasantly.

'*Por qué*? Who's asking?'

'I just need to ask them a few questions about the death of a *gitano*, Paco Maya. He died a few days ago in Sacromonte.'

'Paco!' exclaimed an old gent seated at the bar. 'You didn't –'

'*Joder*! You stupid old fart.'

The brothers stood up quickly. One punched Max hard in the stomach, and the other pushed him over a chair, then they both ran out of the bar. Max lay on the floor gasping for breath. Nobody came to help. He pulled himself to his feet, wiping crushed peanuts and cigarette ash from his trousers.

'How much for the coffee?' he asked the barman. 'So those two goons were Mauricio and Gregorio Espinosa?'

There was a deadly silence.

Max limped back to the church. He had twisted his knee slightly when he fell over the chair. When he got back to his car, the tyres had been slashed. The youths he'd seen earlier were still on the pavement opposite the church, laughing. He phoned the Policía Nacional and explained his situation. Roberto Belén came to rescue him.

'You all right, Max?

'Could have been worse. The car's still got wheels.'

58

'*Verdad* . . . So this is the infamous Almanjáyar. I never thought it was a *gitano* area.'

'Poor bloody *gitanos*. Their caves in Sacromonte got flooded back in the 1950s. They spent twenty years in temporary housing, and then the town hall finally dumped them in Almanjáyar. End of their community, end of their culture.'

'And we have to pick up the pieces,' said Belén. 'What's new? By the way, Inspector Navarro wants to see you.'

'Great.'

Max took out his mobile and called Catalina Maya's number. No reply. Back at headquarters, he went to the bathroom, splashed his face with cold water, straightened his tie and uniform, and then walked to Navarro's office.

'The bastard's going to enjoy this,' Max muttered to himself.

Navarro was at his desk, pretending to be occupied with some report. He kept Max standing, slowly finished what he was reading, and looked up. 'I've got this report from the prison authorities on that *gitano*. The old lag had a dodgy heart. So what the fuck were you doing farting around in Almanjáyar?'

'A reliable witness reported, sir, that the two brothers of Lucía Maya, that's Paco's murdered wife, had threatened to kill Paco as soon as he was out. She's sure they are the ones who had painted *Asesino* on his cave wall.'

'Doesn't mean to say they killed him.'

Max looked at him challengingly.

'Okay, Max. Yes, I suppose we'd better get them picked up. We can nail them for assaulting a police officer. It won't do much good though. And in future, report to me before going off. And learn some basic self-defence, for God's sake.'

Max remained silent.

'Any joy with the old lady or the sister?'

'I spoke to Señora Espinosa, but she wasn't giving anything away. So far, I've not been able to locate the sister, but I have a mobile number for her.'

'Okay. Davila said you've been assigned to another task until Monday. But that doesn't matter. We can close this bloody case as soon as we have the autopsy report.'

Max saluted, then headed for the nearest bar. He felt better when he had finished the red wine.

Back in his office, Max removed his tie and jacket, Googled 'Anti-Globalization Movement' and eventually found details of the conference in Granada, with a list of keynote speakers, workshops and plenary sessions.

There were a lot of talks. 'The Coming Financial Crisis', 'What's Left of the Left in Europe?', 'Women, Migration and Strategies for Self-Determination'. Carlos was giving a talk, 'Saving the Albayzín'. Max smiled. He would try to go to that one. Then he struck gold. On Thursday morning there was a workshop, 'The Women's Movement and Male Violence in Spain', with Catalina Maya, a plenary session on 'Sustainability and the Urban Crisis in Granada: Time for Action' with Francisco Gómez in the afternoon, and a closed session in the evening. A closed session. Drat. That would be the one where they decided tactics for the demo. Okay. There might be a clue to what was planned on the websites of the groups involved.

Mierda. He found lengthy debates on the dialectic of unity and outflanking, non-violent tactics, sit-ins, lie-ins, die-ins . . . Max sighed, remembering his student days. And now he was on the other side of the barricades.

He checked the registration details. It was possible to register at the door, with a ten-euro fee.

Max closed down his computer, and looked out of the window. It was raining again. He walked into the cloakroom where he had left his umbrella. The umbrella had gone. '*Joder*! You can't even trust the cops these days.'

Chapter 8

On Tuesday morning, Max got up early, finished his notes on the conference and then walked through the wet shining streets to work. There was an email from Guillermo in Forensics waiting for him when he got to his office.

'Max. Copy of my report to the judge attached. The actual cause of death was a heart attack, but there's evidence suggesting violence shortly before death. Between the tattoos, lividity and old scarring, the bruising was hard to spot, but the deceased seems to have been restrained. This may not be related to the heart attack, but the judge won't sign it off yet. Looks like you guys are going to have to earn your pay for once. You owe me one. Guillermo.'

Max skimmed through the attachment. His phone rang. It was Navarro.

'Have you read Guillermo's report yet?'

'No, just got it.'

'Davila wants a meeting at eleven. Can you do a preliminary report by then? Guillermo can't attend.'

Max worked flat out for the next two hours assessing and summarizing the reports from Guillermo and the other technical services. He remembered Abbot Jorge's words: 'Don't let the police sweep Paco's death under the carpet just because he's a gypsy ex-con.'

There was no chance of that now.

Max and Belén arrived at Davila's office on the dot of eleven.

'So, what have you got, Max?' said Davila.

'The dead man's name was Francisco Javier Maya Fuentes, known as Paco Maya. He'd been released from jail on Wednesday, first of April, a few days early, after serving a sentence for the murder of his wife Lucía Espinosa.'

Max paused. 'Time of death. The body was found by a Francisco Gómez who claimed he got there about ten minutes before I and my English friend, Belinda Grove, arrived on the scene at 2 p.m. Ernesto and Roberto were there at two-twenty. Forensics took the body temperature at exactly two-thirty and their calculations, taking into account the dead man's weight, clothing and medical history, the floor temperature, air temperature and air flow in the cave, and all other relevant factors, put the time of death at a maximum of an hour and a half, and a minimum of thirty minutes, before Forensics started work.'

'So that puts the time of death between 1 and 2 p.m.?' asked Davila.

'Sí.'

'And you checked vital signs at 2 p.m. and he was already dead when you found him?'

'Sí.'

'Was the man dead when Francisco Gómez found him?'

'Gómez stated that he tried to resuscitate him, but without success.'

'And the cause of death?'

'A heart attack. This is consistent with the prison's report of heart disease. The liver showed signs of damage, probably due to alcohol abuse. There was evidence of past use of cocaine and heroin, but nothing recent. So we can rule out a heart attack provoked by recent substance abuse.'

'But if someone has a heart condition, then a fatal heart attack can occur at any time, can't it?' said Davila. 'And he may have had the heart attack some hours before he died.'

'That's true, sir. And his heart condition was chronic. But the autopsy did uncover some interesting facts. First, there was bruising on his wrists consistent with being tied with

62

string or thin rope. Also, there were marks on the inside of his arms consistent with, say, having his hands tied behind the back of a chair.'

'But we found nothing which could have been used as a restraint, and the chair inside the cave had fallen over, consistent with, as you put it, the deceased collapsing with a heart attack,' interrupted Navarro.

'True, we didn't find any rope or anything similar. Francisco Gómez had a bit of string in his pocket, but not enough for this job. And I'll come to the chair later.'

'Right,' said Davila. 'Some signs of foul play, but this could have happened some time before death.'

'Not quite, sir. Guillermo's report states that the colour of the bruising implies that the deceased was restrained shortly before death, but that could be minutes or hours. He also comments that the heart attack could have occurred immediately before death, or a couple of hours earlier.'

'And we do have *Asesino* splashed on the outside cave wall,' added Roberto Belén.

'That could have been painted weeks ago,' said Navarro.

'No,' said Max. 'The deceased's neighbour, Concepción Cortez, stated that it wasn't there a week ago. She also said that, in her opinion, it was painted by some relation of Maya's wife, probably her brothers Gregorio or Mauricio.'

'They haven't been picked up yet, have they?' asked Davila.

'No, sir,' said Navarro.

'Right,' said Max. 'Fingerprints – mostly they were of the dead man, Paco Maya, and Concepción Cortez, the neighbour who had helped him clean the cave. We haven't been able to get any distinct fingerprints from the guitar or chair, not even those of the deceased, which is a bit odd. Both could have been wiped clean. There were fingerprints matching those of Francisco Gómez, both on the crucifix around Paco Maya's neck and on the wooden box we brought in for investigation. I've been through Gómez's statement, and he claims he didn't touch anything. He was beside the body when I entered the cave, attempting resuscitation, so he could easily have touched the crucifix then.'

'Maybe. But the print on the box? Is there anything missing from it?'

'*Probablemente*,' said Max. 'When I spoke to Señora Cortez, she said that the box held title deeds to Maya's land and cave. But it was empty when we examined it.'

'So Francisco Gómez could be in the frame for this one,' said Navarro, looking cheerful. 'A robbery goes wrong, then he pulls the old first-aid trick when the cops show up.'

'A useful working hypothesis, Inspector,' said Davila.

'I'm not sure,' said Max. 'The incident which may have led to the death could have been several hours before the victim actually died, and the timing's a bit tight for the assailant to have been Gómez, as he states he can account for his movements for most of the day, except for about ten minutes before I arrived on the scene.'

Davila sighed. 'Give us the details then.'

Max checked his notes. 'According to Gómez's statement, he set off to walk to the monastery from Sacromonte at about eleven-thirty with a friend, Steven Gaviero. The friend was with him all the time until they got to the monastery of Jesús del Valle.'

'Is this substantiated?'

'Gaviero confirms this, and states that he continued walking, in the direction of Dudar, on the old track.'

'I see.'

'Francisco Gómez remained at the monastery on his own for a few minutes. We then have six witnesses, including myself, who confirm he was at the monastery of Jesús del Valle between one and one-ten. At around one-ten, Gómez set off to return to Sacromonte. The security guard at the Cortijo de los Angeles saw him at the entrance at one-thirty walking in the direction of Sacromonte, and then the dogs chased him away from the back of the *cortijo* about ten minutes later.'

'I'm not convinced, but go on.'

'Well, sir, we also have evidence of quite a lot of activity close to the cave.'

'Such as?'

'The footprints near the house were indistinct, but we have photos of tyre marks at the bottom of the track. We have two sets of photos, one from the Policía Científica, and the other I took using a friend's camera.'

'A friend?' queried Davila.

'Yes. Belinda Grove. The one who heard the dog. The judge asked me to take some photos of tyre marks, which had been overlooked. But there's something strange about these photos,' continued Max. 'The pictures I took on my friend's camera included tyre marks from a larger vehicle, possibly a 4×4. But I don't see that image in the prints we got back from the lab.'

'Shouldn't worry about that,' said Davila. 'It wouldn't be the first time that our lab mislaid a photo. But let's press on, or we'll be here all day.'

'I have the vet's report on the dog. Judging from the bruises, the vet says it was kicked less than twenty-four hours before our arrival.'

'It must have got a kicking from Maya,' said Navarro.

'But everyone says Paco Maya loved his dog,' said Max.

'That doesn't mean a thing. I love my wife dearly but there's many a time I feel like kicking her,' said Davila, smiling.

Everyone laughed politely.

'*Bien*,' continued Max. 'I have here the report on the location of everything inside the cave. A couple of things strike me. First, the guitar – it was lying face down on a bare concrete floor. That doesn't sound right to me. Hand-crafted flamenco guitars are delicate; no professional musician would maltreat his instrument. Second, the chair was too far away from the corpse for the deceased to have fallen there following a heart attack.'

'Well,' mused Davila, 'folks get clumsy when they've had

a drink or two or something, so the guitar face down probably means nothing.'

'That's true,' said Max. 'But the autopsy showed no evidence for recent consumption of drink or drugs.'

'So that's everything?' asked Davila.

'Not quite. The lab boys say that the ash which I handed over to Inspector Navarro is from a cigarette. I could have sworn it was cigar ash.'

'It wouldn't be the first time you were wrong,' commented Navarro.

'Let's get on with it. Anyone else in the frame?' said Davila.

'The dead man's neighbour said he had previously been threatened by his late wife's brothers, Gregorio and Mauricio Espinosa.'

'*Conclusiones*?'

'Okay. The cause of death was a heart attack, but we have the bruising, the injury to the dog, and the missing documents. Plus the *Asesino* graffiti, and we have a reliable witness who claims the deceased was threatened by the Espinosa brothers.'

'Your point?' questioned Davila.

'Given what we know about our man's state of health, we could probably discount one or two of these facts, but taking them together we have to recommend that further investigation is needed, with foul play probably involved.'

'Look,' said Davila, 'we're overstretched. We can't afford to waste time on an old lag's heart attack. It's up to the judge of course, but I recommend we send him a bland report . . . on the one hand, on the other . . . and forget some of the details.'

'But sir, we don't have much choice,' said Navarro. 'The judge had a damn good poke around the site and said he wanted a thorough investigation. He's bound to follow up any inconsistencies. We'd best keep him happy.'

'I see. What about suspects?' asked Davila.

'My money's on the two brothers, Gregorio and Mauricio Espinosa,' replied Max. 'Why did they run away when I went to speak to them? We could be dealing with a revenge killing.'

'That's too obvious. I know the brothers made a fool of you, Max, but any dodgy *gitano*'s going to scarper when a cop turns up. If there has been any foul play, then the finger points at Gómez,' said Davila. 'And he's already got form.'

'But that's just for trespass and destroying private property during a demo last year. It's not in the same league as murder,' said Max.

'Maybe, but one thing can lead to another,' said Davila. 'Our priority is to check up on Francisco Gómez.'

'But sir, he has no motive.'

'Shouldn't we at least pick up the Espinosa brothers for assault, and question them?' asked Roberto Belén. 'They have a clear motive. And if we don't, the judge will wonder why.'

'All right. We'll put out a general alert for the brothers. They've got form, and we have mugshots on file, so someone should spot them sooner or later. There's not much more we can do, is there?' said Davila. Navarro shrugged his shoulders. 'Max, I have to leave for another meeting. Could you do a report? I'll look at it before sending it to the judge. Emphasize the weak heart.'

'Yes, sir,' said Max. And Davila swept out of the door.

Navarro looked at Max and Roberto. 'That's clear. Concentrate on Francisco Gómez once you've finished with this nonsense on that stupid conference. If it were up to me, I'd kick all these bloody lefties out of Granada.'

'But sir,' said Roberto, 'the judge commented on the graffiti. It wouldn't look good if we made no effort to bring in the brothers.'

'But we've no idea where they might be.'

'Two sources said they are probably holed up in Nerja.'

'Drugs?'

'Could be.'

Navarro paused and frowned. 'Okay. Roberto, you know the cops on the coast. Check if they've been sighted. And if they have, go and get the buggers, but don't waste time. May as well keep this new judge sweet.'

'*Gracias, señor*. We can go after the globalization meeting this afternoon.'

Chapter 9

Teeth cleaned, hair freshly brushed, Max knocked on the door of Comisario Principal Bonila's office at precisely two in the afternoon.

'Ah, Max. Dead on time. Draw up a chair and join us. I think you already know everyone here.'

Max looked round the table. There was Comisario Felipe Chávez, General López from the Guardia Civil, Sub-Inspectora Julia Dahlia from the Media Office, Comisario Alejandro Naranjo from the Policía Local, and Teniente Patricio Grandes from the Mayor's office.

'I do, sir,' said Max.

Bonila continued. 'We're still waiting for Inspector Jefe Davila, always late of course. Help yourself to coffee, Max.'

Max got a cup of coffee from the machine on the side table and chose a couple of pastries from the buffet. He sat down, sipped his black coffee, and waited. The pastries were from a posh caterer. They looked good, but tasted of nothing.

A few minutes later, Inspector Jefe Enrique Davila appeared, bald head shining with the brilliantine he used to keep the remaining strands of hair in place.

'Uhm . . . sorry to be late. I got held up in the traffic.'

'I see,' said Bonila, not offering Davila a coffee.

'You all know why we are here,' he continued. 'I've requested a joint approach to this Anti-Globalization conference and demonstration.'

'*Sí*,' added Comisario Naranjo. 'As far as we can tell, it's a much smaller event than the one in Genoa, but we can't be too careful. And as it's Easter, the Policía Local are stretched to their limit.'

'I agree,' said Bonila. 'We can't be too careful. So we need to ensure good coordination and communication between the three forces. My people in the Policía Nacional will be in charge of the demonstration. The Guardia Civil will be on duty around our monuments. The Policía Local will be busy with the extra traffic and the Easter processions, but they will help if needed.'

Everyone round the table nodded in agreement.

'And as it's Easter the town is full of tourists,' added Teniente Grandes. 'The Alcalde has asked me to insist that we all be ultra-sensitive. After the terrorist incident last year, Granada can't afford any bad publicity.'

'I agree,' said General López. 'But if they think we are weak, they'll just take the piss. We have to show who's in charge.'

'But softly, softly at first, General,' said Bonila. 'Sub-Inspectora Dahlia has prepared a press statement saying that Granada and its police forces welcome this conference, but participants have to abide by the regulations established, and any transgressions will be dealt with accordingly.'

'Yes,' said Julia Dahlia. 'The statement will be going out later today.'

'And I asked Max here to check the Anti-Globalization websites. Max, what did you find?'

'There's a lot out there,' said Max. 'The Anti-Globalization Movement is an umbrella organization of all the groups opposed to the present trends of globalization. It's worldwide, but the movement is strongest in Latin America and Europe. The conference in Granada is a meeting of the European section. But speakers have been invited from all over the world.'

'Can someone explain to me in words of one syllable what this . . . uhm . . . Anti-Globalization is all about?' asked Davila.

Bonila nodded at Max.

'Well, basically they are concerned about unregulated free markets allowing big multinational companies and banks to rip off the poor, oppress women and destroy the environment.'

'I see,' said Davila. 'Or rather I don't, but there we go.'

'So, they are just a bunch of tree-huggers and bra-burners,' said López. 'I don't see them being much trouble.'

Julia Dahlia stared at López incredulously.

'Most will be no trouble,' said Max. 'But the Maoists, the Trotskyites and the Anarchists will be looking for a fight. So it's important that these groups are isolated, and that they don't drag in others.'

'Thank you, Max,' said Bonila. 'Our problem is we may have to defend ourselves. And the whole thing could escalate.'

'*Sí*,' agreed Chávez. 'In my experience, these violent groups are usually put at the back of any demonstration. We need to separate them from the mass of the demonstrators.'

'But what happens if the troublemakers are scattered among the main group?' asked General López.

'That's always a possibility,' said Chávez.

'If there aren't many of them, maybe we could send in snatch squads,' suggested Teniente Grandes.

'That could just make things worse. But it may come to it,' said Bonila.

Julia Dahlia coughed, and turned to Bonila. 'There is the additional problem of the monastery of Jesús del Valle, and the roads issue.'

'Yes,' said Bonila. 'I was coming to that. The Alcalde and the Archbishop are issuing a press statement later today announcing the sale of buildings and land situated in Jesús del Valle to a private developer for conversion into an eco-hotel.'

'An eco-hotel?' said Max.

'Yes, precisely that. An environmentally sound hotel complex. The press somehow found out about this, so the

71

Archbishop and the Alcalde agreed to an early briefing. Teniente Grandes has all the details.'

'*Sí*,' said Grandes. 'The proposed development has the best wishes of Archbishop Doria, and Mayor Olmedo will steer it through the planning process. This is a sensible proposal. The Church gets rid of an unsafe and dangerous building, and the city badly needs more top-quality hotel accommodation, so everybody gains.'

'Do we know who the new owner is?' asked Max.

'The owner wishes his identity to remain private,' responded Grandes.

'Why?' asked Max.

'His right, is it not?'

'I suppose so. But how does this affect our plans for the conference and demonstration?'

'Some idiot leaked the Jesús del Valle proposals to that loony environmentalist, Francisco Gómez.'

'Oh,' said Max. 'He's one of the key speakers at the conference. That means . . .'

'Precisely. The demo could turn into a protest against these developments.'

'These developments?' queried Max.

'I should also share with you that, in return for the cancellation of some unpaid taxes, Archbishop Doria has given the council some land behind the Abadía de Sacromonte which is needed for a road to the hotel. Obviously the hotel will need a decent access road . . .'

'Of course,' said López.

'But as you know,' continued Grandes, 'there's still all the fuss and bother over completing the ring road around Granada.'

'We don't need to go into detail,' interrupted Bonila. 'Our problem is that these radicals now have a concrete focus for their anger, and that could mean big trouble.'

Inspector Jefe Davila opened his mouth again. 'Why don't we just arrest Francisco Gómez now?'

The great and good at the table turned towards him, impressed.

'I can tell you all that Gómez is in the frame for a suspicious death. And even if he's not guilty, we've got enough to hang on to the bugger till this whole thing's over.'

'Great idea, Enrique,' said General López. 'Why didn't you say so earlier?'

'But sir,' said Max, looking straight at Bonila, 'arresting Señor Gómez would only inflame the situation.'

'I agree,' said Chávez.

Davila flushed.

'Okay. Let's leave that for now,' said Bonila. 'Felipe, can you summarize our plans?'

'I've asked Max and Sub-Inspector Belén to attend the conference to identify any potential troublemakers and any changes to the approved format for the demonstration or the march. Julia will be acting as liaison with their press office and has already had a preliminary meeting with them, and I'll be briefing all relevant staff on our side between now and Monday. I have a separate meeting with General López's people tomorrow, and we have a final meeting on Monday morning.'

'Good,' said Bonila. 'Any questions? No. *Vale*. Thank you all for coming. Oh, Enrique, Max, could you both stay behind for a minute?'

The others filed out of the room. Julia gave Max a big smile. 'See you at the conference. Though of course, I won't recognize you without your uniform.'

Bonila closed the door. 'Enrique, Max´s priority is the conference and demo. You´ll have to take over this Paco Maya case. Max can go back on to it once all these shenanigans are over.'

'If you say so, sir.'

'And I'm keeping in mind your option of arresting Francisco Gómez. That was a good suggestion.'

Davila smiled.

'Good. You can go.'

Max walked up the stairs back to his office, dumped his papers, then went to one of his favourite bars in Plaza Trinidad. The pastries at the meeting had been awful. He ordered a *caña* to drink and a tasty *bocadillo* of chicken and anchovies while he waited for Roberto.

The two Granada newspapers were on the counter. He took them both, and sat down at a table with his beer and sandwich. They were both running feature articles on the proposed development of Jesús del Valle, with pictures of the Alcalde and the Archbishop shaking hands, beaming at each other.

'The Conclusion of a Satisfactory Deal,' said *Ideal*.

'A Friendly Handshake Seals a Deal,' said *Granada Hoy*.

There was very little critical comment.

Funny, thought Max. Jorge hadn't mentioned any of this. Maybe that was why he wanted a private conversation . . .

Chapter 10

Ten minutes later, Roberto arrived in the bar. 'Good news, Max. The Espinosa brothers have been spotted in Nerja. I've got the mugshots here.'

'*Excelente*. Let's go before anybody changes their mind. I think this should be a plain-clothes job.'

They left Granada on the motorway to Motril, past the brick and cement factories of Suspiro del Moro, the orchards of the Lecrin valley and then the construction works for the huge new dam below Diva.

'I just don't get it. The river's pretty small so it'll take years to fill up that dam,' said Max.

'They're probably planning a whole new town just here, all the way to the coast. Or it's another white elephant.'

'Chances are it's both, but someone's making money. This valley used to be so pretty when I was a kid.'

'You're local?'

'*Sí y no*. I grew up in Diva, then moved to Scotland when I was fifteen. I came back six or seven years ago.'

'So you really notice the changes?'

'Very much. So, what made you switch from the coast to Granada, Roberto?'

'My wife's a teacher. She's from Granada, and always wanted to get back. She finally got a transfer to one of the Granada schools. But the only post I could get was with you guys.'

'Some people have all the luck. What unit were you in before?'

'Grupo de Delitos Económicos, the Anti-Corruption Unit.'

'*Interesante.*'

'It was. I did a bit of legwork for the guys in the money-laundering team.'

'*Ah sí.* Serious stuff. That wouldn't happen to be the Moby Dick operation, by any chance?'

'*Sí.* It's going to be huge when it breaks.'

'Marbella's going to hell. The council's been a scandal ever since Gil and his pals took over the town hall. And the present lot are even worse,' said Max.

'*Absolutamente.* We've had wire taps on some of the crooks there, and the rot has spread all along the coast. Russian mafia, Latin American mafia, La Cosa Nostra . . . you name it, we've got it. Drug smuggling, money laundering . . . the works . . . on the back of the property boom. And we're pretty sure it's into Granada.'

'That wouldn't surprise me.'

'Marbella's impressive. Everyone's bent. The Alcalde, local politicians, local government officials, businessmen, celebs, the banks, even the police.'

'I'd hate to think it could get that bad in Granada.'

'Max, do you think there could be seriously corrupt cops in Granada?'

'You never know. Why do you ask?'

'I've heard rumours.'

They turned right towards the coast road. The old sugar cane plantations on the plain behind Motril were disappearing as the holiday homes advanced. But round another corner, the hills were still covered in avocado and chirrimoya orchards, and there was the sea, sparkling all the way to Africa.

'Beautiful, isn't it?' said Roberto. 'Enjoy it while you can. In ten years, every square inch of this coast will be covered with concrete.'

They passed the great castle of Salobreña, standing proud on its hill, guarding the old trade routes to Africa. Holiday homes and hotels lined the coast road, and construction sites stretched into the lush green orchards.

'I've got a meeting set up with a friend from the Anti-Drugs Unit from Málaga, a Teniente Luis Barril. He had a meeting with the Guardia Civil in Nerja, so we'll see him as soon as he's finished with the local guys.'

The Guardia Civil was in a pretty nineteenth-century building in the old town of Nerja, in Calle San Miguel. They left the car in the courtyard and walked through an archway emblazoned with the old motto *'Todo por la Patria'*, 'Everything for the Fatherland'.

'Teniente Barril is expecting us,' said Roberto to the desk officer.

'I believe he is in office 34. May I suggest you telephone his mobile?'

A tall, thin man greeted them at the top of the stairs.

'Roberto . . . great to see you. How's Rosa?'

'She's doing fine, and I'm going to be a dad.'

'Roberto! Well done, man, well done. And Granada?'

'Cold and wet just now. I'm missing the coast already. Sorry, Max. Luis, this is my colleague Max Romero.'

Max smiled. 'The desk officer downstairs didn't seem too pleased to see us.'

'There's a problem. A couple of guys in the Guardia got arrested in a drug raid. Madrid and ourselves did the arrest.'

'Vale. I get the picture,' said Roberto.

'So we're not exactly flavour of the month here. Best be careful what you tell them. Anyway, you are looking for a couple of guys who might be in Nerja?'

Max handed over two photographs.

'We're looking for this pair, Gregorio and Mauricio Espinosa. They're small-time dealers in Granada but we need to talk to them about a suspicious death, and we heard they may be here.'

'They look vaguely familiar. I'll check the photo archive.'

Luis spent a few minutes running through a photo file on the computer.

'Thought so . . . got a couple of shots of them going into the Hotel Reina del Sur. We're pretty sure it's a front for some drug baron. The hotel's not far . . . I suggest you check it out.'

'*Gracias*,' said Max.

'Come and see me again,' Luis said to Roberto. 'We'll go for lunch, and I'll give you all the gossip.'

Max and Roberto drove along the sea front, and then inland. Reina del Sur was a gleaming palace, three kilometres out of town, in a prime spot on the coast. The huge lobby was splendid in marble and fine wood, and the reception desk was half hidden behind a grove of exotic plants. They showed the receptionist their badges, and asked if she recognized the two men in the photos.

The receptionist paused. 'I'll have to call *el director*.'

'I'm only asking if you'd seen them,' Max said.

'I have to call *el director*,' she repeated.

The manager came over. Max showed him the two photographs. He looked at them, and shook his immaculately coiffed head.

'Can I see your register?' asked Max.

The manager hesitated.

'It will be easier for you to agree now. Or maybe we'll have to call in the drug squad,' said Roberto. 'And you know what they're like.'

'Okay,' the manager agreed reluctantly.

Max looked down the list of names. There they were, staying in room 64 on the second floor. Max noted down their DNI numbers and the car registration number. They'd been there since last Friday, the day Paco Maya died.

Max pointed at the names. 'Do you know where these two guests are now?'

The receptionist nodded. 'The key is here, so I presume they're out. They are due to check out later today.'

'We need to examine the room.'

'Okay. But I have to come with you.' The manager glanced up. 'Ah. Don Rubén. I'll be with you later.'

Max turned round. Don Rubén was a short, powerfully built man, perhaps in his early fifties, with blue eyes and blond hair. His clothing was casual, but very expensive.

'Right. Thank you, Javier.' Don Rubén turned round sharply and walked out of the lobby.

Room 64 was plush with a private terrace looking over the sea. There was a small bureau desk in the corner. Next to it was a Corte Inglés shopping bag from Granada, and a couple of sports bags had been left lying on a bed.

'They're still here,' said Max. 'Any idea when they might be back?'

'No,' the manager replied, with a shrug of the shoulders.

'Do you have a car park?' asked Roberto.

'It's round the back of the hotel.'

'I'll check the car,' said Max to Roberto. 'You wait in the lobby in case they turn up.'

The number registered to the brothers was a black Nissan Pathfinder 4×4. Max carefully took pictures of the car and its tyres. Back in the lobby, Roberto was enjoying an excellent cup of coffee and a very fine sea view.

'Their car's in the car park. They can't have gone far.'

Roberto had another sip of his coffee. 'What next?'

'I'll have a cup of coffee.'

'The guy who spoke to the manager earlier – that's Rubén Carrington, one of the coast's wealthier residents. We've checked him out thoroughly. But we found nothing.'

Max turned round to order just as Gregorio and Mauricio Espinosa strolled into the hotel lobby. They took one look at him and fled.

'*Policía*,' shouted Max. 'Stop.'

The two brothers ran across the beach. Roberto sprinted ahead, caught up with Gregorio and tackled him at the edge of the sea. Gregorio smacked Roberto hard on the cheek. Roberto winced, but hung on tightly. Max piled in, and snapped on the handcuffs. Mauricio turned up a track that ran down to the beach. Roberto phoned the Guardia Civil.

'They'll be along in a minute,' he said. 'They'll pick him up. It's a dead end.'

They hauled Gregorio to his feet and marched him back to their car. Roberto was right. Fifteen minutes later, a police car arrived with Mauricio Espinosa inside.

'We've got no grounds for detaining them here,' said the officer.

'No problem, they're coming with us,' said Max. 'We'll be in touch.'

The brothers sat impassively in the back of the car on the journey to Granada. They were both good-looking, but not in a pleasant way. Not a word passed between them on the journey. No request to phone wife, family – nothing.

It was after eight when they reached the Granada police station. Once inside Gregorio Espinosa asked to phone his lawyer. '*Mí abogado* will be here tomorrow morning. He has to come up from the coast.'

Max and Roberto looked at each other, amazed.

'All right.'

Navarro was just about to leave work.

'We've got the bastards,' Max told him. 'Their lawyer will be here tomorrow morning.'

'Well done. That should impress the judge. I'll ring Inspector Jefe Davila. We'll interview them tomorrow when their lawyer gets here. What happened to your jaw, Roberto?'

'Gregorio Espinosa hit me while resisting arrest.'

'That could be useful. Get it photographed and logged.'

'Okay, Roberto,' said Max. 'I'm ravenous. Bonila's pastries couldn't feed a rabbit. That's a thought. Barbecued rabbit with garlic. That would be nice.'

Chapter 11

At ten o'clock the next morning, Max and Roberto met the Espinosa brothers' lawyer in the interview room. The lawyer was an older man, impeccably dressed in a dark green coat and a soft felt hat. The business card read 'Pablo Guzmán de Sídonia'. De Sídonia smiled affably at Max.

'I don't think this should take too long. So perhaps we could begin now.'

Max decided to start with Gregorio Espinosa and begin with the charge of assaulting police officers. Navarro and Davila joined them.

Once the preliminaries had finished, the lawyer calmly declared that his clients had already agreed to accept the two minor charges of assaulting a police officer.

Max was taken aback. He turned to Gregorio. 'But if you've nothing to hide, why did you and your brother run away on both occasions?'

'Well, in the Bar los Gitanos, you bloody scared us, pitching up all aggressive like. We're *gitanos* . . . you know what you cops can be like. We've got witnesses.'

'So what happened in Nerja, then?'

'We were in Nerja to pick up a couple of *barras* of dope. We thought you'd come to get us on that.'

'And who was the supplier you were planning to meet in Nerja?'

'Never met the guy. Got this mobile number. Just about to phone when you pitched up. I thought it was a set-up.'

'Do you still have the number?' asked Roberto.

'*Sí*.' Gregorio put his hand in his pocket and pulled out a crumpled piece of paper. Roberto phoned the number on his own mobile. There was no reply, no sound.

'They'll have taken the SIM card out by now,' he commented. 'So where did you get this famous number?'

'Some guy in Almanjáyar.'

'You'd never seen him before, of course.'

'No, never.'

'Gentlemen, gentlemen,' said the lawyer. 'My client also agrees that he was planning to purchase some hashish, but you, for your part, accept that the transaction had not taken place. And he will accept any reasonable charges you might wish to bring against him on this matter.'

'Why didn't you buy the stuff in Granada?'

'We've had a previous conviction for dealing.'

'So instead you drove all the way down to the coast, and stayed in an expensive hotel for five days, just to make a drug deal.'

'That's right. But we were also checking out some plumbing and tiling jobs, you know. We're skilled tradesmen, and the money's good on the coast.'

The lawyer butted in. 'Given that my client is willing to make a confession and sign it to that effect, I would have thought that would be sufficient. And he should now be released until his appearance before a judge.'

'Not yet,' said Max. 'I have questions I want to ask him relating to a suspicious death.'

'And my client is a suspect?'

'No, not at all,' interrupted Davila. 'It's just that we want to clear up a few loose ends.'

The lawyer looked at Gregorio Espinosa. 'My client would like a break in the interview to give us an opportunity to discuss this somewhat new development. We require half an hour.'

'Okay,' said Davila.

Max and Roberto went for a cup of coffee.

'Bugger. That's a clever one,' said Roberto. 'The most we can get them for is two minor assaults and attempting to buy a bit of dope. That's a fine.'

'And Mauricio's story will match up nicely. I can see why that bloody lawyer earns so much. But who is paying him?' said Max.

'Navarro's not been much help,' said Roberto.

'Bugger all.'

'I doubt if we'll get anywhere on the Paco Maya case. They knew him of course, but hadn't seen him since he got sent down. Tragic about his dodgy heart. What a shame.'

They returned to the interview room. Navarro said to Max, 'Can I have a word with you outside?'

'Sure,' replied Max.

'The photo lab technicians have just sent me the enlarged photos of the tyre marks of the car in Nerja. They also found the missing photograph – the one you took on your friend's camera. They match.'

'Great,' said Max. 'We've got the bastard. When he denies being anywhere near Paco Maya's cave, we can nail him. *Gracias*, Ernesto.'

'No trouble, Max. I just want this case cleared up as quickly as possible.'

They went back into the interview room. Max sat down, a smile on his face. He started with the warm-up questions: relationship with Paco Maya, how long had he known him, did they get on, had he seen him when Paco was in prison. Gregorio Espinosa's replies sounded truthful.

'Did you know Paco Maya was released from prison a few days early?' Max asked.

'*Sí*,' said Gregorio. 'My mother phoned. The prison told her.'

'I suppose you never saw Paco after he was released.'

'*Sí*, we did. My brother and I drove over to Paco's cave, the day he got let out.'

'What? So you agree that you both drove over there?'

'*Sí*. We parked our car at the bottom of Paco's track, and walked up to the cave.'

'What car did you drive?' asked Max.

'A black Nissan Pathfinder 4×4. The same one we had in Nerja.'

Max showed Gregorio Espinosa the photograph he'd taken of the car in the hotel car park. 'Is that your car?'

'It looks like it.'

'Okay. Did you see Paco Maya?'

'*Sí*, we saw him.'

'What was the nature of your visit? To congratulate him on being released?'

'Of course not.'

'So you quarrelled?'

'*Sí*, but we had family business to do. My mother wanted Paco to sell his land . . . for Angelita's sake, you know. You have to look after your own flesh and blood. Ain't natural otherwise.'

'I see. And what did he say?'

'He said no at first. But he wanted to do the right thing by his kid.'

'And it was all nice and friendly?'

'Wouldn't say that. Said he needed some time to think about it. So we told him we'd be back. With papers for him to sign.'

'And that's all?'

'*Sí*. That's all.'

'Then what?'

'We drove round to Haza Grande. Told mum exactly what Paco had said. She weren't pleased.'

'And if he didn't sell?'

'We said we'd do our best to persuade him, of course.'

'Like threatening to kill him?'

'No. Of course not. Now he's out, he's got to look after his kid proper, you know. And after what he did to her mother . . . well, he should do the right thing.'

Max looked at Navarro and nodded. Navarro took over the questioning.

'Where were you and your brother on Friday, 3rd April, the Friday after Paco Maya was released?'

'Friday. Before Easter Week? It was a nice day, so we took the old lady for a drive to the coast and lunch. She likes a day out.'

'Nerja?' interrupted Max.

'*Sí*, Nerja. The Hotel Reina del Sur does a great lunch. Mum likes her bit of fish.'

'Any witnesses?' asked Navarro.

'Of course. Loads of people saw us. Loads.' And Gregorio smiled at Max.

'So if you, your brother Mauricio and your mother went to the coast, where was Angelita?'

'Stayed with the wife to play on the bikes with Tomasito and the boys. They're good boys. They look after her, you know.'

'Back to your meeting with Paco Maya,' said Navarro. 'So it all ended nice and friendly, then?'

'I wouldn't go that far. But Paco agreed to consider selling.'

'Okay,' continued Roberto. 'And what time did you finish lunch?'

'About five, I'd say.'

Davila looked at Navarro, who then slipped out of the interview room.

'Then?' said Roberto.

'We ran the old lady back to Granada, and then came back to Nerja. We were going to stay there for a few days.'

'To pick up some hashish later, I presume.'

'*Sí*. And do a couple of plumbing and tiling jobs.'

'Black market jobs?'

'Well, not registered if that's what you mean. There's a lot of work on the coast.'

'So you had no contact with Paco Maya after you saw him on the day he was let out?'

'No. Like I've told you. Mum phoned . . .' He paused. 'On Sunday evening, to let us know he'd passed away.'

Navarro returned. 'I have just phoned the Hotel Reina del Sur. I spoke to the manager, and he confirms that the Epinosa brothers were there for lunch with their mother on Friday. He says the waiters, and some of the other guests, will remember them. Apparently Carmen Espinosa made quite an impression. The lady had a bit too much wine and they were the last to leave when the dining room closed at six.'

'That seems clear,' said Davila. 'I don't think we have any grounds for detaining him. We can charge him for two minor assaults on a policeman, intent to buy marijuana and tax evasion on small plumbing and tiling works.'

Max bit his tongue. He had one more chance to try to nail the bastard.

'Okay, tell me about Paco Maya. You were dealing with him . . . and maybe he siphoned off a bit of coke.'

'I don't know what you're talking about,' said Gregorio.

'That's enough insinuations, Sub-Inspector,' said the lawyer. 'Unless you have proof that my client was involved in the cocaine trade, then questioning stops here. My client has cooperated fully. He has admitted his transgressions, but there's nothing more. You are trying to put words in his mouth, hinting at all sorts of offences he's never been involved in.'

'You've overstepped the mark, Sub-Inspector,' said Davila. 'This session has ended.'

'Thank you, Inspector Jefe. May my client leave now? You have no grounds for detaining him here any longer.'

Davila nodded.

'*Muchas gracias*,' said the lawyer. 'I'm a very busy man. After a short break, I would like us to move on to my other client, Mauricio Espinosa. That should be over with quickly.'

It was. The lawyer and the brothers left together. The lawyer turned at the door and, with a smile on his face, said, 'My clients will of course pay any fine that may be imposed.'

86

The cops got up to leave.

'Romero, Belén. *Un momento*,' said Davila. Max and Roberto stopped. Navarro left.

'What a bloody waste of time that was. Gómez is our man. Got that? Navarro had no business authorizing that trip to Nerja.'

'But sir,' said Max, 'we had to pick up the Espinosas to satisfy the judge.'

'Obviously they've nothing to do with Paco Maya's death. It's Gómez. I'll check his background. You check out his friends at the conference.'

'We will, sir.'

Max returned to his office with Roberto. 'What the hell did you make of that?'

'Sounds like some idiot let that bloody lawyer coach the brothers last night.'

'Clever sodding lawyer,' said Max. 'Roberto, get your friends on the coast to check him out.'

'I'd be pleased to do that, Max.'

'Okay. Gotta go. Taking a friend to el Paso de los Gitanos tonight.'

'Good luck. Hope you don't run into the Espinosa family.'

'So do I.'

Chapter 12

'MUTILATED CORPSES ON MARBELLA BEACH', screamed the headline.

Max scanned the article: 'The victims' eyes had been gouged out, their throats cut, and their tongues pulled through the wound, before they were shot in the head. Police link these deaths to a mafia turf war over drugs and high-class prostitution.'

Max put down his newspaper and poured himself another glass of white wine. Just before ten, he went onto his terrace to check the weather. It was going to rain tonight. Max looked around for an umbrella. *Joder*! The one some cop nicked was his last. Just as he was leaving, his phone rang. He hesitated. It might be important.

'Max, it's Anita. You said you would phone me.'

'Anita, I'm so sorry. I've been rushed off my feet with a murder case, and –'

'We are all very busy. It only takes a minute to pick up the phone and call.'

'I know.'

There was a distinct sniff at the end of the phone.

'Max, I've had enough. Paula told me you have to find another flat, and you didn't even bother to tell me.'

'But it's all very recent –'

'Too bloody bad. You should have phoned. Between you and Capitán González, I've had enough. I've applied for a transfer to Almería.'

'If that's what you want,' said Max.

'Christ, Max. Is that all you can say? You're pathetic. It's over, isn't it? You just don't have the courage to tell me.'

'Look, it's not like that . . . I'm . . . Anita, we could still be friends. I could visit you.'

'Free beach holiday in Cabo de Gata, you mean. No.'

The phone went dead.

Max picked up Belinda at her flat, close by Calle del Pilar Seco. They walked downhill in the lamplight along Calle del Almirante, Calle Aljibe del Trillo, then Calle Guinea where sweet jasmine and yellow Easter roses foamed over high garden walls.

'Max, what's the story about the *cofradías*?'

'Basically, they're men's clubs. They organize the Easter processions, of course, but they do charity work and fundraise for church restoration. From what I can remember, *cofradías* started in the seventeenth century as burial societies, almost died out in the nineteenth century, but a lot were revived in the 1920s, probably to counter the rise of socialism among the poor.'

'But they still seem very popular now.'

'Well . . . the processions are a big tourist draw and young guys seem to like all the macho stuff.'

'Can't understand it, but Granada's a different world, isn't it?'

They turned downhill again at the flamenco club Peña de la Plateria, crossed Calle San Juan de los Reyes, downhill again, past the Moorish houses of the Calle del Horno del Oro and finally reached the corner of Paseo de los Tristes and Cuesta del Chapiz.

'You know, Max, I was on a school trip once, and we went to Seville Cathedral. I'd been reading some Oxfam stuff, and all that gold and silver on the altar really got to me. All stolen from Latin America. Torture and massacres. You know, I felt so queasy one of the teachers had to take me out and get some water.'

'Yes. All that wealth, and it didn't do Spain a bit of good, did it?'

They pushed their way through the crowds lining Paseo de los Tristes, the narrow street beside the river Darro, until they came to the last bridge, a prime spot with a view both of Cuesta del Chapiz and back along Paseo de los Tristes. The far corner above the Roman wall had been cordoned off for the great and good. Abbot Jorge was seated amongst them, his comfortable bulk filling the small red chair.

'Jorge,' called out Max.

Abbot Jorge turned. 'Max. You're in luck. We've two spare seats. Come and join us.'

An usher released one of the velvet ropes surrounding the VIP enclosure and Max and Belinda slipped through.

'Jorge, this is my friend Belinda Grove from Britain. She's moved to Granada and lives near me.'

'A sensible decision to move here.'

Belinda smiled.

'Max, you remember Andrés Mendoza, don't you?'

'Yes, of course,' said Max. 'We met in the Abadía workshop.'

'I didn't expect to see you here, Sub-Inspector, particularly after your remarks about these processions. "A bit over the top" . . . I think you said.'

'Yes,' said Max. 'But Belinda has never seen el Paso de los Gitanos. And she's writing a book on Granada.'

Don Andrés smiled pleasantly. 'Please, Doña Belinda, make yourself comfortable. Los Gitanos is one of Granada's finest Easter processions.' He smoothed the cushions hospitably. 'And this is my wife, Verónica, and her friend Penélope.'

Belinda sat down beside Penélope, and Max next to Andrés.

Penélope was film-star glamorous. Fur coat. Hair piled on the top of her head *a la Cordobesa*. Jewels.

Max turned to speak to Andrés Mendoza. 'And where are you based, Don Andrés?'

'My main office is on the coast. But I also have an office here in Granada, which I'm hoping to make my main base. There's a lot of potential here.'

In the distance, they could hear drums and the harsh melody of archaic trumpets. Then there came the glow of candles as the procession, el Paso de los Gitanos, turned the corner into Paseo de los Tristes. First came the heralds with banners and silver staves, then penitents robed in purple and red, their heads completely encased in high pointed hoods, and musicians, playing a tragic march. Then the great image of Christ crucified and, more splendid still, the blue-robed Virgin on her copper throne, surrounded by candles. Silver tassels shivered as the *pasos* swayed with the rhythm of the tread of the eighty *costaleros*, sweating underneath the velvet canopies.

A young woman next to them in the crowd stared raptly at the face of Christ.

'*Ay, qué guapo*. How handsome he is.'

Suddenly, the procession stopped. The Virgin's crown had snagged on an overhead electricity cable.

'This can happen,' Max explained. 'Let's go and have a look.'

Max recognized the man in charge of the rescue operation, one of the *gitanos* in the Abadía workshop. Two young guys had climbed up on the *palio* to disentangle the Virgin from below. Without success. Two others had gone inside the nearest house, and were leaning over the balcony to lift up the cables.

Most of the *costaleros* were leaning over the river Darro wall, having a smoke. Belinda and Penélope took photos: the costumes, the Virgin's blue cloak embroidered with roses and pomegranates, the carpets of red carnations and purple irises, the burning candles, the carved staves, and the strapping *costaleros* with their red bandannas.

'Is that the original José Risueño sculpture of Christ of the Holy Caves?' Belinda asked.

'No,' replied the Abbot. 'The original is much too precious to move, but this is a fine copy.'

'It's extraordinary, isn't it? Look, Max, the figure of Christ is suspended just by four wooden nails.' Belinda shuddered. 'I do find these hoods sinister; all you can see are the eyes staring out through the slits.'

'Yes. No wonder the Ku Klux Klan borrowed them,' said Max.

The Abbot rolled his eyes. Max pretended not to notice.

Belinda was on her best behaviour. 'Abbot Jorge, I need your advice. I can't go to all the Holy Week processions. Apart from los Gitanos, which do you think is the best?'

'Probably the Brotherhood of the Bell. They march in complete silence apart from the sound of a single bell and the clinking of chains.'

'I'd love to see that. Will you be there, Max?'

'Yes. But on duty.'

The young *gitanos* on the balcony finally disentangled the Virgin from the cables. To a loud cheer, the *costaleros* returned to their positions, and hoisted the Virgin and her throne onto their shoulders. But as the procession approached the corner where it turned away from the Alhambra, the rain came down heavily. Plastic covers appeared as if from nowhere, then to cries of *Olé* the *costaleros* practically ran up Cuesta del Chapiz with their precious burdens shrouded, but shoulder-high again.

'Max, we've got transport waiting in Calle San Juan de Dios. Would you like to come back with us and greet la Virgen at the Abadía?'

'I'm really sorry, Jorge, but I have to go. I'm on duty tomorrow.'

'Are you sure you can't join us, Belinda?'

'I'd love to but I've got an early start tomorrow.'

'Come and see me soon, Max,' said Abbot Jorge.

'I should be free late Saturday afternoon.'

'That would be fine. See you on Saturday, then.'

Max and Belinda set off together in the soaking rain. They

sloshed back up the Albayzín hill, past the fine Moorish houses on Calle Zafra, the exquisite church of San Juan de los Reyes surrounded by cypresses, and back onto Calle Guinea.

'You and that gorgeous Penélope woman seemed to get on,' said Max.

'Not really. She's not my sort of person. Did you know, those earrings were real emeralds? She's a trophy wife, I reckon. Some bloke's got way too much money. And she did rather go on about the Virgin's cloak and her own good taste.'

'She's really beautiful,' protested Max.

'Trophy wives are.'

'What does her husband do?'

'She said he has oil and mining interests in Venezuela and Colombia. They've had problems in Venezuela, but he still seems to be worth a mint. They've got a speedboat at Marina del Este, a penthouse in Marbella, a villa in Frigiliana and goodness knows what else. And now they want a Moorish house in Granada as well. But I didn't exactly take to Don Andrés – cold eyes, you know. And I think those two guys behind them were bodyguards.'

'Why do you think that?'

'I've seen enough thrillers to spot a shoulder holster.'

Chapter 13

It was still raining when Max woke up. He switched on
Radio Granada. Many of yesterday's processions had been
rained off. There were interviews with parishioners in tears
because their own Virgin had been unable to leave her
church. And then there was a dramatic account of the Paso
de los Gitanos. The *costaleros* had carried the *palios* of the
Virgin of Sacromonte and the Christ of the Gypsies, each one
weighing nearly a ton, nearly three kilometres uphill, at top
speed into the Abadía, in lashing rain. Fortunately, no
damage had been done either to the two statues or to the
costaleros. There were interviews with *costaleros*, panting and
utterly exhausted, but proud that they had saved the Virgin
and the Christ.

And then an interview with Abbot Jorge: '. . . and though
the Lord has seen fit to challenge our brave *costaleros* with
foul weather, they were more than equal to it, and they
saved the new cloak of the Virgin from harm. We must give
thanks to our benefactor, and to the Blessed Virgin Mary
who gave such strength to the *costaleros*.'

Max looked out of his window at the steady rain. The
weather forecast predicted there would be rain at least until
the beginning of next week.

He pottered in the kitchen while a pot of coffee bubbled
on the stove, then enjoyed a bacon sandwich. He put on
his oldest pair of jeans, a faded blue shirt, a gardening
sweater, and his mountain jacket. He didn't bother to

brush his hair. But he still looked . . . well . . . respectable.

Conference registration began at ten. The bus from Gran Vía went straight to the conference venue, a dilapidated trade union centre that had seen better days. Outside the main door, there were the usual groups of left-wing paper sellers, but the Brits outshouted all comers.

'The Only Solution is Revolution,' yelled one vendor.

Another seller was trying to deafen his rival. 'Organize, Educate, Agitate.'

Max bought a paper from both of them, just for old times' sake, and then went inside. Bookstalls lined the entrance hall and banners were draped everywhere. The noise and bustle were overwhelming. There was a strong smell of marijuana competing with the odour of cheap disinfectant. He hadn't been to anything like this since his student days. It was going to be a real nostalgia trip. At the registration desk he picked up a form, and started to fill it in.

'Organization, contact telephone number and address.'

He could hardly write in 'Policía Nacional'. He finally put down 'Friends of the Earth'. That should be pretty neutral. And, after giving it some thought, he put the address of his old flat and invented a mobile number. He then joined the long queue waiting to pay and go in. Max found himself in the midst of a group of Trotskyites, arguing furiously among themselves whether the Bolivarian Revolution in Venezuela was a socialist revolution or not. Max smiled. Who cared? All the people of Venezuela wanted were jobs, decent housing, education, and a health system that worked. Just like everybody else.

Max paid his money, handed in his form, picked up a conference pack and went down the stairs to the makeshift canteen. He bought a coffee and managed to find a seat at a long table. The air was filled with cigarette smoke. He gazed around. There were a lot of beards and long hair. And a few dogs. But left-wing conferences sure as hell attracted pretty girls. Max opened his conference pack. Some of the speakers looked interesting, but he'd better stick to his task.

He saw Roberto Belén in the queue for coffee, wearing a suit and tie. What sort of conference did he think he was going to? Then he spotted Francisco Gómez coming into the canteen. Fortunately, Francisco was too engrossed in a conversation with a pretty girl to notice him.

As Francisco and his friend were ordering their coffee, Max slid into another room where more groups had their wares on display. People were milling around, talking animatedly, examining books, pamphlets, posters, trinkets from cooperatives in the Developing World, badges, ecologically sound clothes, and display boards. Groups of people were sitting on the floor, discussing what resolutions to put at the plenary sessions. The political parties were the best organized. They had clearly worked out their resolutions in advance. Democratic Centralism ensured they would all be singing from the same song sheet.

Max sat on the floor by a column and took out his conference programme. Francisco was on in the afternoon, a keynote speaker. Catalina Maya's workshop was in room 4, starting soon.

Room 4 was at the end of a dingy corridor littered with fag ends. The space was already crowded and all the chairs were taken, mostly by pretty girls. Max made himself comfortable on the worn linoleum floor. There were very few men in the room. Max felt even more conspicuous as various girls eyed him up. Then Catalina Maya hobbled into the room on crutches, with Padre Gerardo at her side.

The young priest introduced Catalina, talked briefly about the work of the women's refuge in Almanjáyar, and then handed over the microphone. She was a striking woman, perhaps in her early thirties, slim, with long black hair piled on top of her head and fierce expressive eyes. But her face was lined by suffering.

Catalina Maya spoke without notes, talking about her own personal experience, about the need to break the veil of silence surrounding domestic violence in Spain, and how women had to organize and support each other to get out of violent relationships.

Max was moved by the speech. It came from her heart, from her own experience. Questions flowed back and forth; finally a consensus was reached on putting a resolution to the conference. As Max stood up to leave, Padre Gerardo noticed him.

'El Señor Romero. What a surprise! I never expected to see you here. Let me introduce you to Catalina.'

Max tried not to look embarrassed.

'Catalina,' said the priest, 'this is the police officer I mentioned, the one looking for Mauricio and Gregorio.'

Catalina turned to look Max full in the face. 'Ah, Gregorio and Mauricio.'

'Señora. Do you have a few minutes?'

'Sure. I need something to drink. We can talk over coffee.'

'That was an excellent presentation,' said Max.

'*Gracias*, but will you police ever take domestic violence seriously? I doubt it.'

'We're improving.'

'Very slowly. *Muchas gracias, padre*,' she said to the priest.

'It's the least I can do. I'll see you later.'

She bent awkwardly to pick up her bag from the floor.

'Here, let me take that,' said Max. 'Do you need any help?'

'*Gracias*. But no, I have to get used to managing on my own.'

She hobbled along the corridor on her crutches, Max walking slowly beside her.

'Did you have an accident?'

'Yes. I got knocked off my moped on Friday. I was only discharged from the hospital yesterday.'

So that was why he hadn't been able to contact her.

Max and Catalina made their way slowly down to the canteen, took their coffees, and sat at a small table in a quiet corner. She gave him another searching look.

97

'I won't ask what you're doing here,' she said. 'It's not hard to guess.'

Max mumbled something.

'Padre Gerardo has already told me about Paco, and that you were looking for Mauricio and Gregorio. Paco had a bad heart, you know.'

'We know,' said Max. 'At this stage we're keeping an open mind on Paco's death, but I'm just checking a couple of things because someone painted *Asesino* on Paco's wall.'

'Well, there are many people who feel that five years in jail wasn't much for taking a life.'

'Is that a personal or professional opinion?'

'Both. Lucía was my best friend, you know. We had such dreams. We were going to be famous flamenco dancers. Paco ruined that for me.'

'Really?'

'*Sí*,' she said with a sad smile. 'When I was fifteen, he took me joyriding. He lost control of the car, smashed into a tree, and I broke my leg in two places.'

'I'm sorry to hear that. And Lucía?'

'Lucía was doing well until she got pregnant with Angelita. She picked things up again when she lost the baby fat, and she was getting good bookings when Paco thought she was going to leave him. They had a row in the street outside the Echavira club and my brother knifed her.'

'And Gregorio and Mauricio Espinosa?'

'They're bad news. Very bad news.'

'Would they kill Paco?'

'They threatened to, many times.'

'Would you be willing to testify that they had threatened your brother?'

'Sorry, but I can't risk making a statement, you know, in case anything got back to Mauricio.'

'Of course. But if you think of anything else, give me a call on this number.' Max handed over his business card.

Catalina stood up awkwardly. 'I have to go now,' she said. 'I'm meeting someone for lunch.'

Max waited a few minutes, then walked back to the bookstalls lining the entrance hall. Catalina was already there, resting on her crutches. Max spotted a book of political cartoons which looked interesting. He decided to buy it. As the bookstall holder fumbled with change, Francisco Gómez came down the stairs, crossed the hall to Catalina and hugged her. Francisco took a small red purse out of his pocket. Catalina dropped it into her shoulder bag, then they left together.

Max slipped out of the building, walked to a nearby newspaper kiosk and bought a copy of *Granada Hoy*. The story 'Another Massacre on the Coast' filled the front page. A Marbella hairdresser and his seven-year-old son had been shot when the salon was sprayed with bullets. The assassin's target, a French Algerian mafia boss, had escaped unharmed.

In the nearest restaurant, Max ordered the *menú del día*, and a carafe of wine. As he waited for his food, he checked the conference programme. Francisco was on in the main auditorium at six o'clock. The afternoon sessions all looked a bit heavy. He finally decided to go to the debate on 'The Coming Economic Crisis'. When lunch arrived, portions were substantial, and the carafe was larger than he expected.

At 4 p.m., Max went back to the conference, feeling rather full. The first speaker was a Professor from the Sorbonne. For an hour, the professor droned on: the world faced a crisis of over-production, fuelled by the ending of the ties between commodity production and finance, resulting in a massive wave of short-term financial speculation that would end in a crisis, first in the financial system and then in the production system. Max nodded off. He awoke with a start. Everyone was clapping. The debate had ended.

Somewhat groggily, Max went to the canteen and ordered a double black coffee. He put his hand into the pocket of his mountain jacket. No wallet. He went through all his pockets. No wallet.

'*Joder!*' he said aloud. 'I've been robbed. *Mierda.*'

The woman on the till was not sympathetic.

'Sorry,' said Max. 'I've been robbed. My wallet's gone. I've no money.'

'That's not my problem,' said the woman. 'No money, no coffee. That's the rule.'

The girl right behind him in the queue stepped up.

'Here, let me pay,' she said. 'It's only a euro.'

Max turned. The girl was small and very attractive, with an impish face, curly dark cropped hair, and disconcertingly green eyes. She was maybe in her late twenties, maybe younger. Max read the slogan on her T-shirt: 'So Many Men. So Little Time.'

'*Muchas gracias*,' said Max. 'I'm dying for a coffee.'

They took their coffees and sat together at the end of a long refectory table.

'Were you really robbed?' she asked.

'Yes. Silly me. I had a glass of wine too many at lunch, and nodded off during the talk.'

She laughed. 'I'm not surprised. It was pretty boring. Are you coming tomorrow?'

'*Sí.*'

She picked up her bag, fished out a small wallet, and handed over a fifty-euro note.

'Here,' she said. 'Take this. You can pay me back tomorrow.'

'I couldn't possibly do that,' protested Max.

'Why not? You'll need the cash to buy me a drink later.'

Max smiled. 'In that case, okay.'

'I'm Margarita,' she said.

'I'm Max,' he replied. He looked at his watch. 'I'm off to the plenary session with Francisco Gómez. It's starting soon.'

'I'm going as well. He's great.'

They made their way towards the main hall. A tall guy with cropped grey hair, wearing jeans and a white linen shirt, came towards them. It was Carlos. Margarita gave him a big hug.

'Max, *hombre*. Didn't expect to see you here.'

100

'Day off,' mumbled Max.

Carlos grinned at Margarita. 'I didn't know you two knew each other.'

'We don't. We've just met,' said Max.

'Are you coming to Francisco's talk?' asked Margarita.

'No. I have to drive a couple of folk to the station. It'll be good, though.'

The main auditorium was packed, but Max and Margarita managed to find two seats together at the back.

'You're a friend of Carlos, then?' said Max.

'Sí. I'm really fond of him. He helped me out when I was in a bit of a fix. And you?'

'We're in the same walking group. He really knows the paths around Granada.'

'I might come along one day. Sounds fun.'

Francisco came on to loud cheers from part of the audience. He paced up and down the platform like a caged tiger, black curls gleaming in the sunlight. His speech was a call to arms. The world was facing wars, famine and an unprecedented ecological disaster unless action was taken now. 'Think globally. Act locally,' he kept repeating. 'The time for talking is over. We must act, and act now.'

Then he homed in on Granada. 'The speculators are turning Granada into a concrete jungle. And now the authorities are about to approve the completion of the Granada ring road. They are going to build thousands of new houses in El Fargue, and turn the hill of San Miguel Alto into a giant car park for a new hotel. And why? To make the speculators rich.'

At the end of each example, he yelled, '*Paramos la violencia urbanística*! Stop the concrete!' The audience yelled back at him, '*Basta ya*! Stop it!' And he replied, '*Sí, se puede*. Yes, we can.'

Francisco paused dramatically, and waited for silence.

'And now the Church, supported by the Alcalde, has agreed to sell the monastery of Jesús del Valle and its lands to the speculators. Within five years, the whole valley will

be covered in concrete. So what are we going to do? *Paramos.*
We will stop it. *Sí, se puede.*'

The audience yelled back, '*Paramos.* We will stop it.'

'The time for talking is over. The time for action is now. I propose the following resolutions. One: to assemble on Monday in Plaza Nueva at five in the afternoon to stage a non-violent mass demonstration against the destruction of Jesús del Valle.'

The resolution obtained support from speaker after speaker. Margarita looked pleased. 'I think we're going to win the vote,' she whispered to Max.

Then a bespectacled young man with a posh Granadino accent sprang to his feet. Heads turned towards him. 'Chair, I wish to propose an amendment. Namely, to delete the words "non-violent".'

Margarita leaped out of her seat. 'Chair! Chair!' she yelled. 'This amendment is out of order. It hasn't been put in writing.'

The Chair coughed, and said apologetically, 'Actually it was. I received it at the last minute but I must allow the amendment to be put to a vote.'

Margarita plumped back down. 'It's been rigged. Manipulative bastards,' she hissed.

The Chair then asked the proposer of the amendment, David Costa, to speak in favour. Max started making notes.

David Costa began: 'This amendment is not an amendment in favour of violence. On the contrary, it is an amendment in favour of the right to self-defence. It is an amendment which says we must be prepared for the worst. It would be madness not to come prepared. Look what happened in Genoa.'

He finally concluded: 'After thirty-six years of the Franco dictatorship, are our Spanish police really any different to those butchers the Italians call cops? We must come prepared, with scarves in case the cops use tear gas, and to defend ourselves with arms if they attack us with batons. Vote for this amendment. Vote for your own safety.'

There were loud cheers. The ultra left were well prepared. One after another, confident young guys sprang to the defence of the amendment: tough anarchists from Italy and Greece, Maoists from Germany, Trotskyites from France and Britain, the Anarchist Black Angels from Granada.

The Chair finally called for the seconders of both the original resolution and the amendment to sum up.

Catalina Maya hobbled on to the platform on her crutches to second the original resolution, and spoke as before, from the heart.

'Non-violence,' she concluded, 'means non-violence. To go to a demonstration with weapons means those weapons will be used. People will be hurt, many of them innocent bystanders. I urge you to vote for the resolution, and reject the amendment.'

It was a powerful speech, the more so as it came from a victim of violence. Then to a loud roar of approval from his supporters, a young man called Alejandro Castro was called to the platform to sum up the case for the amendment. He began quietly, welcoming the European tribes in their own languages. He then switched to Spanish, but presented his slogans in French, Italian, German and English.

'We are not advocating violence,' he argued. 'But just as we support the right to resist unjust laws, so we must pre-serve the right to defend ourselves against police violence. And believe me, we will be in danger. It's not just the police we have to worry about. Maybe the Fascist Youth will attack us. For those of us who have grandparents and relatives who fought against Franco, against Hitler, against Mussolini, would we have said to them "Don't resist – be non-violent"? And do you think Franco, Hitler and Mussolini would have respected us for not resisting? Never again. Never again another Genoa. Let us never forget our comrade who was shot dead by the police there. Never forget our injured comrades. We must always defend ourselves.'

His supporters began chanting their slogans, their voices becoming louder and louder.

103

'That's bloody unfair,' said Max to Margarita. 'The Granada police aren't fascist goons.'

Margarita raised a quizzical eyebrow.

'The buggers are going to win, aren't they?' said Max.

They did, but narrowly.

The session ended in loud cheers from the winning side. The Chair then called Francisco Gómez to put forward his second resolution. Francisco came forward, subdued by defeat.

'Resolution Two: to join the Easter Procession of the Virgin of All Beings outside the church of Cristo El Benefactor in Almanjáyar, and march to the church of San Miguel Alto in the Albayzín.'

There were noises of surprise and murmurings of protest in the hall.

Max turned to Margarita. 'Why on earth is he asking this conference to support an Easter procession? This lot look more like a bunch of pagans.'

'Sí, but Francisco is not your normal lefty. He's Catholic. Theology of Liberation, and all that. It's what keeps him going.'

But before Francisco could speak, a guy stood up to propose an amendment to be voted on immediately.

'Amendment: those who wish to join the Procession of the Virgin of All Beings are very welcome to do so. But it is not the business of this conference to offer support to a religious procession.'

The Chair looked at his watch. 'Given the fact that this plenary is already running late,' he said, 'I suggest we move immediately to a vote. Please remember that the next session is closed. Please have your delegate authorization with you, and show it at the door.'

Francisco's proposal was defeated by an overwhelming majority. Margarita sighed, then smiled at Max.

'How about that drink you promised me?'

Chapter 14

Max and Margarita took the little bus from outside the trade union centre into Realejo, the ancient Jewish quarter of Granada.

'Let's start off in Campo del Príncipe,' suggested Margarita. 'A glass or two of *vino* in La Ninfa to get us started, and on from there. And if we end up in Plaza Nueva, it's not far to my flat.'

In La Ninfa, they ordered two Riojas. Max hadn't been there for years. The walls were still covered with old bullfight posters and green and yellow pottery from Níjar. Purple glass grapes clustered on the ceiling like stalactites. An elderly wood oven burned brightly in the kitchen behind the groaning bar, and the owner still displayed the fish, fruit and vegetables for the restaurant above as proudly as his wine. Their table was a tree trunk split in half. The tapa was a plate of raw mountain ham, *jamón serrano*, served with black olives and fresh bread.

'That wine is good,' said Margarita as she sipped it quickly. 'It's been one of those weeks.'

'Yes,' echoed Max. 'It's been one of those weeks.' He raised his glass. '*Salud*, Margarita! Here's to you. And thanks for the loan. I'll get it back to you tomorrow.'

She laughed. 'It's nothing.'

'So what do you do?' asked Max.

'Not much really. I've nearly finished my degree in English Lit. Just the thesis to hand in now. And what do you do?'

Max hesitated.

'Let me guess.' Margarita laughed again, a warm generous laugh. 'You're a cop,' she said. 'I recognized you from the TV a couple of years ago. The famous terrorist case. You looked cute on the box.'

Max blushed. 'I thought my disguise was good.'

'Not really. There is always police infiltration at conferences like this. We were just surprised they sent you.'

'Me too. But the boss needed someone with English, and I'm the only bilingual officer they've got right now.' Max had another sip of wine. 'How come you're not at the closed session?'

'No big deal. It's a delegate meeting. Only two delegates are allowed per group, and I wasn't chosen.'

'Oh, I see. So what would be happening in that session, then?'

'Probably the stuff you really need to know. Agreements on tactics for the demo, slogans, marching order, that sort of thing . . . and of course, the surprise tactic.'

'I see. And what would the "surprise" be?'

She laughed again. 'You really are a *poli*. Don't you already know? Anyway, just between you and me, I've heard they may be planning something outside the Regional Council offices.'

'Interesting.'

'Pity about the conference vote. Some groups from out of town are itching for a fight, so there's bound to be a bit of trouble. But most of the local folk are sound so, provided the cops don't overreact, it shouldn't be too bad.'

'Thanks for the advice,' said Max.

'Make sure you pass it on.'

'I don't suppose you know anything about the guys who put up the amendment supporting violence.'

'A bit. They're local, from the Black Angel Anarchists. They're all right really. They just think they'd look good on the barricades.' She drained her glass. 'Okay, time to move on. Next door is quite good.'

Max paid, and received change from the fifty-euro note. The next bar had a framed newspaper article on the wall: 'Ernest Hemingway Drank Here.'

'Where didn't he drink?' commented Max.

This time they tried one of the best local white wines for a change, the Calvente. The tapa was tuna, salted and sundried, served with a soft cheese. The wine was so good that Margarita ordered more before they had finished the first glass. The second round of drinks came with piping hot slices of *tortilla*, Spanish potato omelette, studded with spicy little green peppers.

'So what's with Francisco?'

'Francisco? He's brilliant. Just so full of energy. He's a volunteer with Granada Verde pretty much full-time, and he also does stuff with the radical Catholics. Most of us can't keep up with him.'

'So does he have a day job?'

'He's a freelancer for an IT consultancy, but he lives very modestly so he can afford to spend most of his time campaigning.'

'And Catalina Maya?'

'She's great. Tragic what happened to her. But she's a real fighter. Never lets it get her down.'

'Yeah. But how come Catalina and Francisco know each other?'

'Know each other? They were an item once.'

'Married?'

'I think so. We'll give the next bar a miss,' said Margarita. 'Their tapas aren't great, but the bar over the square is really nice. It's owned by a countryman of yours, an Englishman called Frank.'

'I'm Scottish,' protested Max. 'And we Scots aren't English. I think I'd better slow down; that's three glasses already.'

'Come on. We've hardly started. I thought you cops are all serious boozehounds.'

107

'Only in detective novels. And the hero tends to be a miserable, divorced git with issues.'

'Have you noticed, cops in books never seem to have family?' said Margarita.

'Lucky buggers. Me, I never seem to get away from mine.'

'Me too. Friends you can choose. Family you're stuck with. My bloody father.'

'What's wrong with him?'

'He's in the construction business. Another damn speculator.'

'I can see the problem there,' said Max.

'Given half a chance, he'd convert the Alhambra into luxury apartments, and put a golf course on top of the Alhambra hill. He just doesn't care about anything or anyone. You get in his way, and you've got problems.'

Margarita put her arm through his, and they made their way to the Bar Paradiso at the end of Campo del Príncipe.

'Do you dance, Max?' she asked as they went in.

'Badly,' he replied. 'Embarrassingly badly.'

The owner welcomed her as they entered the bar. Frank was a big guy from Newcastle who'd come to Granada on holiday, dropped out of college, and stayed on.

'Margarita,' he said in English. 'How are you?'

'No bad,' she replied in English.

'So you speak English,' Max said in English. 'And it should be "not bad".'

Frank turned to Max. 'I wish my Spanish was as good as her English. Complicated language, Spanish. I've been here five years, and I'm still rubbish.'

'*Hombre*, your Spanish is fine. Don't worry about it.'

'If only,' said Frank. 'I still can't get my head round the fact that every bloody noun's gendered.' Frank was warming to his topic. Margarita smiled broadly. 'And look at your bloody verbs, different endings depending on whether you're being matey or polite . . . so many bloody tenses it's untrue. And my school said Spanish was the soft option.'

108

'When you're brought up in it, it's easy,' Margarita said.

Frank laughed. 'If you're brought up in English, so is English.'

'Shall we go now, *guapetón*?' Margarita said to Max.

'Where to now, *guapetona*?'

'Next stop, La Tana, then AjoBlanco. I've known the owner forever. Then there's, well, Puccini.'

'Lead on, Macduff. And damn be him who cries enough.'

'Max . . . it's "Lay on, Macduff, and damned be him that first cries hold, enough."'

'You cheeky wee thing. How come you know *Macbeth*?'

'Because it's one of my set texts, stupid.'

When they walked out into the cool night air, Max remembered he'd had four, or was it five, generous glasses of wine already. But Margarita seemed as steady as a rock. They walked down Calle Mondujár, and round the side of the Convent of las Comendatores de Santiago. La Tana was packed as usual, and they couldn't get a seat. So they stood at the bar and had a glass of Señorío de Nevada with a tapa of spicy *morcilla*, a rich black pudding made with almonds and raisins.

'Margarita, this is great, but I really need to sit down.'

'Okay, let's go.'

They walked up Calle Palacios and into Plaza Santo Domingo. Max pointed up to the fresco of Queen Isabel la Católica in the porch of the Dominican church.

'Just look at that,' he said. 'Her Highness trying to look like the Holy Virgin Mary. Cracking piece of propaganda.'

'Nothing changes,' said Margarita. 'See how the portraits of Che Guevara made him look more and more like Jesus Christ as time went on.'

'Absolutely.'

'Great thing, iconography. Fascinating. Image is everything. Hey, Max – do you remember the Charlie Chaplin film, *The Great Dictator*?'

'*Sí*,' said Max. 'It was great, wasn't it?' And then he giggled. 'Great, great . . . get it?'

Margarita laughed as if it were a really funny joke.

Around the corner they could hear a roll of drums and the shrill blast of cornets.

'*Ay, coño*,' said Max. 'I forgot. Bloody Easter.'

'*Coño*,' echoed Margarita. 'Let's get into AjoBlanco fast.'

Max held her hand, and they dashed between the battered stone lions and down the steps into the cosy basement bar.

'Bloody Virgins,' said Max. 'They're everywhere.'

'Not many of us left any more,' said Margarita, giggling.

The owner, Pepe Caravalho, emerged from his bottle-lined lair to greet Margarita.

'How are you, *hermosa*? And how's Don Faustino?'

'I'm fine,' she said. 'Don't know about my dad. Haven't seen him for a bit.'

Pepe peered at her over the top of his gold-rimmed glasses. 'He was in last week, and he was complaining about the company you keep. He said you've joined an even madder bunch of lefties and he isn't exactly pleased.'

'Sounds about right.'

Max remained silent. He was having a bit of a problem focusing. And he hadn't been introduced.

'All right,' said Pepe. 'Seeing as it's you, I'll get my best red, a Marquesado del Zenete. And the *morcilla* is home-produced, and just right. Made by my sainted mother herself.'

Neither Max nor Margarita was in a state to appreciate the excellent wine or the *morcilla*. They kept laughing at each other's bad jokes. Max was impressed. She was so wild and free, but cultured. And she made him laugh so much.

'I like your T-shirt,' he said.

'Sure it's just the T-shirt? Right. Now for the best cocktails in Granada.'

There was a large crowd in the plaza, waiting for the jewelled image representing la Virgen de la Misericordia to return to her home church.

'Quick. This way,' said Margarita. 'Or else we'll get stuck

110

in the crowd. Puccini's quite a place. They play opera all the time.'

They zigzagged through the back streets to a bar tucked behind the Imperial Church of San Matias. Max had passed it before, but thought it looked a bit exotic. He remained dubious. The place was sumptuous, all soft green velvet, candles, stained glass, gilded mirrors and painted angels. The sound system was playing Bach's Italian Concerto. And then the overture of Gounod's *Faust* filled the bar.

'Bloody dad. He's called Faustino, and he goes and calls his little girl Margarita. He hadn't read the bloody Goethe. Innocent girl sacrificed to the god of power.'

'Well, I had these friends in Glasgow, and they had a wee boy and they called him Tristan, which is fair enough. But when they had a little girl they wanted to call her Isolde. Should have called the poor little buggers Romeo and Juliet and got it over with. Had to finish a whole bottle of whisky with Jamie to get him to change his mind. Talisker it was. Damn nice.'

Somewhat belatedly, Max realized he had made a mistake in ordering another large Lepanto brandy. Margarita was saying something interesting. Something about a novel he had read, *A Heart so White*.

'Bit heavy for my taste. Murder and family secrets. Nothing much seems to happen after the beginning . . . rambles on and on . . .' Max lost the train of his thought.

'Oh,' she said, 'I loved it. The way Javier Marías used the *Macbeth* texts was amazing. It doesn't matter who has actually done the deed; it's the one who planned it that's guilty. "My hands are of your colour, but I shame to wear a heart so white."'

'Who said that? Bloody Hamlet?'

'*No.* Lady Macbeth. Hey, Max, how come you're bilingual?'

'My mother. One of the Maxwells. Scottish.'

'Like Lady Macbeth.'

'Always off somewhere. I hardly see her. She's a musician.

111

Harpsichord. Got a job and buggered off back to Glasgow with my sister when I was twelve.'

'That's sad.'

'Well, could've been worse. Left me with my *abuelo* and *abuela* in Diva . . . but me and my cousin Juan had a good time. How about you?'

'Stuck alone with my dad. My mother – she killed herself.' Margarita tried to suppress a sob.

Max put his arm around her. '*Pobrecita mía*. I'm awf'y sorry . . . that's really sad,' he slurred consolingly.

'Poor mum. Stuck in the house. Dad wouldn't let her work And then if bloody dad hadn't started playing around – but I don't want to talk about it any more.'

Max bounced upright in his warm armchair. 'What the hell was that?'

'Thunder,' said the barman.

Outside, the rain fell as heavily as a tropical storm.

'We can't go out in that,' said Margarita. 'Another one, Max?'

'*Sí*, why not? The same again, that . . .' He peered into his glass, befuddled. 'Some bloody battle. What the . . .'

'Lepanto,' said Margarita.

'Yeah, bloody battle of Lepanto. Don John of Austria. Stopped the bloody Moors, he did.'

'Maximiliano, you're getting very drunk. *Borrachísimo*.'

'You sound just like *mi abuela*.'

'The rain's eased off. We'd better run for it. There's bound to be another storm in a minute,' said Margarita, decisively.

She put on her coat. Max tried to fasten up his worn mountain jacket, but the zip got stuck.

'What the hell. And no bloody umbrella,' he muttered. 'Some fucking cop nicked it. If I catch the bastard I'll –'

'Have you paid, Max?'

'No.' Max went to the bar and handed over all the money he had left.

'*Un poco más, señor*. Short by forty-two euros,' said the barman.

'Bloody hell. That's daylight robbery. What the . . . I don't have any more,' he said, leaning over towards the barman.

'Here's the forty-two euros,' Margarita said to the barman, and she pushed Max towards the door. 'Let's run.'

They set off down the dark, narrow street, the wet cobblestones glistening in yellow lamplight. Max slipped, stumbled and sat down hard in the stream of water pouring downhill.

'Hell,' he said. 'That's my jeans bloody soaked.'

'Don't worry,' said Margarita, helping him up. 'I'll help you get them off.'

Another thunderclap, closer this time.

'Come on, we haven't long. Run. Run, *corre*,' said Margarita.

Max started running, but his legs felt as if they had been cast in concrete. He started to wheeze.

'Wait,' he gasped. 'I need . . . my inhaler.'

He stopped, and took two quick puffs of his inhaler.

'How on earth did you get into the cops? I thought they had strict medicals.'

'They do. Wasn't a problem at the time.'

'Christ, what have I ended up with? *Un poli*, who can't hold his drink, and asthmatic with it. Are you okay to make a dash for it?'

'*Sí*. Think so.'

The rain came down like stair-rods. The streets were deserted, the bars full.

Max wheezed. 'But I could do with another wee dram.'

'No chance.'

They slithered across the marble flagstones of Plaza Nueva, past the fountain, its water playing with the rain, and splashed along the stream of water which filled most of Paseo de los Tristes.

Margarita pointed at the signboard outside a building site. '*Construcciones Azules*. That's one of my dad's . . .'

'Your dad . . . not . . .'

113

'*Sí*, Faustino Azul.'

'*The* Faustino Azul?' said Max.

'*Sí*.'

They splashed up Calle Zafra, paused at a huge sixteenth-century door with a tiny modern lock almost hidden among the ancient metalwork.

'In we go. I share the top floor, but the girls are away.'

They climbed the stairs, Max taking them slowly.

'Are you okay?'

'I'm fine,' he said. 'Just have to . . . careful . . . take everything slowly.'

She laughed. 'That's fine with me. This is it. Thank God, I left some heating on.'

'*Coño*,' said Max, impressed. 'That's some place you've got here.'

'Yes, a friend of my mother's rents it to us. Here, let's get dry. I'll light the wood fire. It's a Salamander, so it shouldn't take long to heat up. I'll put on some music. Do you like Manu Chao? Let me find one especially for you. Here it is, "Mr Bobby".'

They both sang along with Manu Chao: 'This world go crazy.'

'Come on, Max. Let's dance.'

Max felt Margarita take his hands. He swayed from side to side, but his feet failed him and he flopped on to a sofa.

'You got one thing right, Max. You can't dance. Best get those wet clothes off then.'

He felt his wet jeans being pulled down.

He raised his hands as if in protest, and then let them fall.

Chapter 15

It was still raining when Max woke up. He stared at the carved wooden ceiling. His head throbbed. His eyes refused to focus. He closed them again, and then tried opening them slowly. It wasn't his pillow. There was a snore. He never snored.

What? He had no clothes on. No pyjamas. He put out a hand and encountered bare flesh. Warm and smooth. Silky. He shut his eyes again. Refocused. The room swam into view. A lovely big room, but hellish messy.

He sat up with a start. Christ, what had he done?

A black cropped head lay on the pillow next to him, almost hidden underneath the quilt. Max groaned. *Abuela* Paula was right – never drink too much. Bad for your asthma, she used to say. Not just asthma. The head on the pillow stirred, and two green eyes peeked up at him.

'*Buenos días*, Maximiliano.'

Then a roguish smile appeared as a hand pulled down the quilt a little.

'What time is it?' asked Max. 'I have to rush, got a meeting at nine, you know.'

'You men always do.'

Max blushed.

'No need to apologize. I had to do all the work.'

'Do you have any paracetamol?'

'In the bathroom cupboard.'

'Thanks. I – I –'

115

'Go on, rush off. You can get in touch later if you want. If not, it was nice to meet you, Maximiliano. *Un poli* . . . Who would have thought it?'

Max gulped down black coffee and hangover cure, and dressed as quickly as he could manage. He was already late for his meeting with Chávez, and there was no chance of going home to change.

'I'll phone you,' he said lamely.

She laughed. 'You should see your face. Women can take the initiative, you know.'

For once, Max was lost for words. It was still raining. His clothes were still damp; the seat of his jeans was muddy. His head throbbed. And he was horribly late. He ran down to Plaza Nueva and jumped into a taxi.

'*Policía Nacional, por favor.*'

'Reporting a murder, are you?'

The taxi stopped outside police headquarters. Max put his hand into his pocket. Christ. No money.

'Wait here a minute.' Max got out, and ran up the steps. Fortunately it was Pedro on desk duty.

'Pedro, for the love of God, lend me ten euros. I've a taxi waiting outside.'

'*Por dios*, Max, you look rough. Look like you crawled out of a brothel,' said Pedro, handing over a ten-euro note.

Max ran back to the waiting taxi. 'Here, keep the change.'

The lift was out of order so Max sprinted up the stairs, his head thumping with every step, and knocked on Felipe Chávez's door. At least he was reporting to Chávez. Davila would have had a field day.

'Come in, Max. Oh dear.'

Chávez surveyed the muddy jeans, lank hair and deathly pallor.

'You really have gone native. Well, what have you got?'

Max managed to pull himself together, and gave a reasonably coherent account of the conference.

116

'They are definitely planning something to catch us by surprise, sir. But it was decided at a closed session which I couldn't get into.'

'Well, they've already got permission to assemble in Plaza Nueva, and march along the Gran Vía, and down into the university campus at Plaza Albert Einstein. So you think they might change the route?'

'Maybe. My source suggested the probability of a protest outside the Regional Council offices, next to the Jardines de Triunfo.'

'That's useful.'

'Another thing, sir. The conference was full of anarchists and hard guys from out of town. Francisco Gómez put forward a resolution for a non-violent protest, but he was outvoted.'

'That's unfortunate.'

'The militants said they would react only in self-defence.'

'That's always ambiguous. You never know who starts what. So there could be trouble?'

'*Sí.*'

'Did you pick up anything on leaders, then?'

Max fished into the pocket of his mountain jacket and pulled out a sodden notebook. He eased the pages carefully apart.

'I've got two names. David Costa and Alejandro Castro. They're local, the Black Angel Anarchist group. But my source says that the real hard guys are out-of-towners, probably the Italian and Greek anarchists, but she doesn't know them.'

Chávez raised an eyebrow. 'She?' He noted the names down. 'These Black Angels and the other guys – will they be at the back of the demo or mixed in with the rest?'

'I don't know for a fact, sir. But I was told by a reliable source –'

'The same she?'

117

'*Sí* – that they expected the police to infiltrate the conference. So I guess the militant groups are going to be mixed in with the others.'

'That could make life difficult for us.'

'One other thing. I'm afraid I was robbed at the conference. I've lost my police ID card, my money and my credit cards.'

Chávez laughed. 'Some cop. Robbed at a radicals' conference. I ask you. Anything else happen to you? A bit of a hangover, by any chance?'

'No. Nothing. There were some good speeches. Apparently we can expect a major financial crisis.'

'Oh. More budget cuts for us again. You did well, Max. I suggest you go home and get some sleep.'

'Did Roberto Belén pick up anything?'

'Very little, unfortunately.'

'Oh, one more thing, sir. Some of the people from the conference will be joining Francisco Gómez at the Procession of the Virgin of All Beings.'

'So it will be a bigger group than last year. That's useful.'

'I'm sorry it's not more, but nobody was going to spill the beans to some guy they've never heard of.'

'Some girl did, though?'

'Er . . .'

'Thanks for that, Max. And Max, go home quick before anyone else sees you.'

Max managed to squelch along the corridor and check his emails without being spotted. But his luck ran out as he passed Davila's office. The door opened, and Davila emerged.

'What – Romero! Have you seen yourself? You look a disgrace. Get inside.'

'Yes, sir,' mumbled Max.

'Your bum's muddy. No. Just stand there. I don't want my chairs wet. What the hell were you doing? Drinking with hippies in the street?'

'I had to blend into the crowd at the conference.'

'Blend in? You look like you've come from some bloody *botellón*. I've just had a phone call from your famous conference organizers. Someone's handed in your wallet to something they describe as their media centre.'

Davila sniffed and looked down at his notepad. 'A girl called Margarita. Your police card was in it, credit cards etc. But no money, of course. What sort of idiot cop are you to lose your wallet when on duty? I can't tell you how bad this looks.'

'I know, sir. I was robbed.'

'Robbed? A police officer. Of your rank and experience. Robbed by a bunch of long-haired scruffs?'

'They're probably experts, sir.'

'Romero, if I hadn't just had a phone call from Chávez, your arse would definitely be on the line. He said you did a good job. Okay. You're on extra overtime tonight.'

'But sir –' protested Max

'Romero!'

'Yes, sir. Where do we assemble?'

'We? I will accompany the Brotherhood of the Bell from outside their church. And you, my lad, will be with those hippy scruffs and their ridiculous Virgin of All Beings – whatever that's supposed to mean. They leave from that trendy priest's church in Almanjáyar, Cristo El Benefactor, at midnight.'

'But, sir –'

'No buts, Romero. From the look of you, a long walk will do you good. You should join the penitents, and do it barefoot. You'd better go now. I don't want my office covered in mud and smelling like a doss house.'

'Yes, sir.' Max turned to go. Then he remembered. 'By the way, I discovered something which might be useful on the Paco Maya case. It seems that Francisco Gómez knows Catalina Maya very well.'

'Now that really is interesting.'

'I saw them together and someone commented that they'd been married.'

'Leave it with me, Max. I'll chase that up. Gómez swore on a stack of bibles he didn't know Paco Maya. Now why did he do that?'

'I don't know.'

'Because he's lying, Max. And if he's lying on this, he's lying on everything.'

Max squelched back along the corridor and reached Reception without bumping into Navarro.

'Pedro, could you lend me another ten euros for a taxi?'

'Christ, Max. You're not becoming an alky, are you? I know Barcelona ain't doing too well, but there's no need to take it so hard.'

'Pedro, I'm on a mission. Deep undercover.'

'Okay then. Sure I can't join you? You look like you had fun.'

Max laughed. 'I did.'

Back home, he dumped his dirty clothes in the linen basket and had a long, hot shower. The laundry hanging up in the bathroom still wasn't dry and he'd forgotten to pick up his dry-cleaning. All he had that was clean and dry was the pale blue cashmere sweater his mother had given him, not exactly a conference thing. Fortunately his old mountain jacket had dried out. He walked down to the Gran Vía, bought a ham and cheese *bocadillo* from one of the cafés, then took the little number 30 bus to the trade union centre. The conference had stopped for lunch, but the media centre was still open.

'I've come for a wallet,' Max mumbled. 'It was handed in this morning. It's plain black leather, and it should have my ID inside'

'Ah. The cop. We knew the cops would be here, but didn't expect you to lose your wallet. You're very welcome to attend, you know. It would have been courteous to let us know you were coming. We've nothing to hide.'

The man at the desk looked at Max and smiled. 'That sweater's a bit of a giveaway.'

'My wallet, please.'

He opened a desk drawer, took out a wallet and handed it to Max. Once outside, Max checked the contents. Everything was in place apart from his money. And there was something new, a carefully folded piece of paper. He opened it.

'Thanks for everything. I had fun. I owe you 50 euros – my treat next time? Big kiss, Margarita. 658 272930.'

Max smiled. The girl had style.

He walked back to his flat, still feeling pretty grim. The fresh air helped but he felt like death warmed up, despite the coffee and paracetamol. His mobile rang as he was walking up the stairs.

'*Dígame*,' he muttered.

'It's Juan. Are you okay? You don't sound too well.'

'I'm fine. Just a cold. All this rain, you know.'

'Thought I'd phone to give you the good news. I've been accepted by the Brotherhood of the Bell. And I'll be joining *el paso* tonight as a penitent. Isabel is coming to watch. We're staying at Isabel's parents' house in Realejo afterwards.'

'Isabel will be pleased. She's always said you have a lot of penitence to do.'

'Nice one, Max. No, I'll do the hood and all that. But I won't do the barefoot stuff, not with all that dog shit in the Albayzín.'

'That's not real penitence then. I'll probably see you tonight, Juan. I'm on duty. I'm just going home for a nap, then I start again at midnight.'

He washed his face, cleaned his teeth, and then curled up on his bed and fell asleep. He awoke with a start. His phone was ringing. Wrong number. Max looked at his watch. It was nine o'clock already. He could do with a little drink before the procession. He walked down the hill, into the Bodega la Castañeda. He couldn't stop thinking about Francisco. Why had he lied?

Chapter 16

Max sat at the counter bar of the Bodega la Castañeda, staring at the stuffed bull's head above him.

Ramón, the barman, came over. 'Got the blues, Max?'

'Hangover, Ramón, hangover.'

'One of those days, eh? Hair of the dog? I'll get you a *calicasas*.'

'Heavens no, man. A beer will be fine.'

Max gazed at the bull again, and then at the barman. There definitely was a family resemblance.

'Ramón, would a guitarist ever leave his guitar face down on a concrete floor?'

'Never. You kidding? You treat your guitar like a baby. You never, never put it face down.'

A group of fit young guys in identical T-shirts had materialized at the other end of the bar.

'*Un momento*, duty calls. Back in a minute.'

Max's head still nipped. The paracetamol was wearing off.

Once the food orders had been taken and the drinks served, Ramón returned to his usual spot.

'Ramón, do you have a couple of paracetamol?'

'Max, if you work here, you live on them. How many do you want?'

'You couldn't give me a packet, could you? I have a feeling I'm going to need them. I'm on night duty with the Virgin of All Beings.'

'Oh, I thought the Archbishop had banned them.'

'He has. But he can only stop them going inside churches. And now that trendy priest in Almanjáyar and his buddy at San Miguel Alto have got their act together, so I'm going to have to walk from bloody Almanjáyar to bloody San Miguel Alto, right at the top of the Albayzín.'

'*Hombre*, that's some distance. But they'll be going along the Haza Grande road and then round the back of the city walls, won't they?'

'No chance. They're going the hard way, on the old pilgrims' path, straight up the front of the San Miguel hill.'

'You know half their team are girls?'

'*Sí*, and that's probably why they want to do it the hard way.'

'Mark my words, no good's going to come of it. Girls carrying a *palio*. My old dad would be spinning in his grave. Still, the thought of all those pretty girls, all hot and sweaty . . .' And he grinned wolfishly at Max.

'Modern times, Ramón, modern times. At least I'll end up near my flat, so I can crash out there. *Mierda*, is that the time? I'll have to get a taxi.'

Max paid, pocketed the paracetamol, and grabbed a cab at the rank in Plaza Nueva. In Almanjáyar, a large crowd had already gathered outside the darkened church. He noticed Roberto Belén and Pedro having a smoke together as they waited for the procession to move off.

'Roberto, Pedro. Sorry I'm late. Everything okay?'

'No problems,' said Roberto. 'It's a pretty mixed crowd, but they seem good-natured.'

'Where's Chávez?'

'Over there behind the *palio*.'

'Ah, Max,' said Chávez. 'I wondered where you'd got to.'

'I was delayed.'

'Okay. I've put you on the *palio* with the Virgin.'

'That's the last thing I need at the moment.'

'That bad, is it?'

At the *palio*, Catalina Maya was talking to a girl wearing a red bandanna round her crisp dark hair. The girl turned round. It was Margarita, looking as fresh as a daisy. Max smiled weakly.

'Max, I didn't expect to see you here.'

'On duty, keeping an eye on the *palio*.'

'So you can keep an eye on me as well. I'm *una costalera*. In this *cofradía* we do it fifty–fifty. Equality, you see.'

'It's a long way to be carrying that *palio*. It looks bloody heavy.'

'It's high-tech – the underside's aluminium, so it's much lighter than the old ones, but still heavy enough to be a challenge. Max, you do look rough. Cops these days . . . just no stamina.'

'Cheeky thing. I'm fine, thanks.'

As Max took up his position beside the *palio* of the Virgin he noticed Francisco Gómez, splendid in a green velvet jacket, black trousers and shiny shoes, proudly holding a silver mace. Of course, he realized. El Capataz, the Master of Ceremonies.

A Granadino sculptor had designed the image of the Virgin cradling her dead Son as a memorial to his brother, an aid worker who had died in Ecuador. The carving was simple, without sentiment, and Ecuadorian parishioners had made the cloak for the Virgin themselves, telling the story of the Ecuadorian rainforest. A panel showed ranchers burning the forest, another reforestation by local villagers. The cloak was beautiful, but not exactly standard stuff for a Granadino Virgin.

Cycling up and down beside the *palio* were a bunch of kids. Max thought he recognized Angelita and the boys who had been outside *abuela* Espinosa's house. Tough-looking lads, they were, especially the one with streaked hair.

'Tomasito,' a voice called out. 'Remember, make sure Angelita's home before 2 a.m.'

The tallest boy turned round. 'Don't worry, *madre*. I'll get her back on time. There'll be no problems, I promise.'

Max turned to look at the mother. She was a tall, thin gypsy woman, a worn-out beauty. But she was smart in an expensive black jacket and skirt. Her henna-dyed hair was held in an elaborate comb, and she carried both a rosary and a candle. She wore black stockings, but no shoes. She was a penitent who would do the whole route barefoot.

In front of the *palio* of the Christ was a group of green-shirted musicians, mostly carrying guitars, drums or flutes. Father Gerardo and the Jesuit priest from San Miguel Alto, Father Oscar, were talking to the band leader. Behind the band was a group of men, some holding hands. Pedro stood beside the group of gay Catholics, his face a picture of mortal embarrassment.

'Pedro. You've finally come out. Well done, man.'

'Fuck off, Max. *Véte a la puta mierda.* And I bet they're a bunch of poofter Barcelona supporters too.'

Max laughed, and moved down the procession. Next was a group of women in black, all holding candles. Most of them, like Tomasito's mother, were going to walk the whole route, through the long night, without shoes. Further back there was a group of Bolivian and Ecuadorian immigrants, Granadino parishioners in their Sunday best, and right at the back, some lefties from the conference. Nearly everyone was wearing a green scarf and carrying a sprig of rosemary for remembrance. Max walked back to the head of the procession, and took his position by the *palio* of the Virgin.

To shouts of *Olé*, they set off, marching past the bus station, then the huge hypermarket, Al Campo, the Granada bull ring in Plaza de Torros and down to Avenida de la Constitución. Max had another swig from his bottle of water. The barefoot women's feet were already bleeding, but they smiled calmly though the pain. This was going to be a long night for everyone.

The procession stopped on Gran Vía, then marched into Plaza de la Trinidad. A small improvised stage had been placed in the plaza, which rapidly filled up with people.

Father Oscar led a prayer for the heretics, Jews and Muslims who had been burnt at the stake in Granada. The crowd solemnly intoned, 'Amen,' then sang a short psalm.

The procession set off again, with a new team of *costaleros*, as Margarita and her team took a break. Max felt like going up to Margarita and hugging her. She glanced at him, smiled, but stayed with her *costaleras*.

They walked behind the cathedral, into Plaza de San Juan de la Cruz, then into Plaza Nueva, where more people were waiting to join them. From Plaza Nueva, the procession snaked up into the dark streets and the ancient white houses of the Albayzín. Max couldn't stop yawning. And, of course, Pedro spotted him.

'Max, you idiot. There's press photographers all over the place. A yawning cop would look great on the front page of *Ideal*.'

'You're right, man. I need coffee.'

'I've got caffeine tabs. They help.'

'Pedro, you're a bloody saint. *Gracias*.'

Margarita came up to him. 'Max, you look shattered.'

'I'm fine. Just tired out.'

She laughed. 'You could have fooled me. *Vale*. This is my big moment. The San Miguel Alto section. That will be some climb. But it will be worth it, Max. See you at the top.'

The procession halted outside the Convent of Santa Isabel la Real, close to his flat. A cordon of police with Chávez in front stretched across the cobbled street. Francisco went up to speak to Chávez, and then returned to his procession.

'I have just spoken to the police. The Procession of the Brotherhood of the Bell is running late, and they have still to cross in front of us to climb up to the Mirador de San Nicolás. We will have to wait here for a few minutes.'

There were cat calls, and then, 'Why can't those bastards be halted, and let us go on?'

'We don't go near the buggers anyway. The cops are just taking the piss.'

'Bloody speculators.'

'Opus Dei fascists.'

'Let's just go on. Screw them,' other voices called out.

Francisco raised his mace. 'We must let them pass. We all need a rest. So let us sing and rest.'

There were boos and cries of 'Sell-out' from the back of the crowd. But most seemed glad of a break. Max looked around. His flat was so close. But Chávez had a job for him.

'Max,' he said, 'go over to the Brotherhood of the Bell and ring me when they are all up in the Mirador.'

Max trudged to the corner of the Carril de San Agustín. The flickering candles of the Brotherhood of the Bell were climbing up the hill towards the Convento de Santo Tomás. The only sound was the tolling of a solitary bell, and the clinking of chains carried by the penitents. The first light of dawn gleamed pale above the Alhambra, silhouetting a huge cross. There was no sound but that of the bell, chiming in the dark street.

Then a penitent winked at Max through the slits of the purple-hooded mask, and a hand rose in salute.

The Procession of the Brotherhood of the Bell halted at the Aljibe de las Tomasas where *los costaleros* changed shift. Isabel was waiting, digital camera at the ready.

Juan took off his hood, and came over to join them.

'Here,' said Isabel. 'Let me get a photo of you in those robes. Nita and Leo won't believe you did this. This really will be one for the family album.'

She took a few pictures, and then examined them critically.

'There's not enough light,' she said. 'Could you stand by the candles over there? I want some of you with and without that hood.'

Juan walked dramatically over towards the candles. Three men were talking earnestly close by. They turned round, disturbed by the camera flash. Max thought he recognized them, but his eyes were too tired to focus. One was a man wearing the black cloak of the Priestly Society of the Holy Cross, the clergy of Opus Dei.

The priest and the guy in the dark suit pointedly walked away from the lights but the tall, masked man, carrying the silver staff of El Capataz of the Brotherhood of the Bell, walked towards Juan.

'Don Faustino,' Juan called out. 'Come and have your photo taken with me.'

'Don Juan, where is your hood? No photos. Remember the Brotherhood code. We do not disclose identities to those outside. Remember the rule.'

A couple of minutes later, Davila and Navarro sauntered by.

Davila stared at Max. 'Romero, what the hell are you doing here? I thought you were on duty with the hippy lot.'

'Chávez wants me to phone him when you are all up in the Mirador.'

'I see. I'm still chasing up that tip you gave me on Francisco Gómez. My contact will get me the info first thing Monday morning. Ah, there's the lady wife.'

Max spotted Davila's wife, dripping with jewellery and mink.

'I'd better go and have a word,' said Davila. And he disappeared into the mob of fur coats.

Five minutes later Davila emerged, and joined a group of men talking to El Capataz of the Brotherhood of the Bell. It was dark, but Max could have sworn one of them was Teniente Patricio Grandes, adjutant to the Alcalde. Another was definitely Che Navarro.

Eventually El Capataz raised his staff and lowered it dramatically, and the *costaleros* faced their final challenge, the hill leading to the Mirador of San Nicolás. As dawn broke, the windows of the Convent of Las Tomases opened wide, and a choir of nuns sang: '*En una noche oscura, con ansias en amores inflamada* . . . On a dark night, my heart was filled with love and longing . . .'

The Cross of the Brotherhood of the Bell was carefully lowered as the *costaleros* manoeuvred it into the church of San Nicolás. Max phoned Chávez when the Brotherhood and their supporters were safely up at the Mirador then rejoined the Virgin of All Beings.

128

Francisco's procession was preparing to split into two. The heavy traditional image of the Christ was to go along the road, the easier route to the church of San Miguel, but the lighter image of the Virgin of All Beings was going the hard way, the steep pilgrims' path, climbing the front of the hill of San Miguel Alto.

Chávez turned to Max. 'So far so good, but there's quite a crowd at the top already. I'll head off to San Miguel Alto. See you there.'

The smaller group with the image of the Virgin crossed Calle Pages, and into the streets of Albayzín Alto. At the pilgrims' cross of La Rueda, the *costaleros* changed formation and grip for the final stretch. From there, some five hundred steps climbed through the cactus scrubland to the church of San Miguel Alto looming high above them, a sentry post on the ancient city walls. The dawn suddenly turned colder, and a chill little wind ruffled the embroideries of the Virgin's cloak.

Max turned to Pedro. '*Ay dios mío*, it's going to bucket and there's no way they can turn back once they're committed to the hill.'

'*Sí*. We have stop them here.'

Max hurried up to Francisco. 'Francisco, it's going to rain. Those steps will be bloody treacherous. Call it off.'

'I always finish what I begin. We're going up. It's steep, but not far. And the Virgin will protect us.'

'I strongly advise . . .'

But Francisco turned, and shouted, 'Onwards and upwards! *Arribad compañeros y compañeras. Venceremos.*'

Chávez phoned. Things had suddenly turned tricky at the church. A group of traditionalists were determined to prevent the Virgin of All Beings from entering.

The procession of the Virgin toiled up the hill at first slowly and carefully. But then the heavens opened and rain poured down. The *costaleros* speeded up. Suddenly, on a steep incline, there were screams, shouts of panic. The *palio* collapsed and the Virgin tumbled down, crashing on to the

129

hillside. Pedro and Max ran to the *palio*. There were shouts, screams, cries for help. Max, Pedro and the *costaleros* finally managed to lift the *palio* up, and move it away from the crumpled body underneath.

It was Margarita.

She lay still and deadly pale. Max knelt beside her, his own heart racing.

'She's still breathing. *Una ambulancia, rápido.*'

'I've already phoned for one. It's on its way,' said Pedro.

The Virgin lay in the cactus scrub, her crown askew, her cloak torn and muddy. Max fetched the Virgin's cloak and laid it carefully over Margarita, as photographers jostled for shots around the body lying on the path, the collapsed *palio*, and the Virgin lying in the scrub.

'Stand back, stand back. Give her air and for God's sake don't move her. She may have damaged her spine,' Max shouted.

Maite just sat in the mud holding her friend's hand, tears rolling down her cheeks.

Max turned to the nearest *costalero*. 'What the hell happened?'

'I don't know,' he replied. 'We were doing great. Then the back of the *palio* suddenly dipped, the weight shifted and the whole bloody thing came crashing down.'

'*Mierda*. What a mess,' said Pedro. 'Let's start getting statements.'

Max questioned the two men who had been at the back of the *palio*. 'Okay. Diego Elvira and Salvador Lozano. Where exactly were you located under the *palio*?'

'We were right at the back. With all this rain, it was really slippery. We stumbled, and had to let go our grips,' volunteered Diego.

'Both at the same time?'

'We both slipped at the same time,' said Salvador.

'An accident or a coincidence then?'

'*Un accidente.*'

The shrill of an ambulance siren came closer and closer, then two paramedics ran up the steep path towards the fallen Virgin. They lifted Margarita carefully on to the stretcher, and hurried back to the waiting ambulance. It sped away, siren shrilling again, as Chávez arrived from the top of the hill.

'Max, what the hell happened?'

Max explained briefly.

'Okay. Full report on my desk first thing Monday morning. I'll go and deal with the press.'

Francisco sat on the muddy ground in a trance. The rain poured on to his upraised face and streamed down his long dark hair. Then he stood up, raised his arms to the heavens, and cried out to the dawn sky.

Chapter 17

Max finally got back to his flat at 6 a.m. If only he'd been able to stop that damn procession, this wouldn't have happened. He rang the Hospital Virgen de los Nieves, and waited again. Finally somebody answered the phone.

'*Dígame*?' a sleepy girl's voice said.

'*Por favor, mi amiga*. My friend Margarita Azul was admitted a couple of hours ago following an accident. Can you tell me how she is?'

'*Un momento.*'

Max chewed a hangnail till it bled. It was only five minutes before the girl came back on the phone. But it seemed much longer.

'I spoke to the doctor and he said her condition is stable. Your friend is a very lucky girl indeed.'

'Thank God. So she'll be all right?'

'*Sí*. I think so, but I can only give details to close family.'

'*Gracias*. What time are visiting hours?'

'She's in a private room, so visiting is fairly flexible. I suggest you phone first, any time after twelve noon today.'

Max collapsed gratefully on to his bed. He awoke at two, the sun streaming into his bedroom. He phoned the hospital again. It was a different girl this time.

'Señorita Azul? *Bueno*. Afternoon visiting hours are between four and seven, and then later in the evening after eight.'

132

Max brewed a pot of coffee, and slipped two slices of bread into his toaster. He'd need to think about the report on the procession. Those guys could have slipped, but then? No, it made no sense. His phone rang. It was Paula.

'Max, *hijo*,' she said, 'I was so worried about you. It was on the lunchtime news. I heard what happened to the procession. That poor girl. Were you there, Max?'

'I was on duty, *abuela*. It could have been worse, but the girl is out of danger. I'm fine. Don't worry.'

'I'll see you tomorrow then?'

Max had forgotten that it was Easter Sunday. He paused. 'I'll be there. I'd never miss Easter Sunday.'

'Are you sure you're all right? Max. You know how I worry.'

'*Sí, abuelita*, I understand. Everything's all right.'

Max took the bus to the hospital. He bought a bunch of *margaritas*, large Spanish daisies, from the shop outside the entrance and then hurried to the private ward. Margarita lay propped up in bed, a surgical collar around her neck. She was still very pale, and her eyes were half closed. A man was sitting beside her bed, his manicured hand resting on her arm. He turned his head and looked questioningly at Max. He was a big man, with flattened, slightly feline features. His grey hair was combed back, like a gentleman, but his eyes were bloodshot, and his cheeks slightly roughened. Margarita opened her eyes and smiled.

'Max, so nice of you to come. And you've brought flowers. Who said all cops are pigs? *Papá*, this is Sub-Inspector Max Romero of the Policía Nacional.'

Faustino Azul stood up and shook Max firmly by the hand.

'I was just about to leave,' he said. 'She's been very, very lucky. One of the poles of the *palio* took the impact. That bloody *fanático*, Francisco Gómez, is to blame. He should be in jail. And she's to drop all this politics nonsense right now, and concentrate on her thesis. You tell her that, officer.'

Max nodded.

133

'And you, *señorita*, will be staying with me once you are discharged. I'm getting a nurse for you.'

Margarita grinned at Max as her father left. 'That's great. Just what I needed. A wet nurse.' She winced as she tried to sit up. 'So now you've met *mi padre*, Faustino Azul. You can see what I have to put up with. Didn't ask if I wanted to stay with him. Just makes his mind up, and that's that.'

'Parents can be like that, and rich guys are usually worse. But how are you, Margarita? Are you sure you're all right?'

'Bloody lucky. I was admitted with concussion, and I'm bruised to hell, but there are no bones broken.'

'So how are you feeling?'

'Sore. The painkillers make me woozy, and my shoulder looks awful. But it was just a simple dislocation, and they've fixed that already. So I'm okay.'

'That's great. So you could manage to answer a few questions, then?'

'So it's Official Business? And here's me thinking it might be something else.'

'Well, it's that also. But I've a report to write. Could you tell me what happened?'

'I don't really know. It started raining, you remember, and the steps were maybe a bit slippery, but we were doing fine.'

'And then?'

'Well . . . suddenly the weight shifted, and the *palio* tilted and collapsed on top of me. I don't remember anything after that.'

'Do you remember mud or leaves on the path?'

'No.'

'Okay. How well do you know Diego and Salvador?'

'The guys behind me? I don't really know them. They were in the team for only a few weeks. I think Maite knew them. We were really glad when they turned up as we were a couple of people short.'

The nurse returned. 'You're looking very tired,' she said to Margarita. 'You should rest now.'

'Okay,' said Max. 'I've got to go. I'm off to see *mi abuela* tomorrow, and then I'm on duty for your bloody demo on Monday.'

'Thanks for coming, Max. Good luck on the demo. Be careful. Some of the anarchists may be planning something stupid. Make sure the cops don't overreact.'

Max took the bus back to Gran Vía, and walked to his flat. He finished his preliminary report for Chávez quickly. There was time for a walk to the end of the Sacromonte road before seeing Abbot Jorge. The recent rain had left the hills beyond the Alhambra a lush green, and the sun shone on the snowy peaks of the Sierra Nevada in the distance. The doves were out in force, circling around the cliffs below the Alhambra. The bars on the Sacromonte road were filling up with tourists, and there was a crowd of kids on bicycles. He thought he recognized Tomasito. Those blond streaks on dark hair were very distinctive.

Below him in the valley the little river Darro sparkled, full of fresh clean water, and the old white houses under the city walls looked newly painted. Max came to the small square where the steep cobbled paths of Barranco de los Negros joined the main Sacromonte road. He could do with a beer. Music poured out of one of the flamenco bars. Fortunately, Kiki's bar with its pretty terrace was open and quiet. And Kiki knew everything about the gypsy clans. Maybe Kiki had some useful gossip on the Maya family.

Max climbed the short incline to the venerable cave, filled with pictures of Sacromonte in the old days, when it was an impoverished village of donkeys and barefoot children, and memorabilia of all the famous names who had performed there.

'Kiki,' he said. 'How are you?'

'Max. *Amigo*. It's been a while . . .'

'I know. Horribly busy, Kiki.'

'*Una cervecita*? Inside or outside?'

'It's sunny. Outside would be nice.'

Max sat on the terrace, looking across the Sacromonte valley to the Alhambra and the city. Strange how you could hardly see the cathedral when you were downtown, but from here it really dominated the city. Kiki brought out the beer and sat opposite Max. Kiki knew everyone and everything. He must have been handsome in his youth, and with his flowing hair and elegant silk jacket he still looked good.

'So what brings you here on a fine Easter Saturday, Max?'

'Looking for fresh air, sunshine and a glass of beer. After that accident last night on San Miguel Alto, I'm shattered.'

'The Virgin of All Beings?'

'*Sí*. That one.'

'Have you heard anything about the girl who was hurt?'

'I've spoken to her. It looks like she's going to be all right.'

'That's good. But then those kids really shouldn't be doing anything outside the official programme. The Archbishop's already said the police should have banned their procession on health and safety grounds.'

'He would.'

'He does have a point, you know. Proper *costaleros* start training six months before Easter. And having half the *costaleros* girls . . . it's asking for trouble.'

'Well . . .'

'Another *cerveza*?' asked Kiki. 'This one's on the house.'

'*Muy amable*, Kiki.'

Max sipped his beer thoughtfully. A small grey lizard flashed along the wall in front of him, and disappeared into a crack.

'Kiki, I was just wondering. I'm trying to clear up a few loose ends on Paco Maya. A heart attack, you know, but when someone's just out of jail we have to take a bit more care. Can you give me some background on the Espinosa and Maya clans?'

'*Sí*, I know both the families. Greek tragedy, the lot of them.'

'So what's the story?'

'That's a long tale. How far back do you want me to go?'

Max laughed. 'I should have known better than to ask a *gitano* about family history. No, just the recent history. It's the rumours and gossip I'm interested in.'

'Well, there's a lot of talent in both families, and a lot of trouble. *Muchos problemas.*'

'*Sí, sí,* I know about Lucía.'

'That was so sad. The girl could have gone far. She really could, but the family were all messed up. Ever since her parents got rehoused to Almanjáyar, there's been trouble. You know there's a rumour that Paco, Mauricio and Gregorio were dealing?'

'No, I didn't know that.'

'Probably just small-time, working for someone higher up the chain. Mostly *cocaína.* I'd heard the drugs were coming up from the coast around Nerja.'

'Go on.'

'Well, apparently Paco and the Espinosa brothers fell out. It's just hearsay. I don't know for certain, but the story was that Paco was skimming the *coca* to sell on the side for himself. Then Paco and Lucía had a fight outside the Echavira club . . . and, well, you know what happened next.'

'That's useful.'

'I've heard Paco hid a packet just before he got picked up after Lucía died. And the brothers want that cocaine back.'

'And the word *Asesino* painted on Paco's cave wall?'

'Just kids, I think. The brothers wouldn't be quite so stupid. They wouldn't want to draw attention to themselves.'

'Do you think they visited Paco before he died?'

'Max, this sounds like someone's thinking it could be murder.'

'Not at this stage but – and this is confidential – Paco once did me a favour when he was inside, and I want to do the right thing by him. And so does Abbot Jorge.'

'All right. This is for Jorge. One of the locals who drinks here says he thought he saw Gregorio and Mauricio drive by last Friday.'

'Really? Would he testify to that?'

'No way. And he's not sure anyway.'

'And Catalina? Would she do anything to harm Paco?'

'Despite everything that happened, no. Paco was family.'

'How about Señora Espinosa?'

'*La abuela*. That woman could bite with her mouth shut.'

'Did she want revenge?'

'*Sí*, and she told everyone. Sounded like a broken record.'

'Her sons?'

'She nagged them to do something. They might have roughed up Paco a bit to keep her quiet, but kill him? I doubt it. They may be a pair of lowlifes, but they're not that dumb, I tell you.'

'*Gracias*, Kiki. Can you think of anything else?'

'Max, I've probably said more than I should anyway. Another beer?'

'No thanks. I've got to see Jorge soon.'

'Remember me to the Abbot. And don't wait so long next time.'

Max continued his walk. Beyond Kiki's bar, the valley broadened out to market gardens and orchards full of blossom. Along the left-hand side of the road, Max could still pick out the remains of the processional crosses which once marked the route to the abbey of Sacromonte in its days of glory when pilgrims came in thousands to wonder at its relics and honour San Cecilio.

The tarmac road finally gave way to a dirt track that crossed Paco's land on the way to the monastery of Jesús del Valle. Despite the rain, the hills on the left were still dusty, dotted with prickly pear cactus and clumps of grey-green agave lifting up their great poles of desert flowers. But on the right, the Alhambra side, which caught the rains, the trees glowed with new green leaves.

Max stopped at the track leading up to Paco's cave. He walked to a large flat rock straddling a small stream, now running with water. At the foot of the rock, stuck in mud and reeds, was a torn page. He fished it out and examined it carefully. It looked like a child's comic. The date was indecipherable. Max carefully stowed it in the inside pocket of his walking jacket.

It was time to set off back towards the Abadía. At the small bridge, Puente Maríano, he climbed the steep steps that wound their way up to the abbey, sitting atop the hill of Valparaíso. Max pulled the string on the ancient bell at the large carved chestnut door.

'Max, *amigo*. Just in time for a drink of something good,' said Abbot Jorge as he hauled the door open.

'I need more than one,' Max replied.

'Let's go to my study. I've still got a couple of bottles of Cartojal left.'

They went up to Jorge's private study, the Abbot's rough sandals slapping on the stone floor. The walls were lined with books. There was a simple crucifix on his desk, a nineteenth-century lithograph of the Abadía, and an eighteenth-century painting of *El Cristo de los Gitanos* on the walls. Max looked through the books while the Abbot uncorked a dusty bottle of the fine Málaga wine.

'Two shelves on the Lead Books of Sacromonte. I never thought there'd be so much interest in them.'

'Stands to reason, Max. Anything claiming to be such an early Christian text which emphasizes that the Arabs are beloved of God is bound to be hot stuff these days.'

'So you think there's more to come out about them?'

'Somebody should write a thriller about them. It's an amazing story.'

'I'm sure somebody will.' Max sniffed his wine. 'This is really good.'

The Abbot put his glass down carefully on the small side table. 'You have the look of someone who needs to tell me something. The accident at the Procession of the Virgin of All Beings?'

'How'd you guess?'

'My job. So what happened?'

Max explained about the accident, but didn't go into details about his relationship with Margarita.

'I see,' said Jorge. 'So the girl's going to be all right. That's good. She could have died.'

'She was very fortunate.'

'So you think those two guys might have deliberately let the *palio* go?'

'I'm not sure, Jorge.'

'My view is that it was an accident. The *costaleros* simply didn't have the training and couldn't cope with the bad weather. And they should never have taken that route anyway.'

'I tried to stop it, you know.'

'I know, Max, and it's not your fault. It was an accident and no one was badly hurt. Just let it go.'

'I feel responsible . . .'

'You're bound to. But believe me, it's not your fault. A little more *vino*?'

'Please.'

'Right, where have you got to with poor Paco?'

Max gave a brief summary.

'So that's how it is,' said Jorge. 'Remember: don't let *la policía* sweep him under the carpet just because he's a poor *gitano*.'

'I won't, Jorge. And neither will the new judge. But there was something you wanted to talk to me about?'

The Abbot frowned. 'This is just between you and me.'

'*Venga*, Jorge. It's me you're talking to.'

'You know Jesús del Valle, don't you?'

'Like the back of my hand.'

'*Vale*. The Church owns it, but the Abadía is responsible for managing it and getting rents if possible. Anyway, the whole lot fell into ruins and we did nothing about it. I don't know why, but it doesn't really matter now.'

'I was there last week. It's falling down.'

'A while ago the Archbishop came to see me. A businessman had made an offer for the monastery buildings and its lands.'

'Do you know who?'

'The Archbishop wouldn't say. The businessman wants to remain anonymous. But it's a very good deal for the Church. He's offered to give a large sum of money to a *cofradía* to help it repair the back buildings of the Abadía.'

'You mean the buildings which were a school before the fire?'

'Those.'

'And the *cofradía* is?'

'The Archbishop wouldn't say. But in order to sell, the Archbishop needed my signature and the seal of the Abadía.'

'I see. So you agreed?'

'*Sí*. I've been waiting for years to get those buildings repaired.'

'So what's your problem, Jorge? It's common knowledge that the monastery has been sold. It's all over the press. And you've had a really generous offer.'

'*Sí*. But something's not right. A surprising number of my parishioners have sold up and are moving out. Some of them have said that the person who wanted to buy was pretty insistent. And now we have an unknown buyer of the monastery, and an unnamed *cofradía*. It smells, Max.'

'But of what? Nothing illegal's been done. And you can hardly be suspicious about a *cofradía* offering to help the Abadia. The most you can say is it's a bit odd that they are so publicity-shy. Most *cofradías* would want their name in lights over a project like this. But if one doesn't want to . . .'

'Beware of Greeks bearing gifts. Beware of Archbishops bearing gifts. No, something's not right. And Max, I want you to find out what that is.'

'Come on, I'm not a miracle worker!'

'But you're a cop. You have contacts. Just ask around for me, will you?'

'Jorge, I'm up to my eyes at the moment . . . Okay, seeing as it's you, I'll find out what I can. Though I'm sure everything's above board.'

'But if it isn't?'

Chapter 18

'Señorita Azul is asleep,' the nurse said when Max phoned the hospital. '*Sí*, her progress is satisfactory.' Max felt less anxious. He could now enjoy the Easter Sunday family lunch. Should he tell Paula about Margarita? No. Much too soon.

At 2 p.m. he drove through Diva, and on to the Jola road and past the bridge. The car crunched down the drive of the big old family home in its mountain valley. Tiny fruits were already forming on the fig tree by the gate, and the peach tree was in blossom. Paula hobbled out as soon as she heard the car. Her face was streaked with tears.

'*Abuela*.'

'Max,' she said, and burst into tears again.

Max put his arms around his grandmother. '*Abuela*, it's all right.'

'I'll tell you about it when it's just us. Isabel's inside.'

In the kitchen of the old farmhouse, Isabel was checking a large roast of meat.

'That smells good,' said Max. 'What is it?'

'Roast lamb from the Englishman's farm, garlic, white wine and fresh thyme. New broad beans and *serrano* ham in cream to go with it. Then for *postre* it's *crema Catalán* with strawberries. Nita's made some biscuits to go with the dessert. You are honoured. Señorita Encarnita doesn't bake for just anyone, you know.'

Max picked up a tray of glasses, and Paula led him outside where the table was laid.

'So what happened, *abuela*?'

She sat down, her face crinkled, her body sagging with the exhaustion of old age.

'It's so *típicamente español*,' she said. 'They raise your hopes only to dash them again. You know the Alcalde agreed we could excavate the *fosa común*.'

'Yes. I thought that was all agreed.'

'*Sí*. He's an old man and even though he was with Franco, he understood. And he was a friend of my Pedro, so he probably agreed out of respect, you know . . .'

She started crying again. 'I thought I was there. I thought we could dig. I just know Antonio's bones are there. And we could hold a dignified ceremony, and let him rest in peace. I want to do that before I die.'

'You shall, *abuela*. You shall.'

'Not now.' And the tears rolled down the furrows of her cheeks. 'A bunch of men who call themselves judges have said that all excavation of burial places of the Civil War dead is to be put on hold. You know what that means. It could be for ever. And I don't have long.'

'Are you sure?'

'*Sí*. The Alcalde phoned me this morning to say he couldn't go against the judges' ruling, and he's postponed his permission to dig.'

'*Ay*, *abuela*. I'm so sorry.'

'And that idiot Juan had the gall to say he agreed with the judges. "Let sleeping dogs lie," he said. He can be so like his grandfather.'

The children arrived, boisterous and loud. '*Tío* Max.'

Max lifted Encarnita into the air, holding her aloft. 'My, my, you're getting heavy. I won't be able to do this for much longer.'

'*Hola*, *Tío* Max,' said Leonardo. 'Your team's rubbish. Seville'll hammer Celtic in the Final.'

'Oh no they won't,' said Max. 'Tell you what, Leonardo. I'll see if I can get us tickets for the Cup Final.'

'Could you really?' said Leonardo, beaming.

Juan emerged from the wine cellar, nursing two precious bottles.

'Juan, would you like to go to the Seville–Celtic match?'

'I can't go without Leo. He'd be so upset.'

Leonardo gave his father a manly hug. '*Tío* Max says he can get all three of us tickets.'

'That would be great. I think this calls for this season's Seville strip,' said Juan.

'Seville will give Celtic a tanking, won't they, *papá*?'

And all three started shouting about the respective merits of the best individual player, and who would win. Paula sat there, a tired smile on her face.

'*Hombres*, men have such a capacity for the trivial,' she said to Isabel.

'Don't they just. That's enough, come on everyone. Let's eat.'

They all sat down at the table. The lamb was wonderful. Meltingly tender meat, crisp, caramelized skin and fat. Paula cheered up a bit after the second bottle of wine.

'I'll show you the photos of Juan in the Brotherhood of the Bell procession after lunch,' said Isabel. 'He looks so distinguished. Paula didn't approve, but I told her there's no harm in it now.'

'Pah. *Cofradías*. Your grandfather was in at least three. Just an excuse for men to drink and gossip. But I still don't trust them.'

'What's it like being part of the Brotherhood then?' asked Max.

'It's going to be very useful,' said Juan. 'I've already made an excellent investment. A tourism project, just outside Granada.'

'So where is it?'

'Early days yet, so I'd rather not say.'

'Hmm,' said Max.

The strawberries were delicious, and the *crema Catalàn* was fabulous – the very soul of cream and caramel. But

Encarnita's tiny pine-nut and cinnamon biscuits stole the show, as was right and proper.

Isabel finally stood up from the table. 'I'll make some coffee. And I'll get those photos.'

She returned with a tray of coffee and a pile of photos. 'Here they are, Max. Who'd ever have thought we'd see Juan as a penitent?'

'Not me. Though he sure has a lot to be penitent about.'

Max looked at the photos. There was a good one of Juan standing proudly with a big cheesy grin on his face. And here was Juan trying to look serious. Behind him were three men, their faces lit by the flickering flames of the candles. Max peered at the photo. The young man in a dark suit looked remarkably like one of the Black Angel Anarchists from the conference, David Costa. The guy in the priest's cloak was definitely Monsignor Bien. And the third man, the one in the hood, holding the silver mace of El Capataz, was the Don Faustino Juan had annoyed. Why on earth was David Costa, a Black Angel Anarchist, talking to those two?

'Can I keep this photo for a while?' asked Max.

Isabel looked over his shoulder. 'That one? Yes. Keep it. It's not a good one of Juan. And I got those men by mistake. I'll email you a copy if you like.'

'That would be good.'

Max finished his coffee and looked at his watch.

'*Vale,*' said Max. 'Ladies, that was a wonderful meal. And the biscuits, Encarnita, were the best I've ever had.'

Encarnita glowed pink with pleasure, almost as pink as her dress.

'Max, did you speak to Anita?'

'I did, *abuela*. It's finished. We're both sad, but it's all right. She's put in for a transfer. We'll talk about it another time.'

He kissed Paula and Isabel goodbye. Leonardo walked to the car.

'*Tío* Max, you won't forget those tickets for the Seville game, will you?'

'You know, Leo, some people think that football is a matter of life and death. But me, I know it's more serious than that.'

Chapter 19

On Monday morning, Max phoned Margarita's hospital from work.

'*Hola, guapa*. How are you feeling today?'

'A lot better, Max, but they won't let me out yet. It's a pain. They're doing further tests. And I've got to have more X-rays.'

'Nothing serious, I hope.'

'I don't think so. I feel okay, actually, but my father is plaguing the specialists to get everything checked that could be checked. They'll be testing me for leprosy next.'

'Could be worse.'

'I just want to go home, but Don Faustino is still insisting that I stay with him for a couple of days when I finally get out.'

'Well . . .'

'I suppose I ought to go and spend a bit of time with Blanca.'

'Who?'

'Sorry. She's my stepmother. I like her, and she's having problems with my dad.'

'*Vale*. I've got to go to a meeting. It's the final instructions before the demo. I'll try to get over this evening.'

'That would be great. Could you bring me a decent book? My flatmates left me a load of chick lit, and I'm bored already.'

'No problem. I'll see you tonight if all goes well.'

Max hurried to the briefing meeting. Twenty minutes later, Bonila concluded: 'Remember. Stay calm and be restrained. Comisario Chávez is managing the demo from our side. I'm staying here to deal with the media and the politicians. Good luck, men.'

Max, Pedro and the other cops filed out of the building into the waiting police bus. Nobody spoke. A few gripped their batons tightly.

Pedro muttered, 'I've got a bad feeling about this, Max.'

'Me too.'

The bus parked discreetly in a side street close to Plaza Nueva, near the statue of Christopher Columbus kneeling at the feet of Queen Isabel la Católica.

In Plaza Nueva, demonstrators were already assembling, fitting banners to poles, and the vendors for the radical papers were out in force. Chávez had been there for a while.

'Ah, Max. I got your report on the accident. Useful. So you have doubts as to whether it was a genuine accident or not.'

'I do, sir.'

'Right. If you have time, look into it a little more, but discreetly. Keep it away from Bonila. Faustino Azul's convinced him it was an accident, and he doesn't want any more publicity. And Azul is a friend of the Alcalde, the Archbishop, and everyone who matters in this town.'

'I understand, sir.'

'How's the girl?'

'I visited her in the hospital on Saturday, and phoned this morning.'

Chávez raised an eyebrow.

'She's recovering fine, but will be in hospital for a while yet.'

'All right, Max. It could have been much worse. The press coverage has been sympathetic so far. No one is saying we should have stopped the procession.'

'That's good.'

'But the leader writers are having a real go at the radical Catholics. Archbishop Doria's making capital out of the whole thing, and those two priests will get a kicking.'

'That doesn't surprise me.'

'Me neither. Okay, Max. Keep an eye on the guys you picked out at the conference.'

'I'll do my best. But I don't know where they'll be or what they're planning.'

'I appreciate that. All we can do is be watchful. But that tip from your source about the Regional Council building could be useful. If there are problems, we now reckon it will be around there.'

The square was filling up, but numbers were smaller than the police had expected. Gangs of youths in balaclavas were milling around the fountain of Plaza Nueva. There were red flags, black flags, a few green flags, posters tacked to wooden poles . . . 'Stop the Speculators Now', 'Stop the Destruction of Granada', 'Free Palestine', 'Stop the Destruction of Jesús del Valle', 'Women Against War in Iraq', 'End the Evictions'.

To a loud cheer, the demo marched off with a flurry of banners and a cacophony of sounds: whistles, drums, chants and yells. The Black Angels marched as a group, all in black with kerchiefs round their faces.

Suddenly, at the junction of Gran Vía and Calle Reyes Católicos, the back end of the demo peeled off. A bunch of young guys raced down Reyes Católicos, then swerved right towards Plaza Bib-ba-Rambla.

Max dashed after them. Still running, he phoned Chávez. 'Sir. They're heading for the cathedral.'

'*Mierda*. There's still a load of them heading for the Regional Council offices. And there's a gang breaking windows at Plaza Einstein. I'll have to stay here, but I'll send Navarro and some other men over.'

Max and Pedro ran into Plaza Pasiegas, in front of the cathedral. It suddenly filled up with demonstrators. There was only a small group of cops from the Guardia Civil guarding the main cathedral entrance.

'You must all disperse now. You have no permission to be in front of the cathedral,' yelled the *capitán* in charge of the Guardia Civil.

'*La catedral*. Storm the cathedral,' came the reply.

Two elderly priests slowly hauled the huge cathedral doors shut. Then Francisco appeared at the top of the cathedral steps, loudspeaker in hand, his eyes shining with excitement.

'We will occupy the cathedral until the Archbishop agrees to stop the sale of Jesús del Valle. No violence! *No violencia!*' he yelled into his loudspeaker. 'But we will occupy the cathedral. Our companions inside will open the doors.'

'Take over the cathedral,' the crowd yelled. '*Ocupamos la catedral.*'

And to a loud cheer, a green banner unfurled from a window in the cathedral tower: 'STOP THE SPECULATORS NOW!'

A detachment of riot police marched in and positioned themselves in front of the cathedral, their shields up and their long batons clutched tightly. General López of the Guardia Civil arrived and took the loudspeaker from his *capitán*.

'Nobody is allowed to enter the cathedral,' shouted López. 'Disperse, and return to the agreed route.'

'We will occupy,' the crowd roared.

López continued, 'You have no permission to be here. We will not allow you to enter the cathedral. Disperse immediately or face the consequences.'

'*Ocupamos. Ocupamos,*' yelled the crowd.

Max noticed that the ultra left groups had moved to the back of the demonstration, and were pushing the crowd forward, ever closer to the riot police.

'*Mierda*. Pedro, this could get out of hand. I'm going to speak to General López.'

To a loud cheer from the crowd, the doors of the cathedral swung open: groups at the back were still pushing forward. Max reached General López just as Davila arrived, panting.

'Sir,' said Max, 'we must –'

But Davila interrupted. 'General, I have a warrant here to arrest Gómez for questioning on suspicion of murder.'

'Good work, Enrique.' López did not seem surprised by this development.

'Señor General, that might provoke a riot,' said Max.

Davila gave Max a withering look, but López listened.

'All right. We'll wait a little longer to see what the Alcalde advises. If he agrees, we wade in.'

Teniente Grandes appeared at López's elbow. 'The Alcalde's given us the green light. Do whatever's needed.'

Squads of police began to block the side streets. Max caught a glimpse of two youths, their faces hidden by ski masks, edging forward. They stopped right behind Francisco, took rocks out of their rucksacks, and hurled them at General López. The General signalled to the riot police to attack.

'Snatch Francisco Gómez,' he yelled.

The riot police surged down the steps, swinging their batons viciously to beat a path towards Francisco. There were screams, shouts, cries for help.

Max pushed after them. He spotted Carlos and Maite in the crowd.

'Carlos,' he yelled. 'Go and tell Francisco to get the fuck out of here. The cops are going to snatch him.'

Carlos signalled to Max that he'd heard, and he and Maite began to push their way towards Francisco ahead of the riot police.

'Francisco, Francisco. The cops are after you. Get out.'

Maite took out her mobile and began snapping photos. The cops reached Carlos, and one lashed out at him. He fell heavily to the ground. Maite bent over Carlos and screamed, '*Ayúdame*. He's hurt.' Then she picked up his mobile.

151

Francisco turned to retreat, but someone pushed him and he tripped and fell. Baton-wielding police surged forward, knocking those around Francisco to the ground. They grabbed him before he had time to get up, and dragged him to a side street where a police van waited.

A roar of anger arose from the crowd.

'The cops have snatched Francisco,' they yelled. 'Get the cops.'

A Molotov cocktail hit the cathedral doors. It burst into flames. The mounted police edged forward from the side streets. But the crowd was so dense and penned in that they could hardly advance. A Black Angel threw down ball bearings, causing one of the horses to skid to the ground, pinning its rider underneath it. Demonstrators kicked the fallen cop.

Ambulance sirens screeched. Paramedics arrived, trying to reach the wounded.

Max heard Maite still screaming for help. He called out to a paramedic, 'Go and help that man over there.'

Max pushed his way towards Pedro. 'Help me get to General López. He must open the side streets to let the crowd disperse or there will be even more serious injuries.'

Pedro joined Max and together they shoved through the crowd towards General López. They had almost reached him when Comisario Felipe Chávez finally appeared on the top of the cathedral steps. He took one look at the disaster.

'Right, López,' said Chávez. 'We have to disperse this crowd immediately. Most of them just want out. Then we can lift the hard core.'

Chávez gave the order for the police to withdraw from the side streets. The plaza began to empty as people swarmed away.

But from inside the cathedral came shouts. 'Get inside the cathedral. Occupy. Occupy.'

There was a sudden surge forward.

'Fire the tear gas,' yelled Chávez. 'Max. Pedro. Grab that lot in the cathedral and get the doors shut.'

152

Max ran into the cathedral, followed by a bunch of cops. They lashed out with their batons at the young men trying to hold the doors open. Max and another cop slowly hauled the doors shut. Other cops chased the demonstrators along the aisles. One demonstrator stumbled and fell at the feet of the statue of the Virgin of Santa María de la Encarnación. Two cops pounded him as the Virgin looked benignly down. Max ran forwards.

'Stop it!' he yelled. 'Can't you see the kid's out cold already? You'll be up on an assault charge if you're not careful.'

One of the cops turned. It was Inspector Navarro.

'Oh. It's you, Max. Just defending ourselves.'

A camera flashed. Navarro turned, baton ready.

'Don't,' yelled Max. 'She's a tourist.'

Navarro swore, but walked away. Max bent over the unconscious kid, whose dark curly hair was clotted with blood. 'Oh Christ,' he said, and phoned for medical help. Max stood up and looked around the cathedral. There was a knot of hysterical tourists in one corner.

Back outside, tear gas filled Plaza de las Pasiegas and Plaza de Alonso Cano. The ultras, with wet kerchiefs around their faces, were still flinging missiles at the police.

'The cathedral's secure,' Max reported to Chávez.

'Good,' said Chávez. He turned to the riot squad. 'Use the water cannon to knock the last ones over, and arrest as many as you can.'

Eventually all was quiet apart from the complaints of startled birds. There were pools of blood on the cathedral steps. An upturned pushchair lay abandoned. Scarves, kerchiefs, broken cameras, torn banners, banner poles, rocks, stones and ball bearings were scattered all over the plaza. As the last of the protestors were being bundled into police vans, Felipe Chávez stood on the cathedral steps and surveyed the scene of devastation.

'Max,' he said, 'twenty-five years in the force, and that's the worst bloody riot I've had to deal with. What the hell went wrong?'

Chapter 20

It was 5 p.m. when Max got back to his calm, quiet flat. The answerphone light flashed. The message inbox was full. Everyone needed him to phone as soon as possible. Urgently.

The tear gas had affected his stomach. He felt sick and its acrid taste lingered in his mouth. His eyes burnt and the bloody gas had barely touched him. Max stood under the shower for ten minutes, letting the cool water run over his eyes and lips, then cleaned his teeth vigorously. He stood on his terrace for a minute, letting the peace of the Albayzín and the fragrance of its gardens sink in, then started to work through the list of calls. He phoned Maite first.

'Maite, it's Max Romero. Any news on Carlos?'

'It's not good. He's in intensive care. And he still hasn't regained consciousness.'

'God, that's terrible.'

Maite started crying. 'Sorry, Max. I have to go now. I'll be in touch.'

Max then called Paula. Juan answered the phone.

'Ah, Juan, it's you. Yes, I'm okay. Yes, we arrested a lot of them . . . Juan, before we get into a long argument about the good old days when everyone respected law and order or else you got shot, I have to go now. It's been one hell of a day, and I've got a lot of people to call. Just reassure Paula I really am okay, but I'm going out so tell her not to keep calling me.'

Then he phoned Margarita. She was in tears. 'There's a report on the radio. Carlos is in hospital. And Francisco's been arrested. I have to see you. Can you come this evening?'

'I'm on my way, Margarita. Be with you in half an hour.'

Max put Isabel's photo in his pocket, and grabbed a cab.

Margarita was sitting in an armchair by her bed, her face still streaked with tears. Max squeezed her hand as she sobbed.

'Will Carlos be okay?'

'I don't know; it's too early to tell. But he's a strong, healthy guy.'

'Why did it have to be Carlos? He's such a kind, decent man. What happened?'

'Some guys behind Francisco started flinging rocks at the Guardia Civil. Then the cops snatched Francisco and it all went to hell. I don't know exactly what happened to Carlos. He was near Francisco – everyone started pushing and shoving, and Carlos must have fallen.'

'*Ay díos.*'

'I sent a paramedic over to him, so they got him to hospital really quickly.'

'Thanks. But Francisco?'

'My boss turned up with an arrest warrant.'

'But that's crazy. You can't arrest someone just for organizing a demo. Francisco would have been a calming influence. How stupid can you get?'

Max decided not to mention the murder issue.

'But, oh Max. Your eyes are all red.'

'I got a dose of tear gas, I'm afraid. It's okay – they'll calm down in a couple of hours.'

'And you look so tired. Can I order you some coffee?'

'*Por favor.* It's been a bad day.'

A Bolivian girl brought in two coffees, and left quietly.

Margarita sipped her coffee. 'Now I'm really worried about Francisco as well as Carlos.'

'Don't worry. There's no need. I'll find out what

happened. Now, I know it's not the best of times, but would you mind looking at a photo I've brought with me?'

'That's all right, Max.'

Max handed over the photo Isabel had taken by mistake. Margarita peered at it.

'I could swear that's David Costa. You remember, the guy who proposed the amendment against non-violence at the conference. The priest I don't know. But the man with the silver mace, that's my dad.'

'Are you sure?'

'*Sí*, I'm sure. He's El Capataz of the Brotherhood of the Bell. Can't see his face because of the pointy hood, but that's him.'

'But what's he doing with David Costa?'

'I don't know.'

'Costa's a Black Angel, isn't he?'

'*Sí*. Not the sort of guy I'd expect my father to know.'

'Any ideas?'

Margarita frowned in thought. 'Francisco did warn us that we'd be infiltrated once we began to make an impact. That we were taking on powerful interests. Could David Costa be . . .?'

'I don't know. What do you know about him?'

'Not much. But Maite knows Alejandro.'

'Alejandro?'

'You remember, the guy who summed up the amendment against non-violence. He's her cousin.'

'It was a good speech.'

'It was. Alejandro will know David Costa. He'll help. He's a decent lad really. He went from being a good Catholic boy to a revolutionary the minute he got to university.'

'It happens.'

'You'd best ask Maite. Could you just pass my mobile over?' She winced as she tried to stretch over the table. Her arm and shoulder were a mass of bruises.

'It's okay. I've got her number. Any more ideas on those two guys on your *palio*?'

156

'You don't think . . .? My dad said it had been thoroughly checked out and it was an accident.'

'I thought I'd just check it again.'

'I see. You'd better speak to Maite. She knows everyone.'

'So how are you?' said Max, trying to suppress a yawn.

'I get nasty headaches and they're still checking for internal damage. But so far so good. And I want to go home, but I'm running a temperature so I have to stay here a bit longer.'

'You're lucky. It could have been so much worse.'

'Max, you really look exhausted.'

'No, I'm fine. I'm just tired. I feel better now that I've seen you.'

Margarita smiled. 'Me too, Max. So, what book did you bring me?'

'Oh no – with all this bloody demo stuff, I forgot all about it. Sorry. I'll bring something next time.'

'Any chance of a hug? Not too hard.'

He leaned over and kissed her gently. She kissed him back. The fragrance of her perfume almost disguised the smell of hospital.

'Max, you have to go. Get some sleep before you fall over. Ring me tomorrow.'

Max took a cab back to his flat. He was tired, really tired. But he needed to eat. He had a bowl of breakfast cereal, crawled into his warm and cosy bed, and tried to sleep. But he was restless: images of blood on the cathedral steps, an upturned child's pushchair at the bottom of the steps, tear gas and water cannon filling the plaza, Margarita lying pale and still under the *palio*, a youth beaten in front of the statue of the Virgin. And Margarita, naked apart from the Virgin's robe. In a jumbled fashion these images ran in and out of his mind as he tossed and turned.

Then sleep, a deep sleep, finally came.

Chapter 21

Max woke up quite abruptly next morning. He switched on the local radio. There was a report on the riot – the Alcalde was promising a fair and through investigation.

He phoned Margarita. She was worried about Carlos and Francisco, but otherwise fine. The pain from the bruising was less, and her temperature had gone down slightly, so with luck she'd be out soon.

Max hurried to his office and checked his emails. Chávez wanted to see him as soon as he got in.

'You've read the papers today?'

'I haven't had a chance, sir.'

'It could be worse. The media are saying the police had no choice but to defend themselves. But the opposition parties insist that the Alcalde appoint a Committee of Investigation into the riot. Bonila can pull a few strings, so the committee should be reasonably sympathetic.'

'I'm sure it will be.'

'Okay, but this is not to go outside these four walls.'

'It won't.'

'What do you think really happened yesterday?'

'Well, some of the demonstrators clearly wanted a punch-up.'

'And?'

'In my opinion, sir, it was a bit too much of a coincidence that the guys who started chucking stones at the cops had worked their way round to be just behind Gómez.'

'I get the picture.'

'And then General López ordered the police to charge as soon as the first rock landed.'

'I see. Anything else?'

'Well, arresting Gómez in the middle of a demo just inflamed things even further.'

'Not my idea, Max. Davila's sticking to his guns on that one, and he won't lose any friends over it.'

'I see, sir. Any word on a Carlos Ramos?'

'So you know him?'

'He's in my walking group. A really good guy.'

'I'm sorry about him. The last I heard is that he's still in intensive care. Bashed his head when he fell. And what makes matters worse for us, he's a bloody architect. Thorn in the Alcalde's side, you know, but very widely respected.'

'Can you keep me informed if you hear any more on him?'

'Will do. We'll be in trouble over him. Francisco Gómez less so.'

'If I may say so, sir, I think the case against Gómez is quite weak.'

'Let's wait and see. There's also this awkward matter with Navarro. The tourist who took those photos is a German woman, a professor of Spanish Literature in Berlin. She speaks fluent Spanish, so we can't claim there was a misunderstanding. Navarro admits he overreacted, but claims the kid had thrown a stone at him. Is that true?'

'I didn't personally see him throw a stone.'

'Hmm. I'm inclined to let Navarro dangle from the rope on this one. But Bonila won't hear of it. All for one and one for all. Still too much of that shit in the force.'

'*Sí*, sir.'

'Keep this conversation just between us, Max. If you can find out anything on the guys who threw the first rocks, let me know. Right. I'm off to another meeting.' Chávez scooped up the papers from his desk and put them in a folder. 'See you later. Keep me posted.'

159

By the time Max got back to his own office, the telephone was ringing. It was Davila. The great man needed to see him.

'Ah, Max. Come in. Bad business, that demo. What a bunch of thugs. But at least we managed to sort them out.'

'If you say so, sir.'

'Come on, we had no choice but to defend ourselves. I'm sorry about the injuries, especially to our guys. But look on the bright side. We've got that bugger Gómez in the cells for a bit.'

'Can I speak to him?'

'No. From my reading of the situation, you're already too close to the suspect. I'm leaving that to Navarro and Belén.'

'But –'

'Max, I've made up my mind on this. It's for your own good. Trust me.'

'Very well, sir. Has he said anything?'

'No. Swears blind he can account for his movements for all but the last ten minutes. But give us time and we'll get him to talk. You know Gómez and Maya's sister were once married?'

'But that doesn't make him guilty of murder.'

'Not yet. But he lied about this. He knew Paco Maya. And he lied.'

'To protect Catalina Maya?'

'But why would he do that? When I interviewed her, she proved she was in hospital on the day of Paco Maya's death. She has a perfect alibi. No, that makes no sense. And if he lied about that, who knows what else he's lying about.'

'But he has no motive.'

'Yes. That's still a problem. But once we have a motive, we can keep him in longer. He'll break eventually. They always do. Navarro and Belén are with him right now. Gómez was after something in that cave. And he killed for it.'

Max went back to his office with a heavy heart. Davila had made his up mind already. Max sat quietly for a few moments, gazing out of the window and thinking. He was just about to go down to the canteen to get some toast and a glass of orange juice when the phone rang.

'Sub-Inspector Max Romero? It's Catalina. Catalina Maya. We talked at the conference, remember?'

'Catalina. Of course I remember. What can I do for you?'

'It's about Francisco and my brother Paco. I have to talk to you privately.'

'Certainly. Where?'

'I'm at the Hotel Santa Paula on Gran Vía. There are some seats in the old cloister, and there's no one else around at the moment. We could talk here.'

'I'll be over straight away.'

Max hurried out of the office, walked up to Gran Vía and into the Santa Paula. He went down the stairs to the cloister, now comfortable with polished wood and leather sofas. Catalina was sitting in a corner overlooking the courtyard where the nuns of the convent had been buried. Now a fountain sparkled there, and a palm tree cast a pleasant shade. Max went over to join her. She looked tired and worried.

'Thanks for coming so quickly.'

'How's your leg?'

'Oh, a lot better. *Gracias.*'

'What can I do for you?'

'It's Francisco. He phoned me from the police station to say he's been arrested on suspicion of murder.'

'*Sí*, he's being held for questioning.'

'But he didn't do it.' She paused and wiped her eyes. 'I suppose I have to tell you the full story. Unfortunately, the truth's rather complicated.'

'But it would be a good place to start. Have you already spoken to anyone in the police?'

'*Sí.* An Inspector Jefe Davila came round yesterday.'

'What exactly did you say?'

'Just that Francisco and I were married, briefly. Francisco was very kind when I had to get away from Mauricio Espinosa, you know.'

161

'And?'

'That when Paco died, I was in hospital . . . which I was.'

'So did Francisco know Paco?'

'Not really. Paco was in jail when we got married. Things were very difficult with Lucía's family.'

'I can imagine.'

'Anyway, Francisco and I split up a couple of years later. But we're still close friends. He's that sort of guy.'

'And?'

'Paco phoned me the evening he got let out. Mauricio and Gregorio had been round. He was really scared.'

'What had happened?'

'Two things. One was that the brothers were pressuring him to sell his property.'

'Do you know to whom?'

'No.'

'And the other thing?'

Catalina paused, embarrassed. 'A missing packet of cocaine. It wasn't much, but Paco thought of it as a savings account.'

Max raised an eyebrow.

'Well, Paco managed to stall them. He said that he'd hidden it somewhere near Jaén, and the owner of the *cortijo* didn't know about the package, so he'd need some time to sort it. They said they'd be back. And he'd better have got it sorted. So Paco phoned me in a panic. And I went to see him as soon as I finished work.'

'You never told me this.'

'No. The cocaine thing is bad news for Francisco.'

'It is.'

'Anyway, Paco swore blind that the cocaine had been his legitimate share the last time he did business with them, so he didn't want to give it back. He didn't want to flush it down the toilet, and didn't want to hand it over to the cops either. You know, apart from his land, it was the only asset he had. So I said I would look after it for him for a bit, which was probably a silly thing to do . . .'

162

'Not a good idea at all.'

'Yes, but it calmed him down and gave us chance to start thinking things through.'

'So where is it now?'

'In a safe place. And I'm going to get rid of it as soon as I can now.'

'That's good. But didn't you think that the Espinosa brothers would come straight after you?'

'Not likely. They didn't know my brother and I were still in contact. And if they had, I would have just handed it over nice as you like, and then shopped them to the cops.'

'I see.'

'There's another thing. Paco wanted to stay on his land for as long as he could. And he knew he probably hadn't long to live.'

'Go on.'

'So Francisco and I came up with a plan. Paco would transfer his land to me, to be held in trust for Angelita until she was eighteen.'

'Clever.'

'*Sí.* That would put the brakes on any development of the land for at least the next ten years. Then we could sell to a buyer who was interested in conservation, and the money would go straight to Angelita without the Espinosas getting their nasty hands on it.'

'So what did you do?'

'The three of us went to a lawyer the day after Paco was released, got the will sorted out, and drafted the Deed of Gift.'

'And Paco died before the Deed of Gift could be concluded?'

'*Sí.*'

'So what happened to Paco?'

'Paco didn't quite get the details of the land deal. Francisco and I were going round on Friday lunchtime to reassure him about it. Then some idiot knocked me off my moped. Francisco got there on his own and found Paco on the floor

163

of his cave. Francisco tried first aid, then realized he was already dead. And then you and your friend turned up, and he panicked.'

'And you were?'

'I was on my way there when I came off my moped, like I said, and ended up in hospital. Even when I came round, there's no phone reception in the valley, so there was no way could I reach him.'

'That's unfortunate. Can you tell me anything about the red purse which was in Francisco's pocket?'

'Red purse? It's mine. I left it behind when I saw Paco the first time. I was glad to get it back. It's the only photo of Angelita I have, and it's one Lucía took.'

'But Francisco said it was his.'

'Yes, he knew it was mine. He thought I'd been to see Paco earlier that day, and might have quarrelled. So he tried to protect me, pretending that the purse was his and that he didn't know Paco.'

'Not very sensible.'

'Yes, but he doesn't trust the cops. He gets harassed a lot.'

'Do you have any idea why Francisco would look in Paco's wooden box when he knew the title deeds were with the lawyer?'

'I don't know. He might have been looking to see if Paco had left a note cancelling the property transfer. It was only a draft at that stage.'

'Catalina, can I ask you something? Why, given all that's happened between you and your brother, were you prepared to trust each other?'

'You'd understand if you'd known Paco. He did a terrible thing, but it was *la droga, la cocaína*. It makes you paranoid . . . impulsive . . . *estúpido*. Nothing's going to bring Lucía back, but he's my brother, and he has a daughter, and he wanted to do the right thing for Angelita, and protect the valley if he could.'

'You do realize that we have a serious problem.'

'Of course.'

164

'Everything you've said could make things worse for Francisco.'

'I understand. But Francisco definitely didn't kill Paco. I'd stake my life on that.'

'Look, Catalina, I'm prepared to believe you, but I'm not sure my colleagues will.'

'So what can we do?'

'First thing, get rid of that cocaine. Flush it down the toilet. It won't do Francisco any good if anyone thinks there's a drug link. Beyond that I'm not sure. The will really complicates things, you know.'

A mobile rang in Catalina's bag. She took it out.

'*Vale*. I'm on my way. Okay. Thanks, Inspector. I have to go. I should have been at work an hour ago.'

As she limped towards the door, Max wandered into the courtyard. There were gravestones of nuns from the former convent set into the ancient patio. 'Here lies the body of Sister María Elisa de los Dolores González. She entered this convent at the age of 4 years. She suffered a serious illness with great patience and resignation, passing to a better life at the age of 24 years, on the first of September 1887 R.I.P.'

And now this convent was a luxury hotel. So very typical of Granada.

Chapter 22

Max walked out of the Hotel Santa Paula and turned right, and right again into the maze of quiet back streets which still traced the lanes and alleys of the ancient Moorish city. Back in his office he turned on his computer, hoping for inspiration. None came. He glanced at the Dali picture on his calendar: *The Disintegration of the Persistence of Memory*. In art, as in life, nothing is ever as it seems. Max turned his notepad to a fresh sheet of paper.

Gómez, the Mayas and the Espinosas were all connected. Were they connected to anyone else? Max wrote a list of names.

- Francisco Gómez – prime suspect?
- Paco Maya – the deceased.
- Catalina Maya – Paco's sister, once married to Francisco.
- The Espinosa brothers, Gregorio and Mauricio. Want their cocaine back?
- David Costa, Black Angel Anarchist.
- Faustino Azul? Rich builder. Seen talking to the anarchist Costa and Bien.
- Mateo Bien – Opus Dei?
- Salvador Lozano and Diego Elvira – the guys under Margarita's *palio*.
- Andrés Mendoza – very rich. Donated the new cloak to the Virgin of Sacromonte.

He connected those who knew one another with arrows. Five minutes later, he had a list of questions.

1. The Espinosa brothers had a posh lawyer from the coast. How and why?
2. Why did David Costa, the anarchist, turn up in a suit at the Brotherhood of the Bell, talking to Faustino Azul and Mateo Bien?
3. Are Salvador Lozano and Diego Elvira connected to anyone else?

Max paused, tore off the page, and slipped it into his pocket. He also had a major problem with the things Catalina Maya had told him. How long could he hold back on that conversation? He decided to leave it till tomorrow. Maybe something else would turn up before then.

Max phoned Maite to ask for information on David Costa and the two guys on the *palio*. She promised to contact her cousin Alejandro, and get back to him.

Just as Max was going for lunch, the phone rang.

'*Dígame.*'

'My name is Miguel Montero. I'm a lawyer. My office is on Gran Vía opposite the cathedral.'

'How can I help you, *señor*?'

'I was put through to you as the officer investigating the death of Paco Maya.'

'That's right. I am.'

'I've been out of the country for a few days and have only just got back.'

'Ah.'

'Well, I was reading *Granada Hoy* today. And I found a small obituary for Paco Maya. You know he won the Prisoners' Flamenco Song Contest?'

'I understand he was very good.'

'Well, I thought I'd better let you know . . .'

The lawyer paused, waiting for a response.

'*Sí?*'

'I have Señor Maya's will, a draft Deed of Gift and the title deeds to his property in my office.'

'Really? That's very interesting. Would you mind telling me when these documents were drawn up?'

'Almost two weeks ago, just before the start of Holy Week.'

'And the gist of the documents?'

'This would be covered by client confidentiality, but given the circumstances . . .'

The lawyer paused, as if reading from a document.

'It's very simple really. In the event of Francisco Javier Maya's death, Doña Catalina Maya is to become the legal guardian of his daughter, Angelita. And his property is to go to Catalina Maya, to be held in trust for Señor Maya's daughter, Angelita, until she reaches the age of eighteen. The Deed of Gift would have transferred the property to Doña Catalina as soon as a final version was signed.'

'You couldn't tell me who the witnesses are?'

'A Francisco Gómez and one of our secretaries witnessed the will. The Deed of Gift is still in draft form.'

'Thank you. That's very interesting. We'll need a signed statement.'

'Where should I give a statement?'

'If you could come to the Policía Nacional building as soon as possible, that would be very helpful. And please bring these documents with you.'

'I can be with you in half an hour.'

'Thank you. Please ask for me when you arrive.'

Max immediately went round to Davila's office. Davila was flicking through a pile of forms, as usual.

'Ah, Romero. What is it now?'

'A lawyer just phoned. Gómez witnessed Paco Maya's will. The lawyer's on his way to give a statement.'

A broad smile spread across Davila's face. 'Got him. We've got the bastard. Excellent news, Max. Meeting this afternoon?'

'*Sí, señor,*' replied Max.

168

'Right. Bring everything with you.'

The lawyer was waiting for him in reception. Max took his statement, and made copies of the will and draft Deed of Gift.

The afternoon meeting with Davila, Navarro and Belén was quick and easy. Max kept his reservations to himself, and made no mention of his conversation with Catalina.

Navarro kept repeating, 'I told you, Max, to concentrate on Gómez. And I was right.'

'Okay,' concluded Davila. 'We have the motive. No problem getting the judge to extend Gómez's detention period now. We'll get a confession. Well done, men.'

As they filed out, Max asked Roberto for a word in his office.

'So what do you think, Max?'

'I don't feel comfortable with this. You've interviewed him twice. What do you reckon?'

'I don't think he did it. He doesn't seem the type. He's bright, well educated, used to thinking things through. From the interviews, it's clear he's passionate about saving the valleys, but I don't think he would suddenly turn murderously violent just because Maya was having second thoughts about the will. It doesn't feel right to me.'

'Me neither.'

'But then you never know. We're assuming Gómez is innocent just because of our assessment of his character, and that wouldn't carry much weight in law.'

'Absolutely. So what do we do?'

'I don't know. Maybe there's more to this case than meets the eye. I think we should dig around a bit more.'

'Okay. We know there was pressure on Maya to sell his plot of land. And the Abbot of Sacromonte told me that a lot of people around Jesús del Valle and Sacromonte have been selling up.'

'More than you'd expect with this hotel plan?'

'*Sí.*'

'Interesting. Maybe I'll take a trip to the Land Registry.'

Max looked through his notes. 'I think timing could be crucial. Fifteen minutes either way . . .? The security guard's statement could make or break this case. I'll go and check out Gómez's movements with a stopwatch.'

'Okay,' said Roberto. 'Fancy a drink later?'

'Why not? La Trastienda, just off Plaza Nueva, is usually quiet early on. They've kept the old shop in front so it can look really crowded, but there's a bigger room at the back.'

Roberto was already in La Trastienda when Max arrived.

'So you found it?'

'Not a problem. Fancy a bottle of the Rioja?'

Max squinted at the *carta de vinos*. 'Good idea. Works out cheaper anyway. How did it go then?'

'Really interesting. There's a guy I knew in Málaga in charge of the Granada office now. So I got to see a lot of really new stuff.'

'And?'

'Something's up. A hell of a lot of the land around Jesús del Valle has changed hands recently. And in Sacromonte, the Cortijo de los Angeles and all the property close to it has been sold, with the exception of Paco Maya's holding.'

'And the new owners?'

'Different companies, but every single one of them is Gibraltar registered.'

'Well, well.'

'Did you know, Max, Gibraltar has over thirty banks, twenty-eight registered companies, one hundred and fifteen lawyers . . . all effectively outside any financial regulations? It's a giant money-laundering centre. And if you want any info, your request just gets shuffled between Gibraltar and Her Majesty's Government in London.'

'So, it could take months to get any info on these outfits.'

'If we ever got anything hard and fast . . . but all these land sales are more than a coincidence. I'll keep digging when I've got a bit of time. How about you?'

'It all hinges on Gómez's side trip round the Cortijo de los Angeles. Assuming the security guard's timings are reasonably accurate, that detour accounts for at least fifteen minutes. So Gómez should have arrived at Paco Maya's not much more than five minutes before Belinda and I got there, and Maya was definitely dead at 2 p.m.'

'So providing the friend who says he walked with Gómez all the way from Sacromonte to the monastery isn't lying, Gómez didn't have time to argue with Maya, kill him, and destroy any evidence.'

'So if Gómez didn't do it, who did?' Max refilled their glasses. 'Roberto, what do you make of Navarro?'

'Navarro? Honest opinion?'

'Honest.'

'I wouldn't trust him as far as I could throw him. But why are you asking?'

'Well, Navarro and I have had our differences in the past. Major differences. I got him suspended.'

'I heard rumours about that.'

'I wouldn't like that to cloud my judgement.'

'Go on.'

'There's something not right about the way he's handling this case.'

'I'm glad you said that. I thought it was just me. Somebody let that posh lawyer in to see the brothers before we got to interview them. Must have been bloody Che Navarro.'

'Looks like it. Then there's the missing tyre photo, and I'm sure someone switched the cigar ash I found outside Paco Maya's cave to cigarette ash.'

'And then Che pitched up with that photo just when we were interviewing the brothers.'

'Curiouser and curiouser.'

'He could have been bought, you know,'

'That's what I'm thinking. I'll have to talk to Davila on this.'

'Be careful, Max. There could be a simple explanation. Accusing a fellow cop is pretty heavy.'

'I know. But I have to tell Davila about my doubts on the times, so I may as well be hung for a sheep as a lamb. But he won't like it.'

Chapter 23

Margarita phoned Max at eight o'clock on Wednesday morning. She was happy. 'I'm being discharged today.'

'That's great. Do you need a lift home?'

'Thanks, but not now. Dad will be surprised, but Blanca finally persuaded me to stay with them for a couple of days.'

'Is that a good thing?'

'Sort of. It'll be great to have a proper bath, and it'll be nice to see Blanca.'

'But?'

'Dad and I will have a dust-up in a couple of days. So then I can go home.'

'When can I see you?'

'Dad's sending a car round this morning. Give me a ring later on today. With a bit of luck the old bastard will be out of the house early evening, so you could come then.'

'That would be great.'

'Any news of Carlos?

'Maite's been to the hospital. He's making progress.'

'That's really good. Okay. Have to go now. The consultant's just arrived to sign me out. See you this evening.'

Max practised what he was going to say to Davila. He'd almost finished when Maite phoned.

'That's great, Maite. *Sí*, I can see you in the Gran Taberna in half an hour.'

Max walked to the Gran Taberna through the little streets behind the cathedral. Plaza Pasiegas had been cleaned up

173

thoroughly and, apart from a scorch mark on one of the doors, no one would have known what had happened there two days ago. Now he walked along the side of the cathedral, between the Royal Chapel and the Casa del Cabildo, the original University of Moorish Granada, on to Gran Vía, and round the corner into Plaza Nueva. Maite was already perched on a stool at the bar, finishing a coffee. Max ordered two glasses of San Miguel. The beer arrived with a plate of tiny ham omelettes, hot from the pan, the Gran Taberna's speciality.

'Have you seen Carlos?' Max asked her.

'I've just been to the hospital, and he's making progress.'

'That's good.'

'Max, I've got a picture on my mobile. It's a cop batoning Carlos. I'm going to give it to the press, but I wanted you to know about it first.'

'Give it to me, Maite, and I'll pass it up to someone I trust.'

'I'll send you a copy. I've also been through Carlos's own pictures. Look here.'

It was a picture of Francisco Gómez. Right behind him was one of the men who Max was sure had thrown the first rocks. But the stone thrower's ski mask had slipped. Max couldn't be sure, but he looked like Salvador Lozano, one of the men under Margarita's *palio*.

'I recognize that guy. It could be Salvador from the Procession of the Virgin,' he said.

'*Sí*,' said Maite. 'And if you look at the next picture, it could be his mate Diego jostling Francisco.'

Max looked. 'It's definitely Diego. What do you make of that?'

'I don't know. When we were two guys short for the last stage of the procession I asked Alejandro, my cousin, if he knew anyone who could help us out at short notice. He got in touch with David Costa who recommended two guys he said were experienced *costaleros*. They were Salvador and Diego.'

'Did he now? Do you know anything about David Costa?'

'Not much. Alejandro says he joined the Black Angels about a month ago. Apparently he's very bright, and a good speaker.'

'Don't these Black Angels have some sort of vetting system?'

'Not really. There aren't many of them, so anyone with half a brain who turns up gets pushed forward. From what Alejandro tells me, they spend most of their time debating theory and attacking the Communist Party.'

'Nothing much changes. I don't suppose you know what these guys are studying?'

'Alejandro said they're all at the Business School.'

Max raised an eyebrow.

'I know. It's a phase some people go through. Ten years from now they'll all be running banks.'

'*Gracias*, Maite. This is really useful.'

'You'll find out more from the University Registry in the Hospital Real.'

Max paid for lunch, then took a bus along Gran Vía to the University Records Centre, based in the old Royal Hospital. He paused for a moment in the garden, admiring the building's fine Renaissance façade. The statues of King Ferdinand of Aragón and his wife, Queen Isabel of Castile, gazed benignly down on the Moorish city they had conquered in the name of Spain, God and the Holy Catholic Church.

A porter escorted him through sunny courtyards and great carved stone doorways to the Records Office at the back of the building The clerk was reluctant at first, but called up the students' files after she'd seen Max's police ID.

'You can only look at them here,' she said.

'Here's fine,' said Max. 'I won't be long.'

He wasn't long. All three had been to La Escuela de Sierra Nevada, Granada's elite Opus Dei secondary school. Max noted down their present addresses and telephone numbers. The two guys under Margarita's *palio* were staying at the

Opus Dei student residence behind the church of Santo Domingo in Realejo.

At five o'clock, Max phoned Margarita again. A woman with a Bolivian accent answered the phone.

'I'll put you through to Señorita Margarita's room.'

'Margarita,' said Max. 'How are you?'

'Sort of settled in. But I'm still really stiff and sore. And I'm going to be bored out of my mind.'

'I could bring you that book.'

'Would you? My dad's definitely out early evening. Any chance of a good thriller?'

Max put the phone down, a smile on his face.

Back home, he hunted through his bookcases to find something to lend to Margarita. Perfect. The Spanish translation of *Winter in Madrid* by C.J. Sansom. He found a pretty card, one of Lorca's pencil drawings of Harlequin with the Alhambra in the background. Max paused, and finally wrote: 'Hope you enjoy this. It's full of insights into the early years of the Franco regime.'

He paused, wondering how to sign it. Shy boys get nowhere. *'Un abrazo muy fuerte.* Love, Max.'

He slipped the book into a used jiffy bag, splashed some cologne on his face, and walked in the twilight to Margarita's father's house in Realejo. It was an old house up on Cuesta del Caidero, the approach to the Alhambra from the Realejo side. The garden was one of those he had often imagined from the street, with cypresses, a palm tree and sprays of tiny yellow roses which tumbled over the high walls. Somewhere, there was a fountain. Max rang the bell of a small door set into a modest white wall. A uniformed maid answered.

'Señorita Margarita is expecting you,' she said.

Max followed her up the polished wooden staircase to the top floor. The maid knocked on the door.

'The gentleman is here to see you,' she said.

'Come in, Max,' Margarita called out.

She was sitting in a white armchair, wrapped in a large cardigan. Her face lit up when she saw him.

'Max, thanks for coming so soon.'

'How are you?'

The maid curtsied and left.

'You see how my father is,' Margarita said. 'We have to have a maid in uniform.'

'That's the way it is here if you have money.'

'It's so bloody bourgeois. She spends all day dusting and changing the curtains. She should be doing something meaningful.'

'But it's clean, safe work, and if you don't have qualifications –'

'She's Bolivian, and the old git pays her peanuts.'

'Bet she thinks it's better than slogging her guts out in a sweatshop back in Bolivia.'

'Sorry, Max, on the campaign trail again.' She stretched and winced slightly. 'But *hombre*, it's good to see you.'

'I've brought you a really good book. *Winter in Madrid*.'

'What's it about?

'Brits in Spain during the Second World War, and what happened to Republican orphan children.'

'That sounds like it could be interesting.'

Max settled into a heavy armchair.

'Coffee?'

'Please.'

Margarita rang the small silver bell which had been sitting on the side table. The maid appeared noiselessly. 'María, could we have a pot of coffee, please?'

'*Sí, senorita*.' The maid disappeared as quietly as she had arrived.

'Now don't get too comfortable, Max. Dad and Blanca won't be out for long. It's probably easier if he doesn't run into you.'

'That's okay.'

'But there's a good chance they'll be going away to the villa in Marbella for the weekend. So I'll have the place to myself.'

Max smiled.

177

'Anything on Francisco?' asked Margarita.

'I haven't heard anything definite yet. But I'm hoping he may be released soon.'

'That would be some good news for a change.'

'You're looking tired.'

'*Sí*, I'm still on painkillers and stuff to help me sleep. Look Max – it's lovely to see you but you'll have to go quite soon in case they come back early. Hope to see you Saturday. We can have a long talk then.'

They finished their coffee, then Max stood up and gave her a full kiss. '*Chao, guapa.*'

'*Chao, guapo. Hasta la próxima.*'

The maid let Max out. He noticed discreet cameras all over the place as well as the guard outside. Don Faustino was certainly security-conscious.

On Friday morning, Max had a slot in Davila's diary. 11.15 a.m. Clara smiled encouragingly when she buzzed him through.

'Ah, Max. I trust this is important. I'm busy.'

'It is, sir. I thought I should check out a few things on the Gómez case.'

'Oh. I thought that was all pretty straightforward now. Apart from his confession. And that's just a matter of time now.'

'Maybe, sir. But I was worried about the timings.'

'The timings?'

'*Sí*. I've always been unsure –'

'Romero, get to the point.'

'Well, I . . . I thought it best to test the timing. I mean check the earliest time Gómez could have arrived at Maya's cave.'

'I don't see the relevance of all this.'

'I . . . I disagree, sir. I went back with a stopwatch on Tuesday. I tracked and timed all Gómez's movements from when he left me at the monastery, to the time of the second sighting by the security guard after Gómez went round to the back of the *cortijo*.'

'Don't be so bloody long-winded. What's your point?'

'Well, sir, I have the timings written down here. I just don't see how Francisco Gómez could have had the time to kill Paco Maya. The Forensics report clearly states that the time of death was between 1 and 2 p.m. The security guard at Cortijo de los Angeles saw him just before 1.45 p.m., and it takes barely five minutes to get from the *cortijo* to Maya's cave, so the earliest Gómez could have arrived at the cave is ten to two. I was there at exactly two, and the man was already dead. So, I don't see how Gómez could have had an argument with Maya, killed him and disposed of the evidence in the time available.'

Davila stared at Max in disbelief. 'Are you a bloody idiot or something? Maya died of a heart attack, right? Gómez could have assaulted him any time earlier that morning. Maya hangs about unconscious or whatever, and then dies sometime between one and two.'

'But sir, he had an alibi from the time he left his house in Sacromonte until he arrived at the monastery, and two sightings with precise times by the security guard at the Cortijo de los Angeles. It's just impossible for Gómez to have done it either on his way out to the monastery, or coming back to Sacromonte. And if he'd harmed the man earlier in the day, why on earth would he have continued on to the monastery instead of going into town where he could be sure he'd be seen by enough people to establish an alibi of some type?'

'Romero, how long have you been in the force now? Witnesses are never reliable. Fifteen minutes, half an hour one way or the other. *Es igual*. They never have a fucking clue when it comes to it. You are wasting your time and mine. Anything else?'

Max paused. '*Sí*, sir. There's a matter about Inspector Navarro.'

'Inspector Navarro? What matter?'

'Well, there's . . . there's something not quite right.'

'Not quite right? Get on with it. What do you mean?'

Max spoke rapidly. 'From the very beginning Inspector Navarro assumed Maya's death was an accident, and then as the case progressed he seemed to be constantly putting up obstacles to its progress.'

'Go on.'

'Well, I . . . I just think, sir, there's something suspicious about Navarro's handling of this case.'

'What are you talking about, Romero?'

Max summarized his doubts about Navarro. Davila listened in silence.

'Is that all, Romero?'

'*Sí.*'

'You have just suggested that a senior officer might have tampered with evidence in a murder case.'

'I . . . I . . .'

'That is what you are implying, Romero. Inspector Navarro's out of his office until Monday morning. I shall phone him. And you can make your points at a meeting with both Inspector Navarro and myself. That will give you time to reconsider some of the suggestions that you've just made.'

'With respect, sir, all I'm stating are facts. It's the truth I am after.'

'*La verdad*? We have the truth. You can go now, Romero.'

Chapter 24

Just before two o'clock on Saturday, Max put on his favourite white shirt, the Adolfo Dominguez jeans and his black linen jacket. He picked up the CDs he'd bought for Margarita, slipped a book into the bag, and caught the bus to the top of Realejo. This time Margarita answered the door herself.

'I've given the maid the rest of the weekend off.' She nodded at José, the security guard. 'He's all right,' she said to Max.

'How are you feeling? You look a lot better.'

'I'm feeling better, but I'm still a bit sore.'

'I love the top. The colour really suits you.'

Margarita was wearing a rose-coloured silk top, which almost hid the bruises.

They walked across the jasmine-scented courtyard and paused at the fountain. Max kissed her gently. 'Have you any news on Carlos?'

'I phoned Maite this morning. The hospital says he's stable.'

'So that's good.'

'Better, but not good really. I've said a prayer for him, and I'm not exactly a practising Catholic these days.'

'So have I.'

'Strange, isn't it? It all comes back to you in a crisis. I always pray for my friends when they have serious problems, you know. But I would never ask anyone to pray for me.'

181

'I understand.'

The *salon* of the Azul family home was impressive, but heavy. Serried ranks of oil paintings rose above carved, gold-upholstered furniture, and the view over the city was obscured by layers of ruffled lace curtains. There was a laden drinks trolley in one corner.

'Can I get you anything to drink? The orange juice is good, and there's sherry if you fancy something stronger.'

'Orange juice is fine.'

Margarita poured the juice into fine Baccarat crystal glasses.

'I've brought you another book. I think you'll like this one.'

Margarita glanced at the title. *The Soldiers of Salamis* by Javier Cercas. That's the one about the Falangist poet at the end of the Civil War, isn't it?'

'The very one.'

'Thanks. I've wanted to read this for ages. I like your taste in books. Sit in the armchair there, Max, and tell me how you're getting on.'

'Not well. Things are difficult at work.'

'Tell me what you can. Maybe I can help.'

Max hesitated. 'I didn't want to upset you earlier. But Francisco's being held for questioning in relation to the death of Paco Maya.'

'Paco Maya? Catalina's brother? He can't be. No. If you knew Francisco, he just couldn't have killed anybody. Oh, why are you cops so bloody stupid?'

'Stupid some of the time. But not always. I can't go into detail . . .'

'Of course.'

'Look, Margarita, there is a case against him, but it isn't that strong. I'm keeping an open mind. My boss isn't.'

'*Mierda*. Maybe I should have told you this earlier. When I had the mega bust-up with my dad –'

'The one when you were eighteen?'

'*Sí*. I left home and shacked up with Francisco.'

'With Francisco?'

'He's quite something, you know.'

'No, I don't know.'

'Oh, Max. Don't be jealous. It was a long time ago. He's impossible to live with. I was up half the night typing bloody pamphlets and making coffee while he and his mates had long discussions about Deep Ecology.'

'And your father?'

'He hates Francisco. Hates him like poison. Between the campaigning, and corrupting his innocent little girl, he's had the knife into him for years.'

'I see.'

'Anyway. I know Francisco well, and he'd never harm anyone. How could you guys even imagine it? Christ. I need a drink.'

'I'll get it.'

Max carefully pushed the drinks trolley across the polished wooden floor and parked it next to Margarita. She topped up her orange juice with a slug of vodka.

Max explained the gist of the case. But he didn't mention Paco's cocaine stash.

Margarita listened intently. 'So what's Francisco's motive?'

'That's the problem. There isn't one except this bloody will and Deed of Gift. The police are banging on about that stupid lie and how Francisco would do anything to save Jesús del Valle.'

'*Idiotas.*' Margarita sipped her drink. 'Shall I play one of the CDs you brought? How about *Orpheus*?'

'*Sí.*'

The CD slipped into the splendid sound system hidden inside an ornate cabinet. She finished her orange and vodka.

'That's good. I feel a bit better now. Let's organize lunch before we get wrecked.'

Max followed her into the kitchen. Gluck's wonderful opening chorus echoed through the house.

'Do you need any help?'

'I'm fine, thanks. I just have to shove all this in the pan, turn up the heat, and it'll be ready in twenty minutes. Fancy an olive?'

'Thanks.'

While Orpheus descended into Hades to rescue Euridice, pork loin, chicken, squid and Sanlucar prawns followed each other smartly into the pan. Then came Valencia rice, and a precise half-litre of hot, saffron-scented stock. When the rice was almost cooked, she stirred in steamed mussels, *carabinero* prawns, finely chopped parsley, and the juice of a lemon.

'*Vale, mi amor.* Could you set the table in the *torreón*? It's cooler there. Everything's ready in the baskets.'

'You okay with steps then?'

'The physio wants me to walk as much as I can. I'll be fine. I just have to be careful with this shoulder.'

Max set the table in the small tower which rose from the terrace, then carried up the food. The top floor of the *torreón* was open on two sides, one overlooking the city, the other, the Alhambra woods and the Sierra Nevada. Maximum view, maximum privacy.

'Some view you have here. Nearly as good as mine.'

'I must see your flat soon.'

'Compared with this, it's very modest. And I have to move out soon.'

'Well, I could help you look for somewhere.'

Max admired the roof of the *torreón*, carved wood in the *mudéjar* style.

'Is that original?'

'If only. No, probably nineteenth-century.'

'This paella is excellent.'

'Just to prove I can cook. *Mi abuela* always said the way to a man's heart is through his stomach.'

The wine was Blanc Pescador. There were two bottles in the icebox.

'So what did you make of *Winter in Madrid*?'

'Haven't finished it yet. But I'm enjoying it. And I'm

184

learning a lot about my own country. The description of what happened to the Republican orphan children is horrific.'

'It is. It's taken us seventy-odd years to start to get to grips with the Civil War and the Franco regime.'

'And it's often foreigners who are unearthing the stories. Not Spaniards.'

'You know, my great uncle Antonio, that's *mi abuela* Paula's brother in Diva, he disappeared in August 1937.'

'That's terrible.'

'He'd walked to Diva from Granada, and was trying to get to the coast, but he got picked up in Banjaron and was shot a couple of days later.'

'Oh, how awful.'

'We only found out the full story a couple of years ago. We think he was dumped in a *fosa común* outside Diva. The family is still divided over whether we should dig to try to find his bones. As for the Church . . .'

'I know. Incredible, isn't it? I have a great aunt who's a nun in the Carmelite convent down in Plaza San Juan de la Cruz.'

'The Barefoot Order?'

'The very one. We visit her twice a year. And Sansom's book got me thinking. She was adopted. Maybe she was one of those poor babies who got taken from Republican parents and handed over to Nationalist families.'

'Could be. We've all got skeletons in our cupboards.'

'Mine more than most, Max.'

A phone rang downstairs.

'I'll get that, and make some coffee.'

Margarita walked carefully down the stairs. The phone stopped ringing. Then it rang again. She returned, looking shaken and angry, without the coffee.

'Max, oh, Max.'

Max put his arms round her. She wiped her eyes.

'What happened, girl, what happened?'

185

'I picked up the phone in the kitchen, and this guy asked for Señor Azul. I replied that Señor Azul was away for the weekend. The line was breaking up a bit, and he must have thought I was the maid. He asked me to tell Señor Azul that Salvador had phoned. Bloody Salvador!'

'The Salvador under your *palio*? One of the guys who slipped?'

'*Sí.* I'm sure. I recognized the voice.'

Max thought of his list of connections. There was now an arrow linking Faustino Azul to Salvador, and thus to Diego.

'Oh, Max. Don't you get it? My own father sabotaged my *palio*. The mad bastard could have killed me.'

'No way.'

'He bloody did. He didn't know I'd be under the *palio*. I only became a *costalera* when Lidia pulled out.'

'I see. Just sit down, Margarita.'

'I can't believe it. The bastard.'

'Look, there could be another explanation.'

'What?'

'The third guy on that photo I showed you is an Opus Dei cleric, Monsignor Mateo Bien.'

'So?'

'Salvador knows your father. David Costa, Salvador and Diego all went to the Opus Dei school in Granada. And Salvador and Diego stay in the Opus hall of Residence in Realejo. There's an Opus Dei connection.'

'Max, I just don't buy that. I thought you only read good books. The Opus boys are just a bunch of sex-starved idiots. The real connection is my father.'

'Maybe.'

'You told me you have a photo showing Salvador standing just behind, flinging the first rocks at the police. If my father wanted to make a laughing-stock of Francisco over the procession and then fix him up on the demo, he's done really well.'

'Just hang on. Mateo Bien's name keeps cropping up.'

'All right. You should go and talk to that bloody priest then.'

'I will. Another drink?'

Margarita knocked back her glass of wine and stuck out her hand for another one.

'I'll get the coffee,' said Max.

He returned with a pot of filtered coffee.

'I'm sorry, Max. I didn't mean to have a go at you.'

'I still don't see why your father would sabotage your *palio*. Christ knows what might have happened.'

'You have to understand my father. He's impulsive. A bully. And used to always getting his own way. I bet he thought he had a good idea and didn't think it through. If he made Francisco look an idiot, that could have killed two birds with one stone.'

'So your dad's involved in Jesús del Valle?'

'Could well be. My dad – it's not a nice thought to have going round your head.'

'Maybe there's another explanation.'

'No. See, my father, mostly he's a complete shit, but you know . . . he's still my dad. What a bloody family. My mother committed suicide, you know.'

'You told me.'

'He wanted her to be a lady of leisure. But after I started school, she wanted to finish her art degree. My father refused.'

She cried again. Max hugged her tight.

'So mother started taking private art lessons. My father hit the roof when he found out and accused her of having an affair with the teacher. My bloody father. He's always had his mistresses.'

'Why didn't she leave him?'

'Women like her just didn't. Then she got hooked on antidepressants, and finally took too many.'

'I'm so sorry.'

'And my father is treating Blanca the same way.'

'She'll be all right. She's got you.'

187

'Max, your parents divorced, didn't they?'

'Yes. My mother's Catholic, like my dad. But she didn't grow up under Franco. So she had more opportunities, you know.'

'That's good. Hell. If I'm not careful, I'll spend the afternoon moaning. Just change the topic and talk about something nice. Books and music. Let's enjoy the view. Just look at that sky.'

They talked until the sun began to set behind the Alhambra.

'*Vale, guapo*. I think I could manage a little walk. How about we get the bus to Sacromonte for tapas and *vino*?'

'*Sí*. But in moderation, this time.'

Margarita laughed. 'You're really quite sweet when drunk. Shame you can't dance.'

They got off the bus at the School of Arabic Studies, and walked up the Camino de Sacromonte as views of the Alhambra appeared and disappeared beyond garden walls. The cave bar, Pibe, had an empty table and chairs on its outside terrace. Zaíd, the friendly Moroccan waiter, smiled at them both.

'I didn't know you two knew each other. It's been too long since I've seen either of you.'

'*Sí*. Two white Riojas, please.'

Zaíd disappeared into the little whitewashed bar, which had been tunnelled into the hillside, and returned with two glasses of chilled white wine and a plate of cold prawns.

'Do you know, I had a Californian wine producer here the other day. He took photos of this cave, the views of the Alhambra and the views down the Sacromonte valley. He's just sent me an email. He's going to call one of his wines after the bar, Pibe.'

'That's great,' said Max. 'Maybe one day the bar will appear in a book.'

Max and Margarita finished their wine and crossed the road to gaze at the green damask hills caught in the evening light. The lamps of the Renaissance Cordova Palace and its gardens gleamed below them, and the Alhambra, floodlit in green and gold, shone brightly, directly across the valley.

'You know, Max, I once stood here to watch the Paso de los Gitanos. I can't stand the Church. But Los Gitanos is always worth watching.'

'It certainly is. This year, I was with a bunch of VIPs at the bottom of Cuesta del Chapiz.'

'How come you got to sit with the poshies?'

'The Abbot of Sacromonte's a good friend.'

'Really?

'It's a long story. Anyway he invited us over.'

'So who were you sitting with? Anyone famous?'

'Well, there was this woman who looked just like Penélope Cruz. Same first name, too. And a rich lawyer, Andrés Mendoza, with his wife.'

'And Javier Bardem? Gael García Bernal?'

'Dream on, girl. Anyway, the lawyer was there because he'd donated a new cloak to the Virgin.'

'Why would he do that?'

'Dunno. Maybe he thought it would give him a VIP pass to heaven.'

'Weird. How medieval can you get? Better to give money to the poor.'

'But that's Granada for you.'

'Right, one more at Kiki's. And that's your lot, young man. Can't have you getting drunk. You never know what might happen.'

They walked slowly along the Camino del Sacromonte, past the famous flamenco *zambras* of La Faraona, La Fragua and El Rocío. They climbed up the steps at Barranco de los Negros until they came to Kiki's cave with its terrace overlooking the valley to the Comares Tower and the towers of the Alhambra Fortress.

'Good to see you, Max,' said Kiki. 'And you too, Margarita. Didn't know you knew each other.'

'Granada's a small place.'

189

They had two glasses of Kiki's best white, and a bowl of almonds and another of olives.

'Is there anything new on the Paco Maya case?' asked Kiki.

Max glanced at Margarita. 'There have been a few developments. But still no breakthrough yet, I'm afraid.'

'Francisco Gómez has been arrested, hasn't he? I can't say I agree with everything he does, but I tell you, I was shocked. He lives round the corner, you know. Just can't imagine him doing anything like that.'

'I really can't comment, Kiki. But I'll let you know when anything goes public.'

Margarita paid for the drinks, and then they strolled back towards the Albayzín along the Vereda de Enmedio Alto, the narrow cobbled balcony above the cave houses of Sacromonte. The lights of the city glowed below them. They stopped at the Fuente de la Amapola, the Fountain of the Poppy with its poem 'When you drink from me, Your lips are my blessing.'

'Max. Come here,' said Margarita. And she put her arms around him, and kissed him fully on the lips. 'If you can't fall in love in Granada, where the hell can you?'

'Where indeed?'

'*Vale, guapo*. Are you seeing me home?'

'Of course. We'll get a taxi.'

They picked up a cab at the Plaza Nueva rank, and sped through Realejo, along Calle Molinos, and then turned up the hill towards the Alhambra.

'Thanks, Max,' said Margarita, kissing him lightly as they stood outside the Azul house. 'Perhaps I can see you tomorrow.'

'I . . .'

She laughed. 'You should see your face. Just teasing. Come on, you idiot. I'd race you to my bedroom if I could run.'

Max laughed. He laughed most of Sunday.

Chapter 25

On Monday morning, Max knocked on Davila's door and entered. Navarro was already there, sitting comfortably.

'Sit down, Romero. I've already summarized for Inspector Navarro the gist of what you told me. He's very angry and offended. You should have gone straight to him with any doubts, you know.'

'That would have been a little difficult, sir.'

'Most of your issues can be easily settled. There has clearly been a breakdown in communication between you two.'

Navarro sat there, saying nothing.

'This minor detail about cigar ash. Inspector Navarro says you simply made a mistake. When the labs tested it, it turned out to be just cigarette ash. So, you know better than the lab, do you?'

'No, sir. I accept that I made a mistake, and apologize to Inspector Navarro for doubting him.'

'Good. Now the missing photo of the 4×4 tracks. It did turn up in time for your interrogation of Gregorio Espinosa, didn't it?'

'Yes sir, but –'

'*Sí.* The photo did turn up, so what are you trying to imply?'

'I accept it could have gone missing. But to turn up the day we were interrogating the Espinosa brothers . . . it just seemed a bit odd.'

'Odd? Coincidence, you mean?'

'Yes, I suppose so.'

'Good. I'm glad that is cleared up. Now, you claim the Espinosa brothers were coached by their lawyer. So would you prefer us to deny them their legal rights?'

'No, of course not. Maybe I've been a bit hasty in my judgement.'

'Hasty? You are questioning the integrity of a fellow officer. With no evidence to support your assertions.'

'Okay. And I apologize. But there's still the other matter. Between the security guard and other witnesses, Francisco Gómez didn't have time to kill Paco Maya.'

'Well, I asked Inspector Navarro to check out that security guard's statement. It makes no sense for Gómez to scramble round the back of that *cortijo* instead of going straight to Paco Maya's cave. Why would he do that?'

'Gómez said he wanted to check out what was going on with the new owner.'

'And you expect me to believe that?'

'I don't see why not.'

'I'll tell you why not, Romero. The security guard says you lent on him to fabricate that story. We know Gómez is your buddy. We know you warned Gómez at the demo that the police were coming for him. You have been perverting the course of justice to protect an individual with whom you share political sympathies. You know what that means, Romero?'

'What exactly are you suggesting?'

'I have here a signed statement from the security guard saying that he saw Francisco Gómez once, at one-thirty. And that you put words into his mouth to suggest that he saw him again fifteen minutes later at the back of the *cortijo*.'

'I'm afraid it's the truth, Sub-Inspector,' added Navarro.

Max was speechless.

'And we now have definitive proof of Gómez's guilt. Inspector Navarro and I did a thorough search of his flat over the weekend. And Inspector Navarro found a package of cocaine. It was very well hidden, but we found it. That rumour you told us about Paco Maya once dealing is clearly true. So Gómez must have killed Maya and then taken the cocaine.'

'But –'

'Romero, you are hereby suspended from all duties for a week. I'll be generous. On pay. I'll arrange a disciplinary. You may go to your office and collect your personal effects. Do not return until summoned to do so. Is that understood?'

'*Sí, señor*, but –'

'No questions. You may go now.'

Max saluted, returned to his office, and packed his things. He looked at the new image on his Dali calendar: *Soft Watch at the Moment of First Explosion*. That summed it up. Bloody Navarro must have planted the cocaine package. But what the hell was going on with the security guard?

Max returned to his flat and immediately phoned Catalina.

'It's Max Romero. Have you still got that packet of Paco's? You know . . .'

'No. I flushed it all down the loo.'

'*Mierda*.'

'What's up?'

'I'll explain later. So there's nothing left of it at all?'

'Well, it was kept in a cotton rice bag. I put the bag in with my rubbish. It might still be there.'

'Could you fish it out and keep it for me? Don't wash it or anything. Just put it in a poly bag and give it to the desk officer at the Policía Nacional.'

'Sure.'

A rice bag? Of course – storing the powder with a handful of grains would keep it dry. Max hurried out of his flat, walked along Calle Guinea to the Sacromonte bus stop. He was in luck: the bus was due in five minutes. He got off at the last stop and walked to the Cortijo de los Angeles. The two mastiffs were barking in the distance.

'Anyone there?' he called.

The barking came nearer. A man wearing the security company's jacket came round the corner, with one of the dogs on a leash.

'*Buenas tardes, señor*. I'm looking for Fernando Pozo. He works here as a security guard.'

'Never heard of him,' replied the man. 'I only started here today.'

'You don't know where I might find him?'

'*Ni idea*.' He shrugged. 'You can ask Gloria, the boss's secretary. She seems to know everything.'

A crescent moon was out when Max got back to his flat. He poured himself a large glass of white wine, a Blanc Pescador, one of his favourites. He went outside on to his terrace, savoured the clean taste of the wine, its tiny bubbles freshening his mouth.

What the hell was going on? He only had Catalina's word that Francisco Gómez had walked in on a dead body. Yet the land deal gave Gómez a stronger motive. Now this bloody cocaine package had turned up in Gómez's flat. Catalina said she had been given Paco Maya's original stash and had destroyed it. So this new package must have been planted. The whole bloody thing was a set-up. And Davila was too stupid to see that Navarro was running rings round him.

The phone rang.

'Max, it's Roberto Belén. I've just heard what's happened. Can I come round and see you tomorrow lunchtime? I think I might be able to help.'

'Yes, I need some help. I'll rustle up some food. I haven't got much else to do at the moment.'

He phoned Margarita with his news. ·

'Oh, Max. That's terrible. Let's meet.'

'How about the terrace of the Alhambra Palace hotel in an hour?'

'Don't worry, *mi amor*. We'll sort something out.'

Chapter 26

The next morning, Max walked from his flat in Calle María de la Miel through the Moorish Puerta del las Pesas into Plaza Larga. His conversation with Margarita had helped. Her hug and kiss had helped even more. The market stalls were just setting up. Mercedes' old uncle was still unloading sacks of fresh broad beans for their stall from the back of their tiny van, and an enterprising young *gitano* was setting out his wares – live snails that he'd collected in the hills at dawn.

Max bought a copy of *El País* and then walked across the square to Casa de los Pasteles for breakfast. Once he had finished the toast, fresh orange juice and coffee, he sauntered along to Mercedes' stall where he bought fresh asparagus, a couple of local lemons and avocados, and half a kilo of Huelva strawberries.

Just by the stall, a young woman was selling organic olive oil in relabelled beer bottles. It was from her family farm, and their production was so small they didn't have a licence. But the oil was really good stuff, dark green and very fragrant. Max bought a litre.

From Plaza Larga, he walked along Calle de Panaderos to the bakery, Panadería la Solana, and bought a wholemeal *chapata* and a white loaf of *hogaza*, both still hot from the oven. Then to the small Coviran supermarket for some nice brown eggs, a kilo of potatoes, milk and a carton of cream. As usual, Luis was on the till. Today he was shelling fresh broad beans and munching them like sweets as he worked.

'Not at work today?' asked Luis.

'No, it's my day off.'

'Lucky chap. I never have a day off.'

'That's because you never allow yourself one.'

Max strolled back via the Torreón de la Plaza de Charca and the Mirador de San Nicolás. He'd been set up and it was bloody obvious who was behind it – Navarro. The bastard had gone to a lot of trouble to stitch him up. Max walked along the cobbled street to his flat, made himself a cup of strong aromatic coffee, and sat out on his terrace with the newspaper. *El País* had another long article on urban corruption:

'Spain hands out 900,000 building permits every year, more than the UK and Germany combined. These permits are a major source of local government finance . . . and for lining the pockets of corrupt politicians and officials.'

Just before two, Max boiled the potatoes, grilled the asparagus, beat the eggs, and hulled the strawberries. Roberto arrived five minutes late.

'How are you feeling, Max?' he asked.

'Bloody angry. I've been set up and Davila's just going along with it.'

'So what happened?'

Max told him the whole story.

'So, unless the security guard is able to stand by his original statement, you're the one who's committed an offence.'

'*Sí*. I phoned Chávez this morning. He's sympathetic, but he can't do anything unless I can come up with some pretty robust evidence. The judge said the same. I just don't know what I can do now.'

'I might be able to help,' said Roberto. 'You know I told you I used to work for the Anti-Corruption Unit in Málaga.'

'*Sí*, I remember you telling me about the Moby Dick investigation.'

'Well, I'm still working on it.'

'You're what?'

'I know. We think there is something funny going on in Granada connected to the case. My boss asked me to go undercover in Granada. And then this job came up, so my boss suggested I go for it. My wife wanted to come back to Granada anyway.'

'But why didn't you just join our Anti-Corruption Unit?'

'Because we think the head of that unit's been bought. And probably most of his team as well.'

'I see.'

'But the Maya investigation has been really useful. We think there's a lot behind it. Maybe it's the Granada end of one of the Marbella gangs. And if it is, it's big. And we want to get the guys at the top. We think you can help.'

'How?'

'We'd like you to carry on with your investigation on our behalf now.'

'With permission of the department?'

'Without. You have a lot of contacts.'

Max paused. 'What do you want me to do?'

'I want you come to Málaga and meet the head of the Anti-Corruption Unit. He'll brief you. Then using the Maya case as a lead, we want you help us fill in the picture. It could be dangerous. You'd be shocked how many millions of euros are involved.'

'I don't know. Could land me in even more trouble.'

'But it could also help clear your name.'

'That's true. Okay. Count me in. I've nothing to lose.'

'Great. We could go to Málaga straight away.'

'After we've eaten. It's not much. My special tortilla, followed by strawberries and cream. A glass of wine first?'

'Why not? Nice little place you've got here, Max. And what a view.'

'It is, but the landlord is kicking me out. I don't want to leave the Albayzín, but finding something good in my price range isn't easy.'

'Something will turn up. It always does.'

Max went into the kitchen and started to cook the asparagus tortilla. As garlic and potatoes sizzled in the rich olive oil, he poured two glasses of white wine, and took them out on to his terrace.

'You could sit for hours just looking at that view,' said Roberto. 'It's magic.'

'It is,' agreed Max. 'The tortilla won't be long.'

Max returned to his tiny kitchen, carefully turned the tortilla over, and waited a moment.

The potatoes, garlic and asparagus had caramelized beautifully on both sides. 'That was great, Max,' said Roberto, wiping his plate. 'I phoned my boss in Málaga while you were cooking. He's expecting us.'

'Fine,' said Max. 'I'll make a quick pot of coffee, and then let's go.'

They were soon out of Granada, speeding past Santa Fé and Loja on the motorway. The geometric patterns of olive groves and hills stretched before them, all the way to Málaga.

'I checked up on that posh lawyer on the coast,' said Roberto. 'Pablo Guzmán de Sídonia.'

'That shrewd bastard.'

'He's got connections. He's joint owner of a large estate agency based in Nerja and Marbella. He organized the sale and purchase of the Hotel Reina del Sur.'

'To whom?'

'A company registered in Gibraltar.'

'I see.'

'And guess who the other owner of the estate agency is?'

'*Ni idea.*'

'Another rich coastal lawyer with offices in Granada. An Andrés Mendoza.'

'That's interesting. The lawyer who paid for the Virgin's cloak.'

'The what?'

Max explained.

'So that could link both Don Andrés and Don Pablo to the Maya case and maybe the Jesús del Valle affair.'

'So what's the overall picture?'

'It's big and nasty. All the usual stuff. Some company buys land at agricultural value. Their friends in the council get it re-zoned, the company builds houses or whatever, and sells at a huge profit because they don't pay tax anywhere along the line. Now it's gone mega because someone's pumping drug profits through the system. The corruption is immense.'

'So, the local guys with contacts in the town halls have got cosy with the Colombians, the Russians and Mexicans or . . .'

'Yep. It could be any one of a dozen groups, and they're all pretty bad.'

'So who's in the frame in Granada?'

'I'm sorry, but I can't disclose any names. That's up to the boss. We agreed we could say we have suspicions about Che Navarro. We figured that might tempt you.'

'It does.' Max smiled.

'The problem's getting evidence that'll stand up in a court of law. We've had wire taps on a few players for a while.'

'But surely they must suspect you are after them,' said Max.

'Of course. That's why it's taking so long to get the buggers. They know every trick in the book. These guys change mobiles like other people change socks. There are companies hidden by companies hidden by more companies. Suitcases and cardboard boxes of cash. It takes time and patience. You know something is wrong when you hear about a Picasso in someone's toilet. But tips like that don't come up often. We have to be very patient. And it doesn't help when cops are batting for the other side.'

'Like Navarro?' inquired Max

'Maybe. And not just cops. There are politicians, town hall officials and bankers all in the web. But sometimes they slip up and make mistakes. A guy starts to enjoy the lifestyle and, if it doesn't fit with his declared income, maybe he's another player. We keep an eye on who's spending. We have a girl in one of the Madrid art dealers telling us who's buying. You'd never believe the things she's found out.'

They were approaching the Montes de Málaga now, still green from the heavy rains. They drove past the Málaga Botanic Gardens, down into the city of Málaga itself, left the car in a secure parking area near the port, and took the lift up to the top floor of a large modern building.

'*Hola*, Roberto. How are you doing?' asked a striking secretary.

'*Bien gracias*. I'm doing fine, Laura,' said Roberto. 'Granada's a lot colder than here. I miss the company here as well.'

'*Sí*, Granada folk can be so rude sometimes.'

'Granada's famous *malfollada*. Rudeness as an art form. Is the boss in?'

'*Sí*. He's expecting you.'

Inspector Jefe Mario Cruz was a small, brown, wiry man, who fizzed with nervous energy.

'Good to see you, Roberto. So this is Sub-Inspector Max Romero. Pleased to meet you,' he said, shaking Max's hand firmly. 'I've heard about you from Roberto. I also checked up on you with a good friend of mine, Martín Sánchez. He speaks highly of you.'

'Martín? I should have guessed his name would crop up sometime.'

'He's a clever bugger. And doing a good job with Special Branch in Madrid. He's been a great help to us. So Roberto's filled you in?'

'A bit, sir.'

'We've already got useful new information from Max,' said Roberto. 'Remember that lawyer I told you about, the one who organized the sale of Reina del Sur to a company in Gibraltar? Well, his business partner bought an expensive cloak for a Virgin.'

'He what?'

Roberto laughed, and explained about the cloak of the Virgen de los Gitanos and the sale of the monastery of Jesús del Valle.

'Now that is useful. We'll follow it up. Right, Max. I can't give you any names from the Marbella to Nerja probe. Let's just say it's very extensive. And the Russian and Latin American mafias have muscled in. But we're now picking up a bit on Granada. And there we have a problem.'

'Roberto's explained about the Granada unit.'

'And they'll have bought other cops too. But then your murder probe came up with a list of companies we've already had our eye on.'

'That was just luck. Roberto did the legwork on that.'

'But you got the tip about the land sales. And the jigsaw is starting to come together. The name of a leading Granada businessman, Faustino Azul, has cropped up a couple of times.'

'I'm not surprised.'

'Don Faustino's been talking to some of the guys we've been tapping, and we need to know who's on Don Faustino's network. We've had a look at his house already, and he's very security-conscious. His study only looks on to an inner courtyard, so we have to get a bug there somehow.'

Max remained silent.

'You know his daughter. Margarita. Maybe you can persuade her to help us.'

How the hell did they find out about Margarita and me? thought Max. Was nothing private?

Max stared into Mario's eyes. It was Max who blinked first. 'I know her, but not too well.'

'Maybe. We need your help, Max. Will you help us?'

'Sí. But there are limits. I don't want Margarita in any danger. Why don't we break in ourselves?'

'You've seen the guard and the security cameras he's got on the outside. The slightest hint that something's not right and we've lost our man.'

201

'I can't say I'm delighted to help this way. It's asking a lot of her.'

'I know. But in the long run it will be best for her and the family.'

Max hesitated. 'I'll do what I can.'

'Good. I've prepared a file for you. Stay in touch with Roberto, and he'll keep us informed. No more contact directly with us in Málaga. Just be careful. You never know who has been bought.'

'I'll be careful, sir.'

'Right. I'll give you one of our listening devices. This baby is state-of-the-art. We got it from the US Drug Enforcement Agency and it's virtually undetectable. Margarita just has to stick it somewhere outside the window of Azul's study. If it's on a window sill, she can disguise it in a plant pot, or put it in a box. Wood and ceramic are okay, but not metal, of course. It'll overcome the anti-bugging jams, and pick up everything, just from the vibrations of the window pane. Any questions?'

'None at the moment, sir.'

'Good. Pleased to have you with us, Max.'

On the way back, Max explained about Margarita's difficult relationship with her father.

'I don't think you can give her too many details about this operation,' said Roberto. 'Not until we are sure we can get him. He's starting to get worried, and more than a little frightened.'

'I really don't feel good about this, you know.'

'Max, in our experience the family are often involved.'

'Not Margarita, I'm sure.'

'But this is going to blow up sooner or later. And the more quickly we sort it out, the better for the whole family.'

'All right.'

'Why not phone her now? Some of our birds are getting jittery.'

Max called Margarita's mobile. It rang for a while. Then a sleepy voice answered.

'Margarita, it's Max. I hope I didn't wake you.'

'I'm missing you, *hombre*.'

'Me too, *guapetona*.'

'It's nice to hear your voice. Max, I'm worried. I really need to talk to you. Can we meet for lunch tomorrow? I'll pay.'

'No, I'll borrow fifty euros off you.'

She laughed. 'How about the new restaurant just below the Mirador de San Nicolás? They have a French chef.'

'I'll see you there at about two. Tomorrow then. '

'Okay. See you. Lots of love.'

'Perfect,' said Roberto. 'Couldn't be better. I'll phone Mario.'

Mario was very happy.

'*Sí*, Mario. I'll put him on.'

'Max. That's great news. It's important I speak to the girl. I'll be in the bar of the restaurant. If all goes well, bring her over to me and let me talk to her alone.'

'Will do, Mario. But –'

'No buts, Max. Just do as I say. I know what I'm doing.'

Roberto soon approached the outskirts of Granada. 'Let me off at Plaza del Triunfo,' said Max. 'I can get an Albayzín bus from there.'

As Max returned to his flat, the bug felt as if it was burning a hole in his pocket. He picked up his car and drove straight to the offices of Seguridad Victoriano. Gloria was in the front office, still painting her nails.

'Well, well,' she said. 'If it isn't the cute cop. *Oye*. I've been really bad and need a full body search.'

'I'm looking for Fernando Pozo. Do you know where I can find him?'

'No,' said Gloria as Víctor walked into her office.

'Fernando?' said Víctor. 'He resigned. He just phoned to say he'd got something better, came in, collected what he was due, and that was it.'

'Did he say where he was going?'

'No. The job's in Málaga, I think.'

203

'*Gracías*,' said Max. 'You've been really helpful.'

'I'll see you out,' offered Gloria.

Max was about to decline the offer but then had an idea. 'That would be nice,' he said.

Víctor watched Gloria accompany Max to his car.

'I might be able to help you,' she said. 'How about a meal tonight? There's a nice steak house on Plaza del Triunfo.'

'I know it,' Max said. 'Nine o'clock?'

She smiled coquettishly. 'See you then.'

Max had booked a table for two at the Argentinían Steak House, and had asked for it to be at the back. He ordered a bottle of Rioja, medium-priced. Gloria arrived ten minutes later. The red dress had been replaced by a little black number, with a sequinned tiger filling most of the front.

'I've just ordered the wine,' Max said.

'*Gracias*. It's nice to eat out, isn't it?'

'It is, Gloria.'

'*Hombre*. You don't know how boring that office is. And Víctor's a brute. Tried to paw me a couple of times, but I told him where to get off.'

'I'm sure you can take care of yourself.'

'I can, but I'm very sensitive to some warm, soft talk.'

After her third glass, Max broached the subject of the security guard, Fernando Pozo. 'I'm surprised he's moved on. I thought he was happy out at the *cortijo*.'

'He was a bit bored out there on his own, but he liked the dogs, you know.'

'Had he been with you long?'

'Five years. Why do you ask? I thought it was me you're interested in.'

'I am, Gloria. This wine's good. Fancy another bottle?'

'I wouldn't say no. You have *ni idea* of how bored I get in that stinking office. It's not what I wanted, you know. I should've stayed on at school, so I should.'

Max ordered another bottle. She was already quite tipsy. He'd better get his questions in quickly.

'So what happened to this Fernando?'

'Him again? You're not gay, are you?'

'No. But I'd like to talk to him.'

'About what?'

'I shouldn't really be telling you this, but a *gitano*, who lived close to the *cortijo*, died a couple of weeks ago.'

'*Ay! Un asesinato!*' Gloria's eyes shone. 'I do love a good murder. I bet you've some good cases you could tell me about . . .'

'Why don't I pour you another glass, Gloria?'

'*Por favor, gracias.* It was odd with Fernando. No complaints, no nothing. Then these two *gitanos* pitched up at the office. Let's put it this way . . . they were the type you wouldn't like to meet on a dark night.'

'Any idea who they were?

'No. Never seen them before.'

'Go on.'

'Well, they went into Víctor's office. Then they all left in their car. And Fernando was with them when they came back. Fernando didn't say a word to me. It all seemed bit suspect. Fernando and I always had a bit of banter. He wasn't bad-looking, you know, but not my type. I like blue eyes. "Fernando's leaving," says Víctor. "Give him his wages made up to the end of the month, plus a bonus of two hundred euros." Well, Víctor's a mean bugger. He'd never give anyone a cent. So I knew something wasn't right.' She hiccupped loudly.

Max topped up her glass. 'Anything else? Do you know where Fernando Pozo lives?'

'He lives in Almanjáyar, Calle . . . forget now. He asked me for a meal to his place, once. I wouldn't be seen dead there. Víctor's not said a word about it all. He clammed up like an . . . an . . . oyster, and that's not like him at all.' She hiccupped again. 'Oops. I think we'd better go now – I'm feeling a bit dizzy.'

205

'Sure,' said Max. He paid, and helped Gloria out of the restaurant. 'My car's just round the corner. Where do you live?'

'Not far. Just down from the hospital. Here, you'd better take my keys. I might lose them on the way.'

Max drove to a block of high-rise flats.

'*Planta* 5. Number 6D. You are nice. A gentleman. I don't see many of them in my line of business.'

Max helped her into the lift. She clung closely to him as he walked her along the corridor to number 6D. He took her keys out of his pocket, opened the door and they entered a small, but neat flat.

'It's small. All I can afford,' said Gloria. 'Help yourself to a drink, Max. I'll slip into something more comfortable.' And she toddled off towards the tiny bedroom.

Max sat quietly for five minutes. He looked around the flat. There was a modest fitted kitchenette, photos of the family, dolls, a pile of celebrity magazines and cheap thrillers under a small television, a sofa and that was about it.

Another five minutes. Still no Gloria.

He finally got up and checked the bedroom. Gloria was sound asleep on the bed, fully clothed, snoring loudly. Max took off her shoes, covered her up with her bathrobe, and then placed a glass of water on the table. Finally, he turned out the lights and left quietly.

There was a powerful black motorbike parked opposite the flats. There was no sign of its owner.

Chapter 27

The next morning Max drove out to Almanjáyar, straight to Father Gerardo's house.

'May I come in, *padre*? Do you have a few minutes to spare?'

'Please come in. I have an hour before a meeting.'

The priest's small house was next to the church. The study was neat and modern, full of books and pamphlets stacked tidily on office shelving, a plain crucifix on one wall, and a photograph on the desk of Archbishop Romero of El Salvador, assassinated by paramilitaries whilst saying Mass in his own cathedral.

'I was just wondering if you knew a Fernando Pozo.'

'*Sí*, he's a regular at Mass and a friend of Catalina's. He's not in trouble, is he?'

'No, I'd just like to talk to him, that's all. Do you know his address?'

'I do,' said the young priest. 'He lives in the block of flats next to the bar Los Gitanos. You can't miss it. It's first left after the bar, the only blue door on the first floor.'

'So how are things in the neighbourhood?'

'Not good. Everything's being closed down.'

'The work with drug addicts and the women's refuge?'

'*Sí*. And the Archbishop's moving me to some parish in the middle of nowhere. I have been instructed to concentrate on the spiritual concerns of my parishioners, and forget the rest.'

'That's a great shame.'

'It's bad. I'm thinking of leaving the priesthood.'

'I'm sorry to hear that. But I understand how you feel. Have you heard from Father Oscar?'

The priest hesitated, collecting his thoughts before answering Max's question.

'He's in serious trouble, so he's now planning to go back to El Salvador. But before he leaves we're planning to hold a Theology of Liberation Mass.'

'That'll be interesting. I'd like to attend.'

'You'll be welcome,' said the priest. 'I'll let you know when the date is confirmed.'

Max got up. '*Gracias, padre*, for your time. Can I leave my car in your yard?'

'Of course. You should have better luck with it this time. My meeting's here so I can keep an eye on it for you.'

Max walked to the bar Los Gitanos and round the corner to the block of flats where Fernando Pozo lived. It was still early, and no one was about except the postman.

Max knocked on the blue door. '*Policía*,' he called. The blue door opened a crack. 'Can I come in? I interviewed you at Cortijo de los Angeles, remember?'

The door opened a little wider. It was on a heavy security chain.

Fernando Pozo peered at him, his hand firmly on the door. 'No. I have nothing to say.'

'You've done nothing wrong. I just want to ask you a few questions.'

'Like I said, I've nothing to say.'

'Catalina Maya said I could talk to you. We need your help.'

Fernando Pozo opened the door and checked the stairs and the lobby. '*Vale*. I suppose so.'

'*Muchas gracias*.'

Fernando had begun packing his possessions. He found a space for Max to sit among the bags and boxes.

'So you're leaving?' asked Max.

'The van's coming round later.'

'Catalina will miss you. She said you've been a good friend.'

'She's been a good friend to me as well. But I have to leave here.'

'So what happened with Seguridad Victoriano?' asked Max directly.

Fernando stared at the poster of Cristo de los Gitanos, which filled half the kitchen wall. 'I don't know what you mean.'

'You said you're a good friend of Catalina's. She has big problems. This could help her.'

Fernando paused. 'Catalina? Okay, but promise never to let this out.'

'I'll be as silent as the grave.'

Fernando laughed nervously. 'You'd better be, or else it's the silent grave for me.'

'You have my word.'

'Well . . . I was just getting on with odd jobs at the *cortijo*, and then Víctor pitched up with a pair of *gitanos*. I know them. Bad bastards. They don't mess around, I can tell you. They said a cop would be coming round later, and I had to make a new statement saying you'd put words in my mouth about that hippy guy I saw. I had to say he'd never climbed round to the back of the *cortijo*.'

'And you agreed?'

'I had no choice. You don't argue with guys like that. They know where I live.'

'Okay. Could you give me their names?'

Fernando looked at Max incredulously. 'Do you think I've got a death wish, or something?'

'*Vale* . . .'

'*Mira*. You don't understand. They told the boss man, Víctor, to give me two hundred euros then and there, and they'd give me another two hundred once I'd done what they wanted. End of story.'

'I don't suppose you would want to sign a statement to that effect?'

'Was that a joke? *Mira*, I have told you. Now it's up to you, and Catalina owes me one.'

'Do you know the cop who came round to see you?' said Max

'I've never seen him before,' said Fernando, 'He had this strange accent. He wasn't local. Could have been Argentinian.'

'*Gracias*, Fernando, you've been a real help. I'll remember this. If there is anything I can do for you, call this number.'

'I'll see you out,' said Fernando. 'The front door sticks a bit.'

Fernando turned the lock, lifted the door up, and pushed hard. There was a man with an ugly dog in the lobby. Max thought he recognized him. It was the same guy with the dog that he had last seen in the bar, Los Gitanos.

'Give my best to Catalina when you see her,' said Fernando.

'I will.'

Max picked up his car and drove back to the Albayzín. He failed to notice the black motorbike shadowing him, three cars behind.

Max changed into his black Pedro de Hierro jeans, white shirt and the black linen jacket and walked round to *el restaurante* Las Estrellas de San Nicolás, snuggling just below the Mirador.

'Señorita Azul is waiting for you,' said the owner.

He ushered Max up the stairs into a dining room with huge windows looking straight across to the Alhambra. Margarita was sitting at the table with the best view. She was wearing a blue dress, with long sleeves to cover the bruises.

'Blue suits you,' said Max 'You should wear it more often.'

'Thanks. It's your colour too. It goes with your eyes.'

'This is a really gorgeous place,' said Max, admiring the fine carved wood ceiling. 'It's the first time I've been here.'

'Me too. This used to be Enrique Morente's house.'

'I bet he composed his *Suenos del Alhambra* here. With that view you'd be inspired, wouldn't you?'

There was a bottle of wine on the table. Margarita poured two glasses. 'Sorry I jumped the gun with the wine, but the Barbazul's lovely, and they are down to their last two bottles.'

Max glanced at the menu. 'That's fine. I rather fancy the "crumble" of *morcilla* as a starter, and then the slow roast duck.'

'That's what I was going to have too.'

The 'crumble' turned out to be a little tower of the savoury black pudding interleaved with caramelized mango, roasted almonds and a red wine sauce.

'This *morcilla*'s so much nicer than the black pudding in Scotland,' said Max.

Margarita raised her glass. 'To our first posh lunch out together. Here's to us!'

'I'll drink to that. The first of many.'

'On your salary?'

'On both our salaries,' corrected Max.

Margarita leaned over and kissed him on the lips.

'You sounded really upset on the phone,' said Max. 'What's going on?'

'It's my bloody father. Do you know what he's done? Transferred a whole load of properties to a trust in Blanca's name.'

'That's not good. If your father is arrested, the cops might think she's an accessory.'

'I know. Apparently she didn't think anything of it, but yesterday she read something about a case in Valencia where a dodgy lawyer put property into a trust for his daughters, and they ended up in big trouble. Blanca started thinking and got worried.'

'So she should. It's a classic crook's move. Your father must be getting nervous.'

'She asked him about it and he turned nasty.'

'Oh dear.'

'It gets worse. He checked the security camera tapes and found pictures of you coming in and out at the weekend. He

211

knows you're a cop, and he ordered me not to see you again. He was quite threatening. I told him where to get off, and we had a shouting match. So I'm moving back to my own flat tonight.'

Max hesitated. 'I'm sorry to have to tell you this – but your father is in real trouble.'

'Tax dodges, bribery . . .?'

'A whole lot worse. We think a mafia gang on the coast are using his property business to launder drug money.'

'Mafia? *Joder*! I . . . I knew he cut a few corners, but this?' Her face went pale. 'Max, you haven't been using me to get to my father? I thought you . . .?'

'Of course not. It's just that our paths crossed with my job. I can't go into details. But since I got suspended, I've been working with the Anti-Corruption Unit in Málaga.'

'You didn't tell me.'

'I couldn't. And even the Granada cops don't know about it. But the Málaga team have been bugging suspect phones for months, and your father's name keeps coming up.'

'*Mierda*.'

'And Jesús del Valle is turning very nasty. Paco Maya wouldn't sell, and he's dead. The murder's been pinned on Francisco. And it could get worse. Your father and his friends have to be stopped now.'

'Oh shit.' Margarita took a swig of wine.

'Margarita, we think you can help.'

'I don't see what I can do. The old bastard never listens to me.'

'I know. But there's something only you can do. You know how security-conscious he is.'

'*Si*.'

'The Anti-Corruption team want to bug your father's secure phone. That phone blocks out our usual remote monitoring devices, but we've got a little gadget which could pick up conversations in his study, and all you have to do is hide it there.'

'Oh, Max. You mean that lovely weekend, you were thinking of this?'

'No, I was recruited a couple of days later, after I got suspended. Look, I didn't want to involve you, but Mario, he's the head of the Anti-Corruption team in Málaga, thinks your father's a key to getting the mafia gang.'

'Do you realize what you're asking? This is bloody dangerous. And after all . . . he is my father.'

'I appreciate that. But we need to get the guys behind it all. We really need your help.'

'Oh, Max. I get the picture, but . . . oh shit, I can't do that.' She took a large gulp of wine.

'We're very short of time. They could bolt before we get the evidence we need. Please help us. You're brave. You picked this copper's pocket once. You can do it.'

'I really can't help you guys send my own father to jail.'

'Okay. But could you just have a word with Mario? He's the head of the Málaga Anti-Corruption Unit. He badly wants to talk to you. He's waiting in the bar downstairs. Your father's going down. It might help get him a lighter sentence.'

'But . . .' There was a long pause. 'Okay. I'll talk to him.'

Max took her through to the small bar downstairs. Mario was sitting alone, by a large statue of the Buddha, nursing a glass of orange juice.

Max went back up to the restaurant. The maître d' was hovering.

'Is everything all right, sir?'

'My friend has a bit of a family crisis. Could you hold the duck until she gets back?'

'Of course.'

Max had finished the bottle of wine before Mario and Margarita joined him. She was pale.

'I'll do it. I'll do it as soon as the maid goes home, and then I'll move back into my flat.'

'Thank you, Margarita,' said Mario. 'We really are grateful. Believe me, the risk to you is minimal. We'll only

213

need to leave it in place for a few days, and then you can be rid of it.'

'I hope you're right,' said Margarita.

'I hope so too,' said Max.

'It's best if you two aren't seen together until this is over.'

'I suppose you're right.'

'And don't use any of your father's phones. I've got a new mobile for you. Use this one if you need to speak to Max or to me.'

Margarita looked at Max. 'Oh, man. If this goes wrong . . .'

'It won't go wrong,' said Mario. 'We've got everything covered.'

Chapter 28

For two days Max waited. To kill time, he went flat hunting. He looked at one off San Miguel Baja, right at the corner where the bus turned to go down Costa de la Loma. The flat was dark and cramped, and it had a penetrating smell of fried food from the kitchens of El Yunque. He looked at a another just off the Mirador de San Nicolás. It had a view of the side of the church of San Nicolás, which wasn't bad, but the plaza was full of noisy tourists, hippies smoking pot and street musicians until the early hours of the morning. Then there were the flats off Plaza de la Cruz Verde. They had just been tastefully refurbished. But the only one he felt he could afford was tiny. And it had no view whatsoever.

Max deep-cleaned his flat and manicured his plants. He read all the newspapers from cover to cover, and finished Julian Rathbone's *Lying in State*, a novel set in Madrid in the last days of the Franco regime when the old bastard was actually dead but nobody dared admit it. He checked his mobile every five minutes, just in case he'd missed a call.

Then finally, on Friday evening, Roberto rang.

'Meet me in half an hour in the cloisters of Hotel Santa Paula.'

Max hurried to meet Roberto, who was sitting in a corner reading *El País*. There was a long article on mafia killings in Marbella. 'Look at that. Our media office is giving out too much to the press. Coffee?'

Max nodded. 'Any progress?'

'*Sí*. Faustino Azul's under pressure. Andrés Mendoza told him to come up with two hundred thousand Euros fast, as an advance payment for a building permit. And Azul's called a meeting of the guys involved in the Jesús del Valle project.'

'Where? In Azul's offices?'

'No. Believe it or not it's in a *cofradía* building. The Brotherhood of the Bell. Tomorrow evening.'

'The Brotherhood of the Bell? *Dios mio* . . . of course. What a cover.'

'We're planning to monitor that meeting, so we'll be planting the listening devices tonight, about 2 a.m. The street is very dark and quiet, but we have to be careful. Max, could you stand as a lookout?'

'Sure. Where do we meet?'

'In Plaza Santo Domingo at 2 a.m.'

'You're on.'

Just after midnight, Max finally found his dark grey woolly hat lurking among the junk, dust and lost hankies at the bottom of his wardrobe. He put on the hat, old black trousers and a black jumper, and walked down the Albayzín through Realejo to Plaza Santo Domingo, close to AjoBlanco.

Roberto, Mario and another man were waiting near the bar.

'Max, this is Raimundo. He's our technical wizard. This man could listen in to the Pentagon.'

Raimundo smiled modestly. 'I just have some very good kit, that's all.'

'I tell you, if this man went over to the dark side, we'd have to give up.'

The four cops walked round to the back of the church, through an ancient arch, to a quiet side street.

'This is the place,' said Mario. 'We've got the van just round the corner. Max, you stay outside. If you notice anything odd, phone me. If you haven't time, act drunk, and shout "*Viva Málaga*". We'll hear you.'

216

Max leaned against the wall close to an iron-bound door. There was laughter in the distance as the last revellers were chucked out of AjoBlanco, then the hiss and snarl of cats fighting over rubbish. The minutes ticked by. Max looked up the narrow street. A tall dark figure in a priest's cassock and two young men were coming down the street. Max started shouting, '*Viva Málaga*. We're going to win the cup. *Sí*, we are.'

'Not much chance of that, Salvador.'

There was a laugh. 'You're right, Diego. It's Real Madrid's cup this year.'

Max stumbled off as if drunk. He waited until the priest and the youths went inside another old building, then phoned Mario.

'Just had a close shave. A priest I know passed by.'

'The priest's out late. We'll be with you in a minute. Just finishing off.'

'Fine.'

'That's it done,' said Mario as he reappeared a couple of minutes later. 'We'll pick you up behind the Columbus statue, tomorrow at 6 p.m.'

Max returned to his flat and slept until late morning. At half past five, he walked downtown. The surveillance van picked him up behind the statue as agreed.

'I've brought in support from Málaga,' said Mario. 'We still can't tell anyone in the Granada forces. Right. Max and Roberto will stay in the van with Raimundo and me. Max, listen in with Raimundo. You might recognize somebody. We've got camera operators ready. The rest of the team will be waiting in the front and round the back, ready to go in once we've got enough evidence on tape. *Vale*.'

They all nodded.

'Then let's go.'

Raimundo parked the van on a quiet side street near the Brotherhood of the Bell's HQ.

'All clear,' said Roberto. 'None of the guys at the meeting

should come this way. But we can't risk being seen. So, there's no leaving the van until it's all over.'

Raimundo was testing the equipment.

'This is the boring bit,' said Roberto. 'It wouldn't be the first time I've done this all night and we got nothing.'

'Well, I hope we get something today,' said Max.

'I have this gut feeling that we will.'

At 7 p.m. Max could hear voices through the headphones. Faustino Azul was greeting new arrivals.

'So good of you to make it at such short notice, Don Miguel.'

'You said it is an important meeting, Don Faustino.'

'Yes, we have to review where we are and how we go forward. Ah, Don Andrés Mendoza, a pleasure to see you. Was *el jefe* able to come?'

'Unfortunately not. However, he has sent a message which I will deliver to you all.'

'Damn!' exclaimed Roberto.

Then someone in the meeting rang a little bell, calling the assembly to order.

'I believe you all know each other,' Faustino Azul began. 'I have apologies from a number of Brothers. Unfortunately, the gentleman behind the scheme is unable to be here with us this evening. But he has asked Don Andrés Mendoza to read out a statement on his behalf.'

Mario whispered to Roberto: '*Mierda*. No show, after all that effort.'

'But these guys inside can give us names,' said Max.

'Sure, we could probably pick up the small fry. But only Don Andrés and maybe Don Faustino know who the top man is.'

'Maybe if we let them talk some more, we'll get something,' said Max.

'I doubt it.'

The microphone picked up the rustle of paper. Don Andrés started reading.

218

'Welcome, Brothers, to this meeting. I appreciate that many of you wish to know my identity. However, I am convinced that until everything related to our proposed project is completely secured, it is best that I remain anonymous. If we are to succeed in this project, we shall require the assistance of many people in order to obtain all the necessary permits. We now have positive relationships with all these people, but this costs money. Various gifts have been made to secure goodwill, including a donation to the Cofradía de los Gitanos. The Capataz of the Brotherhood of the Bell has agreed to put in another two hundred thousand euros to ensure the success of this venture. But further investment will be necessary. I now appeal to you all to consider increasing your stakes. The return on this will be substantial.'

Faustino Azul opened the meeting to questions.

It was a man with a Málaga accent who spoke first. 'The success of our project depends upon the road connections There is the outstanding problem of the gypsy's property. Has there been any progress?'

'There have been developments,' said Andrés. 'The gypsy is dead, and that bloody Francisco Gómez has caused a few headaches . . .'

There was a mutter of anticipation in the room.

'But, if you don't know this already, Gómez has been arrested for the murder of that very same gypsy.'

Another voice cut in. 'That's excellent news, Don Andrés.'

'And I am confident that once the gypsy's will has been settled, the heir will sell.'

'Can you be sure about that?'

'No. Not a hundred per cent. Nothing in life is ever so certain.'

'So there is still some doubt? Then, Don Andrés, I will delay any further investment until this matter is concluded satisfactorily,' said a man with an educated Granadino accent.

There were mutters of 'Hear, hear.'

219

After a pause, Don Andrés spoke slowly. 'Such caution is not necessary, *caballeros*. It's virtually a done deal. I advise you all to continue with your investments. None of you would want to lose what you have already put in, would you?'

Max recognized the voice of the next speaker. It was Juan. Definitely Juan.

'We should trust Don Andrés' judgement. I am confident he will get that piece of land. And then we should be home and dry. I, for one, will put something extra into the pot. There's a risk involved, but returns promise to be very attractive.'

There was a round of applause. The formal meeting was coming to an end.

Mario rang the guy in charge of the team waiting outside the building. 'The main man's not there. We may as well pick this lot up. We've got enough on tape to show they all know it's seriously crooked. Somebody might just give a lead to the boss. But I doubt it. Okay, men. Get the rich buggers.'

There was the noise of splintered doors, shouts and loud complaints as some of the Province of Granada's most respectable businessmen were handcuffed and escorted to a police van.

'Mario,' said Max. 'Can we talk privately? I need a small favour.'

'Sure.'

'One of the guys you've lifted is my cousin, Juan Romero. He's just a small-scale developer who cuts corners to make a buck. He's not one of the bad guys, just an idiot. If he cooperates, maybe you could put a word in for him?'

'If it's like that, I'll see what I can do. You've been a great help.'

'*Gracias.*'

Max walked over to where Juan was standing in line.

'Max, what the hell are you doing here? Can you tell these goons I've done nothing wrong?'

'Juan, you're an idiot. You've got yourself involved in a huge corruption case. It's serious. Mafia drug gangs . . .'

Juan blanched. He looked like a little kid who had stolen from the church plate for a dare, and then been found out. 'I d-didn't know.'

'You heard what Andrés Mendoza said, didn't you? And you voiced your support for Don Andrés.'

'What should I do, Max?'

'Tell the police absolutely everything you know. Absolutely every detail. I'll put in a word for you.'

Juan swallowed. 'Thanks, Max. Can you keep this away from Paula and Isabel? Please.'

'I'll do what I can. Be cooperative, Juan.'

Max returned to Mario. 'Another thing, Mario. A couple of points Mendoza made rang a bell with me. I can't yet put my finger on them, but they will come back to me. Can I have a copy of the tape?'

Mario turned to Raimundo. 'How soon can you do that?'

'I'll bring it over to your flat tomorrow morning, Max.'

Twenty minutes later, the Málaga team drove off with some very respectable gentlemen in handcuffs, and Max trudged back to his flat. He phoned Margarita's number. There was no answer from her flat. He tried her new mobile, and then the old one. No answers. He kept on trying until after one. There was no reply.

Chapter 29

Max heard the doorbell ringing over the noise of his shower. He shrugged on his dressing gown, padded down the stairs of his block of flats, and opened the front door. Two cops were standing there: Inspector Jefe Davila and Inspector Navarro.

'Max Romero, we are taking you in for questioning.'

'What? Have you gone crazy? It's 7 a.m.!'

'Inspector Navarro will accompany you while you get dressed. I shall wait here. There's no point in trying to run for it.'

'Run for it?'

'I'll follow you up the stairs. Let's go now,' said Navarro.

Halfway up, Max turned. 'Ernesto, what the hell –'

'Just keep going.'

Navarro followed him into his flat, walked into Max's bedroom, opened the window and looked down.

'Good. It's too far down to jump. I'll leave you alone while you dress. Leave your door open. Remember, I'm right outside.'

Max dressed while Navarro wondered around his living room, leafing through his books and papers, opening doors and touching everything.

'Ready?' said Navarro.

Max locked his flat door. 'Ernesto, surely –'

'Just keep walking.'

'No problems,' said Navarro to Davila when they got to the bottom of the stairs.

'Our car's at the top of the street. What sort of place is it when you can't even drive to your entrance?' said Davila.

Max got in the back of the car with Davila. Not a word was said. They took Max to the police interview room. He sat down at a table, facing his colleagues.

'You know your rights, Romero. We have some questions to ask you. It will be best if you cooperate,' said Davila.

'I have nothing to hide. What the hell is this all about?'

'Do you know or have you met a Fernando Pozo?'

'*Sí*. He was the security guard at the Cortijo de los Angeles. I interviewed him about the Paco Maya case. He then came in to sign a formal statement. I witnessed his signature.'

'And you saw him again?'

'*Sí*. I saw him last Wednesday in his home, at about 11 a.m.'

'And what did you see him about?'

'I went to ask him why he'd withdrawn his first statement, and why he claimed I had lent on him to make a false declaration.'

'In spite of being suspended?'

Max felt relieved. So this was what it was all about.

'*Sí*.'

'And when did you see him again?'

'See him again? I didn't. What do you mean?'

'Just answer the questions, Romero. Did you see him again?'

'No, I never saw him again.'

'Come, come, Romero. His front door had been forced. There were signs of a struggle. The deceased had a suitcase, half packed, lying on his bed. Your fingerprints were all over the place.'

'The deceased?'

'*Sí*, the deceased. Fernando Pozo's body was found yesterday, dumped in a ditch off the Carretera de Jaén. He had been shot in the mouth.'

'Oh, no, no. The silence of the grave.'

'The what?'

'He told me he'd been leaned on.'

'Not by me,' interrupted Navarro.

'Someone did. A pair of *gitanos* told him to change his statement, and got the owner of Seguridad Victoriano to pay him off.'

'Come on, Romero. What the hell are you suggesting? That I had something to do with it?' said Navarro.

'I don't know. But I do know something's going on.'

'Insinuations again, Romero.'

'And Gloria Ortega at Seguridad Victoriano – how long have you known her?'

'I met her when I was checking up on Cortijo de los Angeles, just after Paco Maya's death.'

'And?'

'Seguridad Victoriano weren't very helpful.'

'And you've never seen this Gloria woman again?'

'No, I saw her on Tuesday when I was trying to track down Fernando Pozo.'

'And did she tell you where he was?'

'Yes, no . . . not immediately.'

'What do you mean?'

'No, she didn't tell me at first. But then I invited Gloria out for a meal that evening.'

Davila raised an eyebrow. 'And?'

'We went for a steak. Then I gave her a lift back to her flat.'

'And what happened? You tried to molest her?'

'Of course not. Nothing happened. She'd had way too much to drink, and passed out on her bed soon after I got her into her house.'

Navarro snorted. 'We found your prints on a glass of water by her bed, and on her shoes.'

'I've told you I was there. I was just trying to make her more comfortable. I took her shoes off after she keeled over. And when I left I put a glass of water by her bed.'

'Did you touch the bottled gas fire?'

'The gas fire? Why on earth would I do that?'

'Gloria Ortega was found dead in her flat. Asphyxiation. Someone had turned her gas fire on without lighting it. Your prints are on the top of the gas fire.'

'Christ. Poor Gloria. What's going on? I might have touched the top of the gas fire.'

'That's what we want to know. We want you to tell us the truth.'

'The truth?' yelled Max. 'The fucking truth is that I'm being stitched up. By that bastard sitting next to you.'

Navarro stood up, fist curled.

'Sit down, Ernesto. We're way beyond false accusations against a fellow officer now. This is murder, probably a double murder.'

'This is madness. Why would I kill either of them? They were the people who could clear my name.'

'It would be sensible to confess, you know.'

'Confess? Confess to what? I didn't do this.'

Davila switched off the tape recorder. 'Okay. It's time for coffee.'

'I need to speak to Roberto Belén,' said Max.

'Why? Is he involved as well?'

'No. But I need to speak to him now.'

Davila looked at Navarro who shrugged.

Max's mobile rang in his pocket.

'Okay,' said Davila. 'Answer it. We're listening.'

'*Dígame?*'

'Max. It's Margarita.' Her voice trembled. 'I've been kidnapped. I don't know where I am. I don't know who is holding me. I am well at the moment. Tell my father if he says anything to the police, they will kill me. Max, pray to the Virgin of Sacromonte for me.'

The call went dead. Max dropped his phone in shock.

225

'*No*! Oh my God.'

'What's up, Romero?'

'What's up? Faustino Azul's daughter has been kidnapped. I have to speak to Roberto.'

'He's not working today.'

'He is. He'll probably be in the annexe.'

'What the hell's going on? Okay. Call him.'

Max flipped open his mobile. Roberto had been questioning suspects most of the night.

'Max, what's going on?'

'Margarita Azul's been kidnapped. The security guard and the secretary at Seguridad Victoriano have been murdered, and Davila's arrested me. Get Chávez and Mario over here. I'm in interview room B.'

'Oh Christ. Mario's still here. Hang on.' There was a pause. 'Max, Chávez has just come in with the duty judge. We're on our way.'

Davila and Navarro looked at each other in silence.

Five minutes later, Roberto, Comisario Chávez and Inspector Jefe Mario Cruz crowded into interview room B. Mario was still on an adrenalin high. Chávez was fresh and angry.

'What the hell's going on?' demanded Chávez.

Davila got in first. 'Comisario, there have been two murders, and Romero's prints were in both locations. We brought him in for questioning as soon as we had the Forensics report.'

'Fuck all that rubbish. Margarita Azul has been kidnapped. They've threatened to kill her if Faustino Azul talks.'

'Enrique, release Sub-Inspector Romero. Now. I will personally take over these two murder cases. And send me a copy of the tape and a full report. Today.'

'*Sí*, sir.'

'We'd better tell Azul right now. *Mierda*,' said Mario.

'I need to speak to him,' said Max. 'He might know something. Where is he?'

226

'He's still being interviewed in the annexe,' said Mario.

Mario, Max and Roberto hurried out of the main head-quarters building, and into a shabby office block across the plaza.

'Did you get anything?' Max asked Mario.

'We've learnt a lot about how the Brotherhood of the Bell worked. They knew who to bribe, so they oiled the wheels for a whole load of people to get building permits, and used each other's companies for money laundering. It's a real spider's web, but our accountants will crack it eventually. Unfortunately the foot soldiers don't know the man or group behind it all. And they've all got good lawyers. We had to let most of them out on bail last night. The judge agreed we could hang on to Faustino Azul and Andrés Mendoza.'

'My cousin?'

'Very helpful, but probably knows least of all of them.'

'Anything from Azul or Mendoza?'

'I doubt if we can keep them much longer, but we'll get them both on tax evasion, bribery and money laundering. Azul was beginning to weaken and might have given us something useful. But this kidnapping's blown it. And Mendoza was never going to say a word.'

In a small office, an exhausted Faustino Azul was smoking a cigarette. Guzmán de Sídonia sat beside him.

'I think you should let my client go now, officer. He has nothing more to tell you,' said the lawyer.

'Not yet. There has been an important new development,' said Mario.

Faustino stared at Max. 'Sub-Inspector Romero?'

'Your daughter, Margarita, has been kidnapped. If you decide to cooperate with us, we can find her.'

'You're bluffing. That's a nasty trick.'

'No. It's not. I suggest that you ring her mobile. Try the landline. Margarita's flatmates confirmed that she didn't come home last night.'

Faustino turned pale. 'What exactly did she say?'

Max repeated her message. 'You have to help us find her.'

227

'I have no idea. No idea where she is.'

'But you know who's behind this.'

'No idea.' Faustino Azul looked Max straight in the eyes. 'You bastard. You persuaded my daughter to bug my study, didn't you? That's how you found out about the Brotherhood of the Bell meeting.'

Max remained silent.

'You must have some clue,' said Mario. 'For your daughter's sake, give us something. We'll keep you out of it.'

'I told you I have no idea.'

The lawyer interrupted. 'My client has cooperated on everything. You have no choice but to release him now. If you have a case and it comes to court he will be questioned according to the proceedings stated by the law.'

'Wait,' said Mario. 'I'm going to talk to Andrés Mendoza. Max, you stay here.'

Max stared at Faustino. 'All right. The tape's off. Just between you and me. Tell me about the *palio*.'

'You don't have to tell him anything,' interrupted the lawyer.

'It's okay. The *palio*. That was a stunt to embarrass Gómez. Mateo knew a couple of students who might be up for it. I paid them. I didn't know Margarita would be under it.'

'But they could have killed somebody. And the demo?'

'That was a cop's idea. Set up a riot and discredit the protestors.'

'Who was the cop?'

'I've nothing more to say.'

'And Monsignor Bien?'

'A business acquaintance. I have the contract to build the new Opus Dei student residence at the top of the Albayzín.'

'Would you be willing sign a statement ?'

'No.'

Mario returned. 'We promised protection for Andrés Mendoza's family, and Mendoza's agreed to tell us all he knows. Señor Azul, give us the names of the bastards behind

228

all of this. Silence isn't going to help your daughter. You know they won't release her. Maybe they'll rape her a few times while she still looks pretty, torture her a bit, just for fun, you know, then dump her. Maybe she'll still just be alive when they dump her . . . in the sea maybe, or perhaps down a well. You know what these guys are like. You have to help us.'

'Nice try, Inspector Jefe. I've told you all I know.'

The lawyer interrupted once more. 'I have requested three times for my client to be released. This time I have no choice but to make an official complaint.' He stood up as if to leave.

Mario glared at him. 'All right, Azul. You can go now. The judge will be in touch.'

Faustino got up and walked towards the door with his lawyer.

'Your daughter . . .' Max called out at him.

Faustino didn't turn round.

Chapter 30

Max felt sick. The sweet mint tea helped a bit, but not much. Why the hell did he get Margarita involved? She knew who they were now. They wouldn't let her go free. They'd kill her. Just as they killed Gloria and that poor sodding security guard. Max stared at the Alhambra. The towers were bright and fresh in the morning sun, and the blackbird's song drifted from the pomegranate tree in the garden next door. There was a thump and rattle from the street below. The binmen were hauling sacks of trash into their little van. Max picked up his notepad and pen again.

So what did he know? He jotted down a few things. Bugger all really. He went over everything he could remember since the Paco Maya case began. Webs of corruption. Murders. Margarita could be anywhere. And he had no leads.

Max paused. Opus Dei. Faustino Azul and Mateo Bien were connected. Mateo Bien. Bien's name kept coming up. He was the one who advised the lawyer, Andrés Mendoza, to buy the new cloak for the Virgin of Sacromonte. David Costa, Salvador Lozano and Diego Elvira were all Opus boys. Maybe Bien knew what was going on.

Max hurried round to the Opus Dei centre, behind the Dominican church of Santo Domingo. He rang and rang the doorbell.

'*Voy, voy*,' a voice called out. 'I'm just coming. I'll be with you in a minute.'

A sweet-faced old man answered the door.

'Policía Nacional,' said Max, showing his card. 'It's urgent. I have to see Monsignor Bien.'

'He's in prayers. You can wait here,' the old man said, pointing to a plain chair in the corridor. And he wandered off, muttering to himself.

Max looked round the dark corridor. It reminded him of his own Jesuit school in Glasgow, brown paint and a musty smell. On the wall opposite him hung a plain crucifix and a brightly coloured picture of the founder of Opus Dei, San Josémaría Escrivá, surrounded by adoring Filipino workers and children. The caption read, 'Be holy through thy work.'

Max started pacing up and down the corridor. Finally a door opened. Monsignor Bien had finished his prayers. His crucifix was very plain, but gold glittered at his cuffs.

'*Buenos dias*, Inspector Romero. Jaime said you needed to see me. He said it was urgent.'

'It is,' said Max. 'Where's Margarita?'

'Who?'

'Margarita Azul, Faustino Azul's daughter. She's been kidnapped. Where is she?'

'Why on earth would I . . .? You'd better come to my study.'

Monsignor Bien opened a heavy wooden door, and they walked along another corridor until the last door on the left.

'Sit down, Inspector. You seem very agitated. And tell me what your problem is.'

Max had difficulties explaining clearly. His sentences tumbled out. Monsignor Bien listened carefully.

'Inspector, I am very, very sad to hear about the girl, and I shall pray for her safe return to her family. But what you are suggesting is absurd. You seem to think I have something to do with this kidnapping. That I personally, or Opus Dei, helped stir up a riot at the demonstration, or sabotaged that *palio*. Absurd. It's beyond all reason. You've read

231

too many conspiracy books. We are not like that. Your accusations are totally outrageous.'

'But all these connections?'

'Inspector, let me explain in words of one syllable.'

'Sub-Inspector,' corrected Max.

'Right, Sub-Inspector. Let me explain. I know Don Faustino. Of course I do. His company does a lot of work for us. He's just got the contract to build a hall of residence. Faustino put me in touch with Don Andrés Mendoza, who wanted to contribute to a *cofradía*. Abbot Jorge of Sacromonte is an old friend –'

'*Sí*, I realize that.'

'Jorge felt that la Virgen de los Gitanos needed a new cloak. So I introduced Don Andrés to Abbot Jorge.'

'But why la Virgen de los Gitanos?'

Mateo Bien frowned. 'For the simple reason I knew Abbot Jorge wanted a new cloak for the Virgin.'

'But the monastery of Jesús del Valle, the roads . . .?'

'Jorge mentioned that he'd agreed to the Archbishop's request for the sale of the monastery and its lands.'

'To whom?'

'I've no idea. You would have to ask the Archbishop.'

'And the repairs to the back of the Abadía?'

'Abbot Jorge has been trying to raise money for the repairs for a long while.'

'Raise money from where?'

'From wherever. The Church is always grateful for donations. I told Jorge that Opus Dei might consider a gift. But it would only have been a small part of the total repair bill.'

'And the *palio*? And the riot at the demo?'

'I know nothing about them. *Sí*, of course I know the students you mentioned, David Costa, Salvador Lozano and Diego Elvira. They are old boys of our school. I have profound differences with Padres Oscar Alto and Gerardo Arredondo. That's well known in Granada. And there's no love lost between Opus Dei and the Jesuits. There's been a lot of ink spilt on that. But neither Opus Dei nor I myself would ever countenance sabotage or provocation. They're both illegal and immoral. You claim that Faustino Azul paid these students? And that I recommended them?'

'*Sí.*'

The priest shook his head as if to rid himself of something foul and clinging. 'That's a slander.'

'Do you know where these three students are now?' asked Max.

'No. On holiday or at home, I imagine. Both Salvador and Diego have recently moved out of this residence.'

'And Margarita?' Max said desperately.

'Once again, I have no idea where Margarita Azul is. I'm sorry for Don Faustino. And we shall pray for his daughter. But to imagine Opus Dei could have anything to do with a kidnapping. It is beyond belief. We are devoted to spreading the word of God in the world, through good works, prayer and penance. Anything else is fantasy.'

Max felt as if he'd had a really bad session with his old headmaster. He had been too hasty, too emotional. Where fools rush in . . .

'Is that all, Sub-Inspector?'

'Thank you for your time, Monsignor.'

'Just don't rush to judgement again. I hope you find the girl. I'll pray that she is alive and well.'

Max shivered as he emerged into the bright sunlight. Overhead a solitary bird flew from the portico of the church of Santo Domingo.

Back home, he went on to his little terrace with a cup of strong coffee and wrote down exactly what Margarita had said . . .

'Pray to the Virgin of Sacromonte for me.'

He copied the sentence, repeatedly. Margarita was intelligent and resourceful. If she could, she would give him a clue. What was it she had said when they were talking about Carlos? 'I'd never ask anyone to pray for me. But I still pray for a friend in trouble.'

Okay. Then why ask him to pray for her? And why the Virgin of Sacromonte? The Virgin? What were they talking about when that came up?

His doorbell rang. It was Raimundo with the photographs of the Brotherhood of the Bell meeting and a transcript of the tape.

'Hi, Max. I'm so sorry the way things have gone.'

Max sat at his desk, pen and notebook at the ready, and went through Raimundo's material. There was that reference to the Cofradía de los Gitanos. Okay. This must be the cloak, and the promise to repair the building at the back of the Abadía.

There was something else nagging at him. Max closed his eyes and pictured the Virgin's cloak, blue and silver. Blue velvet, richly embroidered in silver thread.

The Virgin and her cloak? Belinda had said something to him about that. Something which had been nagging at him. He phoned Belinda.

'Max. How are you?'

'Fine, Belinda, fine. It's about the Easter Procession of the Gypsies. You were sitting next to a Penélope, a beautiful woman.'

'I was.'

'You said something to me afterwards about your conversation with her.'

'Yes?'

'Can you remember the conversation?'

'It's some while ago now, Max. And –'

'Try. Please try. It's very important.'

'Well, we talked about her speedboat in Marina del Este, her villa in Frigiliana, clothes, life in Venezuela.'

'The cloak, the Virgin's cloak?'

'Possibly. I don't remember now.'

'Try, Belinda. Try.'

There was a pause. 'She rabbited on about the cloak a bit. I got the impression she had chosen it.'

'Do you remember her surname?'

'It didn't sound Spanish. No. Oh dear . . . Baring . . . Barrington? No, that's not it. Carrington. Yes.'

'That's it!' shouted Max. 'Rubén Carrington. The guy at the Hotel Reina del Sur.'

'Max, what's going on?'

'Belinda, I'll explain everything later. Thanks.'

So Penélope chose the Virgin's cloak, not Andrés Mendoza. What did Belinda say Penélope's husband did? This and that on the coast. He'd been in the oil business in Venezuela, had business connections in Colombia. And Roberto pointed him out in the Reina del Sur.

Max phoned Mario Cruz.

'Mario, I think I've got something. Andrés Mendoza's boss could be a guy called Carrington. He may be holding Margarita.'

'Rubén Carrington? Venezuelan guy? We checked him out a month ago, but couldn't find anything on him. Except he has way too much money.'

'Where are you?'

'In your station. I'm still here.'

'So why Carrington?'

'I'll explain. See you in fifteen minutes.'

Mario, Roberto and Max met in the police car park.

Max explained.

'*Vale*. The guy fits the part. He has a British passport as well as a Venezuelan one, so he can pop in and out of Gibraltar whenever he wants,' said Mario. 'We asked the Brits to check up on him, and they said they had nothing. But he's got way too much money for his declared income.'

'We know he makes regular trips to Gibraltar,' added Roberto. 'And the companies buying up property around Jesús del Valle and Sacromonte are registered in Gibraltar. Which doesn't necessarily prove anything, but it's suggestive.'

'Did your friend learn anything else?'

'Penélope Carrington mentioned a speedboat . . . I think in Marina del Este, and a villa in Frigiliana.'

235

'It must be the same guy. Has a luxury fortress outside Frigiliana. He called it Villa Caracas.'

Roberto nodded. 'So what do we do, chief?'

'It's the only lead we've got. We put maximum surveillance on Carrington, and just hope somebody gets clumsy.'

'But we have to act now,' said Max. 'Margarita's life is in danger.'

'We're shattered,' said Mario. 'But you're right.'

Mario phoned Raimundo, then turned to Max and Roberto. 'We're all going to Frigiliana right now. Raimundo and the gang will check out Carrington's place.'

Chapter 31

They drove like demons out of Granada, down the gorge, along the coast road to the Nerja roundabout, then turned back inland towards the mountains of the Sierra Almijara and the ancient Moorish hill village of Frigiliana.

Villa Caracas was a gleaming white pile on the old Compéta road above Frigiliana village, surrounded by cypresses and palm trees. The entrance was a twenty-foot-high secure gate with surveillance cameras. The rest of the security fencing was hidden by flowering vines and bushes.

The police surveillance van was already in the driveway of a half-built villa just across a little valley. The van had been repainted since last week. The logo this time read 'Galvez y McDougall. Servicios Tecnicos'.

Raimundo was testing his equipment. 'This is as close as we could get without being spotted. With luck we'll hear something, but I can only get the rooms with windows facing this way. Better than nothing, though.'

An hour passed. Max was becoming more and more agitated.

Then they heard a man's voice. 'Put her in the car. Then let's go.'

They could hear someone being dragged along a gravel pathway. A car door slammed shut.

'Mauricio, keep an eye on this little slut. Let's go.'

Max started to panic. Mario put a restraining arm on his shoulder.

'Roberto, get this bloody car across their gate . . .'

But the gates of Rubén Carrington's villa swung open, and a 4×4 BMW nosed on to the concrete track, then accelerated rapidly as soon as it hit the tarmac road.

'Shit! Roberto, can we cut them off somewhere?' said Mario.

'Don't know. This valley's a maze of minor roads. All we can do is try to follow them.'

Mario flipped open his mobile. 'Luis, we're after Carrington. A 4×4, BMW. They've got a hostage, a girl. Probably going to Málaga airport.'

They heard a loud explosion. Across the little valley, Villa Caracas burst into flames.

The cops raced along the minor road, then sped past Frigiliana, the 4×4 some distance ahead of them.

'They'll turn at the roundabout before Nerja for Málaga,' said Mario. 'I'll phone again and try to get the Málaga cops to block the road.'

They almost lost sight of the 4×4. But they could just make it out turning left instead of right at the Nerja roundabout.

'Where the fuck are they going? Almería is hours away.'

'The Carringtons have a speedboat in Marina del Este,' said Max.

'*Joder*! He'll try and make it to Gibraltar. And then we're screwed.'

'Luis, looks like they're trying to get to Gibraltar from Marina del Este. Close the harbour, and get the speedboat. See if you can find a helicopter.'

They roared towards Almunecar, the sea a brilliant blue beneath them. They sped past La Herradura, and followed the 4×4 on to a steep road past a large hotel, then down a winding road between villas clad in bougainvillea. There was a pretty white harbour below them with a string of coves beyond. The BMW turned sharp right before the harbour, and braked harshly. Three men and two women tumbled out of the car and started running.

238

'We've got them,' shouted Mario.

But instead of turning down into the harbour, the five ran across the causeway to a small rocky island, and up the path towards the ruined lighthouse.

'*Joder*! Some bugger's got the boat out for them on the other side of the island,' yelled Max.

'Stop!' shouted Mario as the three cops set off in pursuit. '*Policía*. Stop!'

Mauricio Espinosa turned and fired a shot in their direction. The cops dived to the ground. Rubén Carrington signalled to Mauricio to stay on the top of the hill. A bullet hit the ground by Max's foot, and another splintered into a pine tree.

'Christ,' said Roberto, 'I'll have to shoot.' He took aim and fired. Mauricio Espinosa screamed and fell to the ground. Max sprinted up the path. He could see a speedboat bobbing in the water, a rope tied round a rock at the water's edge. There was no path down and Rubén and his group were sliding towards the boat, hauling Margarita close beside them, a human shield. Max scrambled down the steep slope as loose stones clattered down around him. Another shot rang out, hit a rock and exploded.

Carrington leaped on to the boat clutching his briefcase. Penélope jumped next, stumbled and fell backwards towards the water before Rubén grabbed her. As the engines roared into life, Gregorio Espinosa fired back at the cops. Margarita screamed and struggled. But Gregorio grabbed her and jumped, dragging her on board.

The boat lurched violently as it smacked against a rock. Margarita and Gregorio tumbled from the stern, and disappeared in a trail of bloody foam.

Margarita resurfaced, gasping for air. 'Max,' she called out. 'Help!'

'Over here. Grab my hand.'

'Can't . . . No . . .'

Max jumped into the water and seized Margarita's head as she went under again. He pushed her towards the rocks. Roberto scrambled on to the rock at the water's edge, lay face down, and stretched out his arm.

Splashing, spluttering, Margarita found Roberto's hand, and hung on as he pulled her on to the rocks. She lay panting, coughing up water. Roberto then hauled Max, wheezing, on to the rock beside her.

'It's all right. Just breathe. Slowly. Again, that's good.'

'Max . . .'

'Where's the other guy?' called Roberto.

'Got him,' said another cop. Gregorio Espinosa floated up. His arm was torn and bloody.

A rescue boat from the marina nosed cautiously round the rocks, and two guys lifted the injured man aboard.

'*Amor mío*. Are you all right?'

'Max, *un abrazo*,' she said, crying. 'Hug me. Hug me.'

As the speedboat raced towards the horizon, Max held her tight. 'You're safe now. They've gone. Look.' Max made out Rubén Carrington putting his mobile to his ear. Two minutes later the boat was just a mark on the horizon.

Mario clambered down to join them. 'Everyone okay?'

'Okay?' spluttered Margarita. 'You bloody joking? You nearly got me killed. What the hell were you playing at?'

'I said there was a possibility of some danger.'

'Some danger!'

Max felt distinctly wheezy. He stood up, bent over and breathed in slowly. The inhaler must be wet. 'Have you got a clean hanky, Mario?' He dried his inhaler as best he could and tested it. It worked. He took a deep puff and felt his breathing ease.

Margarita sat on a rock, crying and rubbing her shoulder. Max held her close.

'You're all right. You're safe.'

'Oh, Max. I was sure they were going to kill me as soon as they were safe.'

'Well, they didn't, and you're fine. Absolutely fine.'

Mario closed his mobile. 'Right, young lady. We need to get you warm and dry. We have to go back up to the top, I'm afraid. Do you think you can make it?'

'I'm not sure. My shoulder is hurting like hell.'

'Okay. I'll see if the rescue boat can get in close enough. We don't want you in the water again.'

Mario phoned the boat. It edged close to the big rock. A cop threw a line to Roberto who made it secure before helping Margarita to the rock's edge, She cried in pain as two sailors lifted her on board. By the time they got back to the marina, an ambulance had already arrived and two paramedics were working on Mauricio Espinosa.

'Well done, men. Raimundo, you sort out everything here. Roberto, tell the hotel we'll be needing coffee and towels. Margarita, a doctor is on the way in the second ambulance. They'll give you a quick check-up.'

Margarita shivered. 'I'm fine. Honest. My shoulder's bloody sore but I'll go to the clinic in Granada tonight or tomorrow morning. I just need some painkillers.'

'I insist you have a check-up now. I've phoned your father to tell him you're safe. He said he'll speak to you in Granada. But do you want to speak to him yourself now?'

'Not yet. If you've told him I'm okay that's enough. I need time to think. I just want to get home as quickly as possible.'

'Only if the doctor gives you the okay. I'll get fresh clothes and a shower sorted for you in the hotel.'

Fifteen minutes later Margarita was nursing a mug of hot chocolate.

'That's me okay to return to Granada as long as I have another check-up there.'

'That's good. Do you feel up to telling us what happened?' asked Mario. 'The more we know, the better chance we have of getting the bastards.'

'Sure.' Margarita sipped her hot chocolate. 'I got snatched just outside my dad's house. José, our security guard,

241

phoned my flat last night. He said something was wrong with Blanca, and he couldn't reach my father. I thought she'd gone to Madrid, but José sounded in a panic so I dashed round. Then as I walked through the gate somebody shoved a cloth over my face, and the next thing I knew I was staring at this guy with a gun.'

Mario frowned. 'Carrington must have bought the security guard.'

'Seems so. Anyway, they'd got a car inside our driveway, the bastards. Then we drove for a couple of hours and ended up in Carrington's villa.'

'So he didn't attempt to hide his identity?'

'No, which is why I was so bloody scared. Then I had to read their message this morning with them standing over me.'

'I got your reference to the Virgin of Sacromonte, thank God,' said Max.

'I knew you'd remember. I was told to just read the prepared message. But I managed to add the Virgin bit at the end. Carrington was angry, but Penélope calmed him down. Then, he wanted to know who'd bugged my father's office. I told him that it must have been Max.'

'Well done. Did they hurt you in any way?'

'No, apart from when that goon was pulling at my arm. I was locked in a bedroom, but I had food, coffee, all that, you know. Penélope was there, and she was actually pleasant to me. She told me all about the Virgin of Sacromonte and the cloak.'

'Do you think she was trying to help you?'

'No idea. I really couldn't read her. But she did, anyway.'

'And thank Christ for that.'

'The house was sumptuous, you know, just like something out of Hollywood.'

'And then?'

'They said they were going to Morocco. Then there was a phone call when I was with Carrington.'

'Any idea who it was?'

'No. But I got really scared. Carrington just sat there staring at me. Then he told everyone we all had to leave immediately. Things became a bit hectic . . .'

'So you think he was tipped off?'

'It seems like it.'

Margarita sobbed and burst into tears again. 'They were going to kill me, weren't they?'

'You're all right now. You're doing fine. More chocolate?'

'*Por favor.*'

Mario refilled her mug.

'Then we piled in the car, and you know the rest. Can I go home now?'

'Okay. Max, I think you should get Margarita back to Granada. I'll speak to you tomorrow. I'm shattered.'

Max and Margarita took the road towards Motril. Margarita put her head on Max's shoulder. She was shivering. 'Be just my luck to get a cold.' She burst into tears again. 'Oh Max, I was so frightened.'

'I know. I should have said no. But Mario was so insistent. And I honestly thought it would be for the best.'

'I'm not blaming you in any way, Max.'

'So why did you change your mind and decide to do it?'

'Mario was nice at first. Explained how in the long run I'd really be helping my father. But I just kept saying I couldn't do it.'

'And?'

'Then he told me that as my father had transferred property to Blanca, that would make her an accomplice. And she could be in for a lengthy trial along with him and end up in prison. Unless I helped you guys, of course. Blanca's very vulnerable. If she went down I don't think she'd survive it.'

'Bloody Mario. What a bastard. But it's all over now. The cops will need to see you again tomorrow, and the media will be after you. '

'Oh dear. I just can't face that at the moment. Can I stay with you until this all dies down?'

243

'Of course. Mario can say you're recovering in a safe house.'

Max turned inland at the Motril roundabout, drove smoothly between the mango and avocado orchards of the Guadelfeo delta, and then up into the gorge which wound through the mountains of the Sierra de Contravesia towards Granada and the high mountain villages.

'Max, I need the loo. And I could really do with something to eat.'

'Okay. There's a restaurant on the Diva turn-off just before the dam. We can stop there.'

They sat on the outside terrace, looking down the valley with its spiky mountains rising sheer from the narrow gorge. Sunlight filtered through the young vine shading the terrace, and a ginger kitten stalked Max's shoelace.

'You know, Max, I'd really like to get away for a few days. I need out of Granada.'

'Me too. I know, let's go to Scotland. Flights are really cheap at the moment. We could visit my mother, and then go to the Trossachs, Sir Walter Scott country. The rhododendrons and the azaleas will be out. It's so pretty, you'll love it. Can't guarantee the weather though. It's Scotland.'

'I did *Rob Roy* in my course. That would be great. I've always wanted to go there.'

'And we can take the little steamer on Loch Katrine, and walk round Loch Achray where Scott set *The Lady of the Lake*.'

'You make it sound so romantic.'

'It is. Ready to go?' said Max.

'*Sí*. I feel so much better now.'

Margarita tucked herself back into the passenger seat.

'Max, do you have Gluck's *Orpheus* in your car?'

'I think I do. It should be in the glove compartment.'

'I'd like to hear it again. Remind me of the lovely weekend we had together. Honestly, Max, I feared it might have been our last.'

Margarita put on the CD, and rested her head on Max's shoulder.

'Not long now,' he said.

The road turned towards Granada, through the gentle Lecrin valley. Soon Max changed lanes for the turn-off. As he slowed right down, a black motorbike with a driver and pillion rider drew level with them. Margarita sat up, leaning forward to replay the lament for Euridice. There were two shots. Margarita slumped forward.

A red stain spread across Max's shirt.

Chapter 32

Max woke up in hospital. A nurse smiled down at him. He lifted his hand and touched a dressing on his forehead. He felt numb, and cold.

'What's your name, young man?'

'It's . . . it's Max.'

'You're okay,' she said. 'Concussion, cuts and bruising. You've had an accident.'

'What . . .?'

'In a minute. You're all right. Do you feel sick?'

Max shook his head. It hurt.

'That's good. You'll be fine. We gave you something to help you sleep.'

'Margarita . . . the girl?'

The nurse paused. 'I'll just get the doctor.'

She returned with a grey-haired woman who sat by the side of Max's bed and held his hand gently.

'Margarita?'

'There's no easy way to say this. But I'm afraid your friend is dead. There was nothing we could do. I'm so very sorry.'

Max faded into the bed. His eyes wouldn't focus when he opened them again.

The doctor was looking anxiously at him. 'Are you all right? Can I get you anything?'

'No. No, I'm fine.'

'The police are waiting to speak to you.'

'Let them in, please.'

'Are you sure?'

'I'm sure.'

Comisario Chávez, Inspector Jefe Davila, Sub-Inspector Roberto Belén and Inspector Jefe Mario Cruz walked quietly into the hospital room.

'Max, I'm so sorry. This is terrible,' said Davila.

'We're all truly sorry,' said Chávez. 'Are you able to tell us what happened?'

'*Sí*, I'm fine . . .'

Max felt empty. The words of condolence were like little breezes, passing as soon as the words ended.

'So what happened?' asked Roberto gently.

'Everything was going really well. We were on our way back to Granada. We were talking of going to Scotland – she was going to meet my mother. Then we slowed down to turn off the motorway . . . this motorbike drove up beside me with a guy riding pillion . . .'

'Just take your time, Max.'

'I'm fine, Roberto.'

'We've spoken to witnesses, but nobody saw anything useful. Can you describe the men? Describe the bike?'

Max shook his head. 'Not really. They were in black leathers. Black helmets. Big black bike. Nothing distinctive. The driver looked into my window, then Margarita leaned forward to replay a track . . . Christ . . . she saved my life. They'd have shot me too if she hadn't done that.'

The cops stood around, awkwardly. Davila shuffled his feet. 'Uhm . . . Some good news for you, Max. The disciplinary's been binned. A most unfortunate mistake. You've done an excellent job helping to unmask this web of corruption. Bad business. And I've also given some thought to your promotion. I will strongly recommend you to be promoted to Inspector.'

'Just get that fucking Carrington. Get the bastards who did it. Get the lot of them.'

'We'll get them,' said Chávez.

Max rubbed the dressing on his forehead, then shook his head helplessly.

The nurse came over and took his pulse. 'That's all for now. We've got more tests to run.'

'Okay,' said Chávez. 'We've work to do. Max, we will find them. And you're taking some leave when you get out of here.'

'But sir, I want to get back to work. I need to find them.'

'I know how you feel, Max. But it's an order. I've seen men return too soon. They think they're fine, and then they crack up. Believe me, it's for the best. Get away from it all. Take a holiday. We'll find them. Just phone me whenever you like.'

Mario Cruz hadn't said a word. 'He's right, Max. I know this won't do much good, but I'm so sorry. I never expected it to be as bad as this.'

Max said nothing. The cops turned to leave. 'Roberto, could you stay for a moment?'

Roberto looked at the nurse. She nodded.

'Where's Carrington?' asked Max.

'We're pretty sure he made it to Gibraltar. But now we've lost him. Mario phoned the Gibraltar authorities. But the buggers want an official report and request before they'll do anything, and Carrington will be in Costa Rica before we get a reply.'

'So all this "we'll find them" was just bullshit?'

'Maybe, maybe not. Mario said the Minister's been on the phone twice. We're doing our best, Max. The Espinosa brothers are helping with our inquiries. But they don't know much. They're still insisting they didn't kill Paco Maya, and knew nothing about the shooting.'

'Okay. Carrington was tipped off, wasn't he?'

'Could be. We're working on it.'

'Are all of Mario's team straight?'

'I'd swear by them.'

'Then it must be some bastard in Granada.'

'*Si*. Mario's looking into it.'

'I could help.'

'No, Max. You're off duty. Go away for a while.'

Max paused. 'You're probably right, Roberto. I'll try to get away for a couple of days, and then start looking for a new flat.'

'That's a good idea.'

'But Roberto . . . this bent cop in the Granada force. Must be Navarro. But he didn't know about the trip to Frigiliana, did he?'

'Max, this is a difficult one. We're convinced Chávez is the only person in Granada who knew where we were going.'

'Chávez? I don't for one minute . . .'

'I know. He's gone out of his way to help. But I've known stranger things.'

'No. Not Chávez. No way.'

'Think about it, Max. If anything strikes you, phone me.'

'Okay, I'll think about it. And Roberto, you've got all my numbers. As soon as you learn something let me know.'

Roberto hesitated.

'Roberto, promise me.'

'I will, Max.'

The next morning Juan, Paula and Isabel arrived as soon as the doors opened for visitors. Paula urged him to come over to Diva straight away, but he didn't want the women fussing over him and explained that he'd decided to go away for a few days. In the afternoon Maite and Belinda came. They were wearing bright colours, but they wept when they saw him. They both understood why he needed to be alone, and Maite offered him her parents' holiday flat in San José, Cabo de Gata. Max gratefully accepted, and Maite promised to bring him the address and the keys.

'The funeral's tomorrow,' said Maite. 'Margarita is to be buried in the cemetery on top of the Alhambra. None of us have been invited. But none of us want to go. Though I wondered . . .'

'Thanks, I should go,' said Max. 'Do you know what time the burial is?'

'It's at five in the afternoon.'

'Where?'

'In the Patio de los Angeles. There'll be a Mass next week, but we're going to organize our own celebration of her life. It'll be something special. Just like Margarita.'

'I'll be there,' said Max. 'When's your celebration?'

'Don't know yet. Probably not for a couple of weeks. We'll let you know.'

'Thanks.'

'And we've got some good news. Carlos is a lot better. He should be out of hospital in a week or so.'

'That's great. Give him my very best when you see him.' Max winced as he tried to sit up straight. 'Belinda, could you do me a favour? I have to get out of this place. Tell the doctor I'll be staying with you. Promise her you'll keep an eye on me. Promise them anything, but I've got to get out.'

'Will do. Maite, come with me. I don't think my Spanish is good enough for this.'

Belinda and Maite walked round to the nurses' office. Max waited anxiously. The doctor came back with the two women twenty minutes later.

'All right, Max,' she said. 'I'll sign you off. But no rushing back to work. Just take it easy.'

'I will. Belinda will look after me. And I'm going to Cabo de Gata for a few days' rest.'

'That's sensible. You're physically fit to travel, but don't drive for a couple of weeks. Look after yourself. I'll give you some mild sleeping pills, and if you have any problems your doctor will be able to help you.'

His neck and shoulders were sore, his face was cut and bruised, but apart from that he was okay. Belinda fetched her car and they drove up the old Murcia road, through the city walls, and into the back of the Albayzín. She stopped off to get Max some bread and milk, then parked above his flat.

'Are you sure you'll be okay on your own tonight? You can stay with me, Max. I've got a spare bedroom.'

'Thanks, Belinda, but I have to be on my own for a bit.'

'All right. But if things get bad, just call me any time and I'll come round.'

'That's very kind. I'll be going to Cabo after the funeral.'

Max still hadn't wept.

Chapter 33

Pills may help sleep, but they don't ward off nightmares. Especially the ones during the day. Dazed and groggy, Max took a taxi up to the cemetery in the olive groves above the Alhambra. The old cemetery entrance had just been rebuilt. Neat, modern and efficient, it could have been the entrance to an exhibition centre. People came and went, while a group of tourists huddled round a plan of the graveyard, anxious to find the sites which had been used as film locations.

The Azul family mausoleum was in the second section of the cemetery, the Patio of the Angels. Like its neighbours, it was a pompous enclosure, walled and roofed in black marble.

Max stood in the shade behind a ponderous carved angel, out of sight of the official party. As far as he could tell from the suits and furs following the coffin from the chapel, the mourners were just family and Faustino Azul's business associates. Stony-faced elders stood around uncomfortably, but a youngish woman wept bitterly as the casket was placed in the waiting niche. More prayers were said, then Don Faustino locked the mausoleum's gilded gates and his guests walked back to the cemetery entrance.

When the family had left, Max went over to the tomb, bowed his head, and quietly thought of what might have been.

As he returned to the gate, the final limousine purred out of the car park. An elderly gentleman limped out of the olive grove surrounding the cemetery, then stumbled and fell as he tried to cross the low wall between the path and the grove of trees. Max helped him to his feet.

'Are you all right, *señor*?'

'*Si*, thanks, I'm fine. But the Mayor's gone and removed the plaque again.'

'The plaque?'

'*Sí*. Every year we put up a small plaque in memory of the Republican prisoners who were shot against that wall. And every year the Alcalde gets it torn down.'

'I'm sorry to hear that.'

'My father was shot here along with another fifteen members of our town council. There was no trial, no nothing. They shot them like dogs. And the bastards still running the town hall refuse to remove a memorial to the Fascist leader, José Antonio Primo de Rivera, but won't allow a simple ceramic plaque. You know, in 1936 two thousand Republican prisoners were lined up against this wall and shot, and there's no mention of it anywhere. Not in the cemetery guidebook. Nowhere.'

'I can't believe it,' said Max. 'Thirty years after the return to democracy . . .'

'I know. It's hard to believe, isn't it?'

'*Sí*, but this is Granada.'

Max walked home, still thinking about the murdered Republican prisoners. He looked round his beloved little flat. He would have to find somewhere else, so best just to get on with it. It would help keep his mind off Margarita. He phoned a *buscador*, an unofficial estate agent who made it her business to know what was for rent or sale in the Albayzin. Many of the old folk didn't like estate agents, but were willing to trust someone they knew. The *buscador* promised to show Max what was available in three days' time.

The next morning, after another bad night, Max took a taxi to the bus station, and caught the bus to Almería. Soon, the bus was out of the suburbs and on the motorway that slashed through the mountains of the Sierra de Huetor National Park. Max stared blankly out of the window. The groves of Mediterranean pine shone dark green in the late morning sun, but the sight gave him no pleasure. He played some music on his iPod – things he'd listened to with Margarita. Then for two hours he stared out of the bus window, not eating or drinking, hardly noticing the strange lunar landscape of eroded rocks. The bus sped through Guadix with its caves, past the old film studios where the Clint Eastwood spaghetti westerns were made, then on to the dreary, dusty suburbs of Almería. The seat was uncomfortable and his back hurt. Everything hurt. He only had a couple of photos of Margarita, just a couple of bloody photographs and his memories.

They arrived at the Almería bus station just in time for Max to catch the last bus to the little resort of San José del Cabo de Gata. The Easter tourists had left, and the small town was very quiet. Maite's parents' flat overlooked the sea and it was very comfortable. There was a pile of DVDs next to the TV and a bunch of CDs in a drawer, a mixture of classical and jazz.

Max dumped his bag and went out in search of coffee, stuff for breakfast and a bottle of good Rioja. Back in the flat, he poured himself a glass of wine and took it out on to the terrace.

His mobile rang. It was Roberto.

'How are you feeling, Max?'

'Not too bad, thanks. Any progress?'

'We've got the bad guys in the Granada Anti-Fraud Squad, and Teniente Grandes as well.'

'That's good. Any idea who leaked to Carrington?'

'No. Nothing yet. Nothing on Chávez. But the name "Che" has cropped up again.'

'Fucking Navarro. It's him. I'll kill him with my bare hands!'

'I didn't hear that, Max. I'll keep you in the loop.'

That evening Max walked along the beach, and then down

to the small harbour. He ordered the plain swordfish *a la brasa*, a side dish of potatoes and a carafe of white wine. He returned to the flat and sat on the small terrace, gazing towards Africa as the sea turned bright, blazing gold. Sleep was impossible. He sat hot-eyed, creasing the pages of the book he was trying to read. Then dawn was blue upon the waters.

The morning was unseasonably damp, and the sun struggled to penetrate the mist. Max put on his old mountain jacket for the cliff walk to Playa de los Genoveses. He passed the lighthouse and the Guardia Civil building at the end of a promontory, and then turned upwards, through a clump of fan palms around the cliff face before the steep descent to the beach of Los Genoveses.

As he rounded the headland to begin the descent to the beach, the sun faded into swirling mist. And then a chill wind blew in from the sea. His chest tightened. Max rummaged in the side pocket of his mountain jacket for an inhaler. Damn. It was in the inside pocket. Max turned his back to the wind, and fished for his Ventolin. Stuck to the blue cylinder was a muddy piece of paper . . . the scrap of comic he'd found in the stream by Paco Maya's cave. A sudden gust of wind almost blew the paper away. Max hurriedly put it back into the pocket, took a quick gasp of the inhaler, and turned back towards the village.

After lunch he made a cup of coffee, stood looking out at the mist, and then rifled through the CDs. There was a recording of Purcell's *Dido and Aeneas*. He put it on and sat with his coffee in a comfortable armchair, looking out at the mist rolling in from the sea. Purcell's baroque tragedy of Dido, Queen of Carthage, touched him deeply.

For the first time since Margarita's death, Max wept.

The journey back to Granada the next day was easier. He met his *buscador* in the café El Minotauro on Paseo de los Tristes late that afternoon. The flat she had for him was just up from Paseo de los Tristes on Calle Jazmin. It had a view of the Alhambra from one room, but otherwise it was dark, damp and expensive. Not even worth thinking about. And that was all she had within his price range.

Max set off for home on a slightly different route, along Callejón del Paz. He noticed a workman, painting over the graffiti on the outside of a large house.

'What's happening here?' asked Max.

'A new owner,' he replied. 'Doing it up to rent.'

'To rent? You don't know how much?'

'No, but the owner's here. You could ask him.'

The owner came down the stairs to greet him. 'It's two separate flats,' he explained. 'But I'm wanting to rent the place as a whole. You can sublet if you want.'

'Can I see the flats?' asked Max.

'Sure.'

The flats were small, but light and comfortable.

'And here,' said the owner, opening the back door, 'is the garden. A courtyard, and three terraces.'

'Wow,' said Max. 'It's beautiful.'

They walked up to the top terrace, covered with a wooden pergola, and looked across to the Alhambra, glistening in the early evening sunshine.

'And how much?' asked Max. He whistled when the owner gave a price. 'I'd have to rent out the flat downstairs. Can I get back to you?'

'No problem. I haven't finished decorating yet.'

Max took the owner's card. Callejón del Paz was his only chance to get a view and a garden in the Albayzín. And gardening would be good for him. But he'd have to share it. Belinda might be interested.

Back in his flat, Max took out the piece of torn paper he'd found in his pocket on his walk to Playa Genovese. He examined it carefully, paused, then stared up at the Alhambra. It was a kid's comic.

What the hell could that mean?

Chapter 34

Max arrived at police headquarters promptly at nine on Monday morning. He had missed his work. He was even beginning to miss Davila. Sargento Pedro was on desk duty as usual.

'Max,' he said. 'I didn't expect to see you back so soon. I've got something here for you. A woman left a parcel. Striking, she was. Looked like a dancer.'

'Ah, *sí*. Thanks, Pedro.'

Max took the package straight to Forensics. Dr Guillermo had just arrived at work.

'Max, I heard. Are you okay?'

'I'm fine. Guillermo, could you do me a favour?'

'Another one?'

'Afraid so. Could you analyse this bag for me, and if possible date it?'

'Seeing it's you, Max. When do you want the results?'

'Yesterday.'

Guillermo laughed.

Next stop, Roberto.

'You should have taken more time off, Max.'

'I couldn't. I've given a lot of thought to Chávez. He's been good to me. He knew everything that was going on. So yes, he had the information. But I still don't believe he could be the mole.'

'It's hard to believe, Max. But he was the only one in the know. We're tapping his phones. But so far nothing.'

'Navarro?'

'He's still in the frame of course. But we're convinced it had to be somebody higher up. I told Chávez you were returning today. He's not pleased you're back so soon. Don't know if that means anything.'

Max's mobile rang. 'That was Chávez. He wants to see me.'

'We're acting as if everything with Chávez is normal. So don't let anything drop.'

Felipe Chávez and Davila were waiting for him in Davila's office.

'Welcome back, Max,' said Davila. 'A bit better now, I hope?'

'A bit. The break did me a world of good. So where have we got to?'

Chávez explained about the arrests. There was a long list of charges against prominent businessmen and various council officials and politicians – mostly bribery and accepting bribes.

'There's one other thing,' said Chávez. 'This possibility of corruption in our unit. We've arrested Grandes and some members of the Anti-Fraud team. But there's this "Che" on the tapes. Enrique here was explaining that you think Navarro might have been tampering with the evidence on the Paco Maya case.'

'I do, sir.'

'Hmm. Anything else to add?'

'Well, Navarro is Argentinian, and the nickname "Che" has cropped up. So it could be him. I've already mentioned a couple of other things to Inspector Jefe Davila.'

'Sí. Sorry about that, Max,' mumbled Davila.

'That's all right, sir. The murdered security guard told me he'd been leaned on by a couple of heavies, *gitanos*. They said there was no point in complaining to the cops as their boss had connections. High-up connections.'

'Not that a . . . uhm . . . a gypsy would go to the cops in any case,' said Davila.

'Okay. Inspector Navarro knows your disciplinary has been dropped, and you're back to work as usual. But not a word to him about our suspicions,' said Chávez.

'Of course, sir. And Francisco Gómez?'

The two senior cops looked at each other.

'That's a problem,' said Davila. 'The Espinosa brothers have solid alibis for the time of Paco Maya's death, and we have no one else in the frame. To my mind, the death of Paco Maya and this . . . uhm . . . corruption issue seem separate cases. The judge is looking at the reports we've sent him.'

'Yes, but why would Navarro tamper with evidence on the Maya case if they weren't connected?' asked Max.

'If he did,' said Davila. 'Remember the evidence for that is very weak. I don't want us to jump to conclusions.'

'And Azul and Mendoza?'

'They're both out on bail for now. We'll get them on bribery and tax fraud, but I doubt if they'll give us any more on Carrington.'

'Carrington still has all the cards, hasn't he?'

'We've got Europol on the case. They'll be wanting to talk to you, Max.'

'Very good, sir.'

Max's office was much as he left it. He'd bring his plants, calendar, and bits and pieces back in tomorrow. Chávez wasn't acting as if he had anything to hide. Max called up the Paco Maya files and went through them once again.

If the Espinosa brothers' alibi was good, then somebody else must be involved. Person or persons unknown.

Dr Guillermo popped into Max's office. 'That was an easy one. There were traces of cocaine and a few grains of rice in the cotton bag you gave me. We can't date the cocaine, of course, but the bag was barcoded . . . it's about six years old.'

'Thanks, Guillermo. Could you get me that in writing?'

Clara's face lit up when Max stuck his head round her office door next morning.

'Oh, Max. I lit a candle for you. Are you all right?'

'*Sí. Gracias a dios.* Is the boss in?'

'It's good to have you back, *guapo*. He's in his office. He's worried about something. I think the rich widow is cooling off.'

Davila was behind his big executive desk, flicking through a pile of forms.

'Ah, Max. This accusation that we have a rotten cop in our unit is bad news. You may be right about Navarro. Anything you discover, let me know without delay.'

'Will do, sir.'

'He's looking very preoccupied,' Max said to Clara.

'*Sí.* There's something on his mind.'

Max returned to his office and continued reading through the files on the Maya case. Nothing new struck him.

It took a lot of phone calls, but eventually the personnel offices of all the forces in Granada came up with three Argentinians: Inspector Navarro, one in the Policía Local, and one in the Anti-Corruption Unit. Max phoned Roberto once again.

'I checked on that while you were away, Max. We're looking into them.'

'What do you think?'

'Actually, I'm less sure now that Navarro's involved.'

'I'm convinced he is.'

'Okay, Max. Keep pursuing that one then.'

Max took out his pad, turned to a fresh sheet of paper, and began to make notes. It must have been Navarro who planted the cocaine package in Gómez's flat and sent the Espinosa brothers to threaten that poor security guard. And there was the 'Che' reference on the wire taps. Okay, there were two other Argentinians, but that didn't rule out Navarro. Plus there was the old stuff – tampering with the cigar ash, the photos . . . But how did that bastard know they were going to Frigiliana?

Max looked at his watch. He'd promised to have lunch with Maite to discuss the memorial service for Margarita.

They met in Plaza Romanila, behind the cathedral. Maite hugged him tightly. 'We all miss her, Max.'

They sat outside the cafe La Ermita near the statue of the water carrier and his donkey. Maite wanted him to say a few words at the service. All Margarita's friends were going to offer something, perhaps say a few words, read a poem or sing a song. Max eventually agreed to speak. He returned to his office heavy of heart. He wasn't sure about the memorial service, even less so about speaking at it. He'd feel out of place. Better just to plant a tree in Jesús del Valle and leave it quietly to grow. Then he could always come and touch the tree when he needed to.

He sat there musing when his phone rang. '*Dígame*. Oh, Martín. Good to hear from you. I appreciate that. I'll be fine. It takes time, I know. So how's Special Branch then?'

'Do you really want to know?' Martín paused. 'Max, I've got some news for you. You know I've been put on to the Carrington case? I've been pushing to get him extradited back to Spain. He may still be in Gib, he may be in London. I can't find out.'

'I appreciate what you're doing.'

'Well, I've heard back from MI5 to say they honestly don't know where he is.'

'Why MI5? Surely it's a job for Europol?'

'I'm coming to that. Apparently Carrington is on a retainer with MI5.'

'What the . . .'

'*Si.*'

'But –'

'Look, Max. Carrington's one of MI5's main sources of information on the drugs coming out of Colombia.'

'Oh, sweet Jesus.'

'It gets worse. He also keeps the spooks in the picture on Venezuela. Plus he's the Venezuelan opposition's main man in London. And British oil interests would love to see President Hugo Chávez kicked out.'

'So what? We want Carrington for kidnapping and murder.'

'*Sí*. But they've asked us to go easy on him.'

'Jesus Holy Christ.'

'He's given them valuable information on the Colombian drug cartels. The Brits have offered to share that information with us if we back off. The Minister is keen to cooperate. He thinks this can help stop the flow of cocaine into Spain. In the long run that might save lives.'

'And in the long run we're all bloody dead. What about justice?'

'Justice? This is politics. But I thought I'd let you know.'

'Thanks, Martín. But can you tell the Brits from me that if I ever come across that bastard Carrington, I'll kill him.'

'I shall say no such thing. I'll tell the Minister how disappointed you and the police are, but that you appreciate the delicacy of the situation. Keep in touch, Max. And don't do anything rash. We honestly don't know where Carrington is.'

'Still in Gibraltar, I bet. I could pay a visit.'

'Don't be foolish. We're pretty sure he left Gibraltar for London. And from there, who knows?'

'Martín, are you being straight with me? Earlier you said he could still be in Gibraltar.'

'I am being honest. We have a man in Gibraltar of course, and he's convinced Carrington left under another name. And Max . . . Carrington's type eventually come to a sticky end.'

'Maybe, but eventually is not bloody good enough.'

Chapter 35

Roberto phoned Max at his flat that evening.

'*Sí*, I heard about the Carrington deal. But I didn't want to be the one to tell you. Max, we'll get that bastard one day.'

'I hope you're right, Roberto. But you didn't phone about that, did you?'

'No. Something's cropped up on Chávez. Does he know Monsignor Mateo Bien?'

'That Opus Dei creep? Not that I know of.'

'Well, he's arranged to meet him tomorrow. They are driving somewhere. He's picking Bien up behind the Christopher Columbus statue.'

'Christ. My gut feeling says Bien is up to his neck in all this shit. What do we do?'

'Chávez doesn't know my car. We follow them.'

'You're on.'

The next morning Roberto and Max waited, discreetly parked in Calle Pavaneras, next to Plaza de Isabel la Católica. Chávez was the first to arrive in his car.

'Look, there's Bien,' said Roberto as the tall, thin priest in his cassock walked towards Chávez's car. They followed the car as it went down to Carretera de la Sierra, and turned left towards Cenes.

'Jesus, Mary and Joseph. They must be going to the monastery of Jesús del Valle, said Max. 'What's going on?'

But instead of turning up to Jesús del Valle the car sped on to the mountains in the direction of Pinos Genil, then turned upwards again towards Guejar Sierra. Max and Roberto looked at each other in surprise.

'It's a quiet road,' said Roberto. 'We'd better slow down and stay some distance behind them. We don't want them to spot us.'

They went past the Canales dam, telegraph poles still visible where the village had been before it was flooded to build the huge reservoir of water from the snows of the Sierra Nevada. The car bypassed the village centre and stopped at a large prefabricated building on the other side of Guejar Sierra.

Roberto parked under a tree out of sight of the building. 'Do you want me to skirt round the back?' Max asked. 'I could climb over this fence.'

'Not yet. Let's see what we're dealing with first.'

Max and Roberto cautiously approached the entrance.

'What the . . .' exclaimed Roberto. 'Look.'

Max read the plaque on the outside of the building. 'The San Roco Disability Training Centre.'

Max and Roberto looked at each other sheepishly.

'We've fucked up good and proper, haven't we?' said Roberto. 'Chávez must be giving a talk. Let's scarper before anyone sees us.'

'But why go with Mateo Bien?'

'Dunno. But then why not?'

They drove in silence back down the mountain. 'Fancy a *cerveza*?' said Roberto as they approached Pinos Genil.

'*Si*. I need one.'

They sat beside the river, its waters glittering in the bright sun, ducks squawking around the rocks.

'A Disability Training Centre. Bloody hell.' Max shook his head.

'Back to Navarro?'

'*Si*. But I ain't ruling out that cleric yet.'

'Back to the drawing board. You know, Max, maybe there's no connection between Paco Maya's death and all this corruption business.'

'I still think there is. I'll go through the tapes of that meeting of the Brotherhood of the Bell – you never know.'

'Sorry about this wasted trip. I was sure there was something.'

'Me too. Another *cerveza* and a plate of *papas al pobre* then?'

'Best idea we've had all day.'

Back in his office, Max checked the website for the San Roco Disability Training Centre, Guejar Sierra. There was a list of the centre's financial supporters. It included Opus Dei, Granada. Ah well. So much for conspiracy theories.

Nothing for it but to listen carefully to the tapes of the Brotherhood of the Bell meeting. Max stopped the tape at Andrés Mendoza's speech. He'd mentioned Paco Maya's will. But how did he know that Paco had made a formal will? It wasn't public knowledge. The only people who were aware of it were Max himself, Roberto, Navarro, Davila who would have told Chávez, Francisco Gómez, Catalina, and the lawyer who'd drawn it up. Could the lawyer have told Mendoza? Who knew?

Another dead end. He doodled on his pad. A new approach was needed. Maybe Clara might have picked up some gossip, or noticed something. She knew everything that went on in the office. Maybe Chávez and Navarro had become good buddies?

Just after two, Max and Clara met up in the Café Botanico, just by the old Botanical Gardens.

'Max, I was just so shocked. I really don't know what to say.'

'Clara, that's fine. I don't want to talk about it.'

'That's okay then. But if there's anything I can do . . .'

Lunch with Clara was more subdued than usual. But she did her best to make things seem normal, and almost succeeded.

'How's Chávez been?'

'Marta, that's his new secretary, told me he was pretty

upset over what happened to you. And he's working flat out as usual.'

'How's he getting on with Navarro?'

'Che? Can't stand him . . . nobody can. Why do you ask?'

'Oh. No real reason. Let's order. This is on me.'

'In which case, I'll have the steak with wild mushrooms.'

Max laughed. 'On my salary? Okay, you're on. So, what's the gossip while I've been away?'

Clara served herself from the large bowl of baby lettuce with crisp garlic breadcrumbs and anchovies. 'There's even more to our Enrique than meets the eye. He drives out to that posh place, La Veleta, in Cenes for lunch. And guess what?'

'What?'

'There isn't a rich widow.'

'You mean you got it all wrong?'

She grinned. 'It's even better. My nephew, Pepe, started a part-time job as a waiter in La Veleta. Just lunchtimes – he's a student, you know. Well . . . I asked him to keep an eye open for me.'

'And?'

Clara leaned forward conspiratorially. 'Enrique turned up with a young blonde bit. And she looked expensive. Very expensive. Pepe said he could hardly keep his paws off her.'

'Now, that is a good piece of gossip, Clara. Our Davila. Pillar of the Church. Who would have thought it?'

'Not in a million years. There's hope for all of us then. How about pudding and a *digestivo*, Max?'

They gossiped over good coffee and then returned to their offices. Max phoned Raimundo in Málaga on his personal mobile.

'Can you check all the calls made or received by Inspector Jefe Davila and Inspector Navarro from the time we suspected Carrington until Margarita's death.'

'They are your line managers, Max.'

'*Sí*, I think I'm on to something.'

'*Vale*. Mario's got blanket authorization from the Minister, so we should be able to get the go-ahead.'

An hour later, Raimundo called back. Max wrote down the numbers, put the internal phone directory in his bag, and slipped out to a quiet bar. He found a table at the back and started to go through the list. Davila had called Teniente Patricio Grandes in the Mayor's office, and then half an hour later Grandes had rung Davila back. Max checked the times. It was when the cops were on their way to Frigiliana, and Margarita was inside Rubén Carrington's villa.

Back in the office, Max looked again at his notes on Navarro. *Mierda*, how blind he had been. Davila could fit the bill as well as Navarro, maybe better. Jesus, Mary and Joseph! Trying hard to stay calm, Max went to Navarro's office. The door was open and he was alone. Max knocked, and walked in.

Navarro grunted, 'Oh. It's you.

'I just came to apologize, Ernesto.'

'So you bloody should. But given the circumstances, okay. Davila told me you've been reinstated.'

'Looks like it.'

'And he's recommending you for promotion.'

'That's what he said.'

Navarro shrugged. 'Look, I'm sorry about the girl. And I'm sorry about arresting you.'

'That's all right. Argentina's turn for the World Cup then?'

'Sure is.'

They chatted about footie for a while before Max ventured, 'Ernesto, I've been meaning to ask you. Who gave you that photo the day we were questioning the Espinosa brothers?'

'Oh, those bastards. Enrique phoned me to say the lab had found the photo.'

'And the security guard? You know, the one who said I'd put pressure on him?'

'Scared shitless he was. No. Enrique asked me to interview him again, just in case you missed something.'

'Did Enrique tell you where Roberto and I were on the day the girl got shot?'

'No. I don't think he knew. But come to think of it, maybe

he did. He was really pissed off when you and Roberto did a disappearing act. And he said he would phone Chávez to see if he knew where you were. I didn't hear what happened until the next day. What's up?'

'Oh, nothing. And thanks, Ernesto,' said Max. He walked back to his own office, his heart beating against his chest. He had more than enough evidence. He phoned Roberto.

'Max. I think you're right. I'll speak to Mario.'

A long fifteen minutes later, Mario called.

'Max. You're on to something. Do a report for Bonila and give it to him directly. I'll speak to Bonila myself.'

Max took his report and Dr Guillermo's note dating the rice bag round to Bonila's office. Fortunately, the usual fearsome secretary was on holiday. The temp accepted it was urgent and took the report through to Comisario Principal Bonila immediately.

Max went back to his office to wait for Bonila's response. The last time he'd blown the whistle, he'd been squashed, and this was going to be even worse. An anxious hour later, Max was summoned to the Comisario Principal's office

Bonila was sitting very erect at his desk with Max's report open, but face down.

'Max, I've read your report carefully. Inspector Jefe Cruz from Málaga was just on the line. I appreciate the serious-ness of the situation. I would never have expected this of Inspector Jefe Davila. In all the years I've known him, he's been an honest officer.'

'I'm sure he has, sir.'

'Right, I'll speak to him. There may be a simple explanation.'

An hour later Max was in Bonila's office again. 'Sub-Inspector Romero, the conclusions of your report have been proved correct. Inspector Jefe Enrique Davila broke down and confessed. This is extremely serious. He's gone to his office to write out a statement. I'll inform Comisario Chávez.'

268

Max stood at his office window, staring into the street, waiting for something to happen. His phone rang. It was Chávez, asking to see him right away.

'Sub-Inspector, I understand that Inspector Jefe Davila has accepted the accusations made in your report. You know you should have come to me first.'

'I agree, sir, but Inspector Jefe Mario Cruz told me to go direct to Bonila.'

'I see. Do you suspect there might be anyone else involved? Navarro?'

'I don't think so now.'

'Rotten apples in the barrel are bad news. I've even thought my phones are tapped. And that I was being followed.' He looked Max in the eye.

'I know nothing about that, sir.'

'Hmm. Okay.'

'And Francisco Gómez?'

'Let's wait a little longer. Then I'll do a new report for the judge.'

'So Gómez should be out soon?'

'Probably.'

'But we still don't know who killed Paco Maya.'

'That's true. Where have you got to on the Maya case?'

Max summarized the situation.

'All right then, Max. Keep plugging away.'

'Could you tell me – what's the situation with the three students?'

'The *palio* incident's going to be bloody messy if Azul put them up to it himself. Maybe the two priests or Gómez will make a formal complaint. But I really hope they don't, because . . . well . . . it turns out that David Costa was being paid by the police to infiltrate the radicals and give us reports.'

'I wonder who was behind that?'

'The less you know about this the better. I've said too much already. It could be very bad for us if this emerged at the Committee of Inquiry into the demo.'

269

'And Navarro?'

'He'll be reprimanded over the incident in the cathedral, maybe more.'

'Yes, sir. I understand.'

'Oh, and Bonila's worried about Enrique. Could you ask Clara to get him a cup of coffee and keep an eye on him?'

'I'll go round straight away, sir.'

Max went to Clara's office.

'Oh, Max. What's going on? Enrique looked really weird when he came back from seeing Bonila, and he seems to have locked his door.'

'I think he may have had a difficult meeting.'

'I'll get him a *café con leche* from downstairs. He always likes that.'

Max went back to his office and flicked through a memo on recruitment policies. Personnel were concerned about the lack of Muslims in the Granada police force. There were none. Max stood up to stretch his legs. And then he heard a sudden loud bang. A gunshot? Jesus, Mary and Joseph! He jumped to his feet and ran towards Clara's office. She stood shaking outside Davila's door. She'd spilt the coffee down the front of her silk shirt.

'Max?' she said, crying.

Max shook the door. Navarro came running into the office

'*Coño*. What the hell was that?'

It took three men to force the door. Max tumbled into the room. Davila lay slumped at his desk, revolver in one hand, blood splattered all over his papers.

'Get an ambulance, quickly!' Max shouted. But he knew it was too late.

Chapter 36

Max had promised to see Abbot Jorge before the funeral of Enrique Davila. He walked to Puente Maríano, then up the hill to the Abadía.

'Come in, Max. You should have come to see me sooner,' said Jorge.

Max followed him to his study.

'I heard what happened, Max. But tell me yourself now.'

For the next half-hour, Max poured his heart out.

'Max, Margarita would want you to get on with your life. That's the best cure.'

'*Sí*, Jorge. I know, but it's difficult.'

'It is. But just concentrate on getting justice for Paco.'

'And for Margarita. Look Jorge, I've got some questions.'

'Go on.'

'How much do you think the Archbishop and the Alcalde actually knew?'

'Probably very little. No one will ever know now anyway.'

'And Monsignor Mateo Bien?'

'Why do you ask?'

'I know the man's your friend, but it has crossed my mind that he might be involved in all this corruption.'

'No, I don't think so. I don't think he would do anything so wicked.'

'Can you be sure?'

'No one can be sure of anything. He's a Church politician. And he loves power . . . I know that. And a lot of people assume the worst about Opus Dei – the organization is too secretive for its own good. But more than that, no. Mateo's very committed to Opus Dei and he's a genius at getting finance for their social projects.'

'Would one of those be the San Roco Disability Training Centre in Guejar Sierra?'

'His current pet project. Why do you ask?'

'Nothing really. But I'm still not convinced.'

'Then just drop it, Max.'

'But the students who sabotaged the *palio*? They are Opus Dei.'

'They went to the Opus Dei school, and Mateo makes a point of keeping in touch with his former students. Doesn't necessarily mean anything.'

'Jorge, it was sabotage.'

'Idiotic recklessness. But that was Faustino Azul's idea, wasn't it?'

'Just Faustino Azul? And it was more than reckless. It was damn near premeditated murder.'

'It was bad. And Max, I accept I'm part of this whole bloody mess. I was greedy. I checked nothing. When we want something badly we become blind. I was naive. It simply never crossed my mind that the money for the Virgin's cloak could be so tainted. But then it was Mateo who introduced me to Andrés Mendoza.'

'Exactly. Did Mateo know Carrington?'

'Not that I know.'

'And the cloak?'

Jorge frowned. 'Well, I was so busy I couldn't get involved in commissioning the work, so Andrés offered to go to Seville with Mateo to discuss the cloak with the director of the workshop.'

'And could Penélope Carrington have gone with him?'

Jorge paused. 'Perhaps. Mateo showed me the proposed design for the cloak, and I was very happy with it.'

'Do you have the phone number of the Seville workshop?'

'No. But I know it was the Taller de la Viuda de Triana. It's one of the best.'

Jorge was uncomfortable. 'Before you go, let me show you the back of the Abadía.'

They walked round to the fire-damaged ruins behind the Abadía.

'This used to be a school until there was a fire. It's been empty ever since.'

'And this is the building the Brotherhood of the Bell were offering to repair?'

'Sí. But I heard that my dear friend Mateo had plans to turn it into a retreat centre for Opus Dei.'

'And grab your property. How nice of him.'

'Isn't it. Maybe Mateo did a deal with the Archbishop. The Archbishop gets a Cardinal's hat and Opus Dei get their centre.'

'Could Mateo swing that one?'

'Sí. Opus Dei have a lot of influence in Rome.'

'Bien's a right tricky one, isn't he?'

'He is.'

'So what is going to happen with this building now?'

'I don't know. Everything's on hold. But now I've got no money for repairs. And the council will probably go ahead with the roads anyway. But I will fight that.'

'Becoming a greenie?'

'Sort of. There's been too much destruction in Granada.'

Max glanced at his watch. 'Okay, Jorge. Thanks for everything.'

'De nada.'

'I've got to get changed for Davila's funeral. The police choir's a tenor short now so I've been roped in for the funeral. I'm taking Davila's place in the choir. Bloody ironic.'

'I'll see you there, then.'

Max returned to his flat, took his best uniform out of the dry cleaner's bag, and polished his smartest shoes. Another funeral. Bloody Davila. Who would have thought it? An old

Granada family. So well connected. And that's why the bad guys wanted him.

Max phoned the workshop in Seville and spoke to the manager.

'*Bueno*. The cloak for the Virgin of Sacromonte. One of our most important commissions this year.'

'I understand a Monsignor Bien and a Don Andrés Mendoza came over to Seville to discuss the cloak with you.'

'Yes, they did.'

'Were they accompanied by anyone else?

'*Sí*, two ladies. One was Don Andrés Mendoza's wife, and the other, a Penélope something. I can't remember. But she looked remarkably like Penélope Cruz. She caused quite a stir. The girls in the workshop all commented.'

'Can you remember who made the final decision?'

'If I remember rightly . . .' The manager paused. 'The process of commissioning is quite lengthy, you appreciate . . . We ended up with three options, and Doña Penélope strongly favoured the intertwined rose and pomegranate embroidery.'

'Thank you.'

'Nothing wrong with the cloak, I hope?

'No, it's beautiful. Very beautiful.'

The funeral was in the Renaissance church of San Jeronimo. The church was packed. Enrique Davila's family had managed to get him the full works. The police choir were massed on the altar steps. The grieving family occupied the first pew on the right. And on the left were the high ranks of the three police forces, accompanied by the Alcalde and other dignitaries from the Ayuntamiento and the Junta de Andalucia. Behind them were a group of clerics, and then the congregation. The church lights blazed briefly, illuminating the gilded, painted, carved surfaces everywhere. It was only for a minute, but it was long enough for Max to catch Mateo Bien's glance.

274

The bastard, thought Max. He must have known Rubén Carrington as sure as I'm standing here.

The Canon of San Jeronimo, accompanied by two other priests, began the Requiem Mass.

Bonila made a moving tribute to Inspector Jefe Enrique Davila. He made no mention of the case which was gripping Granada, or the suicide, of course. Instead he emphasized Inspector Jefe Davila's dedication to his work, the extreme pressures of that work which led to his untimely death, and his care for the men under his command.

Max coughed, and then concentrated on the bones buried beneath his feet. Jesus Holy Christ. What a farce.

At Communion, the lights of the church came on again as the congregation stood up to shuffle towards the altar. Max checked the row of clerics. There was an empty space where Monsignor Bien had been.

Mierda. Max couldn't leave until Mass finished. Then he'd promised to have a drink with Davila's Homicide Unit.

The team met in the closest bar. It wasn't a great place, but nobody cared too much about that. Clara had been crying. She shoved the crumpled tissue back in her bag, then gulped her mineral water thirstily.

'Oh, Max. It's only just dawning on me what damage Enrique had done. Sweet Jesus, I'm so sorry. And we've been told not to say a word.'

'Me too. Bonila hauled me to his office to promise I wouldn't say a word to the Press.'

'Another drink, Max?'

'Thanks, but I've go to go.'

'Will the truth ever come out?'

'Dunno. It's not the priority.'

At the first opportunity Max made his excuses and left. There were no taxis in the street. Max hurried across town to the Opus Dei centre. This time he'd pin the bastard down until he got the truth. He rang the doorbell again and again. No answer. Max went for a coffee and then tried again. He was in luck. It was the same old man who'd answered the door last time he was there.

Max showed his police card. 'I'm here to speak to Monsignor Mateo Bien.'

'Ah. He's left for the airport. He has a new post in Rome, you know. Such a holy man. He'll go far.'

Max phoned the airport. The Ryanair flight to Milan ML 9347 had departed. It had a connection to Rome.

Chapter 37

It was Sunday, the day of Encarnita's First Holy Communion. Max put the scrap of comic into the pocket of his best suit, and walked down to the Gran Vía. Isabel's cousin, Eduardo, was giving him a lift to Diva. By the time they arrived at Diva's twin-towered church, the organ was playing, and there were crowds of people in the street. Max and Eduardo squeezed into the church.

As the bells rang out noon, three priests in white robes walked down the aisle, accompanied by two altar boys carrying huge candles. Behind them, a younger altar boy swung the ornate silver incense holder enthusiastically back and forth, letting out clouds of fragrant smoke. Then came the supporting players, well-scrubbed boys of seven or eight, dressed in uniforms of the armed forces, white prayer books grasped awkwardly in unusually clean hands. Then came the stars of the show, young girls in white, each carrying flowers and a silver rosary. Their faces were covered by veils, and their hands by long white gloves.

'Look, there's Encarnita,' Paula whispered to Max. 'Doesn't she look lovely?'

'Yes,' said Max. 'Poor kid. The Bride of Christ.'

Isabel looked disapproving, then smiled.

At the end of the service and the Mass, the Romero family gathered on the steps of the church. Paula had to be supported by Juan, her face pale, her body even more shrivelled than normal. She smiled bravely as she kissed

277

Encarnita. Isabel was in her element, the silk roses on her hat dancing as she greeted everyone.

Leonardo appeared at Max's elbow. '*Tío* Max, did you get the football tickets?'

'I did,' said Max. 'I have a good mate in the cops who knows how to find these things.'

Whooping with joy, Leonardo rushed off shouting, 'Dad! *Tío* Max has got us the tickets for the match.'

'Thanks, Max,' said Juan. 'You have made one boy very happy. In fact two.'

The lunch was a banquet, a veritable banquet. Isabel's entire family were there, friends, neighbours, relatives, even the bank manager and Paula's doctor. There were almost as many people in the house as there had been on the day of Grandpa's funeral. Max tried to keep out of the way. He didn't want to put a damper on Encarnita's big day. Nobody wanted to spoil the party. Nobody asked about Margarita. Nobody mentioned the Brotherhood of the Bell, either. It was as if none of it had ever happened. It was better that way.

The afternoon was lovely, so they could have lunch in the garden. Encarnita sat at the head of the top table, stroking the silken folds of her dress, slightly overwhelmed by all the attention.

Leonardo's good behaviour didn't last long. He crept behind the top table and pulled his little sister's hair. Encarnita yelped, spun round and punched him

'Oi! Miss Smellypants! What did you tell the priest then? I bet he gave you five rosaries . . . minimum.'

'No, he didn't,' said Encarnita indignantly. 'I only got two Hail Marys.'

'That's because you didn't tell him all your sins. I bet you never told him about the time you pushed me into the river.'

'That wasn't a sin. You deserved it.'

'Leonardo, leave the poor girl alone. Poor lamb, she's still too young to know what a sin is,' said Isabel.

'Unlike Juan,' said Max.

Juan smiled sheepishly.

Max and Juan finally got a moment to talk.

'Any news?' asked Max.

'Not much. I had to make my statement to the judge, and I've agreed to be a witness for the prosecution. And your friend Mario says they'll try to minimize my role for the papers. But it looks like I've lost my money. We'll be a bit short of cash for a while, but, if that's the worst, I can live with it.'

'You'll bounce back,' said Max.

'Yes,' said Juan. 'I always do.'

Paula looked extremely frail. For the first time since he had known her, Max noticed that she had difficulty in concentrating on what was said to her. Her sharp tongue was silent. And sometimes Encarnita looked bigger than her great grandmother.

As the caterers were clearing away the dessert plates, Paula started crying. Encarnita put her arm around her. 'It's so unfair,' sobbed Paula. 'I read the other day that everyone who died for Franco had been given a proper Christian burial. And now the Catholic Church is preventing dignified burials for the Republican dead, seventy years after the end of the Civil War. How unchristian can you get?'

Max shot Juan a quick glance.

'It's not fair, *abuela*,' said Max. 'But we'll get there in the end. We'll give great uncle Antonio a dignified burial. We will.'

'But why are the judges being so cruel? I don't expect any better from the right wing parties, but the Church, the judges?'

Paula wiped her eyes, and held Encarnita's hand as if that was all she had left in the world. 'Oh, my pretty little girl, I wish I had your energy. I'm really tired. Your *abuela* needs a little lie-down. Max, I'll say goodbye now.'

Paula stood up, moved to give Max a kiss, then slid to the ground. There was a gasp from the guests, and Doctora Ruiz

279

de Cordova walked quickly towards the top table, wiping her hands with a napkin.

Max carried his grandmother carefully to her bedroom on the ground floor, and put her on her bed. She was as light as a feather. Encarnita cried, then held Paula's hand.

Paula opened one eye, then another. She was disorientated. 'I'm cold.'

Isabel put a blanket over her.

'Silly me. What happened?'

'Doña Paula, you fainted. You're all right. Just relax.'

'Oh, Doctora . . . on your day off. I'm making such a nuisance of myself. I'm sorry.'

Young Doctora Ruiz de Cordova shooed the family out, and settled down for a talk with her favourite patient. Fifteen minutes later, the doctor returned to the family.

'She's all right for now. But she really is very frail,' she said. 'She said she has been very tense and anxious recently. I'll go and get my bag and give her a quick check-up. My guess is diabetes, but she should go to hospital for tests tomorrow.'

'That's a blessing,' said Juan. 'She's had a couple of dizzy spells. I asked her to go and see you last week. But she didn't want to bother you, of course.'

The family went back outside to the party, reassuring everyone that there was nothing to worry about. Max and Juan found themselves in the kitchen again as Isabel made another cup of peppermint tea, Paula's favourite.

'Paula's eighty-five now. This mass grave business has worn her out. There's something else, something to do with your grandfather, that's caused her a lot of distress.'

Max looked at Juan, but said nothing.

'I'll take this tea through to Paula,' Max said.

Paula lay propped up on pillows. Some colour had come back to her cheeks. She looked very tired.

'Thanks. My favourite tea. Oh *querido*, I was so frightened for you. I do wish you'd get a safer job. Teaching would be much better for you.'

Max smiled.

'Max, I want you to promise me something.'

'Anything you like, *abuela*.'

'Keep looking for Antonio's remains, and bury him next to me and Pablo. He'd forgive Pablo, I'm sure.'

'I will, *abuela*. Now, you have a good sleep and I'll phone tomorrow.'

And he kissed her very gently.

Max went outside into the bright afternoon sun. Encarnita had taken off her finery, and was playing tag in the garden with a bunch of cousins.

'Can you help me, Nita? I found this bit of comic. Do you know what it is?'

Encarnita examined the muddy bit of paper, screwing her face up in concentration.

It was the comic he'd found below Paco's cave. It had been torn, and all it had on it was the foot of a cartoon cat.

'Yes,' she said. 'It's *Hello Kitty*. I like it a lot.'

'Thanks.' said Max. 'Can you remember this one?'

'Oooh, I'm not sure. But I save them until mummy makes me throw them out.'

'Can we go and check?'

Encarnita's room was not exactly tidy. But under a bear and a bag of sparkly socks was a pile of copies of *Hello Kitty*. The third one down was the picture of the cartoon cat, wearing a kimono. The pictures matched.

Max read the date. It was Friday, 3rd April. The day Paco Maya died.

Chapter 38

The next day was el Día de los Cruces de Mayo, the Day of the Crosses of May, the day when Granada finally forgets the grief of Easter and celebrates spring. There is dancing in the street, and every little girl, and quite a few older ones, wears the traditional Sevilliana, the bright dress awash with frills.

But the central symbol is still the Cross of Our Lord Jesus Christ, crucified. At every corner the little tableaus stand. Street competes against street, patio against patio, plaza against plaza. In fenced-off spaces, with the pavement covered in fresh herbs, there is a display of shawls, brass jugs and bowls, blue Granadino ceramics and farm implements. Often, there is a little altar, but always, in the centre, stands a cross covered in red flowers. And enterprising small boys make crude wooden crosses, and stand on the corners to beg for pennies.

Max telephoned Carmen Espinosa's house. There was no reply. He walked over to Haza Grande. The house was locked up and the shutters closed. The neighbours really, really didn't want to talk. Eventually, he found a woman in a little sweet shop four streets away who had heard that Señora Espinosa had passed away. She'd no idea about Angelita. He phoned Catalina Maya's number. A polite electronic voice informed him, '*Este numero no es disponible.*' Damn.

He tried Father Gerardo's mobile next. It rang for a while. Then a voice said, '*Dígame*. Gerardo speaking.'

'*Padre* Gerardo, sorry to disturb you on your busy day. Sub-Inspector Max Romero here. I need to contact Catalina Maya. I was wondering if you have a number for her. The one she gave me is no longer available.'

'Ah, Max, I'm glad you phoned. I need to talk to you.'

'I would be delighted. But it's quite important I talk to Catalina.'

'She and Angelita are with me right now. Why don't you come round? We're just behind the Hotel Santa Paula.'

Max noted down the address, then walked back through the Albayzín to the maze of narrow streets behind the Hotel Santa Paula. He pressed the button on the door-entry system of a block of flats, and a woman's voice answered.

'Catalina. It's Max.'

'We're on the second floor. Come on up.'

The flat smelled of fresh paint and baking.

'So glad you could come,' said Catalina. 'Gerardo's just making some coffee.'

Max raised an eyebrow.

As they sat down, Father Gerardo appeared with the coffee and a plate of freshly baked biscuits.

'They've come out perfectly,' he said to Catalina. 'Max, Great to see you again.'

'But . . .?' said Max.

'I packed it in, Max. I've left the Church. Or rather the Church left me. I'm going to do a social work qualification. I can do more good there. And the penny finally dropped how I felt about Catalina. And she seems to feel the same about me.' He grinned shyly.

'Congratulations,' said Max. 'You've done the right thing.'

Catalina laughed. 'You know, he's the first sensible boyfriend I've had. And he's great with Angelita. I don't know what I would do without him. I think we'll be fine.'

'Ah, yes. Sorry to hear about the *abuela*.'

283

'I'm not. She was an evil old cow. We're worried what she did to Angelita.'

'That's what I wanted to discuss with you,' said Gerardo. 'I know it's all been difficult for Angelita – the death of her father and her *abuela*, moving in with us – but she's more distressed than I would have expected. She keeps on weeping and is having nightmares. She's not missing her *abuela*, I'm sure. But she mentions her father a lot.'

'Paco? I thought she hardly knew him.'

'That's true. But she goes on about how her *abuela* said her father was an evil man and should be punished.'

'Poor kid. That woman had a nasty tongue.'

'It's not just that. She's scared stiff of her cousins, Tomasito, Rafa and Nico. When we suggested she went to see them, she started screaming about a bicycle trip and how she was left behind. That she wasn't there.'

'Is Angelita in?' asked Max.

'She's in her room,' said Catalina. 'I'll get her.'

Angelita appeared in the doorway, pale as a little ghost, clutching a comic. She looked at Max, burst into tears, and ran to Gerardo who picked her up, put her on his knee and cuddled her.

'No need to be frightened,' Gerardo said. 'This is our friend Max. He's been very kind to your *tia* Catalina.'

Max smiled at the child. 'I knew a lot of people who knew your father. He really loved you, and he was desperately sorry for what he did. He wasn't an evil man. He wanted to take care of you. And he would have done.'

Angelita said nothing. She just stared at him, and clung more closely to Gerardo.

'Your father loved you, loved you very much,' said Gerardo.

Angelita cried again, and dropped her comic on to the floor.

Max picked it up. It was *Hello Kitty*.

'You like *Hello Kitty*, don't you?'

'*Sí*, I get it every month.'

Max took out the torn page he had found at the bottom of Paco's path.

'Angelita,' he said, trying to sound gentle but serious at one and the same time, 'I found this torn page at the bottom of the path leading to your father's cave. There were bicycle tyre marks close by. You were there, weren't you? The day your father died?'

'He wasn't my father,' screamed Angelita. 'He killed my mother. And *mi abuela* said he didn't love me.'

'What do you mean, he wasn't your father?'

'*Mi abuela* said he was a bad, bad man . . . because of what he'd done. I hate him. I hate him,' she sobbed.

'Max, what's going on?' interrupted Gerardo.

'I know,' said Max. 'But I have to find out what happened that day. I'm sorry, but it's very important.'

He looked at Angelita. 'Just tell me what happened that day.'

'I can't,' she sobbed. 'Tomasito made me promise. He said I'd go to prison if I did . . . like my dad.'

'So Tomasito was there with you?' asked Max.

'*Sí*,' she whispered.

'And the others?'

'*Sí*. Nico and Rafa.'

Catalina turned quietly to Max. 'Tomasito and Rafa are Gregorio's boys. Nico's their cousin.'

'Angelita, tell me what happened, what you saw. I promise you won't go to prison.'

'But the boys will. They said they'd go to prison for the rest of their lives.'

'No, none of you will go to prison,' said Max. 'I just have to know what happened.'

Gerardo gave her a tissue to blow her nose. 'It's all right. You're safe here. Nobody's going to be cross with you. The truth doesn't hurt.'

'Tomasito kept saying *mi abuela* was right, that *mi padre* deserved to die . . . after *mi padre* came out of prison.'

'Oh dear,' said Max.

285

Gerardo and Catalina looked at one another.

Angelita started to cry again. Gerardo hugged her tightly. 'It's all right, *cariño*. You'll feel better if you tell us what happened.'

'I can't. Tomasito will hit me. I promised I would never tell anyone.'

'I'll make sure he doesn't touch you,' said Gerardo. 'You won't have to see him ever again unless you want to.'

'I can't,' Angelita screamed.

'But you were all there that day, weren't you? The day your father died,' said Max gently.

'*Si*,' she sobbed. '*Si*.'

Gerardo stroked her hand. 'Just tell us what you can remember, and we'll go for an ice cream and watch the dancing.'

'So you were with the boys that day?' said Catalina very gently.

'*Si*. We went out on our bikes. But my bike won't go fast, and they wouldn't wait for me.'

'So what did you do?'

'I got to my dad's path, but nobody was there. Then I started walking up the path. The boys came running down, shouting, "We gotta go. Run. Run."'

'So what happened then?'

'We all ran down the path. They jumped on their bikes and left me behind.'

'Why didn't you go with them?'

'I had mud on my new shoes. *Mi abuela* would batter me when I got home.'

Angelita started crying again.

Gerardo held her close. 'She can't batter you any more. Nobody is going to batter you ever again.'

Angelita smiled. 'I'm thirsty.'

'I'll get you some milk, nice and cold,' said Catalina.

She returned with a glass of milk. Angelita drank thirstily.

'See, you're a lot better now. So what happened to the mud on your new shoes?' said Catalina.

'I sat on the big rock by the stream and wiped my shoes with a bit of my comic.'

'So you didn't see what happened up there?' asked Max.

Angelita wailed, 'No, I didn't. I didn't.'

'But you know what happened? They told you?'

'No. I can't tell you. I swore by the Virgin of Sacromonte I'd never tell.'

'But you can tell me,' said Gerardo. 'You can whisper.'

'No, I can't. We cut our fingers, and mixed our blood, and swore we would never tell anyone.'

'It's serious,' said Max, very quietly, looking at Catalina and Gerardo.

'Come on, angel,' said Gerardo. 'I think this girl deserves an ice cream. A break will do us all good.'

Gerardo took her hand, and headed for the ice cream shop.

'Christ,' said Catalina. 'I knew Francisco had nothing to do with it.'

'My God,' said Max. 'How old are the boys?'

'Tomasito's thirteen. Rafa's a year younger. Nico's maybe ten, but I'm not sure.'

'Oh dear. So young.'

'So where does this leave poor Angelita? She wasn't there, so nothing can happen to her, can it?'

'No, nothing can happen to her. In any case she's well under age.'

'And the boys?'

'We still don't know what they did. I'm not sure Angelita will tell me. But we're going to have to talk to them all. I'll make arrangements to interview them.'

'Angelita as well?' asked Catalina.

'I'm afraid so. You can sit with her and we'll have a child welfare officer there too.'

'Gerardo and I will take Angelita,' said Catalina.

'That's fine,' said Max. 'Maybe she'll tell you more later.'

'Leave it with Gerardo. He's used to confessions.'

'Okay,' said Max. 'I'll have to go into the office, and get this set up as quickly as possible. Make sure she doesn't go anywhere near her cousins or their families. Keep her off school.'

By Wednesday afternoon, Max had it all in place to start interviewing the boys. They turned up at the offices of the Fiscalia de Menores, all looking younger and smaller than Max remembered them. They sat uncomfortably on high-backed chairs, tugging at clean collars. Mothers were in skirts and best jackets. The red-haired woman, Gregorio Espinosa's wife, looked worn, weepy and very tired. Her sister, Nico's mother, was agitated and defensive.

All three boys stuck to their story that they had gone cycling above Haza Grande and were nowhere near Paco Maya's cave. Young Tomasito Espinosa was already a hard man in the making. He'd picked up the tricks of the trade from his dad, Gregorio. His brother Rafa was just as tough. But Nico was less sure of himself.

Max hoped Nico would give a clue, but they wouldn't budge from their story.

The Fiscal called for a break. A secretary arrived with coffee for the two women and Coke cans for the boys. Max walked with Miguel Cortes, the Fiscal, to his private office. 'Max,' he said, 'I don't think we can question them for much longer.'

'Damn.'

The receptionist rang through. 'Señora Maya has arrived with Angelita Maya and Señor Gerardo Arredondo. Señor Arredondo wants to speak to Sub-Inspector Romero privately before Angelita's interview.'

'Thank you, Emilia. We need to keep the two families well apart. Ask Señora Maya and Angelita to wait in Verónica's office, please.'

Gerardo was ushered through to the Fiscal's office. He was wearing jeans and a jumper, but still managed to look vaguely clerical.

'Angelita's told me everything she knows.'

'That's great. Do you think she'll tell us the full story?'

'I'm not sure. She's crying all the time, terrified of what the boys will do to her if they think she's a sneak. But maybe if one of the boys confesses . . . that will make it easier for her.'

The Fiscal smiled. 'That's okay. The boys won't need to know that she's made a statement.'

'And once I have more information, I'm sure I can get Nico to speak out. He's on the verge of tears,' said Max.

Gerardo had made some notes. 'Well, poor Angelita really believed all that *abuela* stuff about how evil Paco was, and how he deserved to be punished.'

'Poor kid.'

'Anyway, *la abuela* told everyone in the family that there was a reward for anyone who got that bastard Paco to sign and sell his land. And Tomasito wanted one of those little motorbike things.'

'Bloody hell. So what happened?'

'Angelita doesn't know everything. But the boys met Angelita coming up the path to Paco's cave as they came running down it, shouting "Paco's dead. Get the hell out of here!"'

'So she doesn't know what actually happened at the cave?'

'That's correct. And later on the kids swore their famous oath to never tell anyone where they had really been that day.'

The Fiscal turned to Max. 'That's not enough to take this to the judge, you know.'

'But there's more,' said Gerardo. 'Nico said something to Angelita later. Paco was going to get them a drink. So Paco was alive when the three boys got to his cave.'

'*Díos mío.*'

'I know.'

'I shall get Nico to tell the truth now,' said Max.

Catalina, Angelita and the child welfare officer went quietly to the Fiscal's office. Angelita made her statement.

'Thanks, Gerardo. We might have cracked it.'

'I'm used to confessions. Not that much difference between a priest and a cop, is there?'

Max smiled.

'Catalina, *querida*,' said Gerardo, 'you take Angelita home. I'll wait here until Max has finished.'

The Fiscal agreed to give Max another half-hour with Nico. It would have to be a case of tough love.

'Nico,' Max began, 'Rafa has told us quite a lot. He's admitted you all cycled over to Paco's cave that day.'

Nico looked frightened. His mother glared at Max and the Fiscal, but kept quiet.

'We have photos of bicycle tyre marks taken on the day your uncle Paco died. We can easily prove they came from your bikes.'

Nico turned pale.

'Rafa said you three boys went up to Paco's cave. He was alive when you arrived, wasn't he?

'No. No,' screamed Nico.

'He was going to get you a glass of water,' said Max.

'He wasn't. He was dead when we got there. He was dead.'

'Nico, we saw the glasses. Just tell me the truth. You'll feel a lot better,' said Max.

'It wasn't me. It was Tomasito's idea.'

'So what happened?'

'We'd seen this film on TV. The bad guys put a plastic bag over this guy's head to frighten him. And he told the baddies where the money was.'

'And then?'

'Tomasito said we could do that. Get Paco to sign a piece of paper to sell his land to give the money to Angelita. Tomasito said we'd all get rewards from *la abuela*.'

'So what did you do?'

'We all went off into Sacromonte on the bikes.'

'With Angelita?'

'*Sí*, we'd promised to look after her. But she's dead slow

on her bike. I wanted to stay behind to help her. But Tomasito . . . he said no, she'd catch us up later.'

'So, Angelita never got to Paco's cave.'

'No.'

'And then?'

'Paco knew who we were. He was all friendly. Said he'd get us a drink. And then we jumped him, tied his hands and arms behind the chair, and Tomasito put this plastic bag over his head.'

'And then?'

'He kicked around a lot. Then sort of fell. We got the bag off quick. Rafa started screaming, "He's dead. He's dead." Tomasito said we had to put him back inside the cave. So we untied the rope and put Paco, the chair and the guitar inside the cave. Tomasito said we had to wipe everything clean, and take the plastic bag and string with us. We shut the door and ran.'

'And Negrito, the dog?'

'He wouldn't stop barking. So Tomasito kicked him.'

'Do you still have the string and plastic bag?'

'No. Tomasito got rid of them.'

Nico put his head on the table and cried. His mother put her arms around him.

Max got up and left the room. Gerardo was waiting in the corridor.

'He's confessed,' said Max. 'There was no need to mention Angelita. *La abuela* – she got her revenge, didn't she, Gerardo?'

'Yes. She planned it.'

Max looked out of the window on to the busy street below. Something Margarita had once said was floating below the surface of his memory. Yes. Lady Macbeth's speech. 'My hands are of your colour, but I shame to wear a heart so white . . .'

'Max, what's likely to happen to the boys?'

'Hard to say. They're all under age. So probably not much these days.'

'Funny, isn't it? Paco died because a boy wanted one of those awful kids' motorbikes. And that opened up a whole can of worms.'

'It did, Gerardo, it did.'

And in the office of the Fiscalia de Menores, two mothers wept.